Mary Hocking's many novels include *March House*, *He Who Plays the King*, *Look Stranger!* and *The Mind has Mountains*. She lives in Lewes in Sussex. *Indifferent Heroes* is the second part in a trilogy, of which *Good Daughters*, the first volume, is already available in Abacus. The third part, *Welcome Strangers*, will also be published by Abacus.

Also by Mary Hocking in Abacus:

GOOD DAUGHTERS

Mary Hocking

INDIFFERENT HEROES

First published in Great Britain by
Chatto & Windus The Hogarth Press 1985
Published in Abacus by Sphere Books Ltd 1986
27 Wright's Lane, London W8 5SW
Copyright © 1985 by Mary Hocking

Printed and bound in Great Britain by
Collins, Glasgow

I would like to acknowledge Kate Caffrey's *Out in the Midday Sun* and Ray Parkin's *Into the Smother: A Journal of the Burma-Siam Railway*. Also, help received from Dr Serge Hackel, arch-priest of the Russian Orthodox Church, and Reader in Russian Studies at the University of Sussex.

I

December 1939

At any other time, Alice Fairley would have been overcome by the poignancy of the school carol concert. She was acutely sensible to poignant occasions. The war, however, was too newly begun to permit of backward glances at past ways of life; so she looked with dry eyes at the girls sparsely distributed in the hall beneath. Although she had only been in the WRNS for two weeks, it was difficult to imagine what it had been like to be a pupil of the Winifred Clough Day School for Girls.

Yet for ten years she had been a pupil here, popular, but unremarkable in her achievements; although one of her teachers had told her that she had a gift for expressing the English language. Class photographs showed her as a podgy child, with a good-humoured face and long, plump pigtails. Her face was thinner now; and although the corners of the mouth flicked upwards, apparently amused, some memory of recent illness lingered in the eyes.

The school, too, had had its vicissitudes. Only a third of the pupils was present, the remainder having been evacuated to Dorset, where they were presumably joining in a carol concert conducted according to the alien traditions of their host school. The Headmistress spent much of her time travelling between the separated parts and trying to preserve the identity of the whole.

Miss Blaize, that Wagnerian figure who had ruled the lives of the pupils for so long, appeared much tested by her experience. 'My dear, I do believe she's crying!' Daphne Drummond whispered to Alice when, with a sound as of wind stirring the topmost branches of a forest, the depleted ranks rose to sing bravely, 'Wake, oh wake, for night is flying'. Alice could see her sister, Claire, towards the back of the assembly, her face alight with that rapt wonder which she could assume with the striking of the first chord of music, while lesser mortals were taking a deep breath. She was one of the few people whom Alice knew who could sing and look like an angel at one and the same time.

As the triumphant music was flung out – in exultation at the release of cramped limbs and the knowledge that the term was now practically over – a closer examination of Miss Blaize's creviced face would have revealed something more extraordinary than tears. Miss Blaize, gazing from cavernous eye-sockets upon the pupils for whom she had had such high hopes, thought of the doomed culture which they represented, and was aware of the tide of evil surging beyond the walls of the building. She raised her head, eyes burning, and braced herself to take the shock, like a great liner going down with all its lights blazing.

Alice and Daphne were in the gallery, which was allocated to the Old Girls on this occasion. The concert had finished earlier than usual, at half-past three. It was a dull day and the light was fading already. Alice and Daphne helped two members of staff to put up the black-out at the windows. Irene Kimberley, who had been sitting on the far side of the gallery, joined her friends. She was the most intellectually able of the three girls and was now at London University. The staff, however, made little distinction in their greetings. Although academic success was important, the school cherished all its pupils. The teachers were interested to learn that Alice was now a Wren, and that Daphne was learning to drive so that she could 'do ambulance duty if nothing more exciting turns up'.

'You must be the first of our pupils to join up,' the history mistress said to Alice. 'Why aren't you in uniform?'

'The Wrens haven't got uniforms yet; there's been some sort of hitch.' It would have been the only time she had ever been demonstrably first in anything at school. Appropriate, perhaps, to finish as she had begun, without creating undue attention.

Soon after four, the three girls made their way out of the building, secure in the belief that they would never return, since the war was going to change everything. They had little notion of what would happen to them, but the idea that they could ever again be subjected to the tyranny of routine was inconceivable. Even more inconceivable to Daphne and Alice would have been the idea that the school, on which they were now turning their backs, had shaped them for the rest of their lives. They imagined themselves to have sloughed off its influence like an old skin.

The street was dim; darkness seemed to come much earlier now that there was so little street lighting. It was a murky evening. 'No celestial firmament on high tonight!' Irene said as they strolled towards Holland Park Avenue.

'Do Wrens serve at sea?' Daphne asked Alice.

'I don't think so. Not at present, anyway.'

'I suppose it will be the same in all the services. The men will do the exciting things. I want to learn to fly. How am I to manage it?'

'I think you may have to modify your ambitions.' Irene spoke tartly, conscious of her exclusion from the world of action.

'This is one time when anything is possible,' Daphne retorted. 'And I propose to take full advantage of it.' She was a trim, compact young woman, not noticeably more vigorous than her companions. An acceptable scholar in the Winifred Clough mould, but capable, on occasions of her own choosing, of surprising staff and fellow pupils. She had a mental alertness combined with physical agility which could produce startling results on the sportsfield – no rounders match could be considered lost while she had still to bat. Her friends had little doubt that she was well able to suit actions to words.

Irene said, 'Flying would probably be rather dull once you had done it a few times – like driving a bus.' She walked hunched forward, her chin muffled in a long woollen scarf; she had been to the library before attending the concert, and had books tucked under one arm. She was very small and Alice thought she looked like a fourth-former.

Daphne left them at Notting Hill tube station. Alice was going to the home of her sister, Louise, in Holland Park. Irene, who lived near by, walked with her down the tree-lined avenue. They had walked here often in the past, when it had seemed that Irene had the brighter future. Today, she wondered if academic success was what she wanted. She was perceptive enough to know that the time for decision is not long. Unlike her friends, she was aware that the person she would be for the rest of her life was already shadowing her.

'How does Louise feel about all this?' she asked. 'You in the Wrens and Guy in the Army?'

Alice had not considered Louise's feelings. But Irene remembered that, not so many years ago, they had envied Louise, who was so attractive that life would surely shower her with favours. Then, Louise had attracted Guy, become pregnant, disgraced her family, and married in haste. Now, whatever excitement might be ahead for her sisters, Alice and Claire, Louise would be tied to the Home Front and the care of her two children. Her youth had been over and done with so frighteningly quickly! Irene supposed Alice had not noticed because Louise was her sister and, the Fairleys being a close family, they grew into these things together, day by day. In three years' time, I shall be nearly twenty-two, Irene told herself, and I shall have done all my growing up in school and college. Does that make me better off than Louise?

'You will write to me, won't you?' she said to Alice.

'I shall write so much you'll get tired of reading the letters,' Alice responded warmly. 'However many people I meet, I shan't make any friends like you and Daphne.'

'You'll meet far more men than I shall.'

Alice hoped so, since this was a chapter in her life too long deferred.

She parted company with Irene at the corner of Norland Square. For the first time, she found the darkness unpleasant and longed for the familiar light of the lamps. She had been ill in recent years: a breakdown occasioned by the disappearance in Germany of her friend and neighbour, Katia Vaseyelin. It had been Irene as much as anyone who had helped her through this nightmare period when she had not wanted to go out of the house, or to meet people. Irene had been understanding but not invariably sympathetic; and Alice had learnt that one of the tasks which friends perform for each other is to mark the boundaries of behaviour. Without Irene's occasional crisp disapproval, she doubted whether she would have come through so well. Now, as she saw her friend's figure swallowed up in darkness, panic threatened her again. A few dimmer lights had been installed in the main road, but the side street into which she ventured nervously was a black hole. At one time, this strange new darkness in the city would have excited her; but since the disappearance of Katia, the unknown no longer drew her so trustingly forward. There was always the fear that she might glimpse, out of the corner of an eye, something grotesque being hurried out of sight.

Her pawing hand touched a hard surface. Involuntarily, she apologized, and then, her fingers coming to the gaping mouth, realized it was a pillar box. She laughed shakily, and, steadying herself with a few deep breaths, walked on, rehearsing how she would make an amusing story of this encounter when she got back to the Wren cabin tonight. The others would have stories to tell, too. She looked forward to seeing them again. They were the people who were important to her now.

She remembered the day, two weeks ago, when her call-up notice had come. On that same day, people all over the country, whom she had never met, had received the same call. In towns and villages of which she had never heard, they, too, were preparing to leave their homes for the place of assembly. Here, they would be kitted out for their journey. For them, as for the pilgrims taking the road to

4

Samarkand, the great gates would open and they would pass on their way, no longer strangers, but people joined in a common enterprise, with their own exclusive language and rules for the road. How eagerly she had set out! The old life had fallen away as the sleepers ran together behind the train. Now, the strangers were already comrades: a new landscape stretched indefinitely ahead of them. As she thought of this, she felt a thrill of excitement and forgot about Katia – and Irene, too. Her family and friends belonged to a world on which she had turned her back.

It was, however, a family party which Louise was giving. Now that Guy and Alice had joined up, who knew when they might be together again? Family meant Louise and her husband Guy; the Fairleys; and Ben Sherman. There had been some argument as to whether in England Ben would have been considered a relative. 'But it's not an English relationship,' Louise had pointed out. 'It's Cornish.' Cornish relationships, it had been agreed, were as intricate as those recorded in the Book of Numbers.

Guy's parents were not present. Mrs Immingham had not got over the fact that her son had had to marry Louise. Her intractability suited Louise well enough, and harmed only herself and her husband.

It was Louise who opened the door to Alice. 'Hallo, Dumpling!' She was plumper than Alice now; but dominance established in childhood tends to remain unchallenged, so that Louise would always have a special licence to comment adversely on her sisters' appearance, because she was the attractive one. 'You can read a story to James and Catherine,' she said. 'I'm afraid you'll be a great disappointment to them, though. They were longing to see Aunt Alice in uniform.'

If they were disappointed in their Aunt Alice, their father must have delighted them. Old Grandmother Fairley said to Ben Sherman, 'What about Guy, then? Don't he look handsome?' She sounded huffy, as though the King's uniform was something Guy had designed for himself for reasons not entirely meritorious.

As she said this, Guy happened to look across at them. He smiled. Ben thought the smile slid like icing down a cake. But then Ben, who had no time for social niceties, was not a great smiler.

'What's 'e done to get a pip?' Grandmother Fairley asked, revealing more military knowledge than Ben had given her credit for.

'OTC plus six months' service. Then, of course, he has that certain blend of shy, deprecating charm which is generally supposed to conceal essential qualities of leadership.'

5

'Who can you be talking about?' Louise had joined them.

'Your husband.'

Ben did not think Louise had cause to object. She had once said of him in his hearing, 'He is bound to do well at the Bar with his natural capacity for rudeness.'

Louise laughed. 'You're just jealous.'

Which irked, because he had once loved her. He shrugged his shoulders. 'I'm not interested. If they want me, they will have to come and get me.' He had a promising career ahead at the Bar, and the war was an infernal nuisance. Even so, if it had to be, it had to be; and he was not best pleased that Guy should have been commissioned before he himself was out of civilian clothes. He narrowed his eyes, studying Guy and trying to visualize how he would look with a bit of mud and blood on that immaculate uniform. He had to admit that, pointed in the right direction and told to fire, Guy would probably acquit himself as well as the next man. England was moving into an era where want of self-interest and common sense would be highly valued. Guy Immingham was undoubtedly of the stuff of which such heroes are made.

Grandmother Fairley, now so frail that she could barely move a foot without having to pant for several minutes, had drawn on that reserve of energy which she kept for things she really intended to do, and had bullied her daughter, May, into bringing her here in a taxi. She had been enjoying herself up to now, but felt that insufficient attention had been accorded her by Judith Fairley, her daughter-in-law.

'Where's your mother, then?' she said to Louise.

'Do you want her?' Louise beckoned to Judith.

'This is a sad day for you,' the old lady said accusingly when Judith joined her. 'It don't matter about me. I'll be in Glory soon. It's all the young ones that worry me.' She gazed at them without evincing strong liking.

'I expect they'll manage well enough.' Judith could never refrain from disagreeing with her mother-in-law.

The old lady turned away to take a sandwich proffered by Guy. 'I'm surprised at you going before you have to,' she said. 'What about your poor children?'

'He's doing it for his wife and poor children,' Judith said briskly, thus preventing Guy from saying the same thing more sententiously. He smiled at her. He was very happy. He had found life in an accountant's office increasingly difficult. Now he had a greater sense of purpose and a renewed belief in himself. The uniform played no small part in this, not because it enhanced his lanky good looks – he was not vain – but because it gave him that sense of belonging which he had had at school.

'Our hope is that Guy and his comrades will not be let down by mismanagement at home.'

All eyes turned to Stanley Fairley, who was at his most portentous, bushy eyebrows almost, but not quite, masking pebbly eyes full of foreboding, lower lip thrust forward. The voice crying in the wilderness, however, is often least heeded by those best placed to hear it. The boys at his elementary school might accord grudging respect to his utterances; the congregation at the Methodist chapel might be forced, beneath his searching gaze, to examine the state of their souls: Stanley Fairley's dear ones regarded him with expressions ranging from affectionate tolerance to barely concealed impatience. For many years letters had issued from his home in Shepherd's Bush to the Prime Minister, the *News Chronicle*, the *Methodist Recorder*, warning of the danger posed to European civilization by Adolf Hitler. There had been times, as his children grew older and more daring, when they had complained of 'having Hitler for breakfast, tea and supper'. There was no need now of such warnings; but Stanley Fairley was not the man to relax his vigilance because events had proved him right.

Judith said, 'Not Neville Chamberlain today, my love.'

'Not Neville Chamberlain at any time, if I had anything to do with it.'

'But you won't get rid of him this afternoon,' Louise said. 'And it is probably the last time we shall all be together this year, if not the next.'

Her easy assumption that their separation could be measured in months silenced him. He talked a great deal about the First World War, but it was usually the amusing episodes which he recounted – his feelings when he had passed his plate up too late for a second helping of Christmas pudding; the time when the makeshift platform collapsed just as the general was telling them all to 'bear up'. The darker memories could only have been shared with his old comrades, nearly all of whom had been killed. Ben, sorry to see him silenced, said, 'All this must bring back memories.'

'I went through Ypres, Passchendaele and the Somme,' Mr Fairley informed Ben, alert eyes waiting for the reaction as though it was the first time he had ever divulged this fact.

'You've seen it all before, then?' Ben affected surprise. He was fond of Mr Fairley and saw no harm in humouring him.

Louise said to her mother, 'We're in the trenches now! We'll be knee deep in mud for the rest of the evening.'

It was Claire who put a stop to Stanley Fairley's war reminiscences. She arrived from school with a stack of music under one arm, and immediately took centre stage. 'We got the phrasing all wrong, it was *awful*,' she said dramatically, as though the carol concert, and her own performance as a member of the choral society, must be uppermost in the minds of all present. 'You'd think it was simple enough.' She sang a few bars, '"What child is this, who laid to rest, on Mary's lap is sleeping . . ."' She had a notably pure voice.

Her father looked tenderly at the earnest little face framed by the abundant red hair. He heaved a sigh, the full force of his emotion now concentrated on the family gathering.

Judith watched her daughter with affection not unmixed with scepticism. Stanley, who expected a lot of his children, must insure himself against disillusion by equating expectation with performance. In spite of one or two shocks over recent years, he still persisted in the hope that, since he could not change, they would adjust to his need. Judith saw her children's faults clearly, but did not worry about them unduly. Hers was a stabilizing, if not always sympathetic, influence. 'You've got a button coming loose,' she interrupted Claire's recital. 'Come here, before you lose it.'

Stanley Fairley said to Louise, 'Where is Alice?'

'She's reading to the children.'

'But she should be here with us. They should all be here.'

Louise got up. 'You can have the kids. But Alice is going to help me in the kitchen.'

When the children came running into the room, it was Ben who claimed their immediate attention. He delighted in young creatures; only those old enough to compete with him got the rough side of his tongue.

In the kitchen, Louise was studying her sister. They had been good companions, but Louise had been unable to understand what had happened to Alice during the last few years. 'I can't see why she has worked herself up into this dreadful state about Katia,' she had said to Judith. 'It's not as if there is anything she can do about it.' Louise did not believe in crying over things which could not be undone. Had she been different, her marriage would have suffered. She said to Alice, 'There's someone here I recognize.' She was delighted to see that sunnier companion she had loved so well. 'Welcome back.'

Alice, who felt she had changed almost out of recognition during the last weeks, wished she had been issued with uniform to clothe her new personality.

'You're going to like it, then, are you?' Louise asked.

'It's marvellous! I've never felt so free.'

Louise made a wry face. She had purchased freedom at a greater cost. Now, it seemed that she, who had first broken the mould, was to be the prisoner while Alice became the venturer. She was not a grudging person, however, and as she looked at Alice, she had real hopes for her. Alice's was not a beautiful face. But where did beauty ever get a woman save into trouble? This was a good-natured face, more ready for laughter than tears; the face of someone with whom men would feel comfortable. Men were going to need quite a bit of comfort in the coming months.

'Mind you make the most of it.'

'Yes, I must, I must!' Alice meant this with all her heart, and yet she had really very little idea of what it was she expected from the war. It sometimes seemed to her that life was like a film shown the wrong way round; so that when the war was over, she would come back to this moment in the kitchen with Louise, and she wouldn't know until then what it had all been about.

Louise said, 'No more nonsense about Kashmir?'

Alice frowned. Kashmir, that hidden house in Shepherd's Bush, had had a special significance for her in her adolescence. She had had glimpses of it from the branches of a tree in the garden of her home. It lay, surrounded by green lawns and gardens, walled like a city, beyond the boundaries of time, beckoning, unattainable. At this stage in her life, Alice was concerned with the attainable. She said, 'I don't think about Kashmir now.'

'That's all to the good. You were a bit dotty about it once. In fact, you have had a number of dotty spells. So watch out.'

Alice went into the larder. By the time she came out carrying a bowl of trifle, Louise had turned her mind to more immediate matters. 'Did you know that Mummy plans to learn to drive an ambulance?'

'Mummy!' Ambulance driving should be left to young people like Daphne.

'And Daddy, of course, is going to win the war on the Home Front.' Louise spoke with more affection of her father than her mother.

'And you, Louise, what will you do?'

'I shall look after the children and knit socks for soldiers.'

9

Alice laughed, sure that life would always have something special in store for Louise.

'It's all very well for you to laugh.' Louise handed Alice a tray with the trifle on it and individual jellies for the children. 'What excitement can there be here when everyone who is young and healthy has gone rollicking off abroad?'

They went back to the sitting room where their father was talking about the sinking of the *Rawalpindi*. 'The gallantry of that little ship . . .'

'She wasn't a little ship,' Ben said irritably. 'She was a converted liner – 17,000 tons, in fact.'

'She was no match for battle cruisers,' Stanley persisted.

'Her armaments weren't,' Ben conceded. 'But she was a bigger boat.' He could foresee years of heroism ahead, and was resolved to take an early stand against it.

'Granny's taken her teeth out,' James said, sidling up to his mother.

'Well, don't look, darling,' Louise replied. 'I expect she's got a pip stuck. She'll put them back soon.'

Catherine was sitting astride her father's leg, playing 'Ride a Cock Horse to Banbury Cross'. Guy's adoration of the child was almost painful to see. Claire was being nice to Aunt May in a rather lofty way, illustrating the fact that she was the clever one of the girls by talking about a Neanderthal site in Acton. Aunt May, pleased and bewildered, was giving little gasps, interspersed with inappropriate titters.

When they had finished eating, they gathered round the piano to sing. Claire played, and the children occasionally reached out a hand to press down a note. 'We must sing Ben's song,' Alice said. Ben's song was 'Marching through Georgia'. He had once claimed that his American father had been a descendant of General Sherman. This afternoon, for some reason he could not understand, it seemed important to put Alice straight on this matter before she departed to play her part with those who go down to the sea in ships, and do business in great waters.

'I'm not really related to him.'

'Oh Ben! And I always believed it.'

'You mustn't believe everything a man tells you, Alice, or you'll end up in trouble.'

He, too, had grown up in a strict Methodist home, and now, in spite of himself, there was a shade of puritanical severity in his tone. Alice flushed. Really, she thought, Ben was becoming rather tiresome. Or perhaps she was more sophisticated? She had once been impressed by him; with that hooked nose and chiselled mouth and general air of controlled ferocity, she had imagined him to be a person one could trust in a tight corner. But might not other qualities be more serviceable? How much of life is spent in a tight corner? She turned away and joined in singing, 'We're Going to Hang Out the Washing on the Siegfried Line'.

Stanley Fairley, more than a shade puritanical, did not like the song although he approved of the sentiment. He followed Louise out of the room when she went to prepare the children's bath.

'I would have liked us to sing a hymn,' he said. 'I suppose that would spoil the party?'

Once, he would have insisted, and that would have been an end to it. But the foundations on which he had based his authority had been shaken, first by Louise's pregnancy, and then by the disappearance of Katia Vaseyelin. He was more prone than ever now to fits of depression, when he tended to look helpless and vulnerable, as the very dominant can if the power which drives them inexplicably fails. Louise was touched to see him so tentative. She admired him because, however wounded he might be by life, he would always rouse himself for another attack. She did not regard the targets of his attacks as important. Louise would have identified wholeheartedly with Don Quixote: it was the tilting which signified, not the windmills. Now, she laid her cheek against her father's and said, 'Of course we shall sing a hymn.'

When they returned to the sitting room, she announced, 'We're going to sing "Eternal Father" – for Alice, now she's a sailor.'

They all sang, and Ben, once he had decided it was a bit of a joke, put an arm round Alice's shoulder and gave voice in a lusty baritone:

> 'O Trinity of love and power,
> Our brethren shield in danger's hour;
> From rock and tempest, fire and foe,
> Protect them whereso'er they go . . .'

'Are you coming home with us, darling?' Stanley asked Alice when the party broke up soon after six. 'Rumpus would love to see you.'

'I've got to be back in quarters by ten, and I'm meeting Ted at the Corner House first.'

'Is that your old Zeeta's boy friend?' Louise asked.

'He's in the Rifle Brigade now.'

'How sickening!' Claire exclaimed. 'I shall marry a pacifist.' When they reached the main road, she insisted on hurrying ahead, saying she must take Rumpus out for his walk.

'Look after yourself, my love,' Judith said to Alice.

'I'll be all right. But if anything ever did happen, you wouldn't have to be sad, you know. This is the most important thing in my life.'

'I expect we'd squeeze out a tear,' Judith said drily.

Stanley groaned. 'Don't speak of such things!'

After they had seen Alice on to her bus, Judith and Stanley decided to walk home; and Claire, who in reality was too nervous to go far on her own, joined them. Stanley was excited by the evening and wanted to relive parts of it which had particularly moved him. Judith was thinking of the family breaking up. She comforted herself with the thought that it had held together despite Louise's bombshell, so it would probably survive the present dislocation.

She had sometimes wondered how long Louise would continue to love this rather dull young man, and she had thought she had seen signs of tension. Now, here he was, bright as new in his uniform! She hoped Alice would not come home with something of the same kind in navy blue. Give me Ben any day, she thought; cross-grained he might be, but there was the makings of a man there!

'It was a very good evening, wasn't it?' Stanley said, as they came to their own home. 'We're a lucky family.' He did not look at the house next door where the Vaseyelins, who were not a lucky family, lived.

2

---

3 September 1939–February 1940

On the Sunday that war broke out, Alice and Claire had stayed home to listen to Mr Chamberlain's broadcast, while their mother and father went to chapel. On this momentous occasion, Mr Fairley was content that his daughters should be involved in the affairs of the material world while he and his wife attended to matters spiritual.

Mr Chamberlain sounded very sad, and Alice and Claire sat in the living room looking solemn as they listened. When the air raid siren sounded almost immediately after the broadcast, they put saucepans on their heads, and sat in the cupboard under the stairs. Alice was surprised by her own composure. Soon, however, she began to feel rather silly. Claire, who did not like enclosed spaces, said she would 'rather die than stay here any longer'. They went into the front garden. Jacov Vaseyelin was leaning over his gate. He pointed to the sky where a barrage balloon was lofting itself like some heraldic creature floating on its back. 'Pretty!'

The man who lived in the house opposite was herding his complaining family into a car. He called out to Alice and Claire, 'You had better come with us. We're getting out into the country.' He was in a panic. They looked at him with disfavour, and declined the invitation. Later, when their parents returned from chapel, calm and smiling, they felt proud of them, as though a battle had already been won. The all-clear sounded without anything having happened. Mr Fairley said, 'I expect that was just to get us used to the idea.'

Soon after this, Jacov and his brothers went out. An hour later, Mrs Vaseyelin arrived at the Fairleys' front door to say she had mislaid her front door key and could not get into the house. Stanley Fairley had to climb through the larder window. This was not the first time he had had to do this.

Mrs Vaseyelin's difficulties did not stop with her front door key. She ran out of money. At one time, this was something she would not have acknowledged. Gradually, however, the barrier of pride which had held her aloof from her neighbours was breaking down. She would come to the Fairleys late in the evening, asking if they could lend her money for the gas meter. Stanley Fairley would oblige, but when she had departed he would rage about her behaviour. A compassionate man, he was aware that his anger was out of all proportion to the provocation.

If ever there was a woman in need of Christian charity, that woman was surely Mrs Vaseyelin. She seemed one of those marked from birth for ill-fortune. Her father was Heinrich Steine, a German Jew, who married a Russian girl who had Jewish blood. The daughter of this union was blessed with a Slavonic beauty – broad cheekbones, big, hollowed eyes, and a quite unexceptional nose. As a child she spent much of her time with her grandparents in Russia. Here, she met and married the youngest son of Count Gregori Vaseyelin. His parents made no secret of their antipathy for the Jews. Consequently, communication with the German family had almost ceased by the time that war broke out in 1914. It was only with the coming of the Revolution that the importance of relatives abroad – and rich ones, at that – became apparent. Although Stefan Vaseyelin was reluctant to live in the same country as his wife's parents, he was prepared to accept financial assistance, on the grounds that in the past the parents had 'done little enough for their daughter'. The Vaseyelin family struck camp in Lithuania. By this time, their beloved daughter, Sonya, was dead. They had one other child, Jacov. A daughter, Katia, was born in 1920. By 1923, warned that their lives were in danger, they had fled to Poland. Here, twin boys were born. Soon, they again had reason to fear for their safety. Avoiding Germany, as a matter of pride rather than prudence, they came eventually to England in 1926. Nine years of deprivation and fear – and the close proximity of young children – had put intolerable strains on a marriage which required, if it was to survive, a spaciousness of living in which the partners could be distanced from each other. Mr Vaseyelin lived apart from his family, leaving his wife to cope with a situation which was quite beyond her capabilities.

The trials which she had undergone had drained her vitality. By the time she came to live in Shepherd's Bush, she seemed insubstantial as a ghost, leaving only a faint trace on her surroundings. So she continued for many years. Then, in 1936, came the news that her Jewish parents had been taken away by the Nazis to an unknown destination; and her surviving daughter, Katia, who had been staying with them, had also disappeared. At first, it seemed the shock had loosed her already tenuous grip on life. Then, a year later, Anita, the old family nurse, who had accompanied her through all her trials, died, leaving her bereft of her one support. Surprisingly, instead of withdrawing entirely from the world, which would have been sad, but no inconvenience to anyone save herself, she began to make her presence known.

She involved her neighbours not in her grief, which might have been interesting, but in the minor mischances of her daily life, which was tiresome. The woman who had only ventured out in the evenings to meet her husband after he had finished playing the violin outside a tube station or the Shepherd's Bush Empire, had been a source of mystery and speculation. The person who was forever in need of small change, or help over a lost key, a misplaced milk book, was merely a nuisance. They thought she was going to pieces. In fact, she was making a last attempt to claw her way back to life, to find some point of reference, a human contact. Unfortunately, at this time, most people were overloaded with worries of their own as war drew nearer – the gas masks were handed out, the sandbags began to pile up, the Anderson shelters were delivered. How could they be expected to notice that a struggle of a different kind was taking place in this alien, wraithlike woman? At the most, she met with exasperated kindness; but no arms were outstretched, no doors flung wide. And indeed, had this happened, it was doubtful whether she would have known how to respond. When one well-meaning neighbour took her to a meeting of the WVS, she told Judith Fairley disdainfully, 'The people were very boring and spent the evening packing clothes for evacuees.'

Stanley Fairley reacted to Mrs Vaseyelin as if she had the plague. He knew that he must not turn from her if he was to retain his self-respect; but whenever he was in contact with her he feared her slow contagion. In her house, he experienced something akin to panic. The Vaseyelins were victims. A sense of impending evil hung around their house. Mr Fairley was much concerned with matters of right and wrong, on which he was usually ready to risk a pronouncement; but he was not well-equipped to deal with evil.

'She must have money!' he fumed to Judith, after one late evening visit from Mrs Vaseyelin. 'Jacov is supposed to be so successful in the film world, now.' He adhered to the view that films, by and large, were sinful, and that the wages of sin were invariably high.

'I'm never sure what Jacov actually does,' Judith said. 'And, in any case, I don't think Mrs Vaseyelin is short of money so much as company. She comes in here when she gets desperate.'

He gazed at her in dismay. 'You're not going to ask her in?'

'No.' Judith was not in the habit of asking her neighbours in. She was prepared to help when help was needed, and to keep an eye on the house to make sure that Mrs Vaseyelin was up and about. Further than that, she had no intention of going. Years of running a house had made her ruthless in the matter of ensuring that her time was not wasted.

The subject of the Vaseyelins came up when Ben Sherman was visiting the Fairleys.

'I don't know what she will do when Jacov is called up,' Mr Fairley said. 'He does a lot of the cooking.'

Mrs Vaseyelin took no part in the running of the house. The shopping was done by the twins, Boris and Nicolai, who were in their last year at school.

'Do they get a good meal?' Ben asked. He was not so much concerned with the welfare of the younger Vaseyelins as with Judith's refusal to be involved. There was a gritty determination in Judith which Ben admired. She was holding out against the demands of universal motherhood; just as he was holding out against the idea that young men should be in a hurry to join up before they were conscripted.

Judith said, 'They have school lunches. Jacov sees to that. And when they leave school, they'll be in the Army — being fed like fighting cocks, if Guy is anything to judge by. He's put on half a stone since he's been lolling about at that camp.'

'It won't last,' Stanley warned.

'Why not? We've called Hitler's bluff and he's got no cards to play.' Ben wanted to believe this. He was thinking of his future as a great defence counsel. It was a role which appealed to him, not primarily because of his sympathy for the underdog, but because it seemed to offer more in the way of attacking expert witnesses — policemen, doctors — all of whom he saw quailing as he rose to cross-examine. The war was a diversion, unnecessary and irrelevant.

At the beginning of the new year, Guy was still 'lolling about' in camp. It was only at sea that Great Britain was already demonstrably engaged in a war. 'We should attack!' Mr Fairley fumed. 'What are we about, sitting here waiting for Hitler to come to us!' He himself was not sitting about. The elementary school of which he had been headmaster had been evacuated to the West Country. Arrangements had, however, to be made for the education of the not inconsiderable number of children who remained behind — their parents convinced that Hitler posed a less potent threat to their children's well-being than the unspeakable deprivations of rural life. Nowhere was this view held with greater tenacity than in the slum dwellings. Mr Fairley, not by birth a Londoner, had a great respect for such staunch unreason. He proceeded to create a post for himself as the Borough's teacher in over-all charge of the education of non-evacuated children.

Ben Sherman was by this time engaged in a diversion which had put the war and his career in the background. He was in love.

Several years ago he had had a brief argument with Daphne Drummond about Mosley, whom she much admired. At the time of this encounter, it had crossed his mind that he would like to teach this young woman a thing or two. No opportunity presenting itself, nothing had happened to damp down the spark of interest which she had aroused on that occasion. Then he met her unexpectedly in London, early one January evening in 1940. She was walking down Piccadilly, and paused in the shadow of the Ritz before stepping into the last of the daylight. Perhaps he had worked too hard, become a stranger to delight. At the moment when she walked from shadow into late sunlight, he felt a yearning so intense it jerked him out of his stride.

His first love had been Louise, who had attracted all eyes. As he recognized Daphne Drummond, he had the feeling that she was *his* discovery, rare, exciting, but with a certain detachment which he imagined would not make her immediately attractive to other men. When he stepped to her side, she said, 'Hullo, Ben.' They had had distant glimpses of each other over the years, and she found nothing surprising about their meeting on this occasion. It did not surprise her that he should ask her to have tea with him. She was not much given to surprise.

'What price Mosley now?' he asked, when they were seated in a tea shop.

This did earn him a raised eyebrow. It had been four years since that conversation, but he spoke as though they were still confronting each other in the Uxbridge Road. She paused before answering, unhurriedly reassessing him. Then she said, 'That's taken you a long time.' The reply dispensed with those preliminary stages of a relationship which Ben had hitherto found so wearisome that his interest seldom survived them. The war was undoubtedly responsible for cutting out much of the tedium, but he had an idea she would always be quick and positive – or decisively negative.

Later, as they walked towards Green Park, he said, 'When can I see you?'

'You're seeing me now.'

'Next time.'

'Are we through with now, then?'

In the park he investigated how far he might go. She seemed to enjoy the ensuing tussle more than his embraces. He could tell that these were games she had played before. He might consider Daphne Drummond to be unique, but for her Ben Sherman was a male who conformed to a familiar pattern. We'll see about that! he thought grimly.

He did not, however, make much progress. Their play, increasingly rough though it became on subsequent occasions, was part of an exercise which she seemed to find invigorating as a brisk country walk, bringing colour to her cheeks, brightness to her eyes, but giving her heart little trouble.

He planned ways of seducing her. The time of year was not propitious. It was well-nigh impossible to seduce an active, warmly-dressed young woman in a park, if she hadn't a mind to it.

Then, one evening she assumed herself too much in command. They were saying goodnight at the front door of her home in Shepherd's Bush. Ben noticed that only the windows at the top of the large, double-fronted house were blacked out. The servants were in bed. The rest of the house appeared to be empty.

'Are your folk away?'

'Yes.' Provocatively, she enumerated, 'Mother and Cecily are staying in Bucks because Mother is terrified of the guns on the Scrubs, which she seems to think are trained on our house. My father is in the Navy now, and Angus seldom honours us with his presence.' She turned to insert her key in the lock. He moved close. 'Oh no you don't, Ben!' She wriggled free of his grasp and snaked through the doorway. She would have slammed the door on his wrist, uncaring whether she did him injury or not, but he was the stronger.

As she faced him in the hall, something he had not seen before darkened her eyes. The realization that she was afraid excited him. He picked her up. In spite of her compact strength, she was a light burden. 'You can call for the servants, if you like.'

He knew which must be her bedroom – he had stood in the road often enough, staring up at the dim outline of her figure before she drew the dark curtains.

In the bedroom, she said quietly, 'Put me down, please, Ben. I have to take my time.' He put her down but held her close, pressing his body against hers. Her limbs were trembling. She said, 'Let me go. I don't intend to cheat.' In spite of her undoubted agitation, the tone of voice fell something short of entreaty. He unbuttoned her coat, and

18

eased it from her shoulders to the ground. The curtains were not drawn across the window, but it was a dark night, lit only by occasional flashes from the trolley-bus wires. She put a hand against his cheek. 'You must be patient with me. It won't work otherwise.' He was touched by this first show of weakness. He had wondered if she was a virgin; now that there seemed no doubt of it, impulses which were chivalrous stirred in him. But when he tried to reassure her, she pushed him away. He banged his shin on the bed post. Pain concentrated desire. The moment of tenderness was short-lived.

'There must be a candle, or a nightlight . . .'

'By the head of the bed.'

While he pawed his way along the bed, she undressed. The nightlight was shaded and gave only limited illumination. He lifted it, and looked round. She was standing by the bed, naked. He felt his throat constrict. In hollows beneath shoulders and ribs, and under the curve of the belly, the flesh glowed with the dusky lustre of a grape; while breasts and hips, swelling in the soft light, seemed themselves to be luminous, and the nightlight only a pale reflection of the body's radiance. The air was charged with energy. He was still as if his heart had ceased to beat. Could he have moved, he would have fallen on his knees before her.

She said sharply, 'Be quick, damn you!'

He put the nightlight down with shaking hands; the softened wax glistened in its cupped holder. He began to undress. In the road a bus lumbered by. A woman shouted, 'There's a pillar box here, Fred. Mind the pillar box, I say!'

Daphne laughed unsteadily. 'Do you think Fred's hit the pillar box?'

He came to her and laid his hand on her shoulder. She caught her breath.

'It will be all right,' he said.

'I can't.'

'It will be all right!' he repeated less gently.

'I can't, I tell you! I thought I could, but I can't . . .'

He was not accepting denial now that he was so fervent for her. When he pushed her down on the bed, she fought with a ferocity for which he was unprepared – no prudishness this, it might have been her life that was at stake. In the street, the woman was wailing, 'My glasses, Fred! I say, I've lost my glasses!' Daphne thrashed and moaned; she muttered words under her breath, her head strained away from Ben, as though there was someone in the darkness whom she was entreating. He was shaken by the violence of her resistance.

But when he released her, she put her arms round his neck and whispered, 'Yes, yes!' He was clumsy; her fingers clawed his shoulders and drew blood. Altogether, there was more blood than pleasure. While he dressed, she cried.

'You can cry for both of us,' he said, savage with disappointment. But her crying was quiet and very private. He might have played no part in what had happened.

His previous encounters had shed only a dim light on the psychology of sex, and such understanding as he had came from reading the exploits of others – from which he had gained the impression that it was more usual for the man to regard the woman as object than the reverse.

He sat on the edge of the bed, determined to salvage something. 'What is this all about?'

She hunched over, away from him. 'The maids will hear.'

'I can't leave you like this.'

'Can't leave me! Whoever do you think you are? Get out of here.'

He went. 'You're best rid of that!' he told himself as he stumbled down the short drive.

Something crunched beneath his feet on the pavement. He bent and picked up the frame of Fred's glasses. A warden who was passing told him that the last bus had gone.

The long walk to his lodgings seemed the loneliest in his lonely life. Moments of panic seized him as he groped his way down dark, unrecognizable streets. 'I can't go on like this!' he kept repeating, as though things had been going wrong for some time before he became involved with Daphne. But they hadn't, had they? He had been doing fine – he had got a good degree, they thought well of him in his chambers, he was twenty-five and at the start of a brilliant career. Why should he feel the weariness of a man who has taken a wrong turning, and has been urging himself on, while all around him the townscape becomes more and more unfamiliar? In the course of his journey, he asked the way of a lamp-post, fell over a dustbin, and collided with a policeman. The policeman, who had come off duty, was pleased to accompany him.

'You must get very lonely,' Ben said.

The policeman said he was a Baptist and the Lord Jesus walked with him. Ben, brought up among people who talked like this, felt homesick for a way of life long since rejected. When they reached his lodgings, the policeman put a hand on his arm and said, 'You are not happy, brother. I can tell that.' His earnestness was all the more impressive for his not being visible. 'And you never will be happy until you take your trouble to the Lord.'

'It's not the kind of trouble I can "take to the Lord",' Ben said uppishly.

The policeman was not impressed by claims to sin of a superior order. 'You read your Bible! There's all the sin you could wish for — murder, rape, incest, and none of it meriting more than a few words. When I hear people boasting about their sins, I long to sit them down to read the story of David. Now there was a splendid sinner!'

In his room, Ben opened the Bible at random. The first words that met his eyes were: 'He that is wounded in the stones, or hath his privy member cut off, shall not enter into the assembly of the Lord.' He threw the Bible on to the floor.

He was fiercely angry that he had been given a moment in which he had glimpsed something beyond expectation or understanding, only to have been betrayed by this wilful girl. For several weeks he avoided Daphne. Then, remembering Louise's pregnancy, he became anxious. Eventually, he telephoned her, and asked her to meet him for a drink.

She came, a spring in her step, from the direction of Green Park. Her cheeks were rosy from the cold, and she greeted him with such spontaneous good humour she might have been his sister.

'Is everything all right?' he asked when they sat down with their drinks.

She accepted his meaning without self-consciousness. 'I had a scare. But I drank half a bottle of gin and had a hot bath.' She might have been relating how she had shaken off a cold. 'We'd better take precautions next time.'

'I didn't think there was going to be a next time.'

'Don't be silly.' She looked at him, neither bold nor defiant, but direct. 'You want to, don't you?'

'But you?'

'I've just said, haven't I?' At such moments she seemed the least equivocal person he had ever met.

It was little better next time. She fought with the same searing desperation. Whatever it was that gripped her, there was no doubting the genuineness of her emotions — her anger, fear, disgust, pain, her hideous grief, were not feigned.

'You don't want this, do you?' he said angrily afterwards.

'Yes, yes!' She beat at him with her fists. 'I do! I do!'

He put his arms around her, holding her close against whatever it was that threatened her. 'What *is* this?' he whispered, at a loss.

'I'm going to be a whole person.' The words came through clenched teeth. 'And this is the way it's done, isn't it?'

He knew then that he was being used in some way he could not begin to understand. It was a good enough reason for having nothing more to do with her; but it became his reason for seeing her. He would not part with her until he had made her need him. He pictured her clutching at him, begging, beseeching, pouring out secrets he no longer had any wish to hear in a vain endeavour to hold him. She quivered to please him, the sweat larded her body. When he was confronted with the reality, it was bracing as winter frost.

The family was still away. He saw her every night that week. Although she was a mischievous, high-spirited companion, there was none of this blitheness in her love-making – only a grim struggle against what seemed, at the very least, a natural disinclination.

He could not get her out of his mind. Hitherto, he had placed the women who interested him in two categories – those whom he might marry, and those whom he could treat lightly. Daphne was not a person to be treated lightly – as had been the French waitress, Marie, and the cinema usherette, Cherry, both of whom gave their favours indiscriminately. On the other hand, she was not the kind of woman he intended to marry.

Although he was ambitious, Ben did not think in terms of marrying well. His American father had gone down on the *Lusitania* when his son was a year old. Lizzie Sherman had worked hard, taking in lodgers, doing dressmaking, to give her son a home and a future. She had loved him dearly; but there had not been time or energy for demonstrations of affection after she had fed and clothed him, and kept house for the lodgers. He, inheriting her stoicism, had accepted this. Occasionally, he would speak of the things they would do together when he was a man and able to support her. She had listened wryly, already feeling her mortality in her leaden stomach; but she had never laughed at his dreams. Grieving, he still saw her as she had been in her last years, worn and ill. Time had not yet restored to him the happier, more resilient young woman who for a few brave years had succeeded in making an adventure of misfortune.

Ben respected women, particularly those who had to work hard. From such, he was resolved to find a wife. Unfortunately, a capacity for hard work was not in itself stimulating. In the days when he had been attracted to Louise, love had been a matter of shining eyes and floating hair, of inconsequential laughter and a certain proud carriage of the head. Daphne was not beautiful in that spell-binding way; loving Daphne seemed a matter of perversity more than anything else.

When she asked him to a party at her home, his first inclination was to refuse. 'My father is on leave,' she said. 'Why don't you come? You used to be friendly with my brother Angus, and he'll be there. And Irene Kimberley – you have met her at the Fairleys.'

Ben, with Mr Fairley in mind, thought he would find it awkward to meet Lieutenant Commander Drummond. But he went because he was curious. His scruples soon disappeared. It was difficult to imagine this handsome, urbane man being discomposed by a little matter of his daughter's seduction. Ben listened with impatience to Drummond telling a story about a pilot who had landed on the wrong aircraft carrier. '. . . until he was in the mess, when someone said "There's only one thing wrong with that, old chap – this happens to be the *Victorious* . . ."' Although Drummond had not been to sea, he nevertheless contrived by his dry, laconic manner to give the impression of one who, had he chosen, could have recounted more costly misadventures. He himself might be casual, but he left his audience to assume gallantry and quiet courage. Now, in his forties, he was good-looking still, but his face had the high colour and broken veins of the drinker. He had affected the style of the Fleet Air Arm pilot, wearing his hair longer than regulations permitted. In civilian life, he had thought it imperative to be well-groomed, but the gold braid on his sleeve had a worn look – Ben thought he probably rubbed it with emery paper. He moved from one group to another, off-hand, disparaging, carelessly amusing. He was the sort who would speak lightly of the deaths of other men.

Ben sipped his drink, contemplating something offensive to say. A few minutes later, as the Commander proffered cigarettes, he asked, 'Weren't you a supporter of Mosley at one time?'

Drummond saw no need to parry this thrust. 'Still am, old man, still am! No apologies for that! He would have done a lot for this country, if only he'd been given his head. Got rid of the trash – know what I mean? He made a few miscalculations about Hitler, of course. Not that I'm one of those who think that Hitler is a monster.' He looked to where his son, Angus, was talking to Irene Kimberley, and raised his voice. 'We'd be wise not to smash the Germans. If we do, we let the Russkies in.'

Angus went on talking as though he had not heard; Irene, flushed, responded rather more vivaciously than was required.

Ben tried to think of something offensive to say about Hitler; language, however, proved inadequate to this task. The best he could manage was, 'Hitler is a raving lunatic, and the sooner he is smashed the better.'

Drummond said smoothly, 'You'd better do something about it then, hadn't you, old son?' He patted Ben's civilian shoulder and passed on. A few of Drummond's naval comrades laughed.

Angus and Irene joined Ben. 'It never does to take on my father,' Angus said. 'He is so utterly sure he is in the right, it makes him quite impregnable. My one hope is that he will step on a live shell – I don't think he would cope well with dismemberment.'

Irene glanced at him sharply; and Ben, not for the first time, was taken aback by Angus's hatred of his father.

'What are you talking about so intently?' Daphne asked, holding out a plate of olives.

Angus said, 'I was predicting that our devil-may-care father will get a VC without a hair of his head being touched.'

She shook his arm affectionately. 'Brother dear, you mustn't be tetchy and spoil our lovely family party. Tell us about your exciting life at the Foreign Office.'

Angus's rather sombre face relaxed. He was as handsome as his father when he smiled, and rather more distinguished. 'That enquiry was nicely timed. The Foreign Office has decided the Army has the greater need of me.'

Ben thought, the sardonic tone notwithstanding, it was typical of the Drummond male that he should think in terms of there being a particular need of his services. Angus and Daphne moved away to impart the news to their sister, Cecily. Irene sighed. 'Straight out of Dornford Yates!'

Ben said, 'They seem an odd family.'

'Odder than you think.' She did not elaborate. Before Ben could pursue this, Mrs Drummond came up to them. Fragile and elegant, she was mistily draped in the style of another period.

'You're Alice, aren't you?' she said.

'No. Irene.'

'Ah, yes.' Her manner suggested it was vulgar to remember names, let alone faces. She talked with a distracted air, flashing distraught glances around the room, as though expecting that at any moment something untoward would occur. She had the look of a superficial person on whom someone has leaned too heavily. 'You're in the Wrens, aren't you?'

'No, that's Alice. I'm at London University.'

'Oh?' Mrs Drummond wrinkled her forehead, not sure what might be said of London University. 'Neither of my girls seems that

24

way inclined. Daphne talks about flying aeroplanes.' She looked at Ben, apparently expecting him to advise on this extravagance. 'I can't think where she gets it from.'

Irene said, changing the subject, 'We hear Angus is going into the Army.'

'Angus!' Mrs Drummond's voice rose sharply. 'Oh no, that's not possible! He's at the Foreign Office, doing very important work that he can't even talk about. They would never let him go.'

'I expect I was mistaken,' Irene said hastily.

Mrs Drummond looked at her, alerted to the truth by this attempt to retract. 'It's very silly of me.' She made a pathetically inadequate attempt at dignity. 'Other people's sons will go.' She bit on this thought, her eyes closed. It was plain she believed other people had less need of their sons.

Commander Drummond came and put a glass in her hand. 'Splendid news about Angus, my dear! I know how proud you must feel.' His eyes were bright with mirth. It was apparent to Irene and Ben, standing close to him, that it was his wife's distress which gave rise to this jubilation. 'We must all drink to this!' He held his glass aloft and made an announcement in a ringing voice. He might, Ben thought, have been referring to something of real significance – like the United States declaring war.

Mrs Drummond considered her glass as distastefully as if she had been invited to drink poison. A reasonable alternative occurred to her. She said, 'No, I shall not drink to it.'

Her husband stared at her in astonishment – rather as though one of the maids had made a lewd gesture. He was at a disadvantage, his usual methods of getting his own way not being open to him with a room full of people. He decided to ignore his wife and proposed a toast. While he drank, Mrs Drummond raised her glass high, and poured its contents over his head.

It was, as Irene remarked to Ben, a fitting end to the evening. Ben had agreed to see her home. Angus had said to him, 'I dare not leave my mother.'

As they walked down the drive, Irene looked back at the house. 'I don't like to think what is going on in there.' Her tone suggested she would very much like to know.

Ben said, 'I expect they are trying to repair the damage to the King's uniform!' Wine stains weren't in the same category as worn gold braid.

'That will be the least of their problems, I fear.'

Now, cloaked in the anonymity of darkness, she was prepared to

25

say more. But although he was curious, he was reluctant to take the first step into her knowledge. To defer the moment, he said, 'I didn't know you knew Angus so well.'

'Oh, no one *knows* Angus. He's fathoms deep, or so he would have one think.' They walked in silence for a few paces, then she said, 'What great store we set by knowing, don't we? I'm sure half the troubles of the world would be solved if we were more ignorant.'

'We'd certainly have a shorter life expectancy.'

'But you're in the law, not medicine. So ignorance is much more profitable, surely?'

Her mind leapt ahead of topics. She did not bother to elaborate on her remarks, just assumed her hearer would follow her leaps. Ben thought she was probably highly intelligent. From what he remembered of her at the party, he imagined she was equally highly-strung — a diminutive creature, with big eyes which drowned the small face. In contrast, Daphne had seemed sturdy and down-to-earth. At the moment when he thought of Daphne, Irene's flow of talk suddenly petered out. They seemed to share a common unease, as though there had been no intervening conversation. He said, 'Even so, being friendly with Angus and Daphne, you must know the Drummond parents quite well.'

'I've made it my business not to know them.'

'Why do they stay together if they dislike each other so much?'

'For the sake of the children.'

'He didn't strike me as the self-sacrificing type.'

The desire to make her point overrode discretion, and she answered, 'To be precise, it's for Daphne that he stays. And I think *indulge* would be a better word for his activities.' She surely can't mean . . . Even as the question formed in his mind, she said, regretting her lapse, 'Of course, I'm not saying anything has actually happened . . .'

'No, of course not.'

Neither wanted to continue the conversation. It was a bright, frosty night and they walked quickly, soon reaching Norland Square, where she lived. She said, 'Come in and have a sandwich. You must be starving — I know I am.'

He said, 'Thank you,' reluctant to be left with his own thoughts.

As she opened the front door, a voice called, 'Is that you, Irene?' The voice was confident, the enquiry more an acknowledgement that the house now had its full complement.

Irene led Ben into the drawing room. Her parents were seated in easy chairs one on either side of the hearth. An unrecognizable substance, unrelated to coal, was burning, giving out smoke and a smell not unlike manure. Mr and Mrs Kimberley were reading, unperturbed, he the newspaper, she a book. One had the impression that they had been quiet for a long time. Ben could not remember when he had last come into a room where there was such a profound sense of peace. It not being his peace, he immediately felt defensive, as though a statement had been made about his own turbulence. Mr Kimberley looked round the side of his paper, and Mrs Kimberley turned her head, keeping a finger on the page of the book. The greeting was without effort. Had Ben not been there, nothing else might have passed between the three of them.

Mr Kimberley, registering the intruder's presence, smiled, politely uninterested, as Irene made brief introductions. Mrs Kimberley looked at him benevolently over the rim of her spectacles.

'They didn't feed us,' Irene said to her mother. 'I'll make sandwiches.' There was a wry exchange of glances between mother and daughter. The housekeeping here was not as efficient as that of the Fairleys – nor, apparently, as important. There was amusement in Mrs Kimberley's unspoken acknowledgement of deficiency as she followed her daughter into the kitchen.

Mr Kimberley and Ben were left to make the best of each other. Ben looked up at the mirror over the mantelpiece, which gave him a good view of the room without his seeming to stare. It was a long, uncluttered room, furnished in a style to which he was unaccustomed, elegant, but not ostentatious. The furniture had the appearance of having been used by more than one generation of Kimberleys. Age had darkened the pictures on the walls, giving added obscurity to wild seascapes and craggy moorland. Ben imagined the pictures must be valuable, since, in their dingy state, there seemed little else to commend them. But if the Kimberleys lived well, then they were used to it. Nothing here was on display, or called for comment.

Mr Kimberley said, 'We've boarded the *Altmark*. Did you know?'

Ben realized with surprise how little he had thought about the progress of the war in recent weeks. The *Altmark*, he recalled, was the auxiliary of the *Graf Spee*.

'Apparently she had several hundred British merchant seamen prisoner on board. The first they knew of it, was someone crying "The Navy's here!"' Mr Kimberley handed the paper to Ben. 'Nice for their families; but I'm afraid it won't do the Norwegians much good.'

Ben said, 'You think Hitler will invade?'

'Well, of course he will.' Mr Kimberley was mildly surprised by the fatuity of the remark. Ben bowed his head over the newspaper.

The sandwiches, when they arrived, had a mashed filling tasting of paraffin. The tea was even more unpleasant. Mr Kimberley, who was watching Ben quizzically, said, 'Do you like it? It was sent to my assistant by some relatives in South America. It is supposed to have healing properties.'

'I don't much like it,' Ben said.

'No, I think I'd prefer not to be healed myself.'

There was silence while Ben and Irene ate. This was a house of frequent silences which had no need to be broken. For guests, however, it was acknowledged that something different was required. Mrs Kimberley asked, 'How were the Drummonds?'

'As usual. He is like one of those awful bounders in Buchan.'

Mr Kimberley said, 'Sapper, surely?'

Buchan acceptable, Ben noted, Sapper not.

Mrs Kimberley said to her husband, 'Ben is a barrister' – having put him in possession of this fact, she left him to deal with their guest accordingly. Mr Kimberley mentioned several well-known names. He did not seem to expect Ben to be impressed. Ben found conversation with someone at once well-connected and unconcerned about it rather unnerving, demanding as it did a similar detachment on his part.

Yet, uncomfortable though he had felt in their presence, when he left the Kimberleys he found that, despite the black-out and the piles of sandbags, the world seemed a saner place. Frost had silvered the pavements and the bitter air took his breath away. He could not keep any line of thought going. Ideas took shape in his mind against which he had no defence. By the time he reached his lodgings, he knew that whatever he might have felt for Daphne, there was no way forward.

Irene wrote to Alice later that week, 'I have been out with Angus Drummond once or twice. Nothing serious, just that we found we both like Mozart. He took me to a party at his home the other evening – too much to drink and nothing to eat. I am sorry to tell you, Alice, that Drummond *père* is now a Lieutenant Commander – aren't you ashamed of the Navy? It must have been a wangle – he's quite old. I hope he never comes your way. Could you bring yourself to salute him?

'Angus is going into the Army, doing something rather hush-hush. There is a certain inevitability about people's lives, I begin to suspect. It is so *suitable* that Angus, who never gives much of himself away, should be doing secret work. Daphne seemed a bit subdued, I thought. Perhaps she had a cold. She looked what Mother would call "peaky" and too bright about the eyes.

'You will never believe me when I tell you who upstaged the gallant Commander at this scintillating party – *Mrs* Drummond! I hope I can convey something of the piquancy of that moment when . . .'

Mrs Drummond's gesture notwithstanding, the main impression which Alice gained from the letter was that Irene's social life was more interesting than her own. The mansion in which she was quartered was on the fringe of a small town in Hertfordshire, and the only outing was to the village pub, where the company was not lively. The pub was mainly frequented by Scottish soldiers who drank heavily, all the while subjecting the female company to intense and gloomy scrutiny. At closing time, they lurched towards the females whom they calculated best suited to their purpose. 'Ye're a fine lassie,' one brawny sergeant, pausing in his passage, assured Alice. 'But there's nae the time – ye ken?' He patted her shoulder, and stumbled off into the arms of a neat little ATS corporal with demurely downcast eyes and a face like one of the junior miss models in a Weldon's pattern book.

Alice was in the paradoxical situation of wanting to be the sergeant's choice without wanting the man himself. Obviously she had a lot to learn.

Conversation in the cabin at night assumed experience of men. Many of the girls were from homes not unlike Alice's own, and she wondered how they had come by such extensive knowledge. Soon, she realized it had been acquired in the few weeks since they left home. They had discovered themselves to be possessed of gifts which had lain unused, waiting just such a time of freedom. Freedom extended the range of their giving. Only a year ago, their encounters would have been limited to their own kind, but now the field had widened considerably. From being Pat and Jean and John and George, they had become archetypal men and women. The language of the day favoured principalities and powers. Had not Chamberlain said, 'It is evil things that we shall be fighting against . . .'? In such circumstances, men who were about the stern business of killing could hardly be expected to observe the niceties of a well-ordered peacetime society. Alice's companions had adapted to this situation. Ideas of virtue and discretion had been cast aside with the same ease with which they had surrendered their civilian identity cards. Their experiences seemed to have had little adverse effect on them: inno-cent, wide-eyed, retaining all the freshness of the 'nice girl', they recounted with amusement the various attempts to rid them of their virginity. A few even admitted to not being virgins. If this was done with style, it ensured respect. Style was all-important. Girls who went into the first field with a man were regarded as 'sordid'. West End hotels were not sordid, and had not yet become a joke.

There were, however, three girls who maintained their virtue at little cost to their popularity. Each had a fiancé to whom she was completely devoted; but in his absence allowed other men to take her out – provided it was understood they were to be 'just friends'. The 'just friends' status won for them treatment of such a superior order – dining at the Berkeley and country house week-ends – that Alice regretted her own refusal to become engaged to Ted Peterson before he joined the Rifle Brigade.

In answer to a letter from Alice, Irene wrote, 'No, I'm sorry to disappoint you. But I am *not* falling for Angus Drummond. I'm not taken in by these reserved men who give the impression of being very deep. Men who are interesting are usually only too pleased to demonstrate the fact. Our relationship is based entirely on Mozart.

'And speaking of men who don't hide their light under a bushel – did you know that Ben is going out with Daphne? Quite surprising, that . . .'

Alice was more than surprised.

Most of her life she had accepted occupying second place, a not uncomfortable position. In her friendships, she had not been possessive; at home, she had not competed for her parents' attention, as had Claire. If there was one thing on which she could modestly congratulate herself, it was that hers was not an envious disposition.

All this changed when she read Irene's letter. It was not, of course, that she was in love with Ben. It was simply that he was *hers*; and not only by virtue of their being distantly related. It was she who had struck up a friendship with him when she was staying with her grandparents in Cornwall, and – findings being keepings – he had belonged to her ever since. They had seemed to have an unspoken understanding of each other's moods and problems. He would sometimes say, 'Alice is my girl.' Although this was meant, and accepted, as a jest, it was nevertheless a statement of a particular affection which he made no effort to conceal. He was reputed to have been enamoured of Louise, but he had not treated her with that special warmth he reserved for Alice. She never felt it was something she had to earn: he liked her as she was. This was the most precious thing of all – the feeling that in the eyes of one person at least, she was intrinsically likeable.

He had had girl friends. But as Alice had never met any of them, she had never been obliged to measure their likeableness against her own. But Daphne was different. Daphne was one of her oldest friends, and that Ben should find something in her that he had not found in Alice was shockingly hurtful. Hitherto, her friends and family had belonged to a charmed company of people interweaving in some mysterious dance. It would never be the same again, now that these two had waltzed away on their own. She realized, what most of her contemporaries had known long ago, that even those whom we love can on occasions be a threat.

It did not stop with Daphne and Ben, this pain. By their choice of each other, they had excluded her. And Irene, by her very presence at the party, had become a part of this conspiracy. She had seen them together, watched their faces as they looked at each other. Try as she might, Alice could not imagine how Daphne looked at Ben, or Ben at Daphne – but Irene knew. Oh, it was incredibly wounding, this *knowing* of theirs! She was being left behind in the maturing process. She had never questioned the precise nature of her relationship with Ben – or, indeed, with any other young man of her acquaintance. She had thought they would remain constant until, at some undefined future date, she was ready. The readiness she had seen as happening, rather than as being achieved by any effort of growth on her part.

They were all moving away from her. Would they, with a careless backward glance, say to one another, 'I wonder where poor Alice got to?' The more she thought about it, the more she imagined herself, by the very fact of her falling behind, to be a topic of conversation. How could she face them again, now that they had humiliated her in this way?

She wondered what Mr Drummond made of it all. When she wrote to Irene, the only reference which she made to the party was 'Mr Drummond must have been put out about Ben and Daphne.' She was tempted to ask how he was taking it, but felt this betrayed too great an interest. No doubt Irene, who knew about the nastiness in the Drummond household, would tell her in any case. But Irene seemed more concerned with Angus and Mozart, and did not refer to the matter again.

Alice decided that she, too, must put it behind her. Her knowledge of life might be limited, but her knowledge of films more than made up for this lack. Although she liked love stories to be poignant, she had never – even in the worst days of her addiction – liked them to be lingering. She resolved that the next time she met Ted Peterson, she would tell him she had decided to become engaged to him.

But – alas for dinners at the Berkeley and country house week-ends with men who were 'just friends' – when next she telephoned Ted's home for news of him, his father told her that his battalion had moved. 'We think he's on the Continent, but we don't really know.' He spoke as of a place as far removed as Antarctica.

The war was beginning at last, with friends and relatives to worry about. Yet, as she went about her duties, Alice had a feeling of unreality, as though she was waiting in the wings for something to happen on an empty stage. The nature of her course – she was training to be a coder – was a contributory factor; but primarily it was her surroundings which made her feel unconnected with the play of events.

The baronial hall in which she was quartered was a mysterious, slightly creepy place. It had not been built to house over a hundred service women. For one thing, there was too much circulation space – winding corridors and long galleries which were difficult to heat, and in whose labyrinthine meanderings it was all too easy to mislay personnel. The scale was wrong, too. The ceilings were lofty and there was a tiresome echo which tended to ridicule commands. The fireplaces all appeared to have been designed for roasting oxen; the small stoves placed in them became derisory comments on the inadequacy of the heating. Above all, the house had the effect of making the present occupants seem unreal as amateur performers in a setting unsuited to their limited talents.

This friction between the house and its inmates produced a feeling of unrest in Alice, reminding her that there were as many dark corners as sunlit gardens in the world of the imagination. At night, after the cheerful talk of men and sex, there was an awful darkness. Even after they had taken down the black-out and the steely moonlight penetrated the room, it was no better. The house was indifferent to them. It had stood for a long time; the wood and stone had endured, but the people had come and gone like shadows. Alice lay and thought of all the things people were doing even now, preparing to blow up cities and change the map of Europe. Yet they had so little time. The cavalier in the canvas at the turn of the stairs would probably outlast them all, as he had already outlasted painter and sitter.

For a time, there seemed a danger that her illness would recur. Then, at last, she was kitted out. One morning she looked at herself in the speckled mirror. Her collar was commendably stiff, the tie neatly knotted at her throat. Navy blue suited her. She made a vow. She would not look into this darkness any more. This was *her* time of life and she would bend all her energies to making the most of every moment.

3

April–August 1940

In April the Germans invaded Norway. 'It's a rugged country,' Stanley Fairley said to Judith. 'The Germans won't be able to fight in that sort of territory.' In May he was telling her what splendid fighters the Dutch were. Guy had had embarkation leave in March. Louise thought he was probably on the Continent.

Whatever the resolution of the Dutch, it was obviously time to take the war seriously. Mr Fairley decided that the loft must be cleared.

'If we are bombed, it will be cleared anyway,' Judith pointed out, visualizing all the dust which would be blown through the house. 'Why not leave it till then?'

He frowned at this levity. 'All that stuff up there is a fire hazard. We are risking not only our own lives but those of our neighbours.' As the house on one side had been standing empty ever since Mr Ainsworth, their elderly neighbour, died, there did not appear to be any immediate risk to anyone there.

'And goodness alone knows what the Vaseyelins have in *their* loft!' Judith said.

'Very little, judging by the furnishing of the rest of the house,' he retorted. 'Refugees don't hoard possessions.'

He uttered the word 'possessions' as though it was itself a rebuke.

'I still don't see why you want to do it. You refused to evacuate. You said Hitler wasn't going to turn you out of your home. Now, you are preparing to turn out your home for him!'

'This is only a small thing.'

'But why, having refused the big thing, surrender over the small?'

'We are not surrendering, Judith! Simply taking necessary precautions. I can't think why you are being so inconsistent. You have complained a hundred times that there is too much stored away in the loft.'

It was true. Stanley was the one who cared about the bits and pieces of the family framework, she was the casual one. Her disquiet did not seem reasonable, even to herself. She said, 'Do it if you must, but don't leave a lot of rubbish in the back garden. War or no war, we don't want the place looking like a junk-yard.'

He was excited by the prospect. Once, it was he who would be annoyed because Judith must go about household duties when he wanted them to sit quietly together. But he had become very restless and seemed to welcome any diversion; while she was the quieter of the two, giving an impression of strength at the centre.

They set about the task one Saturday afternoon when Alice was home on forty-eight-hour leave, and Louise had come for the day. It was, after all, a family affair, the loft being full of tokens of the lives of Fairleys for generations past. Louise had left the children with Guy's parents. 'I'd have brought them with me if I'd known,' she said, rather surprisingly, since usually she had little time for sentimentality.

Alice had a boy friend with her, a young Pilot Officer in the RAF. He was enthusiastic about the project when he saw the contents of the loft. 'This will be a real treasure hunt!'

'We're not looking for treasure,' Judith said drily. 'Only throwing it away.'

'It is the least we can do.' Stanley Fairley wondered how she could speak like this in the presence of a young man who might be called upon to throw his life away.

The young man appeared to have no sense of his imminent sacrifice. He wasted a lot of time trying on the clothes in the dressing-up trunk and striking attitudes. Family parties in his home had been restrained affairs, and his present uniform was the nearest he had ever come to wearing costume.

Louise looked through the old photograph albums, lingering over the pictures of herself and her sisters when they were young. Her own children asked for their father continuously. She had to be brave for the three of them and accepted this without complaint; she had grasped eagerly what life gave, and now set herself to meet its demands as readily. But the news was bad, and Guy somewhere in the thick of the fighting; she seemed to tremble inwardly much of the time. She could hardly keep the tears back when she came unexpectedly upon snapshots of herself and Guy, taken on that hilarious occasion when the Women's Bright Hour had been tipped into the sea. There was Guy, leaning against a breakwater, looking self-conscious in a blazer, the young face smooth as almond paste!

Judith, looking at her, guessed something of what she was going through. She remembered waiting for news from the Front. How lucky she and Stanley had been! She prayed it might be so, too, for Louise and Guy.

Claire was protesting that this was 'all stupid'. Judith said, 'Then go downstairs, and let us do it.' But Claire remained, kicking at old dolls and broken chairs, complaining, 'Who wants to keep all this rubbish anyway!' More than her sisters, Claire found this exercise upsetting. She feared change. Her aggressive behaviour betrayed the longing to revert to childhood and be comforted.

The dog, Rumpus, who had been allowed to join them, rushed from one person to another, tearing at discarded curtains, barking furiously at the old rocking horse. Like most of the Fairley dogs, he was more loved than trained, and became increasingly hysterical.

Alice worked methodically with her father, enjoying herself. Much of what was found she had already committed to her diary, and she did not need the actual objects to spark memory. In fact, the objects tended to be disappointing. She had remembered the masks, given by an unimaginative aunt, as more frightening than they seemed now that her sophisticated sensibilities rejected the merely crude. Yet, that Christmas, she and Claire had been so terrified, they had huddled together in Alice's bed – until they fell out, bringing down the centre light in their parents' bedroom beneath.

Louise said, 'Oh, the shells! The pretty things!' She held one to her ear and listened to the roar of the sea, thinking of Guy, and how he had romanced about the windjammer, *Herzogin Cecilie*. How vulnerable he was, even still! Had she been unkind to him sometimes, she who was not a dreamer? 'I shall take these for the children,' she said. 'They will love them.'

'We're supposed to be getting rid of things,' her father said.

'If I take them, you *will* have got rid of them.'

He paused over a studio photograph of a fierce old woman in a mountainous hat. 'Great-aunt Agatha! Now, Claire, you were saying only the other day you couldn't remember seeing a picture of her, and I knew we had one somewhere. Here she is!' He held it up proudly. 'A terrifying old lady. I went in dread of her when I was a boy. She once locked me in the cowshed all one day for some minor misdemeanour. I don't think we can throw her away.'

'But you're throwing photos of us away,' Alice laughed.

'I don't need photographs to remind me of you, darling.' He reluctantly consigned Great-aunt Agatha to the pile. Judith rescued her and studied the austere face from which Stanley's eyes looked out.

Stanley was hesitating over an even older photograph of Great-

36

aunt Eleanor, who had dwindled to death in an asylum. It seemed that some honour was due to the photograph which had not been paid to the unfortunate woman in her lifetime.

'We have madness in the family, you see,' Alice said to the Pilot Officer.

'Yes, indeed!' He was much impressed.

'You know, we could make things with some of this.' Louise had become practical, bending over the dressing-up trunk.

'That stuff is so old it will fall to pieces if you wash it,' Judith said.

'Not that black taffeta! That will go on until the end of time. And look at all this lace!'

The young Pilot Officer watched her as she held the black lace against glowing face and chestnut hair. His eyes travelled slowly down her body with a look almost wounded, as though she had hurt him without warning.

Claire gathered Rumpus into her arms, trying to soothe him, and he licked her face frantically.

Alice held up a woollen doll's bonnet. 'Do you remember Daddy dressing him up in this, and a nightdress, to stop him getting pneumonia when he was run over?' She put the bonnet on Rumpus and even Claire laughed.

Judith, to whom it usually fell to supervise enterprises of this nature, sat in a broken wicker chair and let them get on with it. Stanley was enjoying himself. This is as good as stirrup pump drill for him! she thought wryly. The dismantling of the loft disturbed her. It had about it something of the confusion of abandoning ship. These were more than random accumulations which were being tossed aside; they were important just because they had accumulated. People who are settled accumulate. 'Refugees,' Stanley had pointed out, 'don't hoard possessions.' She looked at her family, piling up photographs, old painting books, shawls and fans, toys and dolls' furniture, a sampler worked by Aunt Meg, and sketches of the ships in which their Cornish grandfather had sailed, and she wondered at their wantonness. We grew out of this, she thought; it's a part of us, our history. It is important to know where we came from, to have glimpses of the people from whom we sprang. It helps to explain us to ourselves. But how could she expect them to understand, when she herself had only recently become aware of it? She noticed that Louise was making a collection of items – not all of practical value – to take with her. Alice, judging by her absorbed expression, was committing them to memory. But Claire, who most needed the security of the past to balance the intractable present and unknown future, was

37

simply letting go. She called Claire to her. 'There's nothing to stop you keeping anything you particularly want in your own room.' But it was never possible for Claire to make choices easily, so she stamped her foot and said, 'Throw it all out!'

Later, downstairs, dusty and hungry, they sat talking over late supper until the time came to put up the black-out. Soon after this they were disturbed by Mrs Vaseyelin. On the day when they had been throwing out, Mrs Vaseyelin had decided to add to their possessions. She had brought them a carton of candles.

'We have so many,' she explained, standing in the dining room with her booty at her feet. 'For the icons. Anita must have hoarded. Please to have these.'

Mr Fairley frowned down at this tainted source of light. Judith briskly thanked Mrs Vaseyelin and offered tea. Mrs Vaseyelin declined, but sat on the edge of a chair.

She was wearing a black coat, shiny with age, and a little black hat with a veil. The Fairleys had never seen her outside her house without a hat. Her sparse hair, insecurely knotted at the nape of her neck, was a rusty black. The hat, the shabby coat and the dyed hair seemed as mustily theatrical as the items in the dressing-up trunk. But to Mrs Vaseyelin they represented the last remnants of her dignity.

Louise said impulsively, 'May I take some of the candles, Mrs Vaseyelin? They'll be so useful.'

'Please.'

She looked at Louise with eyes hungry for something that could not be put into words. Louise sat beside her. A gulf of time and culture separated them. It was too late to reach out now; if anything could have been done for this woman, it should have been done years ago. But Louise, once she recognized a need, was determined. 'You have never been to see me, Mrs Vaseyelin – in my home, I mean. And I don't think you have seen the children. Won't you come? Come to tea one day next week.'

The invitation perceptibly alarmed Mrs Vaseyelin. The most she could have accepted would have been a glass of sherry and a dry biscuit. She could have fed on that for days. She said, 'Yes, yes – next week . . .' She got up, and was preparing to take her leave before a firm date could be mentioned, when there was a commotion in the street.

Mr Fairley went to the front door. A warden was standing in the Vaseyelins' garden shouting, 'Put out that light!' Behind him, a number of surprisingly angry people had collected. A full moon lit the scene of the offence.

'I think you must have left a light burning,' Mr Fairley said to Mrs Vaseyelin.

She stood at the gate, bemused by all the angry shouting. Someone said that the Vaseyelins were spies, that for years she had gone out every night to meet the man for whom she spied. Mrs Vaseyelin accepted this philosophically, as though it was only to be expected.

'You should be ashamed!' Mr Fairley shouted, but was stopped from saying any more by a clod of earth which hit him in the mouth. Fortunately, Jacov Vaseyelin came along the road in time to take over the defence of his mother.

Jacov was not as well-equipped as Mr Fairley for the rough and tumble of open debate, but he had a better sense of theatre. It was a chilly night, and he was wearing a long overcoat with a fur collar which he had borrowed from the studio property department. It gave him bulk which normally he lacked. He put his arm round his mother, and addressed the warden. His mother, he said, suffered from an obscure complaint. She was unable to tell dark from light, and would not, therefore, have realized that there was a naked light showing in the house. He delivered himself of this with such panache that the unlikely statement carried the same authority as if he had spoken of the disease of the Romanovs.

The warden consulted Mr Fairley. 'I don't know about dark from light,' Mr Fairley said, spitting blood and mud. 'But she is certainly odd.'

After a brief lecture from the warden, and a promise by Jacov that he would himself be responsible for the black-out in future, the crowd, now diminished to the status of extras, withdrew muttering rhubarb imprecations.

'A disgraceful affair!' Mr Fairley said later when Jacov had joined them in the sitting room. 'I hope your mother was not too shocked.'

'I think she thought it was *your* light they were angry about.'

'*My* light!'

'You left the front door open, Daddy,' Louise told him.

Mr Fairley, prepared to be magnanimous, was not pleased to find himself culpable. But although his family might be amused, Jacov treated him – as he invariably had – with the utmost respect. Mr Fairley transferred his displeasure to the crowd. 'The war is supposed to be bringing people closer together. If those are the sort of people we have as neighbours, I'd as soon not know them.'

'They live down the far end of the road, in those mock Tudor houses,' Judith said.

'We have been clearing our loft,' Louise told Jacov. 'Have you got much in yours?'

'I don't think I've ever been up there.'

'Then you must investigate. Just think – it is probably full of the clutter of past owners since time immemorial.'

'From 1880, at least,' her father said.

Louise shrugged – this being time immemorial as far as she was concerned.

'We've emptied out the dressing-up trunk,' Claire said. 'Do you think the film studios would like some of the clothes?'

'I could ask them.' He would never remember to do it, but both he and Claire thought the matter settled.

Alice came and sat beside Jacov. 'That beautiful scarf you gave me wasn't in the trunk,' she assured him. 'I shall never throw that away.'

He squeezed her hand, and they sat feeling close in spirit while Jacov tried to remember what scarf she was talking about. After a few moments, he said, 'How handsome you look in your officer's uniform.'

'I'm not an officer, Jacov. Just a Wren.'

'But you are most handsome all the same. Will you come out with me?'

'Would you take me to the Berkeley?'

'Of course. I would be proud to accompany you.'

She looked at him to see whether he was making fun of her or himself. It did not really matter. Nothing mattered when one was with Jacov, and anything seemed possible – even dining at the Berkeley. She turned to the Pilot Officer, meaning to explain to him that Jacov was a very old family friend, but it was not necessary because he was listening to Claire talk about the moral stature of Sir Stafford Cripps. Claire's idea of attracting a man was to let him know how clever she was.

Louise said, 'I'm going to make tea.' She put a hand on her mother's shoulder. 'Don't come fussing around me. I can manage.'

After a few minutes, Mr Fairley followed her into the kitchen.

'Are you feeling mis?' he asked, reverting to the language of her childhood miseries.

Gratefully, she confessed, 'Isn't it stupid? Just seeing Claire and Alice, each with a man by them . . .'

He handed her the tea caddy. 'It won't be like it was in the trenches. They'll never throw life away on that scale again.'

He seldom spoke of the bad times; and, herself an optimist, Louise accepted his comfort. Lives would be lost, even if not in their millions, but Guy would survive. Belief in survival was a necessary part of surviving.

'I wish I had more to do,' she said. 'Men have all the *doing*. I bet Mummy missed you more than you missed her – you were too busy trying to keep alive.'

It was nearly midnight when the Pilot Officer left. Alice went down to the front gate with him. It was quiet now. In the sky, a single searchlight lazily exercised itself. 'I hope you didn't find it too dull,' she said.

'Dull!' It seemed he was delighted with the eccentricities of her home life.

'We're really very ordinary,' she assured him. But he insisted it was all quite bizarre. It amused Alice, who had spent so much of her childhood in search of the bizarre, that someone should think she might have found it at home.

Ted Peterson died in the Rifle Brigade's gallant stand at Calais. There was little alternative but to be gallant, since it had been decided there should be no withdrawal – time was needed, and the defenders of Calais must buy it. He felt no bitterness, but an intense surprise when eventually he realized that for him this was the end of the affair: so messy and inconclusive. As life drained away – he took a long time to die – he thought about Alice and coffee at Zeeta's. He was trying to catch the waitress's eye; dimly, he could hear Alice saying, 'It doesn't matter; it doesn't matter, now.' His mind circled as he struggled intensely with the waitress, and the voice kept repeating 'it doesn't matter, now . . .' Then he was on the rugger pitch, struggling through mud with a leaden ball at his chest, and all around there were people telling him it didn't matter, now. But he would not relinquish the struggle, so convinced was he that something *did* matter, if only he could hold on to it.

Guy Immingham, in the Field Artillery, had also been buying time, engaged in manoeuvres to halt the oncoming German Army. But he was more fortunate than Ted. His division was ordered to withdraw from Lille at a time when it seemed likely that it would be completely cut off. They fell back in what Guy supposed would be described as 'good order'. The corridor to the sea was still open and they headed for Dunkirk.

It seemed to Guy that he had been under attack for as long as he could remember. As when one is sick, one has no memory of good health; or the summer seems a mere fantasy in the iron grip of winter;

so exhaustion and confusion had become the natural condition of life. Nothing beyond his immediate duties made sense, and it wasn't always easy to make sense of them, either. Defeat was something for which he was unprepared. He believed in his country in much the same way as he believed in his school and his marriage. He equated all three with the Right Way. His life had been quiet and well-ordered and it had never occurred to him that Right would not triumph. As the transport rolled through the night, he looked at the crowds of refugees, cluttering the roads, only moving out of the way as the wheels of a truck brushed against them, some shaking their fists and crying out abuse which the driver returned with interest. These are the people we are fighting for, he thought in bewilderment. What will happen to them when we are gone?

In the dawn light he glanced across open fields stretching towards the horizon. He was visited by the delusion, as beguiling as the mirage in the desert, that somewhere out there was a place that would be utterly quiet, where not a blade of grass would stir; a place where one could lie and breathe in the good smell of the earth. In a brief moment of imagination, he understood that a man might desert, not because he was a coward, but because no price was too high to pay for a few moments' peace and quiet. Of course, he felt no such temptation. This was a foreign countryside haunted by unknown tribes with alien customs; he felt safer with his own kind — quite apart from the fact that he preferred death to dishonour.

By the time they reached Dunkirk, they were well aware that they were involved in retreat on a large scale. Even so, they were staggered by their first sight of the beaches. 'They're never going to get this lot away from here,' a sergeant said to Guy.

Guy replied firmly, 'Something will happen.'

'It will take a miracle!'

Guy believed in miracles.

In the Channel, a naval officer looked down from the bridge of his destroyer at a paddle steamer waddling like a pregnant duck with a motley brood of ferries, tugs and small motor cruisers. 'Strewth! I reckon we've got everything that can float down there!'

There were times when it did not seem enough. Guy was a long time on the beach. 'It was like waiting for the last bus, afraid that the queue exceeds the passenger capacity,' he told Louise later. 'But I was always sure I would get away.'

The Poles, in whose company he was eventually taken aboard a pleasure steamer, had no such confidence. As they saw it, Englishmen were being saved in preference to foreigners; they forced their way on to the boarding craft at gun point. One of them had eyes staring from his head, as though something in his mind had blown, permanently dislocating his features and distending the eyes outwards. Guy, looking at him, felt he was seeing a man's sanity peeling off like skin from a burn.

He watched the line of the sea rising and falling gently, and the pattern of shells and searchlights. It was not Death who seemed now to be the enemy, but the constant bombardment of noise, and too-brilliant light flashes. The sound of the guns began to form into a rhythm, accentuated by the darting light, like a demoniacal patter song. He realized that if he did not break this relentless rhythm of the mind, it would be there always. From the depths of his being he wrenched up the counter-rhythm of the psalms – 'God is our hope and strength, a very present help in time of trouble . . .' It was a battle as desperate as any he had so far fought.

The pupils of Winifred Clough Day School for Girls had evacuated to Dorset. Over 300,000 men had been evacuated from the Dunkirk beaches. Temporary arrangements had to be made to rest exhausted troops. Some were sent to Dorset.

This raised a delicate issue for Miss Blaize. Her pupils had been left in no doubt that their future role was to serve the community; and they saw no reason why this should not immediately be interpreted in terms of ministering to soldiers. Certainly, Miss Blaize would not have wished it to be said of her girls that they had flinched from their duty. The question resolved itself into what, in these circumstances, constituted duty? The soldiers, having passed through an unpleasant experience, might express themselves in a manner unsuited to the ears of schoolgirls; might, in the heightened emotional situation, go so far as to make gestures, even demands . . . Miss Blaize would not have said of Tommy Atkins 'chuck him out, the brute', but she was not wholly of the 'thin red line of heroes' persuasion. She decided that it would be acceptable for the older girls to help in the canteen, provided they remained in the kitchen, and were not exposed directly to the soldiery.

Claire's friend, Heather Mason, went to the canteen in the company of the two Misses Courtenay with whom she was billeted. She had no intention of obeying Miss Blaize's directive. She could not imagine her working-class mother hiding herself in the kitchen in such a crisis. Heather was not patriotic in Miss Blaize's terms – 'sod the Union Jack!' was her response to flag-waving. She was, however, deeply concerned for 'our lads'. In her mind's eye, she peopled the army with the faces of 'our Jim' and 'our Harry' – hundreds of thousands of dear, familiar faces, all turned towards her. She longed to cheer and comfort them.

She was a tall, bony girl whose body seemed always to be making gestures of nonconformity towards whatever clothes she wore. She had none of the demure prettiness of many of her schoolmates. Her skin was poor, and she had a big mouth from which words tended to tumble all too recklessly. Her main claim to attention – and a sufficient one – was her violet-blue eyes. No polite indifference masked Heather's feelings. Whatever her mood, it was expressed immediately in the eyes – teachers who had displeased her were startled by their angry glitter, just as they were alerted to pranks by the eyes' unholy glee. While the WVS ladies contrived to look unconcerned as they worked in the stinking, steaming room, and turned a gentle, cowlike gaze on the soldiers, Heather gaped her horror and revulsion. It seemed it was just one face that was before her, a face that belonged in a macabre pantomime, caked in white clay with razor-cut lines beneath eyes and mouth. In contrast to the deadness of the skin, the red-rimmed eyes burnt like hot coals.

'Go away, if you don't like it, dear,' the elder Miss Courtenay said quietly. 'But don't let them see you looking like that. They still have their pride, you know.'

She did not know. She saw no sign of pride or of any human feeling. She did as Miss Blaize had requested; she went into the kitchen, and helped at the sink. As she was leaving with the Misses Courtenay, more men were arriving. At first, they all looked the same; then, she found a particular face taking shape in her mind. Before anyone could stop her she had rushed up to one of the men.

'I'm Heather Mason,' she cried urgently, shaking his arm. 'Claire's friend.'

He looked at her, stupefied. She thought he had not taken in what she was saying, that the Misses Courtenay would come and hustle her away before she could make him understand. Then the blistered mouth began to work, and at last words came. 'Tell Louise I'm safe.'

'Oh, I will! I will!' She spoke as though she would surely jump on a horse and ride through the night. In fact, she wrote to Louise, assuring her that 'they all look pretty awful, but he's no worse than any of the others.'

For this assurance, Louise was duly grateful.

When Guy came home on leave he tried to persuade Louise to take the children to her maternal grandparents in Cornwall for the duration of the war. This she refused to do. In her opinion, air raids were likely to be a less exacting experience than minute-to-minute contact with one's kith and kin, however well-loved. As hers was the stronger personality, her view prevailed over Guy's.

Guy was uneasy on other counts than the safety of his wife and children. He had always been resentful of anything in Louise's life which he could not share. He did not object to her close family ties, since he himself was now accepted in the family circle. Music was another matter. Music meant a lot to Louise and nothing to him. When she went to a concert, or even when she played the gramophone at home, he was aware that she had drifted into a territory he could not enter. He could tell from her absorbed face that this was where her treasure lay. That she should find joy where he had no place, filled him with dismay and a sense of betrayal. He had no joy other than in her and the children. He loved her so much he would not have entered the Kingdom of Heaven without her beside him, hand in his. He found excuses for turning off the gramophone, and when she wanted to go to a concert he would discover that this happened to be the only evening he could take her to a film they both wanted to see.

Now he would be away for a long time, perhaps for as long as a year. If she remained in London, he would find it hard to imagine what she was doing at any given moment. The secret places of her life would be extended; not only might she be attending concerts, but engaging in a number of other activities which he, by virtue of his absence, could not share. While he had been at work in London, he had not worried about what she did in his absence; his only thought had been that she would be there with the children when he returned from the office. But now that he would no longer see her each evening, it became very important to feel that in some way he was still in her life. If she was in Falmouth, he could imagine her doing things which he himself enjoyed – accompanying her grandfather to the harbour, taking the children for country walks, perhaps going over on the ferry to St Mawes where he himself had spent so many happy holidays . . . And not much in the way of music.

'You get on with winning the war,' was all that she would say when he tried to persuade her. 'I shall manage very well.' But he did not want her to manage as well as that.

Jacov Vaseyelin, who was with them on one occasion when Guy was on leave, said, 'I will look after her.' They all laughed. They had known one another a long time, and were aware that Jacov, gentle and endearing though he might be, was not very good at looking after people. It was in the Vaseyelins' house that Guy and Louise had conceived their first child, and brought such shame on themselves and their families. While Guy had no regrets about his marriage, he now felt ashamed of their first sexual encounter. Jacov was undoubtedly a bad influence. He would not, of course, see himself in that light. He was much too unassertive to try to influence anyone; nor did he care sufficiently about people or ideas to wish to manipulate. It was his lack of knowledge of the rules which governed society that made Jacov an undesirable companion. Guy's perceptions seldom ran to anything as dangerous as danger; but the more he thought about Jacov, the more he came to believe that he was a dangerous person. There was something of the clown in him. And while clowns were all very well in a circus, who would want one let loose in his home – a person in whose hands everything tended to come apart?

Guy returned to his unit. The country awaited Hitler's next move with more composure than its circumstances would seem to warrant. Defeat had indeed become a miracle. Ben saw an American documentary film showing goose-stepping soldiers marching across a map of Europe. First Norway was branded with the swastika, then Holland, then Belgium, and France. The marching men assembled at the Channel. But a hand came out in a gesture which said 'So far, and no further!' There was a glimpse of the naval sleeve with two rings of gold braid. The people in the cinema cheered. Ben thought, 'If I don't get involved in this now, I'm going to be left out of something all my generation is experiencing.' He did not think the Navy would suit his style. He opted for the Army – there was no false nonchalance about the Army.

Churchill said, 'We shall fight on the beaches, we shall fight on the landing grounds; we shall fight in the fields and the streets . . .'

Down came the street names, the signposts, the names of railway stations. Up went the street blocks, the anti-tank posts. Weapons of surprising ingenuity were conjured up out of household articles.

Jacov, who looked foreign, and whose phraseology was sometimes unEnglish, suffered at this time. He was sent down to Sussex with a film unit to do a documentary for the Ministry of Information. He lost his way in the small market town, and went into the post office to ask for directions to the council offices. No one would oblige him. The clerks gazed mutely at a poster which read 'Careless talk

46

costs lives'. Soon after he left the post office, he was approached by a policeman who had obviously been warned about him. Even after the production of his identity card, he was regarded with suspicion. It was the mention of film work which saved him. Allowances were apparently made for film people, who were notoriously eccentric. Moreover, several foreign actors had 'chosen' England. The atmosphere became jovial; and Jacov and the policeman parted company after exchanging the names of Anton Walbrook and Conrad Veidt.

It was the same story in the house where he was temporarily lodged. 'Did you see *The Mortal Storm* – just before war began?' his landlady asked him. Jacov, willing to please, said he thought he remembered it.

'Oh, that ending, when James Stewart carried Margaret Sullavan across the frontier! Dead, she was, of course. I cried for a week after that.' She paused, a duster in her hand, and stared out of the window where a cattle truck full of land army recruits was passing slowly by. 'Freya, wasn't that her name? Lovely, she was!'

Superimposed on the scene beyond the window, he saw the Shepherd's Bush Empire, and Katia pushing her way to the front of the queue to see Margaret Sullavan in *Little Man, You've Had a Busy Day*. He had not been able to bring her face to mind until this unguarded moment; but now he saw all too clearly her desperate urgency for experience. Anita had often rebuked her, 'You'll be grown up soon enough, and then you will wish you hadn't been in such a hurry.'

'That's one thing about foreigners,' the landlady said later to her husband. 'They don't mind expressing their feelings. You wouldn't find an Englishman knocked all of a heap over *The Mortal Storm*.'

'No,' her husband said, 'and I hope you never will.'

While Jacov was in Sussex with the film unit the first daylight raids took place. People watched the dog fights, and cheered as the German bombers came down in flames. Sometimes they made mistakes, and cheered as their own fighters came blazing down.

There were ominous signs, though. After a bad raid on Croydon, Judith and Stanley persuaded Claire to join the school party in Dorset for her last year. Although, on her departure, she hugged them as if she never expected to see them again, she was not sorry to go. The house seemed strange without Alice at home. It was not nearly so satisfying to play the piano whenever she chose without anyone to compete with for its use. She looked forward to joining Heather in Dorset. Under Heather's influence, she had questioned many cherished beliefs. Lately, she had found herself left with the questions, without the delight of Heather's company.

For days after Claire left, Rumpus stood on the chair by the window, front paws on the sill, listening to the footsteps coming along the road. Occasionally, when he pricked his ears, Judith would say, 'It's no use, old boy. The children have all gone.'

4

September 1940–April 1941

Saturday, September 7th was a beautiful day. The blue of the sky was softened by the faintest haze of autumn. There were only a few feathered wisps of cloud. Angus Drummond, waiting in Knightsbridge for Irene, experienced that heightened awareness which now seemed to touch all things with magic. He was early, deliberately so. The sight of Irene on the way to meet him, but as yet unaware of his presence, was precious. He wanted to remember her as she was now, to be able to close his eyes and see her walking unconcernedly in the street. In fact, he rather preferred her at a distance. Although he got a sensual satisfaction from looking at her, he had no very strong urge to go to bed with her. He had not been tempted in this way since his final encounter with Katia Vaseyelin.

Irene came into view, wearing a blue linen dress with a primrose scarf round her shoulders. She had that verve which is sometimes the gift of diminutive people, in whom all energy is concentrated in a small frame. Her combination of quick liveliness and inner repose excited him; it seemed as if she had the secret of life, while his own reserve was but a mask behind which was concealed terror and confusion.

Now, she was looking in a dress shop window. He sensed that she, too, was enjoying the moment before meeting, prolonging the agonizing thrill of expectation. When she saw him, she would greet him with a gaiety of spirit which had no need of excitable hands and babbling tongue.

They had tea in an expensive restaurant where it was still possible to get delicacies if you were prepared to pay. 'Do you enjoy looking forward to meeting me more than actually being with me?' he asked.

She looked startled. It was seldom he made a remark which might lead to intimacy between them. A slight flush coloured her cheeks. Then, her image seemed to tremble in front of him; he had a sense of such volatility, her very substance might be changing and another woman emerging. He regretted the question and said hastily, 'I only meant generally speaking. Travelling hopefully and all that . . .'

She said, 'I hadn't thought about it.' She felt he had excited her only to snub her. Aware of her distress, it occurred to Angus that she might be falling in love with him. He did not want his love – or whatever it was he felt for her – to be requited. To break the silence, he said:

'I saw Alice in Hertford the other day. She seems to be enjoying herself.'

'Yes. She is much better now.'

'I never knew what was wrong with her.'

'She had some sort of breakdown – all to do with Katia Vaseyelin. Nightmares and things.'

He was not surprised at the turn of the conversation, nor did he regard it as coincidence but as something he had himself invited. He said, 'Nightmares?'

'Katia being hounded down, men running after her with evil intent, calling her a dirty little Jewess. That kind of thing.'

'Yes, I can imagine that.' It was, after all, exactly what he himself had done.

'I don't think I can,' Irene said.

As they went into the street, the air raid siren began to wail. He put a hand on her elbow and she looked up at him, lively again. 'Think of it! We are all involved in one thing at this moment – everyone in this city!' She did not think how separated they might be soon, when some drew in their breath of relief as others gave out their last.

They heard the drone of oncoming planes, a relentless throbbing which seemed to spread across the whole sky. No preliminary skirmish! 'This is an air raid!' Angus exclaimed, as if the warning had betokened something other. He urged her forward. 'We'll make for the tube station.'

'Must we?' She was unconcerned. 'I'd like to watch.'

'They mean business this time.' He steered her in the direction of the tube station. As they walked, something shifted subterraneously, once, twice.

'Were those bombs?' Irene asked a warden.

'Yes, but not very near, or you'd have heard them come down.'

The tube station was crowded with late shoppers and early revellers. Hours passed. It became dark. A few people sang 'There'll always be an England'. Irene worked her way to the steps and looking up saw something like a silver bird held in the crossed beams of searchlights. 'How sinister!' she exclaimed, and felt a primitive fear of this thing which would rain destruction. She did not see the young face peering down, and had no feeling that it was he who was the killer; any more than he, as the bomb load was released, saw the women and children who would be obliterated. They were creatures in a dance and the dance had taken them over. There was nothing personal about it.

'How strange it all is,' she said when she returned to Angus. 'I'm rather enjoying it, aren't you?'

He shrugged his shoulders. 'Someone is getting a packet.' He was neither in nor out of the experience. It had never been so clear to him before that he existed in a kind of limbo. The only reality was Katia Vaseyelin. He could not rid himself of his guilt because she was not here to forgive him, to say, as she might well have done, that he had done little more than make a pass at her. He had held it to himself for so long now that it had assumed proportions too dreadful to speak of. He felt his own complicity in the plight of the Jews, just as he had felt responsible for the miseries of his mother who had stayed with his father 'because of the children'. These things should have belonged to his past. The darkness was behind him; yet, day by day, he moved towards it, like a person out of time.

Irene was saying, 'As far as air raids are concerned, I suppose I haven't lost my innocence yet.'

'I don't ever remember being innocent.'

'Oh Angus, really! Aren't you indulging your melancholy just a little?'

He winced at her astringency.

A man near them said, 'It's the Palace they're after.'

'Wellington Barracks, more likely.'

'It's much further away, the other side of London. Only reason we can hear them is the river. They come up the river, see? Can't black-out Old Father Thames.'

'Where the bloody hell are our guns?'

Cigarettes were passed round. People told stories. Gradually, the singing changed character. Half in and half out of sleep, Irene heard 'Roll me over in the clover' for the first time.

Early in the morning, the all clear arched over them like a blessing.

'They say it was the East End,' Irene wrote to Alice. 'I don't even know where the East End begins and ends. All I know is Limehouse and Chinamen; and Bethnal Green and Percy Harris. Yet while the raid was going on, I felt we were all part of one tremendous experience! I suppose the Eastenders will feel much the same about us when our turn comes.'

Alice, who had not experienced a raid, did not like the idea that the turn of West London would come. But all too soon, Irene was writing, 'It is quite amusing. They hit all the railway lines – they could hardly miss, could they, we have so many! And the next day, the people whose prime concern is usually to get out of work, were fighting like mad to get there somehow. My father's office was hit and his assistant, who is usually too bored to breathe, actually climbed through a window because the door was blocked by masonry. And all the chars turned up on time! I wonder if anyone has told the Germans what a bloody-minded lot we are!'

The train came slowly out of the tunnel as though it knew it had done something wrong and might not be well-received. It travelled very slowly and almost silently towards the platform. Its reluctance was terrible to see. The guard stood ready for it, looking as though he would give it a good thrashing.

'Bomb on the line?' Ben asked.

'Could be.' The guard was not prepared to give the train the benefit of the doubt.

It was packed with service personnel. Ben had to wedge himself in the toilet with two other soldiers. 'Is your journey really necessary?' the placard asked. He wondered that himself. The train was over an hour late. Unlikely that Daphne would be waiting for him.

He had been in the Army for several weeks, and it was some time since he had seen her. She must long ago have assumed that all was over between them. In which case, it was unlikely she had ever intended to meet him tonight. As the train crawled on its way, he told himself he had been granted a reprieve. For one reason or another, she would not be there. He would not be able to tell her that he had finished with her; and his puritan conscience would not allow him to take the coward's way out and put it in writing. Nor could he simply let her drop out of his life. So, since every ounce of anguish must be extracted from this situation, the parting would have to be deferred until his next twenty-four-hour leave.

She was waiting beyond the ticket barrier. How typical of her that she spared him no pain!

'I was late, too,' she told him. 'There's a raid on.'

They walked up Victoria Street towards Westminster Abbey. The guns were sounding off and bits of shrapnel pattered around them – if the enemy didn't get you, our lads probably would! She seemed unconcerned, but he did not like it very much; he saw no point in being killed for the sake of bravado.

They had drinks in a pub in Whitehall where there were a lot of naval officers drinking heavily to keep up their courage. No doubt they were brave enough at sea, but on shore they were as breezy a bunch as one could hope to come across.

'What would your father do if he found out about us?' Ben asked.

'He would kill me.' She sipped her gin and lime reflectively. 'Or you. But probably me.'

For months he had been telling himself that he had misinterpreted Irene's words, only to find the conviction of their truth growing within him. Yet, even at the last, he had hoped. He said, 'You can't be serious. What about marriage?'

'He would accept that. But not being "trifled with".' She took a sip of her drink and ran her tongue around her lips. 'He was very fond of me.'

It did not strike him then that she spoke of her father as though he was dead. His only concern was to dispel his doubts. This was why he had had to see her again, because he could not go on with that question in his mind. He said, 'How fond is fond?'

She spat at him, 'Not that! Never that!'

He stared at her, uncomprehending. She turned her head away, shutting that damned door into her private world. She was only five foot three, and small-boned at that. Why had he ever allowed her to make herself so impregnable? She said, 'I'm sorry – we're misunderstanding each other. I suppose we always have.'

She looked down into her drink. For a moment, he thought she would continue, that the conversation would take a totally unexpected turn; then, as if someone had switched on a light in a dark room, there would be order and wholeness again. But whatever was in her mind, she found no words to express it; and while he waited, he lost that sense of urgency which might have enabled him to sweep aside her defences. She put her drink down and said, 'You can give me a cigarette – and then get on with it.'

'What do you mean?'

She waited while he lit her cigarette. 'You're quite different tonight. I sensed it as soon as we met.'

'You wouldn't lose by being more feminine and less challenging.'

'They go together, do they – femininity and being unchallenging?'

'Constant provocation can be wearing. Just make a note of that.'

'Oh, sick it up, Ben!'

He picked up his tankard, which was empty, and went to the bar. The building shook and the lights went out, and came on again, almost immediately — but not before the Navy had dived for cover. For a moment, he hoped that something dreadful *would* happen, throwing them into each other's arms and smashing down all the barriers. But he knew that beyond the barrier there was limitless disgust. He would not be satisfied until she had given him explicit details, and once she had done this, he would never feel the same about her. He ordered beer for himself and another gin and lime for her. He felt sick and wondered whether he could keep another beer down. He could see her sitting alone; she seemed to burn with a sullen fire and he did not think she would ever be alone long. God, but this was hard! It is one thing to renounce something of which you are already beginning to tire, quite another matter when you still have a strong need of it. But his sense of self-preservation was strong, too, and would carry him through worse moments than this.

Daphne watched Ben as he stood at the bar. Hitherto in their encounters, there had always been her father casting a shadow over him. Now, as she looked at him, a new person seemed to be coming together, as though he was being formed before her eyes. Not *our* sort of person, she noticed. That face is so tough and yet unsophisticated. Not much grace of movement, but that is because he is impatient, afraid of being left out. He is like a scrawny dog, tugging at its leash, anxious to get round the next bend, over the brow of the hill. The world is full of smells and sounds that must be explored! What might one learn from such a person, so eager for life? What excitement there could be in exploring together! The things which are fearsome, when part of a solitary pursuit, can be transformed if shared; just as losing one's way on a moorland walk as the light fails can become high adventure, if one has the right companion. She saw all this clearly, as though a mist had lifted the moment that she knew she had lost him.

'There is no point in going on, is there?' he said, when he put the glass down in front of her.

She sat still for a time, and he was surprised to see that the colour had drained from her face. Eventually, she said, 'Not from your point of view, no.'

'What is that supposed to mean?'

The Navy had taken refuge in song. ' "And if one green bottle, should accidentally fall," ' they roared, ' "There'll be six green bottles, hanging on the wall." ' What a bloody mess it all was, Ben thought, the whole, noisy human race!

She was looking self-possessed now, but no longer provocative. 'I'm sorry, Ben. You've had a bad time with me.' Just as if she had

54

woken from a nightmare, and was acknowledging that she might have disturbed his sleep! 'It's not your fault.'

And that was all. He had wanted her to protest and tell him that she could not live without him. After all, she had used him and so, presumably, she had needed him. He wanted to be able to tell her that whatever it was she had needed from him, it was no longer available.

There were two green bottles hanging on the wall when they left the pub. The raid was still on. He insisted on seeing her home and she submitted. As they walked through one of the noisiest barrages London had yet known, she said passionately, 'Whatever made you join the Army? Don't you feel you want to be up there?'

'They don't seem to be much in evidence tonight, our gallant boys in powder blue.'

'Oh, not for the fighting, but the way it must feel to take off, be free . . .'

'They're not in the least like that when you meet them. Their patter doesn't compare with a London bus conductor's.'

'Irene said it would be like driving a bus. Maybe you're both right. But there must be some new things to do.'

He sensed how strong was her urge towards the future – already, he was unimportant to her. If they had been in a bedroom, instead of walking in a London street, he would not have been responsible for his actions. How many men kill a woman simply because it seems the only chance of getting through to her? His body ached with the effort of controlling his rage. When they parted, he barely listened when she said, 'You've helped me a lot, Ben. You may not believe it, but it's true.'

As he walked away, he said savagely to himself, 'That's more than I can say for you!'

Daphne, watching him go, was aware of a new kind of pain. In the days that followed, she gave way to the pain, explored it, tended it, exulted in it. She lost weight, and looked with interest at her gaunt face in the mirror. But she would only allow a certain time to this grief, a proper period of mourning. Then she would cast aside the drabness, and new life would begin. It was already stirring deep inside her. She nourished the grief because the new life was growing out of it.

The raids continued, and each morning Alice and many of her companions would hurry to the telephone booths to phone home and reassure themselves. The death of Ted Peterson had distressed

Alice. He had been killed before she knew him well enough to know for whom she grieved. His death had opened up the possibility that other deaths might follow, even those of Guy and Ben. What she had not been prepared for was worrying about her parents.

Londoners, it seemed, accepted the blitz and were resolved that it should interfere as little as possible with their lives. Alice's parents slept under the dining-room table; Louise and the children in the basement; while Irene and her parents, after a brief, unsatisfactory spell in a neighbour's shelter, went up to bed as usual.

Alice hoped she would show equal phlegm during her first leave in London. Before that, however, on November 14th, she went on forty-eight-hour leave to stay with a Wren friend whose home was near Kenilworth.

It was evident from her conversation that Felicity Naismith came from a superior background. Her life before the war seemed to have consisted of one endless hunt ball; only the fact that men had changed their habitat had driven her to pursue her hunting activities in the WRNS. While other girls went to some trouble to establish the fact that they were the pursued, Felicity nonchalantly claimed to be the biggest manhunter of the Western World. Felicity liked Alice because she was not puritanical, which was a revelation to Alice, who had always thought she *was* puritanical. Alice hoped she would be able to live up to Felicity's expectations, whatever these might be.

The Naismith house was just outside Kenilworth. It was a Tudor building, rambling and uncomfortable, with stone floors and not much heat. There was a pervasive smell of damp. Alice was given a bedroom to herself, which presented problems as there were servants, and she was not sure whether she should make her own bed. Mrs Naismith, a sharp-featured, aloof woman, seemed totally preoccupied with the problem of finding a four for bridge. 'Do you play?' This was the only remark she addressed to her guest during Alice's stay in the house. Felicity telephoned several men, but it seemed the Army had claimed them all. 'This is getting serious! I shall apply for an overseas draft.' She went off to the stables and left Alice to her own devices, which resolved itself into an attempt to keep warm.

After a meagre lunch, Felicity went riding – presumably in pursuit of such men as the Army might have overlooked. Alice walked into Kenilworth in the interests of keeping warm. The golden retriever, McGregor, accompanied her. He was quite the nicest thing about the Naismith household.

It was getting dark when she returned, and she hurried because she did not like being alone in the country lanes. A mile from the house, the siren went.

Mr Naismith was away seeing a client in Gloucester. He did not return until the afternoon of the 15th. He was in a furious temper. This appeared to be a more or less permanent condition. Anger had consumed the flesh leaving a scarecrow body, and a face the features of which were moulded into a perpetual snarl. Any major misfortune which affected him, however marginally, was regarded as having been engineered with the express purpose of causing him inconvenience. He had only to spend twenty-four hours in Gloucester for the Germans to bomb Coventry! As soon as he set foot in the house, he announced that he must go to his office to get the Akroyd file.

'Lady Akroyd can hardly blame you for the raid,' Mrs Naismith pointed out.

'I don't give a damn whether she blames me or not. That file represents ten years of my time.'

'You'll have to have a cold supper if you go, otherwise we shall have trouble with Ellen.' Mrs Naismith put this forward as a consideration to be weighed in the balance against ten years of time.

'To hell with Ellen! She doesn't run this house.'

'She runs the kitchen. And it's not hell she will go to, but the Connaught Hotel.'

'At her age!'

'Because of her age. The factories take all the younger staff.'

They went on arguing over tea. It was obvious that nothing was more important than convenience to either of them. The war represented a series of inconveniences, some grosser than others.

Felicity said, 'It must have been rather dreadful, Pa. The horses were terrified. I had to go down and soothe Emelda.'

'You will have to come with me.' Emelda's condition alerted Mr Naismith to other complications. 'I expect there will be all sorts of obstructions.'

Felicity brightened at the prospect of encounters with uniformed authority. 'Alice will come, too.' She acknowledged her friend for the first time since their arrival. 'Alice is game for anything.'

Alice, cold and hungry, felt anything preferable to staying in the house with Mrs Naismith.

It was getting dark when they set out, and what enthusiasm Alice had for the expedition soon dwindled. Felicity talked to her father about local people. 'That's the Plunketts' Farm. What happened to Ralph? The Army can't have taken him, surely? It needed a crane to hoist him into the saddle. And what about Desmond Pusey – him with the one glass eye and the other roving?' Mr Naismith took no notice. He drove crouched over the wheel, his lips drawn back carnivorously as though he was eating into the oncoming landscape.

It never grew completely dark. What had seemed a sunset glow in the sky grew fiercer as they neared Coventry. They were now passing people getting out of the city in whatever conveyance they could find. They saw one family trudging wearily with some of its possessions piled on a wheelbarrow. Alice thought that Mr Naismith would turn back, but he only said, 'Bloody place is on fire!'

'Should we be doing this?' Alice asked when they reached the outskirts of the city. Even for this situation, unfamiliar as it was, rules must by now have been formulated.

'What do you mean – "should we be doing this?"' He turned his head, the better to direct his impatience at her, and the car swerved across the road. It didn't matter, by now there was no other traffic. 'We *are* doing it!' He hauled savagely at the wheel; the car skidded, and then – disappointingly from Alice's point of view – righted itself within inches of colliding with a lamp-post.

They came across a makeshift barrier of planks placed across chairs obviously intended for infants. This enraged Mr Naismith. 'Hitler hasn't taken over this country yet! Move those damn things out of the way.' Felicity got out and moved the barrier, which proved only too portable. Alice, who had spent so much of her childhood eagerly anticipating the moment when she would find herself in forbidden territory, looked around in desperation for a figure of authority to emerge from the buildings, which now began to rear up like huge pieces of charred coal. But the chaos was such that had Adolf Hitler elected to view his handiwork in a car travelling from the Kenilworth road, he might well have got into the city unchallenged. They passed groups of men in steel helmets digging in the rubble, while others lifted bundles about which Alice did not care to speculate. This was something which was happening to other people, like a picture show; only in this situation, you were moving and the show was static. The tunnel of horror at a fairground, that was it! As long as you kept moving, you left the horror behind. Mr Naismith understood this much at least – he kept the car moving.

They were near the centre before they were stopped by a young soldier who appeared in front of the windscreen, waving his arms.

'Get out of here!' he shouted. 'You can't go back, though. You've just driven past an unexploded bomb.'

'Then where do you suggest I go?'

The soldier didn't care. 'You'll have to go ahead. Take the first turning that seems possible.' He walked away, and they could hear glass breaking under his feet.

Smoke and grit had blackened the windscreen of the car. Mr Naismith drove hanging out of the side window; this, and the rubble, made for erratic progress. Ahead, there was a burning building; they could see firemen standing high up on a ledge but there was no sign of the fire engine. As they came nearer, the wall buckled and fell inward, taking the firemen with it. Mr Naismith said, 'How am I supposed to tell which way to go now?' The car bucketed over charred wood and broken glass; the air was full of bits of flaming rag, some of which blew into the car. Mr Naismith closed the window; and Felicity and Alice used gloves and scarves to extinguish the sparks.

'It won't set the petrol alight, will it?' Alice asked.

'Fire certainly *does* ignite petrol. Petrol, in fact, is a very inflammable substance, if not *the* most inflammable.' Mr Naismith wrenched at the wheel, and the car skirted a cavity and lurched into a side road. There were buildings still burning on either side. For a hundred yards they were driving in a maze of flames. Then they came to a clearing where buildings – mercifully for their purpose – had been completely flattened.

Mr Naismith stopped the car in order to wipe grit from his eyes. 'Disgraceful!' he said, glaring back at the burning buildings. Until this moment, Alice had been so absorbed in the matter of her own survival that even her terror had been kept in check. Now that they had stopped the process of identification automatically began. In the light of the car's headlamps she could see a tricycle lying on its side and an up-ended swivel chair. These objects affected her more than the bundles removed from the debris and the vanishing firemen. The rubble began to move, cascades of brick and dust bounced into the road. Alice screamed and Felicity shouted, 'It's all going to come down on us! We'll be buried!'

Then, out of the dust and smoke, there appeared the figure of a woman, a shawl around her shoulders, picking her way delicately as though anxious not to get her feet wet on a rainy day. She waved to them and came slowly alongside the car. They saw a thin face with a beaky nose and hatchet chin. The eyes were remarkably bright. Mr Naismith got out of the car. She said, 'I suppose, in these circumstances, we can dispense with introductions.'

'Madam, if you want an introduction, I am Leslie Naismith of Naismith and Hurrell, solicitor and commissioner of oaths. I should be greatly obliged if you were able to indicate where in all this debris I might find my office.'

'Yes, I expect you are experiencing difficulty.' She spoke in the amused voice in which she might have addressed a foreigner who had lost his way in Harrods. 'I am afraid none of the premises in the centre of the city are standing. Nor any people, either, I would imagine. In fact, I think I am probably the only person left in Coventry. They told me that I must go – but they wouldn't wait for me to fetch my cat.' She twitched the shawl aside to reveal the trusting face of an old tabby. 'You, sir, as a solicitor, will appreciate my position. We had entered into a contract. He agreed to keep me company, while I, for my part, promised to take care of him.'

Mr Naismith said, 'Madam, I am prepared to take you *and* your cat out of Coventry, provided you will kindly show me the way to my office.'

'Out of Coventry!' she echoed disdainfully. 'But I intend to stay. They won't come again. It would be a waste of their munitions. What else is there for them to do?' She turned away.

Alice watched her making her way over the mounds of rubble, carrying her cat. Where was she going? Had she been searching for the cat, and, now that she had found him, was there a home for her to return to? Even if there was, would she have food or water? When Mr Naismith started the car, Alice had an urge to jump out and go after the woman; but she did not do anything so foolish.

They passed a pillar-box half buried in smashed wood and glass. Beyond was a section of a house, the staircase still standing. Then, suddenly, a huge wall broken by gaping windows loomed above them; and, rising above its fallen walls, the great spire of the cathedral thrust into the lurid sky. Beyond the cathedral was another blasted church. Out of this devastation appeared words, seeming, in this weird light, to hang in the air: 'It all depends on me: and I depend on God'. It was only subsequently that Alice found out that the words had been painted on a board nailed across a broken window. She gazed at them in awe, thinking, the gates of hell shall not triumph! Mr Naismith felt otherwise. 'First that lunatic woman and now this mumbo-jumbo! It's unhinged their minds.' This particular piece of 'lunacy' seemed to convince him of the hopelessness of his search. In a city which had so lost its sense of proportion, there was unlikely to be sympathy for his quest. 'At least I know where I am now,' he dourly acknowledged this debt of gratitude to the cathedral. After which, in spite of diversions, he drove out of the city.

Although they opened all the windows when they were in the country lanes, it was impossible to get rid of the stench of burning. The condition of the car tyres probably contributed to this.

'Mama will never forgive you if you wreck the car,' Felicity said. 'She won't be able to get to her bridge parties.'

Mr Naismith drove on, emitting a tuneless dirge through clenched teeth, as though finding sardonic pleasure in being himself engaged in destruction of a minor order. He only spoke once. 'Damn fool woman! Crazy, of course, God damn and blast her!'

'I don't suppose she did feel she could leave her cat,' Alice said. 'I don't think I could leave Rumpus.'

She did not see the woman as foolish, but as standing for something defiant and human amid the wreckage. She wrote this and more in her diary that night. Then, when she had put the diary away, she fell almost at once into a troubled sleep. She dreamt that a huge tidal wave was bearing people past her; and as she stood on the bank, she was being asked to jump, urgently, not to safety but into that very torrent which was hurling people to what must surely be their destruction.

The blitz became as much a part of London life as queueing for food and scrap metal collection. Alice was never in London long enough to get used to it. 'Is there a raid on?' she would ask, nonchalantly, as she showed her pass to the ticket collector.

'Just a firework display, love. There's an old German geyser puts one on every night for us.'

Whether the raid had started or not, there would be people bedding down for the night in the tube station. Their world was quite distinct from that of the people who waited for the trains. They chatted to one another, but they never spoke to the train users who manoeuvred around them, nor did they ever look at them. The train users paid no attention to them. It was as if they were people of different races, irreconcilable as settlers and nomads.

Alice enjoyed the camaraderie of the train journeys, the jokes and occasional songs. The dramas could be amusing, too, in retrospect. In the darkness, it was difficult to see the platform. Once, when the doors on both sides of the carriage were opened by mistake, she got out the wrong side. She was hauled to safety, shaken and dishevelled, by a burly Petty Officer who shouted to the guard, 'Whoa! Jenny overboard.'

But as soon as she left the shelter of the tube station at Shepherd's Bush, it was a different matter. The bus service had become highly idiosyncratic. 'Any more for the mystery tour?' the conductor would say cheerfully, as the bus set off on a long detour through unfamiliar areas. It was only too easy to get on the wrong bus – one which had never had the intention of arriving anywhere near your destination. There could be nothing worse than being lost in a strange neighbourhood in the blitz. Alice went home on foot.

There was relief if the raid had not yet started. But this was immediately followed by intense anxiety to get home before the siren went. She did not go down the Uxbridge Road, but took a quicker, more lonely route, through the residential area. As she hurried along, she would tick off the stages of her journey – Derwentwater Road and no siren yet, Saddlers Way coming up . . . She made targets. If she got as far as the high wall of Kashmir before the siren went, she would be all right. It was that staple ingredient of all good thrillers, the race against time. How she had enjoyed it in the cinema, had longed for such excitement in real life: and how unpleasant was the actuality!

Usually, the siren sounded before she reached home. The gunfire would start immediately; and then would come the drone of the engines with their broken rhythm, like a missed heart beat. If she had been in a shelter with others to share the experience, she could have borne it better. It was the necessity of going on alone through the empty streets which gave the experience that quality of the personal which was so terrifying. She ran and the planes hunted her down. Sometimes, before she was due to come on leave, she had a nightmare. In the nightmare, the planes hunted her down; she ran, and Katia ran beside her through unfamiliar streets.

She did not admit her fears to her parents, and she refused to telephone on her arrival at the main line station. Her father would insist on coming to meet her if she did that. She was determined to see this through on her own. The night journey, the threat to her safety, the need to break from her parents were, in some obscure way, all one.

Yet now that the bombs were falling around them, her parents were more dear to her than ever. Unfortunately, as so often happens with our imperfect loving, they were also more irritating. They asked the wrong questions about service life, made the wrong assumptions and, worst of all, the wrong jokes. Her father would insist on using service slang, and talked about pilots coming down in the drink. It was excruciatingly embarrassing. This was not his war.

Then there was the matter of her new personality. The attitudes and language of service life were different from those of civilian life. She had changed beyond recognition, but they seemed not to notice. They expected to see the old Alice; and the maddening thing was that the old Alice *was* there, waiting just inside the front door every time she came home. The fight with the old Alice was as bitter as any. She left exhausted at the end of her leave. Then, as soon as she turned the corner and could not see the house any more, she realized how dear her home was to her. The further she travelled from it, the more it increased in value.

Her father found less to displease him now that Churchill was Prime Minister; with the affairs of the country in good hands, he could devote himself to local matters. 'I have insisted that while I am on ARP duty there shall be no reference to "Huns" or "Bosche".' He appealed to Alice, 'I hope you don't find people using that kind of language?'

'We don't talk about them at all.'

Her parents could not seem to understand that the progress of the war was not a topic of conversation if you were actually engaged in fighting it.

Her remark made a greater impression on her father than she had imagined. 'She is right, of course,' he said to Judith after she had left them. 'We *are* becoming obsessed with the war.'

'You could leave the ARP,' she suggested.

'Don't be facetious.'

He determined that during his working hours at the school, and on duty at the ARP post, he would discourage too much talk about the news of the war. It came as a surprise to him to find that, once he himself desisted, there was a marked change in the level of discussion. In a very short time, he learnt that at night, on the pretext of fire watching, the town hall was turned into a kind of harem for the benefit of one of the chief officers; and that a fellow warden had a list of houses which he visited regularly in search of unexploded bombs. 'Pretty tricky some of them – judging by the state he's in when he comes back!'

And, in my own way, am I any better? he asked himself, as he walked home from school one warm spring evening. All my energy has gone into hearing: I listen to the news, I listen for the siren, the planes, the swish of bombs coming down, the sound of falling masonry. I no longer *see* what is around me.

He looked around him. And there it was, a luxuriant world of blossom and tender green through which he passed day after day without noticing! It did not bring to his mind lyric poetry, it pierced him in the genitals. He stood in the middle of the road, gasping with shock. I have missed something, he cried; not now, but all my life! Before the bombers, there had been other irritations; always there had been something buzzing around in his mind. 'I have been a contentious man; forgive me!' he said to the cherry tree. 'What am I to do about it?'

He walked on, throbbing with the pain of this awakening. Year after year, he thought, this glory has unfolded before my eyes, and I have not allowed myself time to feel and respond. I am in too much of a hurry always. And immediately his mind rushed to take charge of this situation before it got out of hand, questioning, analysing, seeking to construct a new way of living which he would test, expound, and then be hurt and angry if others failed to grasp its significance. Oh God, he groaned, I am too contentious! Heal me!

He rushed to tell Judith, but she was out driving an ambulance. He closed the side gate, and then let Rumpus into the garden. He played with an old bone until the dog's hysterical gratitude abated; then he sat on the bench under the oak tree, and Rumpus sat panting at his feet. Here were the springs of my life, he thought, looking up through the tracery of leaves. The temple of the living God. Why have I not seen this before? It is because of my sin, my besetting sin of contentiousness. Well, at least I may have saved my daughters from that — by bad example. How often he had heard Judith say warningly, 'That's a Fairley failing. Watch it!' But had she meant this *particular* failing? Had she, with her unanalytical mind, been able to pinpoint it? His thoughts began to race. He groaned, and Rumpus nuzzled against him. 'At this rate, I shall destroy what peace there is out here, old boy!' He looked at his hands, clenched as so often; felt the tautness of lips, the stiffness of stomach muscles. 'We shall have to do something about this; but we'll give you a drink of water first, shall we?'

But he did not move. He sat in the garden until at last the peace did seem to calm his fretted mind. The darkness came. The siren wailed. Rumpus deserted him, and went to quake under the kitchen sink. He heard the bombers coming over, but he remained at peace. He had just begun to believe he had achieved a new state of life when Mrs Vaseyelin knocked on the front door.

All his devils returned to tear at him as he listened to Mrs Vaseyelin explaining, as though it had never happened before, that she could not find her front door key.

'Come into the dining room,' he said. 'You can turn out your handbag, and then I expect you will find it.'

She turned out her handbag. Neither of them really expected she would find the key. Her hands were shaking and he realized this must be very humiliating for her, with him standing by like the schoolmaster he was. Suppose she broke down and said she could not go on any longer? It was becoming apparent that this was the case, but he did not want the full realization to come to her while she was in his house. He recalled that there was brandy in the cupboard under the stairs where they had put their iron rations. It was only to be used when needed for medicinal purposes, of course; but this could surely be counted such an occasion. He found tumblers – it would seem boorish not to join her – and poured what he took to be the correct amount, the equivalent of a glass of sherry. He found dry biscuits, put them on a tray, and presented his offering to Mrs Vaseyelin. She sat up very straight-backed, and bowed her head before extending her hand. He was surprised, looking at her, that the mere sight of the brandy should be so therapeutic.

He had chosen to remain in the dining room, which was a more formal setting and one which, he hoped, would not encourage her to linger. But he had, of course, already encouraged her. She sat, cradling the tumbler in the palms of her hands, warming the brandy; while he wondered what had led him so suddenly to eschew the total abstinence he had practised all his life. Mrs Vaseyelin looked as near to being happy as he had ever seen her. She began to talk about the past.

'When I am young – you understand?' Mr Fairley acknowledged the possibility of Mrs Vaseyelin's youth with a courteous nod of the head. 'I visit an aunt in St Petersburg. There is some sort of wine, prepared especially for her – I think you call it a cordial?' (Mr Fairley took her word for this.) 'It was . . . ach! an abomination; pink, very heavy and so sweet! It stick to the teeth. Always, I am given a glass as a special treat – you, also?'

'Mine tasted of liquorice,' Mr Fairley recalled.

'Once when I visit my aunt, there is this foreign woman with her – a very old actress, who is long past famous. Her face . . . so made up!' Mrs Vaseyelin threw up her hands and the brandy rocked about in her glass. 'You do not imagine her face, the make-up is thick as syrup. While this woman talks, I empty my glass into what I think a flower pot. But it is this actress's hat. And when she puts on the hat, the cordial runs down her face. All that pink stickiness mixed with that syrup make-up. It is like sunset, all the colours of . . .' She paused and Mr Fairley said, 'the spectrum.' She nodded.

'I run out of the room. They think I am terrified; but I am laughing. I laugh so much – oh, how I laugh . . .' She stared at the brandy, enormously surprised by laughter.

Mr Fairley, looking at her, realized what an opportunity he had missed. There, living next door to him, was this woman, who must have the most interesting memories of Imperial Russia, and all they ever talked about was locks and bolts! All that must change. How constantly life presented new opportunities! No more contention. He would listen to this woman; day by day, he would draw her out, bring her back to life. Yes, yes, that was it! Resurrection. *That* was it! They would ask her in to supper. Judith must arrange it. Undoubtedly she had done more interesting things than pour sticky liquid into other people's hats. This was only a beginning.

When they had finished their brandy, he fetched his screwdriver while Mrs Vaseyelin waited for him in the hall. They walked down the drive and into the Vaseyelins' garden. The brandy glowed within them and Mrs Vaseyelin, perhaps still thinking of the naughtiness of her youth, watched unconcerned while Mr Fairley inspected the front door lock. The thing to do was to try to lever the door open, but this was not immediately clear to him, and in any case the screwdriver was not the correct implement. He tried inserting the tip in the keyhole. The brandy had not made him any more dexterous, and he was having some difficulty when the bomb came down. Mr Fairley, who had pushed at so many doors during his life, now found them all open to him and passed through, taking Mrs Vaseyelin with him.

The burial service was held a few days later. Ben had obtained leave to attend, but Guy was already at sea, his destination unknown. The mourners could have wished for more male voices to swell the singing as the coffin was carried slowly down the aisle.

> 'And so beside the silent sea
> I wait the muffled oar;
> No harm from Him can come to me
> On ocean or on shore.
>
> 'I know not where his islands lift
> Their fronded palms in air;
> I only know I cannot drift
> Beyond His love and care.'

Near the back of the chapel Alice saw Irene and Daphne standing side by side, both tearful. She recorded with detached interest that crying at funerals is apparently one of the things which friends do for one another. Even Daphne.

Louise walked immediately behind the coffin, beside her mother. Judith moved with care, as though the very act of walking was unfamiliar and would take some time to master. Her surroundings also seemed unfamiliar; at each step she advanced further into a strange landscape. It was as if it was she and not Stanley who had died. The streets and shops, the passers-by, were no longer invested with reality; their existence had depended on her authentication, and now that this was no longer forthcoming, they ceased to have any identifiable form or function.

Three cars were drawn up to the kerb. Judith and Louise got in the first car. Aunt May was waiting on the pavement with Grandmother Fairley in her wheelchair. The old woman's younger daughter, Meg Braddon, stood beside her, trying to look at once detached – because she was not a believer – and sorrowing, because she was concerned about her mother, even if she hadn't liked her brother all that much. The impression she in fact created was her habitual one of a person striving for order in a high wind. Ben and Harry Braddon helped Grandmother Fairley into the car. She flopped on the seat, gasping, 'Oh Lord! Lord!' Aunt May said, 'You've been very brave, Mother.' The old woman turned away from her daughter. 'You're a silly woman, May. Always were.'

The rest of the mourning party stood on the pavement, leaving until the last minute the time when they must observe one another's grief at close quarters. They were waiting for the minister. A dog trotted between them, sniffed around the car, and cocked a leg against the front wheel. He had rubbed up against paintwork and had a red streak on his side. Claire was reminded of another paint-marked dog to whom her father had always referred as 'the green dog'. She wept, and Ben comforted her. Alice stood apart. A youngish man, who had been one of Stanley Fairley's sea cadets, spoke to her. 'He was a great man, your dad. Kept us boys off the street.' Alice could see his adam's apple working; he was evidently very distressed. She looked at the men standing, bare-headed, hunched into their coats as though it was winter; and she was surprised to realize that these men had loved her father.

They had loved him for his faults, rather than the virtues he so longed to possess. His intemperate nature, his rash declarations and subsequent humiliating retractions, his frequently misplaced enthusiasm, and his vulnerability, had endeared him to his fellows, most of whom risked rather less of themselves in the day-to-day business of living. His unceasing struggle to live the Christian life in an unChristian world, was an inspiration. They applauded his refusal to give up.

Most of the women, other than his family, had found him an abrasive, angular man. They whispered surreptitiously while they waited, and studied the faces of Judith and the girls to see how they were taking it. Mrs Immingham, who had lost her only joy to the Fairley family, experienced a sense of quiet satisfaction, as though the bomb had been the instrument of divine justice. She thought how heavy Judith's features were – now that all her liveliness had deserted her, the woman was really quite ugly.

Louise called to Alice, 'Go and see if Mr Hurrell is coming.' She thought he was absent-minded enough to forget that the service was only partly completed. Alice went back to the chapel to find the minister. The small, bare room was almost empty now, but one person was still sitting hunched in the back pew. Alice was surprised to see that it was Jacov. He wept, and something other than grief seemed to flow from him and darken the area around him. It was the crying of one who will never be comforted. It seemed odd, when one considered the terrible things which had happened to his family, that he should be so affected by the death of his next door neighbour. She stood hesitant in the presence of this desolation so far beyond her understanding. The minister, coming out of the vestry at that moment, went to Jacov and put a hand on his shoulder. Alice said, her face averted, 'Please tell him to come with us. There is room for one more in our car.'

The minister joined Stanley Fairley's Sussex relatives, the Braddons, and Mr and Mrs Immingham in the third car. The cortège set off.

Jacov said tonelessly, 'He was my first English friend.'

Claire looked out of the window. Last week her father had been with them, and now he had gone. It did not seem at all credible; the whole episode was as ridiculous as if he had disappeared in a puff of smoke, like a genie in a pantomime – the kind of event which could only happen on stage, where unlikely things are allowed because people suspend disbelief. In her mind, she ran through the events of that dreadful day, thinking that if only she could make a small alteration at some point, none of it would prove to have happened. He would be restored to them. For Claire, as for the others of her family, the battle to accommodate loss had begun. The mind had arrived at the scene of the disaster, but the feelings were a long way behind. It would be some time before the whole person could be assembled again.

The sun came out as the procession made its way towards the grave. The cemetery was hemmed in by industrial buildings in one of which men could be seen working at machines, while in another a woman in an overall turned the handle of a duplicator. The sun shone on the glass windows, on the concrete, the gravestones and the weeds breaking up the surface of the path. There was not much in the way of vegetation, only holly seedlings and a stunted hawthorn, now in full flower.

It was noon; there was no softness of shadow, the graveyard was all light. But this light gave no warmth to stone, aroused no sensual pleasure as it touched the skin. It was at once penetrating and detached; showing up with equal clarity the weeds growing in the cracks of uncared-for tombs and the threadbare assumption of pious solicitude.

'May light perpetual shine on them . . .' The words came to Alice with new and disturbing significance. Opposite to her she saw Mrs Immingham, every vestige of conventional regret stripped from the puffy face so that she stood transparent in her jubilation. It was as though this was all there was of her; while, near by, Ben was nothing but his anger. And Claire, Louise . . . ? Alice closed her eyes because she did not want to see this light shining on her sisters. It was there behind her eyeballs; there was no escape from it. Light perpetual . . . Oh, poor Daddy! Nowhere to turn, no corner in which to escape from this relentless enquiry. The light broke up the ordered surface of her mind; she tried to assemble scraps of comfort, but there was nothing there, not one shred of comfort. Whatever Death and Resurrection were about, they had nothing to do with comfort, and the hope that our loved ones are around us, lurking somewhere just out of sight. She had never thought about light in this way before – yet what else discovered the dark deed, laid bare the secret sin, unmasked the false and broke down the last defences? The newly dead must be totally occupied trying to shield themselves from light perpetual.

Louise stood with her head held high, eyes shining, remembering the words the minister had spoken in the chapel: 'As gold in the furnace hath he tried them, and received them as burnt offering, And in the time of their visitation they shall shine, and run to and fro like sparks among the stubble . . .' Yes, yes! she thought, *that* is what I wish for him. It seemed that he was still with her, that this was the last thing she had to do for him, and that it must be done well. The fire seemed to leap in her, too. '. . . and such as be faithful in love shall abide with him: for grace and mercy is to his saints, and he hath care for his elect.'

While they shovelled the earth over the coffin, she felt his spirit rise into the light. As soon as the service was over, she walked among the people, thanking them, as he would have wished. This was his day, and nothing must be neglected. Personal grief could wait until tomorrow.

Ben said, looking across the bleak little cemetery, 'I hope all the trumpets sounded for him on the other side.' He flung the remark out as a challenge rather than a pious hope, as though anticipating opposition and giving notice that he was himself prepared to do battle with whatever Force might seek to deny Stanley Fairley this tribute. Alice was repelled by his anger. She felt that he was using her father's death to satisfy some need in himself, just as Mrs Immingham had. She avoided him.

Judith looked at the wreaths, mechanically reading the messages. The funeral director said, 'I will let you have a list of names,' and she thanked him. Jacov came to make his farewell.

'I felt he held the world on his shoulders,' he said.

'I think he would like to have done,' she acknowledged drily.

'You will come back with us, won't you, Jacov?' Alice asked politely.

'No. They will be upset if I am away long.'

Alice had a momentary vision of him and his brothers standing around the coffin, silent, while candles flickered. She must have seen such a tableau in a painting – or perhaps a Russian film? She walked down the rows of tombstones to where Louise was talking to the minister.

'Have we done anything about Mrs Vaseyelin?'

Louise said, 'Yes, I've seen to the flowers, and I shall go to the funeral.' She sounded competent and cheerful. Alice stayed with her because she knew that Louise was self-sufficient enough not to demand a similar response from her; whereas Claire would expect the echo of her own sobs.

They walked back to the waiting cars; Louise and Alice pushing Grandmother Fairley's wheelchair, while Judith walked behind with Aunt May and the Sussex relatives. Alice could hear the Braddons trying to persuade her mother to go down to Sussex.

'Have you seen the house?' she asked Louise.

'It's like a crushed match-box. I wouldn't go there if I were you, pet.'

Where *would* she go when she came on leave? Alice wondered. The thought of having no home seemed the worst thing of all.

'The flowers were beautiful, weren't they, Grandma?' Louise said. 'And it's not easy to get them now, even in the spring.' The old woman did not answer.

They went back to Louise's house. Later, when all the visitors had gone, Claire and Alice looked through the letters of condolence, while Judith sat staring into the empty grate, her face dull and lumpish. They could hear Louise talking to the children in their bedroom.

'I don't know how Jacov had the nerve to come,' Claire said. 'If it hadn't been for his mother, Daddy would still be alive.'

'No,' Judith shook her head. 'Rumpus was killed in the kitchen, and if Daddy hadn't been with Mrs Vaseyelin he would have been soothing Rumpus.'

But Claire was a long way from being able to accept the incredible fact of death. 'He would have taken Rumpus down into the cellar,' she said.

Her face dissolved in an agony of grief. It is quite genuine, Alice thought dispassionately, looking at her sister. She was always sick at once if she ate anything that disagreed with her; I was the one who couldn't bring it up. She drew her writing pad towards her. 'Shall I answer the ones from my friends and their parents, Mummy?'

'Yes, that would be a help, darling.'

Alice wrote. Claire read the letters through, weeping when she came across particularly touching tributes to their father. Louise began to sing to the children. Judith sat unmoving.

Before she went to bed, Alice had a few minutes alone with Louise in the kitchen. 'What will you do?' she asked. 'Will Mummy come to live with you?'

'She would hate that, and so would I. We're both too strong-minded to live so close. I think she ought to stay with Aunt Meg and Uncle Harry on the farm. There will be work for her to do there. Uncle Harry says they are so tired at the end of the day, they just go to bed. So there won't be much opportunity to fall out. I'll go with her for a while with the children. She won't go otherwise.'

There was no air raid that night. Alice and Claire lay in bed in that unnatural hush, waiting for the siren. Alice said, 'Do you remember how we hated coming to Shepherd's Bush, Claire? We could only bear it with the help of our make-believe family in Sussex. Now our real family will be in Sussex. Why does everything happen the wrong way round?'

They talked about this, each putting out feelers into the unfamiliar territory which lay ahead, seeing how far it was as yet safe to venture; what they must take with them, and what must be discarded.

Claire said, 'But it *will* come right, won't it? The family will be more important than ever now.'

Alice looked at the moon shining through the branches of the plane tree beyond the window, and wondered whether a time would ever come again when they would be entirely thankful for moonlight, which had proved itself as favourably disposed to destroyers as to lovers. She said, 'I suppose a lot will depend on what Mummy does now.'

The silence stretched out, tormenting the nerves so that one longed for the certainty of the siren.

Claire said forlornly, 'At least, we'll always have each other.'

While they slept, Jacov and his brothers kept vigil beside their mother's coffin. Alice would not have recognized the place where they stood as a church. It was a room in a private house, upon which had been superimposed the necessary trappings of the church – the altar, sheltered behind a rudimentary icon screen, together with a preparation table and a bishop's seat. These, set side by side with the three-piece suite and mahogany sideboard, gave an effect as bizarre as if a fairground had put up its booths in a suburban living room.

The hearthrug had been moved to the centre of the room, and Mrs Vaseyelin's coffin had been placed on it, a strange resting place for one who, in life, had been alienated from such homely comfort. The coffin was open, and they could see that indeed, as St Paul had said, 'Death is a gain.' Although her body had been smashed, Death had been kind to Mrs Vaseyelin and had left her face unmarked. As he looked at her, Jacov was reminded that his mother had known happiness; and it was easy for him to anticipate the first words of the burial service, 'Blessed is our God.' Her face had something of the serenity of the young woman who had looked expectantly from the window of her grandparents' house in St Petersburg, at a time when it had seemed that beauty would be sufficient to bring her joy for the rest of her life. It had always set her apart from her children, this fact of having so much to regret. All the time that they had known her, she had seemed abstracted; a person absent from the place where her life was really lived. It had sometimes seemed she was a being fallen from Paradise on whom it would be improper for them, poor earthly creatures, to intrude. They had never come to know her and never would now.

It was impossible for Jacov to understand how hard his mother had, in fact, tried; he could not know the cost of her frail striving to live for the sake of her children; how, every morning, she had to make an effort to open her eyes. On the days of her headaches, on the days when she would not get up, on the days when she turned her face to the wall, she *was* fighting in her own fashion. Suicide had been a constant temptation, which she had steadfastly resisted. Her life had been more than a long backward glance; and it was in triumph that she lay here now.

But he knew none of this. He searched for something on which to rest his mind, and found nothing. In the candlelight, her face wavered like a face under water. She is at peace, he told himself — it was a concept beyond his understanding and brought him little comfort. Perhaps now she was with her daughters, Sonya and Katia? Sonya, perhaps. As he recalled, Sonya had been a true Russian. Katia, alone of the children, had resembled her Jewish grandfather, a thrusting creature, full of restless energy. He could not imagine her lying, still and composed, as his mother was now. He would never be able to think of her as at rest.

The twins were silent, standing close together, each holding a candle. What they felt, he had no idea. As first one blow and then another struck their family, so they withdrew further into their private world. To Jacov, they seemed incomplete, aspects of each other, and yet not adding up to one entire person. Sometimes he was not sure which was which and it didn't seem to matter.

Their father, Stefan Vaseyelin, who had joined them, as he always did for anniversaries and deaths, wept. Leaning forward in the candlelight, he resembled the figurehead at the prow of a skeleton ship, the white hair frothing like sea-spray about the massive skull which seemed to exist independently of the shrunken body, tapering into the shadows. He had something of the grandeur of the archetypal mariner who can never again put into port. Jacov thought how odd it was that, in spite of his desertion of his family, he should make it seem that grief was his prerogative, drawing it greedily to himself, leaving nothing for his sons. The validity of his grief was somewhat marred by the fact of his weeping so frequently, usually for himself. He had cried throughout the twins' only birthday party. His store of self-pity was fathomless. Jacov, not given to making judgements, reminded himself of his father's unexpected courage. A man of his rank, his dignity, who had known the Czar, to play the violin outside the tube stations and picture palaces! Unlike others, similarly afflicted, he did not sponge on anyone, owed no man anything in terms of money. Jacov had only once visited him in one of the houses where he had lodgings. His room had been cheerless and bare — no vodka bottles, even. The only thing he cherished was his violin. Watching his father weeping, Jacov wondered why the dead moved him when the living failed to make any claim on his emotions. It was all in the past — the answer to everything about his mother and father was locked away in a past that he knew little of. Their children had been a cruel complication of their already complicated lives. The mother, at least, had tried to care for them in spite of her unsuitability. The father had simply walked away. Yet, the violin playing must have helped to provide for them. Jacov, unprepared for hatred, as for any strong emotion, set himself to respect his father for this.

But he could not love his father. He had loved Mr Fairley because Mr Fairley wanted to be loved. It distressed him to think that the misfortune experienced by his family might now overtake the Fairleys. Their home had been smashed, the father killed; the war would separate the girls. What would be the outcome?

Mr Vaseyelin cried out: 'Christ is risen and the demons have fallen. Christ is risen and the angels rejoice . . .' In the light of the candles, his three sons looked down, impassive, like figures in an icon, not the likenesses of real people.

Outside in the street, footsteps hesitated, negotiated a barrier, went on briskly. A girl's laughter shrilled briefly. Further away, there was the rumble of a train. Unconnected noises. Nothing connected. Stefan Vaseyelin played his violin outside Earl's Court station, the Shepherd's Bush Empire, Olympia; he made no connection between the places. To him, they were islands on which he stood to play. And even Jacov, who went often to London, had never realized that he could easily walk from Piccadilly Circus to Leicester Square. For him, too, nothing connected.

Yet, the tableau they made, standing around the still figure in the coffin, had the unity of people drawn together by a master hand; something fixed within the flux of life. It was the fussy little room which seemed insubstantial; the noises in the street of no more consequence than a dog barking at shadows.

5

October 1941–February 1942

Ben, leaning on a rail of the troopship, reflected that ever since he joined the army he had had no elbow room. He hoped Africa would provide space, if nothing else. This apart, he expected little from the Dark Continent, and had no appetite for desert life. His knowledge of the desert was gleaned from *The Seven Pillars of Wisdom* and *Beau Geste*, neither of which he had found either credible or congenial. He thought Lawrence a charlatan, and Beau Geste an upper class twit. His perceptions might be different from those of Alice, who relied on the film *Pepé le Moko*, but they were no more authentic. It would have surprised him considerably to know that it was Alice, and not he, who would have the opportunity of revising the picture. He was at the beginning of a very long journey.

Guy was in the desert. His letters to Louise barely disguised the fact that he was enjoying an unfamiliar freedom. Louise had shown one or two of these letters to Ben, who had been unexpectedly touched by their innocent high spirits. He had also noticed the strange lack of physical fear, which made him more aware than ever of the large question mark hanging over himself.

He had not tried for a commission, an odd decision from one so ambitious. Louise had teased him that it was easier to criticize from the ranks, and there was some truth in this. There was also the fact that such sympathies as he had were with the underdog. But what really held him back was an uneasy feeling of having already gone too far from his roots.

The sea was lively, with ridges that formed and dissolved and formed again, shifting mountains with sides of silk and peaks frothed with lace. He watched the other ships in the convoy. The nearest one seemed to have a particularly vocal complement; it sometimes sounded as if they had an entire male voice choir on board.

'Welshmen – all from my valley,' a cheerful voice said at his elbow.

'How can you possibly tell?' Ben asked, amused. At this stage of their acquaintance he regarded this man as a compulsive story-teller rather than an inveterate liar.

'They have a particular lilt to their voices, see?' Gomer Tandy was a jocund, plumped-up little robin of a man, guaranteed to liven up any gathering, and generally popular. One might have imagined pleasing others to be his one aim in life; their happiness the only reward he asked.

'Here's our entertainment come now,' Tandy said to Ben.

Boat drill was carried out regularly, but always gave rise to a certain amount of confusion, so that it had come to be regarded by the soldiers as a welcome break in the monotony of the voyage. On this occasion, members of the Royal Navy draft were taking part. The sailors scrambled into one of the rowing boats while two of their number stood by waiting the order to lower the boat. 'Going to get your feet wet, are you?' Tandy shouted. This remark distracted the attention of the harassed young officer in charge of the exercise, and he neglected to give the command 'out pins'. He had two men of different types at each end of the boat – the one a stickler for the letter of the law, the other a believer that it was the spirit which counted. The spirited sailor took out his pin, and the other did not. The boat assumed the vertical, scattering its occupants upon the face of the waters. Amid much shouting of commands and counter-commands – and cheers from the watching soldiers – another crew was mustered and a boat launched without mishap. As it rowed towards the men overboard, it appeared, however, to be getting lower in the water. 'We're sinking, sir,' a voice called desolately. 'Nonsense! You can't possibly sink!' came the angry reply. The boat laboured on until the rowers resembled some antediluvian seabird flicking its wings perilously on the surface of the waves. Presently, rowing ceased and bailing ensued. 'They haven't put the bung in!' Tandy leant against the rail, crying with laughter. Eventually, after an apoplectic old salt had elbowed the incoherent young officer out of the way, the occupants of both boats were rescued. 'We know what we're in for now, if we run into any trouble,' Ben said.

There was not much to laugh about during the next two days. Enormous seas built up. Even the crew was sick. Worse than this, German submarines had wreaked havoc on a previous convoy and soon the ships were steaming through a sea so laden with wreckage that at times it seemed they were making their way amid the ruins of a sunken city. It was only too easy to hear the cries of drowned men in the howling wind. Ben had not tasted fear until now. In an emergency, the crew would be at their posts. The men on draft were cargo.

As soon as it became calmer, Ben went on deck. It was late afternoon and the light was beginning to fade. He felt very queasy, but grateful to be alive. The voices of the male voice choir drifted across the water, a little more subdued. Ahead, a spray of altocumulus looked like a sheaf of corn laid across the sky. There was the least emphatic of swells, and the deck moved as though the ship was carried on the back of a slow, deep-breathing animal. Somewhere near the water line a galley hand was throwing out brown cardboard cartons and remains of uneaten food. Many of the soldiers had gone below; but not far from Ben a man from his own unit was sitting on a pile of emergency rafts absorbed over a piece of paper. Ben had not taken note of him before. All soldiers, by nature of their uniform, tend to look fairly ordinary chaps. Geoffrey Burt would have looked ordinary whatever clothes he wore. He would have been the casting director's choice for the Geordie on a night out, the Paddy in the shebeen, the fisherlad on his boat, the collier walking his greyhound. The only adjustment that might have been needed was an occasional change of headgear, a cloth cap, a sou'wester, a tam o'shanter. He would have done well in advertisements, too, because although the face was ordinary, the disposition of the features was sufficiently individual to hold the attention – the distance from nose to mouth rather longer than usual, the eyes not quite aligned, giving a wry cast to the face. At the moment, as he gazed at the view before bending over the paper, his face expressed the mild good-humour of the man presented with a brimming beer tankard.

Ben, looking over his shoulder, saw that he was sketching. 'Pictures from the ark?' he asked.

'That will do nicely for this series.' A school-teacher's response this, Ben thought, rewarding the apt pupil whose initiative must be encouraged. 'Are you good at captions? I could do with a collaborator.'

'You're doing very well on your own,' Ben said shortly.

'In fact, I'm not doing at all well. I'm lonely. That's one of the reasons that I do this.' He spoke so easily of loneliness that Ben knew it was not a condition which troubled him.

'What are the other reasons?' Ben put the question as if Geoffrey Burt was a witness whom he intended to discredit.

'I've got a bit of a talent, I suppose.' From the evidence on paper, Ben was not disposed to challenge this assertion. 'Mainly, it's because I'm so bloody scared. Not of all this . . .' He swept a dismissive hand towards the sea and the long line of ships with the cruiser weaving ahead. 'I'm scared at finding myself in the Army –

even more scared of losing myself. I've always done work that I was suited for until now.'

'You're not alone in that.' Ben was quick to put down presumption.

'No, of course not. But that makes it worse in a way. We all sweep each other along.'

'The students really educate themselves?'

'Exactly! Though I doubt if Sergeant-Major Quarry sees it that way.'

'Why didn't you apply for a commission, if you feel like that?'

This time it was Geoffrey who asked the question. 'Why didn't you?'

Ben looked at him thoughtfully. 'You have just given the answer to that, haven't you? I was afraid of losing myself.'

It was becoming very cold. Geoffrey folded his drawing carefully. He had made an offer and it had not been taken up; perhaps he regretted this, but it was not of much significance. Ben was dismayed to find that it mattered to him. He said, 'I'd better see the other stuff you've done. That is, if I am to write some captions.'

Geoffrey had done a few drawings each day of his service life. They were neither particularly imaginative, nor sharply satirical; no appeal was made to the emotions, and there was no message. They were exact, factual records of people and places. In spite of the horrors of this voyage, there were no dead men, and no bloated human bodies floated in the water. 'I haven't seen a dead man yet,' Geoffrey said.

'Not even in the blitz!' Ben registered astonishment.

'I come from Herefordshire. How many dead men have you seen?'

Ben was surprised to realize, on reflection, that he had not seen a single dead body; he had simply constructed one from his glimpses of rubble and the bent figures of stretcher bearers.

'Don't worry!' Geoffrey grinned at the consternation in Ben's voice when he made this admission. 'It will come soon enough.' He fingered his drawings and said, without looking up, 'Well, what about it, then? Will you add a few lines? Whatever you feel – your impressions in words of what we see.' There was shyness in his manner now.

Ben, too, experienced that awkwardness which can be felt at the beginning of a friendship. He said, 'But nothing much happens each day.'

'Even monotony has different stages.'

78

Ben studied the drawings. As he looked at the figures at the start of the voyage, he saw that naked anxiety rubbed shoulders with brash exuberance, while resentment and pride jostled with an eager desire to please and a frantic wish to get the hell out of it. Gradually, as one day succeeded another, wariness crept into the faces, so that, although each kept its individual identity, one began to notice a certain family resemblance.

'It will help to pass the time,' he said. 'But it will have to be what *I* feel, even if that doesn't always match the drawing.'

'Fair enough.'

It was not easy. The drawings, although unelaborated, were so exact that they demanded something which matched their authenticity. It surprised Ben that, with his training, he should have to work so hard to find a few apt words. Geoffrey noticed the anger which invested everything Ben wrote. There had been little cause for anger in his quiet, orderly home, and, for the first time in his life, he felt that, although his parents' means were modest, he had had a privileged upbringing. He did not envy Ben his anger, but accepted it as a corrective to his own amiability.

They reached Halifax congratulating themselves that they still had not seen a dead man. In spite of several alarms, there had been no submarine attack. At Halifax, they were transferred to another ship. It was here that the brigade parted company from its transport; but the men were not to discover this for some time, and were thankful to have survived the first stage of what they still imagined to be their journey to Egypt.

Once more, they headed into the Atlantic. This time, sea-sickness was the worst discomfort they were to experience. They had rounded the Cape before rumours began to spread that they were not bound for Egypt, but Malaya. A certain mild hilarity greeted this. At the ship's concert, a man with a good baritone voice sang 'The Road to Mandalay'. There was a sketch entitled 'From Southampton to Singapore by way of the Seven Seas and Five Continents', which gave an opportunity for much bawdy humour involving harems, and bazaars, grass skirts and hula-hula costumes. Records of Bing Crosby and Dorothy Lamour were played; and Ben and Geoffrey contributed a number entitled, 'The Navy will get you there, provided the Army tells them where'.

As the ship steamed on, more rumours circulated. The United States fleet had been sunk at Pearl Harbour. It seemed inconceivable, even allowing for the fact that the Yanks did not rate very high as seafarers, that they should allow their ships to be sunk by the Japs,

who were known to be so short-sighted they could not tell a
battleship from a whale.

Eventually, they arrived at Mombasa, where they spent Christmas.
On Christmas Day, Hong Kong surrendered. After Christmas, they
sailed to Singapore, where they disembarked without guns and to
discover that they had no transport. They were issued with tropical
kit and little else which would be of use to them. Two days after
disembarking, they were sent to the Malayan mainland to reinforce
troops supposedly engaged in holding the Japanese advance north of
Johore. As they marched north towards Ayer Hitam, it was apparent
that the Japanese advance had been more rapid than had been
expected. Soon, they found themselves part of a retreating army.

They had little idea where they were going or what they were
supposed to be doing. But during their long voyage, they had become
soldiers, to the extent that they assumed someone else to be responsible for their fate. The realization that, on this occasion, no one had
the slightest idea what was happening had not yet dawned on them.
They had come to this so unprepared that the distant hills and
surrounding jungle seemed a garishly inappropriate backcloth for a
camp show, which might at any moment be rolled away and replaced
by something more seemly. In fact, it was the rain which blotted it
out. They slipped and slid and fell. When he was vertical, Ben walked
with head and shoulders thrust forward, as though in haste to get a
head start on competitors. Geoffrey thought that if they threw this
man to the lions, he would strive to be first in the arena. 'A proper
countryman's mile this is going to be!' he warned Ben, and paced
himself accordingly. Tandy trod carefully, working out ways of
survival with each step he took. 'You've got to keep up, boyo,
because these buggers aren't going to carry you unless you've done
yourself a real mischief. And in this place you might die of that. But a
damaged arm wouldn't come amiss – no question of *your* carrying
anyone then!' Whatever their private thoughts, their faces wore a
look of stoic indifference.

It rained intermittently, so that at one moment they could scarcely
see before them, and the next the landscape steamed luxuriously in
sunshine. The troops ahead of them were ambushed, which must
mean that the Japanese had almost surrounded them. They were
subjected to attacks by dive bombers. At some time in the appalling
confusion, their brigade broke up into scattered groups. Ben, Geoffrey and Tandy found themselves in a unit of twelve men led by a
harassed lieutenant who told them they must make for the Causeway
at Johore Bahru, although he plainly had little idea how this com-

mendable aim was to be achieved. They scrambled up hills made treacherous by the rain. They walked through a rubber plantation where a hysterical planter told them he would have them court martialled if they did not get off his land. They ran out of food; they drank water which made them ill; they had no protection against insects and leeches, and no medical supplies. They were constantly in hiding from an enemy who was prepared to wage war on bicycles if this was the best mode of transport in this terrain.

The transition from farce to tragedy was so swift, they could not have said where the one ended and the other began. For the last few miles of their journey, they waded through bog. Ben and Geoffrey were stretcher bearers by this time, and they were weeping with exhaustion as they crossed the Causeway into Singapore. Tandy trudged beside them, nursing a broken arm. Two weeks later, on February 15th, Singapore surrendered.

One of Ben's most vivid memories was of an Argyll piper playing his men across the Causeway just before it was blown up, to the tune of 'Hieland Laddie'. Beneath Geoffrey's drawing, Ben wrote, 'Incident on the road from Bannockburn to Singapore.'

Shortly before Ben set out on his long sea voyage, Guy landed in Egypt. He, too, had had a long voyage, taking in Iceland, a detour into the South Atlantic to avoid submarine attack, a stay in Durban, before finally arriving in Egypt in the middle of August 1941. He had recently been promoted captain. Although by virtue of his service with the BEF he might regard himself as a veteran, his experience of fighting had been mainly in retreat. He looked to the desert warfare to rectify that.

By November, he was engaged in the fighting around Tobruk and was mentioned in dispatches for conspicuous gallantry while withstanding a tank attack outside Sidi Rezegh. He was himself surprised by the sheer exhilaration he experienced on this occasion. He felt no temptation to retreat, and, being unafraid, seemed to have ample time to calculate the situation. As a result, his gun crews held their fire until the last possible moment before engaging the enemy with some success.

He was living through a period when audacity seemed to pay high dividends, and he felt himself invulnerable. 'When I was a boy,' he wrote to Louise, 'I used to think the cavalry represented the ultimate in courage and daring. But I now see that as a sort of Wild West fantasy. All the cavalry did was to hurl itself unthinkingly forward (do you remember the amusing description of Sergius in *Arms and the Man*?). The real heroes, the people who display the greatest nerve and the finest capacity for cool judgement, are those who await the charge . . .'

He found rather more difficulty in commanding men off the field than on it. When they paused for a brew-up on a long journey, he would walk among them, trying to resolve the problem of seeming to be one of them, yet remaining their officer. He succeeded in looking rather like the King at a boy scout camp, shy and awkward, singing 'Underneath the Spreading Chestnut Tree' and having difficulty in co-ordinating the hand movements with the words. His conversation veered unpredictably between the mildly vacuous and the earnestly pretentious. He was overawed by one of his sergeants, a dour, leather-faced man, who took so long to reply to any remark addressed to him that on the occasions when Guy was rash enough to venture an opinion, he imagined it being filtered through the finest of hair sieves in order to test its veracity. It was a test which he had the feeling of constantly failing. He would sooner have found favour with Sergeant Baxter than be awarded the VC.

Sergeant Baxter notwithstanding, army life suited Guy. It had a great simplicity: the sensations aroused were pure — fear, ecstasy, thirst, pain. Modern warfare tended to eliminate that other ingredient, hatred. Guy was not a natural hater. The strange lack of confrontation — the opposing forces dispersed over wide spaces, engagements being more in the nature of intermittent clashes than fixed battles — had the effect of distancing the enemy so that at times he seemed almost non-existent. Above all, Guy was grateful for the lack of complexity in his new life. The things which had most disturbed him in civilian life had miraculously been removed from him: emotional conflicts between people he loved, responsibility for intricate negotiations at the office, the need to live on different levels — with his office colleagues, his clients, his wife and children, his parents; none of these troubled him here. There was a well-tested framework of decision-making in the Army, even if the results were sometimes deplorable. He might be called upon to die, but he was not likely to be unduly tested by alternatives. And if there was one thing the Army did effectively, it was to create a pattern of behaviour which went with the uniform: you had to be very determined if you were to be regarded as 'unacceptable' or 'different', both conditions which Guy dreaded. He worked hard, got on well with his fellow officers, and was considerate to his men; it gave him the feeling of a unified life. And there was the unexpected bonus that he did not appear to be afraid of death.

As a result of his state of mind, each of his letters home had the clarity of a painting, bold in outline and full of light and strong colour.

Alice wanted to serve abroad. This was not well received by her family. Claire had joined that part of the school which had been evacuated to Dorset. Her letters were frequent and unhappy. It was to be expected that she would be dismayed. Judith's distress was understandable. What Alice had not anticipated was the strength of Louise's disapproval. Alice thought Louise was being very unfair. She had stood resolutely by Louise in her time of trouble, and had assumed that whenever she herself needed support it would be forthcoming. It was her first experience of the painful truth that it is no use making investments of this nature. Love and loyalty must be given unconditionally, not as a loan to be repaid at the first call.

'Daddy would understand,' she told herself. The dead can always be relied upon for support. Granny Tippet also understood. 'You must go, Alice,' she wrote. 'Your Mother didn't hesitate to leave Falmouth when she had the chance.'

Quite apart from the question of loyalty, Alice found the decision a difficult one. She needed the protection of her mother and Louise, both of whom were strong and resilient. But however staunchly they might try to steer her through her troubles, there would be the wreckage and the rubble, and her father and Katia, to haunt her. It would all be grey and despairing. Alice wanted to find a way ahead that did not lead through the darkness. 'Abroad' appeared to be the answer. It seemed, however, that there must always be a cost to venturing, and that sometimes it is others who have to pay it. She would gain at the expense of her mother's pain. This made her feel guilty, but not guilty enough to renounce her opportunities.

She was called to an overseas drafting board. The First Officer who presided was a woman every bit as daunting as Miss Blaize. Miss Blaize had had the air of one who has gazed on a scene of the utmost depravity; this woman looked as if she might actually have participated in it. The bags under her eyes reached almost to the tip of her nose, and her mouth twisted down in saturnine folds. She asked Alice whether she liked social life; and Alice, realizing that this woman was committing her to something very different from Miss Blaize's life of service to the community, said emphatically that she did.

Friends later assured her that this had been the crucial question. 'My dear, they'd never have sent you abroad if you had said you *weren't* sociable – not with all those hungry men out there!'

Her mother and Louise were still in Sussex with the Braddons. They helped her to shorten the skirts of her tropical uniform when she spent her embarkation leave with them.

'Just be careful out there,' her mother said. 'You haven't been about much.'

'We've been through all that. We've had lectures on the way the heat arouses the passions, and the need to talc between our toes, and we've been inoculated against everything except rabies!'

Alice had been in the WRNS for two years and gave the impression of being an old hand at almost everything. Her appearance suggested assurance. Judith had watched her doing her hair that morning. The hair was well-brushed and, offset by the dark uniform, seemed more golden than sandy. Alice drew it well back and rolled the ends up over a stocking so that it covered the tips of her ears and the nape of her neck like a draught excluder. She seemed as concerned to achieve this well-padded effect as she had once been to plump out her pigtails. There was no need now, though, to tell her not to waste time. Her fingers worked quickly, sticking hair pins in with precision. She knew what she was about. 'How's that?' she asked when she had finished. But it was of herself that she asked the question, not her mother. She turned her head from side to side. 'Not too low on the collar. It would pass muster, I daresay.' She was wearing her uniform because most of her civilian clothes had been lost when the house was bombed. 'I managed to wangle some lengths of material,' she said. 'I'm hoping I can get a few things made up out there.' Men would notice her, Judith realized in surprise. The eyes were forthright. An uncomplicated girl, they would imagine; wholesome, but not without a bit of sauce.

The atmosphere between them was strained. Judith was aware of that tenacity of purpose in Alice which had always irked her. Grief had unbalanced her and she was as difficult to please as Stanley had been at his most unreasonable. It angered her if people made a fuss and it upset her if they did not; when they avoided talking about Stanley she wondered how they could be so unimaginative, and when they did talk about him they chose the wrong moment and she thought them insensitive. That Alice should choose to make this break so soon after her father's death hurt Judith; although she herself had made a break by coming to Sussex when she could have stayed with Aunt May and Grandmother Fairley.

Louise was jealous. Her body cried out for the pleasures which Alice would experience. As she stitched up the heavy cotton skirt, she saw the fiery sun go down beyond the window. The first breeze of evening stole into the room; she felt its coolness between her body and the flimsy stuff of her dress. She went to the window, smelt the scented air; the breeze lightly lifted her hair, moved the sleeve of the diaphanous dress so that the outline of the arm was visible beneath it. A shiver of delight ran through her. The sun had warmed her whole being, giving not a superficial tan but a glow of the flesh. Someone was coming into the room, anticipation of him began at the base of her spine . . . She looked down at her red, chafed hands holding the heavy cotton. What will become of me? she wondered.

It was a November afternoon, and the light was fading. Soon they would have to put the sewing aside because the only light was from oil lamps. The farmhouse, which had so enchanted them as children, seemed an uncomfortable place now. Beyond the window the land rose in blue-green folds towards the black line of the Downs. They could hear the children talking to someone in the stables; they at least sounded happy.

'They are probably fraternizing with the enemy,' Louise said.

'What are the Italians like?' Alice asked.

'They work hard.' Louise was noncommittal, aware of her mother watching her as she answered.

'I wouldn't mind living in the country,' Alice said.

'You don't know what you want.' Louise rounded on her angrily. 'First you wanted to live in Holland Park, now it's the country; and when you've been in the desert, I suppose you'll want to live there, too! It's never-never land with you – Kashmir and the like.'

'I don't often think of Kashmir now,' Alice said.

Later in the evening, Alice ironed the dresses in the kitchen, while the others listened to the news on the wireless. She worked by the light of a candle. The oil was used sparingly because Meg Braddon said every time she lit the lamp she thought of the men who died in tankers. While she was working, there was a gentle knock on the kitchen door; when she opened it, one of the Italian prisoners of war was standing there. He seemed awkward, confronted by her. He was very dark, like a gypsy, with sad black eyes which flicked quickly about the room while he asked, haltingly, for water. Alice filled the jug which he handed to her and he went away looking disconsolate.

The candlelight flickered in the draught from the door. Alice remembered holidays with Claire when they had gone to bed carrying candles, pleasurably afraid of the leaping shadows. What companions she and Claire had been then! Outside in the yard, one of the dogs was barking, a note of alarm in the sound – perhaps the Italian was still moving about, or he could hear a fox. She thought of

Rumpus. 'He must have been terrified, all alone . . . the poor little dog!' The small grief touched upon a deeper, buried grief, and she cried as she had been unable to in the past weeks, repeating desolately over and over again, 'Oh Rumpus, Rumpus . . .'

Alice sailed, and Judith and Louise settled down to life in Sussex at the Braddons' farm.

Meg Braddon had faded gold hair, parted in the centre and bundled loosely into a knot at the nape of her neck – a style suited to someone who 'never has time to think of myself' as she was constantly saying, thus giving her hearers the uncomfortable feeling of themselves being too self-concerned. Her face, however, was far from meek; if she had no time to think of herself, she had plenty to discover the shortcomings of others. She was a strong, energetic woman and needed to be, for life on the farm was hard. Most of the day she wore Wellington boots and an old coat which looked as though it belonged to someone else, and had been snatched up in headlong flight to some emergency in the yard. She had the manner of one always on her way to an emergency.

Judith wondered whether the emergency might not be Harry Braddon. Harry was a man of implacable goodness and calm. He believed the best of his fellow men, and was an uncompromising pacifist who dismissed as propaganda stories of Nazi atrocities and persecution. If incontrovertible evidence, which conflicted with his views, was presented to him, he accepted the fact without exploring the consequences. 'A terrible thing,' he would say, whether of a brawl in a pub or an undisputed massacre. 'But it is not for us to allocate blame.' He was opposed to violence and bloodshed among his fellow men, but such sentiments played no part in the decisions which he made regarding livestock or vegetation. He was a ruthless, efficient farmer; and a friendly, courteous man, completely impervious to the opinions of others. Judith thought that Meg had probably solved the by no means easy matter of living with him by opting for constant activity. By late evening they were both too tired for speech, let alone an exchange of views, and went to bed where, it would seem, they enjoyed the untroubled sleep of the physically exhausted.

They certainly did not wake to noises in the yard as Judith sometimes did; nor did they heed the barking of the dogs. If ever she referred to this, Harry said, 'foxes' and Meg said, 'You are not used to country life, Judith.' It would have been useless to tell Harry that she suspected the Italian prisoners sometimes escaped from their camp and returned to the farm after dark. Even if this had been the case, he would have seen no reason to interfere with their freedom of movement, provided *they* did not interfere with his livestock.

Louise cherished her aunt and uncle because they did not try to justify themselves; they did not seek the sanction of society for their behaviour, or submit their ideas for the endorsement of scholastics. They were, she said, 'originals'. She admired the way they worked, expending themselves from dawn to dusk, asking nothing in return but sufficient energy to face the next day. When she began to teach Lucio English, she saw no need to mention the fact. She, too, was an original.

During the day, Louise helped with the housework, while her mother worked in the kitchen. Her mother was a better cook than Aunt Meg, who was glad to be relieved of indoor work. Louise saw Lucio when she gave the men their meals, or went to call the children in from the fields. This did not allow much time for English learning. One evening, he came to the kitchen door when Louise was doing the ironing. 'Are you playing hookey?' she asked him. He was flirtatious, but not difficult to restrain. She enjoyed the practice of what once had been so familiar a game.

The farm had seemed a place of endless possibilities when she had come to it on holiday during her childhood. Then she had counted the precious days, dismayed at how they rushed by. Now, the farm had become a prison and the days passed relentlessly the same, offering no escape from tedium. The fields, where she had once felt so free, were green walls sealed by a grey November sky. The long line of the Downs, which had made her spirits soar as she gazed from her bedroom window in the first light of the morning, now grimly marked the limits of her horizon. Her uncle had a ramshackle car, but this was only used in dire emergencies; even had there been no petrol rationing, Aunt Meg would never have let it be used for pleasure because of the sailors dying in tankers. There was a long walk to catch the one bus a day into Lewes, and little to occupy her there until the bus returned late in the afternoon.

The children, playing in the yard and 'helping' with the animals, experienced the ecstasies she had known as a child; they needed her less than ever before. Her main occupation was keeping them dry and clean, which was not easy with so much mud. There was a mysterious mechanism in an outhouse which produced hot water on the rare occasions when her uncle had a mind to operate it. Most of the time water had to be boiled on the kitchen stove. Aunt Meg assured her that it was all a great improvement on conditions in her young days. She sounded as if she was looking back to a more splendid past. An inappropriate attitude, Louise thought, for a woman of progressive ideas; but then, as far as Aunt Meg was concerned, things material must be extracted from progress as chaff from the wheat.

Judith cooked with grim determination, seeming to welcome the challenge represented by the recalcitrant stove and the shortcomings of the store cupboard. She was in no need of assistance, having been mistress of her own kitchen all her married life. Louise was cold, often wet, always lonely and bored.

She went for a walk every day, not so much for the bodily exercise as to exhaust the anger building up within her. Whatever happens, she vowed, I will not become one of those sullen, frustrated females. The spectre of such a woman was her enemy against whom she must fight resolutely. When she returned as the light faded, she played hide-and-seek around the house with the children. They became hysterical with excitement. Normally, she would not have encouraged this.

'It's not good for them,' Judith said, looking at her daughter's flushed face, aware of an excitement of a different order from the children's.

'They go to sleep more quickly afterwards.'

'*And* have nightmares!'

The beginning of December was wet, too. Rain fell on yeasty mud; there was a smell of wet straw and dung. Louise walked down the sodden lanes; at each step she felt the pull of the earth as she released first one foot, then the other. The rain was soft on her cheeks. One afternoon, Lucio walked with her on some errand he had fabricated. The hedges were webbed with misty rain; overhead, the dun sky was porous as a soggy sponge. When it came on to rain more heavily, they stood in the shelter of a stone wall. A cottage had been here once; people had lived, bred and died in it, their world bounded by the hedgerows and woods which defined the limits of the farm. Now there was only the chimney wall left standing as their memorial. Lucio put an arm round Louise and drew her close; his other hand fumbled with the buttons of her raincoat. The rain was drumming down, turning the drenched path into a muddy river. While Lucio kissed her his wet fingers were exploring beneath her jumper. She gasped at their cold touch and he laughed delightedly. She strained away from him. The rain cascaded on to her upturned face, taking her breath away. His fingers circled her stomach and the treacherous muscles twitched and jerked as the tight knot in her stomach began to ease; spasms shook her body. At the same time, she experienced a sense of fluidity and a rising wave of colour. She cried out 'No!' and, surprising herself as much as him, wrenched away. He was angry. They heaved and struggled, cursing, laughing and slipping in the mud until they had exhausted themselves.

When he saw that she would continue to resist, he released her. They leant against the wall while the rain stung their faces, and trickled icily between the seams of their garments. She let him lick the water from her face, like a thirsty mariner.

It was after this that she began to go out at night to give him English lessons. He felt the need building up in her, and he was patient – she was his only hope and he could not afford to risk losing her.

But what was *he* to *her*? The weather had changed. On clear nights when he bent over her, the stars in his hair, the moon on his shoulder, he was some mythical creature conjured up by a maiden's secret dreams. What was she doing with this madness, she who lived for the day and had so little time for the fantastical? In the daytime, she would barely have recognized him. He had no identity; and when she was with him, she herself seemed to lose identity. It was a part of the compact between them.

She was not a person who could live in two worlds. His darkness, his foreignness, began to invade the day. The house took on a new aspect. It no longer bore the imprint of her uncle and aunt – a place stripped of pretension, bare, clean, smelling of beeswax and carbolic. She could remember a time when, during the day, light seemed to reach into every nook and cranny of the house; it was full of the sunlight which had been a constant factor of her childhood. Now, it belonged to the night and the owls. The candles and occasional oil lamp lit only a small area, and beyond was shadow and darkness. People bent forward into the circle of light and then receded; she saw the busy fingers moving, but there was no face, no body.

How different this was from the feeling Guy had aroused in her! When they first met, and in the early days of their loving, the world had seemed so bright and jewelled, so sparkling. She remembered how he had looked at her, with such wonder and delight, with such tenderness. Where was tenderness now? Yet, although she had no interest in him as a person, nor he in her, she began to realize that Lucio had more power over her than Guy had ever had. If she could tease and torment, arouse and disappoint, so could he. All day, she thought of nothing but his hands on her body. She could have shrieked at the children when they demanded attention. She avoided her mother. Her mother knew.

One morning when she looked in the mirror, she saw a face that was heavy and sullen: the face of the enemy. She needed help. Always before there had been someone she could talk to – usually Alice, who was a good listener and tended to confirm her attitudes. She decided to talk to her uncle.

She knew that her uncle had advanced ideas. When she had conceived out of wedlock, her parents had had to make a reappraisal of their whole view of life. Harry, who believed that sexual experience should come before marriage, had been unconcerned. Judith had said tartly, 'He didn't have sexual intercourse with Meg before he married her, and I sometimes doubt if he has had it since! Anyone can have ideas; it's the putting into practice that gives rise to problems.' In this, she was unjust to Harry. The responsibilities of advanced ideas weighed heavily upon him. Had they gone hand in hand with enjoyment, he would have been nothing but a Bohemian. So, having eschewed 'thou shalt not', he must measure up to the puritan in self-denial. The life which he and Meg led was harder than it need have been; not only was pleasure more unfavourably regarded than in the Fairley household, but an austere regime of clothing, eating and drinking was enforced. More than that, thought itself must be examined with increasing rigour as the years wore on, and there was less and less occasion for amusement and light-heartedness. To be trivial was worse than to be Bohemian. Meg and Harry carried a heavy burden. It would have been asking too much of them to see that, while refusing to make moral judgements, their whole attitude to life implied a considerable judgement on the way that most people ate, played, housed themselves and passed their time.

Louise had little idea what she was inflicting on her uncle when, as she washed her Wellingtons under the tap in the yard, she said, 'I'm finding it difficult without Guy.'

He paused, watching the water easing the mud off the sole of her boot. She waited, imagining that he was summoning all the considerable forces within him to her aid; whereas, in fact, he was searching for a form of words which would not put anything in to her mind. Eventually, having decided that this could not possibly influence her, he said, 'Yes, I am sure this must be so.'

'I miss him physically,' she went on, supposing that he was trying to draw her out. 'Other women go to dances and meet people. I can't see that that is harmful. I expect Guy goes to dances when he gets the chance. We can't live like monks and nuns until the war is over, can we?'

The introduction of the cloister deflected him from the uncongenial subject of dances, and he said, 'No, I should hope not!'

'I still have feelings. All that doesn't just stop because Guy isn't here.' She wondered how much her uncle guessed. He was gazing into the far corner of the yard, a brooding agony in his face. It was the expression she once remembered seeing on the face of the contralto singing in the St Matthew Passion – she had not been able to decide whether the singer was grieved by the crucifixion or dissatisfied with the lower register of her voice.

'Yes,' Harry said. 'War does present young women like you with great problems.' He was more at ease now that he had found a theme. 'This is forgotten all too easily amid the talk of heroes in uniform. And the children – to all intents and purposes they are fatherless; but who thinks of them?'

It was a rhetorical question, but she took it personally. 'They're happy enough,' she snapped. 'But what am I to do?'

He winced. 'My dear!' He really was fond of her – or had been when he last saw her with any clarity, as a lively girl. Rather a lot of water was being wasted; he bent down to turn off the tap. '*Are* there any dances held near here?' He screwed up his eyes as if to winkle out some elusive fact from the depths of memory.

'I'll soon find a dance! But ought I to go?'

'Ought?' He was on firm ground here. 'Oh, Louise, *ought* is a word we should never use where others are concerned.'

'I'm not others. I'm your niece.'

'My beloved niece.' He put his arm around her shoulder. 'Look into your heart, my dear. You have always had your own kind of wisdom.'

'It's not my heart that is troubling me.' Her heart knew the answer. Guy could not be harmed if she had an affair, provided she did not cease to love him. Love has no need of sexual fidelity. It would have helped her, however, if she could have talked this over with someone who was capable of understanding this great truth. There are times when even the most strong-minded person can be in need of support. Surely her uncle must appreciate this.

Her uncle looked at his boots, gloomily contemplating desire. Had she already committed adultery, he would have been the first to denounce the first person to throw a stone. But as he gathered that adultery was in prospect, rather than retrospect, he was at a loss. In fact, he was in the same position as any other loving uncle, of being reluctant to say anything for fear of making matters worse. 'You must be Louise,' he said. Inspiration came at last. ' "This above all: to thine own self be true, and it must follow, as the night the day, thou canst not then be false to any man." '

Louise, not herself short of this kind of inspiration, responded:

> 'Come to the stolen waters
> And leap the guarded pale
> And pluck the flower in season
> Before desire shall fail.'

'Ummh . . .' Harry said.

There, Louise saw, they must leave it. His mind lay hidden, limpid and clear and – she was sure – pure as a mountain stream. She would not forgive him for refusing to allow her to drink of it.

Yet perhaps something had been said, either by her uncle or by William Shakespeare, which was of value, because she did make a decision shortly after this conversation.

Judith precipitated matters when she asked one morning at breakfast, 'And how is Lucio's English getting on?'

She looked, not at her daughter, but at Meg and Harry, challenging them to acknowledge what was happening.

Louise looked at her mother and did not answer. She admired her mother at this moment.

Harry said, '*Is* Louise teaching Lucio English? That is very kind of her. These men must be so isolated, cut off from their own homes.'

'And the comforts of home,' Judith said.

Meg, who had begun to clear the table, said, 'Louise, I hadn't realized! My dear, we must make things easier for you. Why don't you use the little sitting room? You could take *several* of them in there, couldn't you? Lucio *and* the others.'

Harry said, 'Yes, I don't think we should distinguish between them.' He went into the scullery, and soon they saw him striding across the yard.

The children scampered after him, and Judith followed, shouting to them to put their Wellingtons on.

Meg collected crockery and walked towards the door. 'I think I could provide paper and pencils – or crayons. We have a stock of things I used to keep for all of you when you were children. Those were good times, weren't they, my dear?'

Louise remained sitting at the table. When her aunt came back to see what was keeping her, she said, 'I can't stay here any longer, Aunt Meg. Mother and I aren't compatible at close quarters. I'll go back to

London with the children. The bombing doesn't seem so bad now.'

Meg said, 'You know best, my dear.'

The decision had not ultimately been difficult. Lucio represented something too dark, too much a betrayal of herself. But the need was still there, and the resentment.

6

February–June 1942

'He makes you feel so at home in his company,' Alice wrote to Irene from Alexandria. 'I have never enjoyed being with anyone so much. Just having his arm around me is bliss; nothing more than that, as yet – he isn't the sort to rush things. I think we shall probably see quite a bit of each other. He never pays any attention to anyone else when he is with me. Jeannie says he looks at me as if he could eat me, but she always exaggerates. You can talk to him about all sorts of things that really matter – slum clearance, birth control, books (I'm afraid he doesn't like Charles Morgan). He tells me I'm a bit too serious and he is gently teasing me out of it.

'You would like him, Irene. When you first meet him, he's just a tiny bit of the light comedian type – slight, fair hair, easy voice, charming to everyone. But I'm sure there is more to him than that. The maddening thing is that just when you think you are getting to know him, you come up against an odd reserve. Up go the shutters! I've heard from fellow officers that he can be moody. He has a sense of his own dignity, too – at parties he never lets himself go like the others. And though I appreciate his refusal to make himself silly with drink, I sometimes feel it is a kind of vanity more than a matter of principle which holds him back. I have a suspicion that if it wasn't drinking – but some innocent clowning – he still wouldn't enter in fully. This self-consciousness makes him a little less of a hero, but much more intriguing.

'I am discovering what an awful beady-eyed little toad I am. Even though I like him so much, I can't help seeing things about him, such as: that his charming, thoughtful treatment of others is in part a tribute to himself. It's not that he wants to win other people's admiration, so much as that he has to satisfy the high standards he has set himself. I think he may be a rather complex person, and I can't understand what it is in me that attracts him!

'I'm in love, Irene; I'm in love, I'm in love!

'And I'd best be careful. Did I tell you the talk we had from the chaplain on the ship? "Men don't look after goods they get cheap," he informed us. "You don't value anything you can buy at Woolworth's. So if you want to have your fun, don't be hurt if you get let down." You can't have it straighter than that.

'I'll have to stop soon. I'm going to meet him this evening, and that means catching a tram. I'm quartered in a convent, of all places for a good Methodist to find herself! They are Belgian nuns. Absolutely sweet. We haven't any Flemish (or whatever it is — Walloon?) and they haven't any English. We make big, gauche English signals at them, and they flutter back exquisitely at us. The convent is some way out of the town, and we have naval transport to take us down to the harbour when we go on duty; but at other times we catch a tram, where we sit in the first-class compartment. Can you imagine a first-class compartment on the tram to Shepherd's Bush Green? So, later, when I have washed and changed I shall catch the tram and meet him in the garden of one of the big hotels. We shall have a couple of drinks and then we shall go for a walk along the Corniche. How I wish we could walk there forever! He is an intelligence officer. So he may be here for a while, but you can never tell. Some of the girls have had three boy friends in as many weeks. A boy friend is essential, otherwise you aren't doing your duty by our gallant fighting men. Imagine trying to feed the five thousand with only a hundred odd Wrens and you will get some idea of the dilemma.

'Now I have run out of paper and almost out of time. I'll write again soon. I am longing to hear *your* news. I haven't had a letter from you for weeks, so I suspect one has gone missing.

Love,

Alice.

'P.S. His name is Gordon Stafford. He's not handsome like those wonderful men in posters – "Back up the man on the bridge"; but he has light blue eyes that can twinkle very invitingly, yet somehow manage to make it quite clear just where you are expected to stop short of the presence. We'll have to see about that!'

Alice put the letter on the floor and rubbed the palms of her hands on the counterpane of the bunk where she was crouched. Then she lay back and watched Madeleine. Madeleine was making up. As soon as she got the grease on her face, it melted. Madeleine persisted. Kathleen Miller, the other occupant of the dormitory, said, in the rather preaching voice she adopted whenever she spoke to Madeleine (it was her form of self-protection), 'There's nothing wrong with sweat, Madeleine.'

'How right you are!' Madeleine sketched a haughty eyebrow. 'Let us all look to the day when it will be accepted that women too can sweat. We may not live to see it, but we can work for it – sweat for it, indeed! And it *will* come. *We* may not sweat unconcernedly, but our daughters will.'

Kathleen went out of the room. Madeleine lightly painted her mouth. 'Why waste lipstick when it will so soon be removed? But then the same, of course, applies to clothes. Oh dear – has she gone? A pity. I'm sure she would have had something uplifting to say. Do you think we might keep a book of her sayings – the daily thoughts of a humble soul? Or perhaps "humdrum" would be better. She's not really humble. She thinks she has a special place reserved for her in heaven, whence she will look down on me writhing in the pit.'

'The front row of the stalls, surely?'

'That was rather good, Alice. How unexpected you can be sometimes.' She began to brush her hair.

Alice thought how exciting Madeleine's life must be. And yet, even in the company of Madeleine, there was a strange sensation of waiting for it all to begin. In some ways, our life is like that of the characters in a Jane Austen novel, she thought. Then, there were the preparations for the visit – which gown to wear, which ribbons for the hat – the coach drive, the anticipation as the characters neared their destination, the all-too-short enjoyment of the occasion, the exchanges and speculation on the return journey. Then home and all to do again another day. While now, there is this party on board ship, the pressing of clothes, brushing of hair, application of lipstick, mascara, the arrival at the dock, going up the gangplank ... Madeleine would look around, attract the man of her choice, perhaps go to bed with him. Then, when his ship sailed, it must all be done again – another ship, another evening, another man. It was as though all life was a rehearsal for the great occasion; or a series of sketches by an artist who would eventually get it right.

'And what are you looking so soulful about?' Madeleine asked.

'I was thinking about Jane Austen.'

'That will get you nowhere with that man of yours. He is the kind who keeps the Jane Austen type of heroine waiting for years and years. You will end up like that ailing female in *Persuasion*, being brave and enduring when you are definitely past your best.'

Alice did not point out that the Jane Austen heroine usually got what she wanted in the end. Instead, she asked, 'Don't you like Gordon?'

'I think I might be able to like him quite a lot if I put my mind to it. But it would never do. I have been around with too many men.

Gordon is a shade exclusive, I suspect. He had a little run with Gwenda and dropped her when he found out her soul was no more unblemished than her face.' She gave a theatrical sigh. 'We have to pay the price, you know, for our sins – since Kathleen isn't here to say it.'

Alice had looked forward eagerly to meeting attractive men, but had not been prepared for the excitement of being with such interesting women. She thought Madeleine quite the wittiest person she had yet met. Not everyone was so admiring. Madeleine was pale with crisp ash-blonde hair and narrow grey eyes which missed nothing. She had a sharp mind and a sharper tongue. The young subbies were frightened of her. 'What's wrong with her?' one of them had asked Alice. 'Why does she talk so odd?' Madeleine needed a man with a good head on his shoulders and quite a bit of enterprise.

Less daunting, though every bit as effective, was Gwenda. She was dark with a heart-shaped face, demure blue eyes fringed with incredibly long lashes clotted with mascara, and a dreadful complexion. 'You would think her skin would put any man off!' Madeleine said. But Gwenda's eyes made promises which her figure suggested she would be well able to fulfil. She was the one who drew men to her the moment she walked into a room. She could be a good companion to another woman when she had nothing better to do and was generally liked. She was quite as intelligent as Madeleine and there was considerable rivalry between them.

Jeannie claimed to be passionate and unconcerned with the small change of life – which may have explained why she never washed her neck. She had hair the colour of corn which is waiting for the reaper, worn piled precariously above her big, freckled face. Madeleine said she was 'the most consistently radiant person I have ever encountered. She should carry a sign warning that too much exposure to her may do one a mischief.' Jeannie was warm and affectionate to all her women companions, although everyone knew she was more likely to poach then either Madeleine or Gwenda. This, she explained, was because, having such a warm nature, 'I'm not calculating like those two; I have to *respond*.'

'All in the genies, I suppose,' Madeleine commented.

Jeannie was probably the most successful of the trio yet, in spite of her warm nature, men seemed not to like her but to accept her as one of the necessary challenges of life.

To Alice, these three were the great courtesans of their time. Yet none was beautiful. Beauty seemed a hazard for a girl. Inertia often went with it, Alice noticed; girls expected it to work for itself.

Perhaps, in the more leisurely days of peace, it had; but now there was less time for its magic to take effect. A little more determination was required. One thing which Madeleine, Gwenda and Jeannie had in common was determination: the other was a strong sexual urge and the ability to enjoy their affairs.

Those who sought to emulate them were not so fortunate. There were several girls who tried to force themselves into the mould of men's expectations and got not an ounce of pleasure in return for their not inconsiderable pain. Their example seemed to Alice to be relevant to herself. 'I am never going to be a courtesan,' she thought, 'so I might as well stay the way I am.' This sensible decision was made in the knowledge that Gordon Stafford seemed to like the way she was.

While she was riding in the tram on her way to meet him, she resolved to ask him more about himself. So far, it had been she who had recounted stories of home and family; he knew about the death of her father, about Louise's marriage, and about Miss Blaize and the Winifred Clough Day School for Girls. He, on the other hand, gave only a few details of his life and background each time she saw him, as though his history was something precious that could be dispensed only a drop at a time. She admired this reserve, and felt herself in a position of trust when he told her he had been a scholarship boy who had gone to Cambridge.

As he stood waiting for her in the hotel courtyard, it was easy to see why Alice was sometimes puzzled by him. His face had a certain charm that might have been boyish, save that boyishness suggests the forthright, whereas in this face something – either diffidence or fastidiousness – tempered spontaneity. Lovers proceeding to their rendezvous can still display all the symptoms of delighted surprise at their first sighting of the beloved. Gordon Stafford did not react like this. When he first saw Alice, the face muscles stiffened and the eyes hooded: so might another man have reacted to a threatened blow. The wariness was only momentary, then the slow smile eased his features, although the eyes reserved judgement of the occasion until they had kissed and were walking towards the hotel.

Alice herself was not yet able to throw restraint aside immediately she greeted a man, so she was grateful for what she took to be Gordon's forbearance. It troubled her, though, that later in the evening, when she had got over her wretched shyness, he was the one who seemed to hold back. I rebuffed him earlier on, she thought regretfully, and now he feels he has to be careful with me. She attributed to men a considerable capacity for understanding and sensitivity; the idea had not yet dawned, even as a distant cloud on her horizon, that most of them were capable of going fairly directly for what they wanted — and that there was something odd about those who failed to do this.

Gordon pointed. 'The barrage balloons are going up.'

She did not look. Nor did she take note of the subterranean movements which told of heavy mortar fire. Life itself must be held suspended, certainly Rommel and the Afrika Corps must keep their distance, until something had been decided between herself and Gordon. She had been in the service long enough to know that wartime friendships — so quickly made — did not long survive separation. Out in the desert one of the major encounters of the war was being fought; men were dying — Guy was out there, might be dying, too — yet all that mattered was herself and Gordon. The world had become a very small place and they were the only people in it. She knew that this was monstrously selfish, but could do nothing about it.

By the time they were walking along the Corniche, the blue sky had darkened to violet and they were aware of the absence of light in the town, where a black-out was in force. Alice, looking away from the town at the vivid sky, exclaimed: 'I never knew there could be such colour until I came out here.'

'This is nothing.' Automatically, he deflected the conversation, like a man shielding himself from the force of the wind. 'You should see the lake of Galilee at sunset.'

She immediately transferred her delight to the contemplation of Galilee. 'Yes, I must, I must!' The thought that she might miss anything was unendurable.

They stood looking across the sea as the darkness came down and the moon dappled the water with silver. Gordon said, 'You're so enthusiastic, Alice.'

'That sounded a bit reproachful.'

'No, it's charming. Only I can't let go of my feelings. If I do, they just go soaring away — like a child's balloon. I'm left behind feeling cheated.'

'Can't you soar with them?'

'Only at my peril. I get carried away and come down in some very uncomfortable place — right out there.' He pointed away from the moonlight to where the water was dark and wrinkled as a snake.

'Gordon, you shouldn't think about being safe until you're forty at least! This is the first time round.'

'What do *you* know about being unsafe?' His arm had been round her waist, now it moved involuntarily; his hand stroked the line of her thigh.

'You're not fair!' she protested.

'Fair? Alice, what a very long way you have to travel!' He bent to kiss her. Voices called out of the darkness and there was laughter as other couples walked by. He kissed her again. She was ready for him now; slowly, her reserve melted, and she felt she had, in fact, swung out over the sea and the motion of the balloon was carrying her, swinging and dipping. She clung to him, while above his head the moon tilted vertiginously. At last, he held her away from him. 'Well, I don't know about you!' He looked at her in surprise.

They walked on in silence. The night breeze was getting up. They could hear the boom of the sea in the hollows of rock and, further away, the distant boom of guns. Once, he took her hand and swung it high above their heads and laughed delightedly. On the way back, he kissed her more passionately and told her that he loved her. Alice kissed him, tasting his flesh. She had seen other lovers going about this business with a dedication she had found repellent; but then she had not understood the burning necessities of loving. Now, she was made free of this mystery. Gordon had done a great deal for her.

When they came back to the town, she was struck by how quiet it was; only the never-ending rumble of traffic on the desert road. There were few people about. The black-out seemed to have subdued the noisy town. Perhaps this disconcerted Gordon. She had hoped they would walk slowly back to the convent; but he said, looking round him distractedly, 'Let's find a dance, shall we? It's not too late.'

'Yes, all right.' It was not what she wanted, but the promise of music playing while his arms were round her made up a little for the disappointment.

They walked through a dingy quarter of the town where as many as fifteen people might sleep in one room of a crumbling house. Gordon drew her close to his side as they passed filthy bundles of rag propped in doorways. They had both been dismayed at the callous way in which service personnel spoke of the Egyptian poor. 'I've had to revise my ideas about Empire,' Alice admitted.

'I never had any positive feelings about it. I was a pacifist for a time. My idea of war was of men bayoneting each other. When I examined it, I wasn't sure whether it was the bestiality of it – or the fact that I should be terrified if someone came at me with a bayonet – that put me off the most. I didn't feel able to give myself the benefit of the doubt.'

'So you joined up?'

'Yes. The Navy, though – no bayonets!'

In her dreams, she had imagined someone bold and brave, with very positive ideas about Empire, who would charge fearlessly with bayonet in hand if need be. She was quite prepared to dispense with that dream.

In spite of their sympathy with the poor of Alexandria, they would be glad when they came into a better part of the town. In anticipation, they began to walk more quickly. Then, suddenly, turning a corner they came upon one of those scenes like a shot from a film, where people come late upon an incident – the vehicle pulling away, the characters left behind looking after it, uncertain which way to go themselves now that the drama has been gathered up to continue elsewhere. The remnant, in this instance, was naval.

'Has someone been hurt?' Gordon asked.

'A Wren.' Alice recognized one of the signals ratings. He hesitated, eyeing her. The other sailors stood behind him; their faces, fish-white in the moonlight, told the story he held back.

'Was she dead?' Alice whispered.

'Very.' By way of confirmation, one of the sailors turned aside and was sick. 'A couple of Aussies found her. It wasn't them, though, We was behind them all the way from the bus.' The sailors had closed ranks, shielding Alice from the sight of something on the pavement.

'She shouldn't have come along here alone,' Gordon said.

'She didn't stay alone.' The quiet venom in his voice was in itself more frightening than anything else.

Alice was uncomfortably aware, while they talked, of people watching from doorways, leaning from windows. The dark eyes watched, curious but detached, as though the English naval personnel were exotic specimens contained in some invisible bubble of atmosphere; a phenomenon to be observed, but unrelated to them.

Gordon said, with warning in his voice, 'There's no point in hanging around here. You can't do anything about it.'

As he and Alice walked on, the sailors remained where they were, bunched together, waiting silently until they had gone out of sight. Alice was conscious of Gordon's uneasiness, and of his helplessness. The Commander for whom she worked, a small, straight Navy man with the belligerence of a Cagney, would have got the men back to their quarters with one rasping command. Gordon lacked not only rank, but the belief that this could be done. Momentarily, she saw him stripped of his enigmatic charm – a slight young man who had been forced by the war into a wholly inappropriate setting. Why was it that men with so much idealism were not more effective? What was the good of caring if you couldn't influence people and situations? What, in fact, was the point of talking of the power of good, when on all sides goodness seemed so powerless?

'They'll go and get blind drunk, and break up some perfectly harmless café!' she said angrily.

Gordon did not answer. He held himself stiffly and walked a little apart from her, angry that there should be a witness to his humiliation. She realized, from his reaction rather than from her own observation, that he should have stood his ground.

The taste for dancing had gone. They caught a tram and bade each other a subdued farewell outside the convent. He watched until she had disappeared into the building.

The news had already got round. The dead girl was Edna Baxter, who had slept in the large dormitory adjacent to Alice's own — not an especially daring girl, but one who tended to be late. The girls were shocked, but already asking, 'What did she go down there for, anyway? She must have known . . .'

Gwenda, genuinely upset, said, 'Cutting corners as usual. She told herself it would only take her a few minutes; she'd be all right if she hurried, and didn't stop for anything . . .'

'She was with me at Pompey. We shared a cabin.' Small claims to fame were already being staked.

The next day, when Alice was having tea in the signals office at stand-easy, the sailors were talking about Edna.

'Was she a mate of yourn?' one of them asked her.

'I knew her, but not very well.'

She looked round for the sailors she had seen the night before, but they were not on duty this morning.

'Some of our lads settled that score,' the sailor said.

'How — settled?'

The leading seaman came over at this point, and something in his manner made the sailor edge away. Alice said, 'What did he mean, hookey?'

He swilled tea round in his mug, not meeting her eyes; he was a quiet, grave-faced, gentle young man. Alice could see he was very uncomfortable,

'You don't mean . . . they *couldn't*!'

He looked over his shoulder to where the sailors were grouped, talking in low voices. 'This isn't our sort of country. It wouldn't be safe for women like you if the wogs thought they could get away with it.'

'But they won't *know*, hookey! How would they connect it? This isn't a village, it's a huge town.'

'The word gets round, Alice.' He was no more convinced of this than was she, he was bolstering himself up.

Alice sipped her tea. It all seemed unreal, Edna's death and this other death. Edna had taken a short cut, probably because she was late, and had paid the penalty; the unknown Egyptian had done nothing to merit his death beyond just being there when a scapegoat was needed. All that Katia had done was to be Jewish. Rage boiled up in her. 'I hope they are caught and court martialled!'

Hookey looked shocked, and said in a hushed voice, 'You mustn't say that kind of thing, Alice. Don't let people hear you. It was just a wog. You can't change things.'

'I don't want this tea.' She went out of the room. She would not spend stand-easy with them again; she would go without her tea. That would be a gesture of some sort.

She told Gordon about it later. He withdrew into himself; he had anticipated this and no doubt felt a personal responsibility. 'There was nothing you could have done,' Alice told him. This was true, but it was not enough to absolve either of them from guilt. He seemed unable to share his guilt with her. All he would say was, 'Men do all sorts of things you can't understand, Alice.'

The girls at the convent were divided in their reactions. Jeannie said with some satisfaction, 'Matelots may be a grouchy lot, but they always look after their own'; while Madeleine commented, 'My God! And we call ourselves civilized!' The others seemed most concerned with trying to identify the sailors; once they had done this — '*I* know that fellow!' — they lost interest.

The darkness which Alice thought she had shaken off came down again. She was aware of the many things it was better not to see — the poverty, the cruelty to animals, the hungry children, the diseased and crippled. For a time, these became the only things she did see.

She was aware of how fractured was her understanding of living. When she was growing up, she had known that people were starving while she was cared for and cherished; she had put money in boxes, but by doing so had not effected a reconciliation. Reconciliation had not been possible. Now, there was *her* war, which she, like many others, had been determined to enjoy because it offered an undreamt-of freedom; while, in Europe, people disappeared, like refuse swept into a sewer, never to see the light of day again. Here, in Egypt, she found the darkness encroaching. And she must fight the darkness for the sake of her own survival. Yet, by doing so, must she acknowledge the need for a fractured understanding? What alternative was there?

She had another of her bad dreams. In the dream she saw her home after it had been bombed, the chimney still standing. The chimney dominated the dream, towering high above the wreckage; smoke belched from it, blowing ashes into the sky. There was something obscene about the chimney which filled her with terror. Yet it was not for her father and Mrs Vaseyelin whom she cried out in the dream, but for Katia, who had not been there when the houses were bombed. Her waking mind was unable to make the connection between Katia and the chimney.

The next day she went into the convent chapel when it was empty. As she said her prayers, she closed her eyes tightly so that they should not dwell on the images and candles and other idolatries. Her mind formulated questions to which there were no answers. In spite of the quiet coolness of the place, she experienced a profound sense of uneasiness, of being drawn beyond the sheltering walls which had encircled her in childhood. Was this sense of danger related to the Roman Catholic faith, which she had been told had sinister drawing powers, or was there something else, something inherently danger-ous which lay beyond the safe harbour of childhood?

When Singapore fell, the number of prisoners of war might have presented a problem to a people more charitably disposed to men who have surrendered than the Japanese. The town was badly damaged, however, and there was plenty of work to be done. In time, they would devise more onerous work for their prisoners.

Ben had been in hospital with fever during the last week of fighting. The hospital had been stormed by Japanese troops, who had killed everyone in sight. Ben had been out of sight at the time.

The military prisoners were housed in the jail and Army barracks at Changi, some fourteen miles' march from Singapore town. At Changi, where nearly two hundred men were crowded into a room which had once served as sleeping quarters for thirty, Ben was reunited with Geoffrey.

'I thought you must be dead! We heard about the hospital.'

'I was in the store,' Ben told him. 'I went there in the hope of stealing quinine – everyone was stealing. The Japs flung open the door and had a quick look. I was behind the door.'

When the slaughter was over, he had crawled out of the building, and had been fortunate in being picked up by two Australian soldiers. Less fortunately, his brain appeared to have recorded in minute detail the sights and sounds of those dreadful moments in the hospital and now insisted on a replay whenever he had a quiet moment. 'What about you?' he asked Geoffrey, hoping his would not be a less ignoble story.

Geoffrey had little idea what had happened to him, only a confused series of images driven like a stake into his mind: a nurse shot down as she fetched water from a standpipe; English soldiers looting a hairdressing salon, spraying one another with perfume; groups of Australians sitting aimlessly on the edge of the pavement, smoking; frantic civilians, who still imagined they enjoyed some sort of privilege, threading their way disdainfully among the troops; Chinese traders hawking their wares as if nothing had happened; smoke and flames, and a burning oil slick looking incredibly beautiful as it moved slowly down the river; a captain in the Argylls weeping over the body of a dead child. From now on, death would be recorded in his drawings with the same factual precision as bridge building or a sunset after the monsoon.

The atmosphere in the room was foul, the noise oppressive. Ben and Geoffrey were lucky to be near a window. They could see wooded hills which looked deceptively cool in the moonlight, like a fairy tale landscape, ambiguously inviting.

Ben said, 'We must get out of here.'

'We can't, Ben. Even if you were strong enough to make the attempt, it would be madness.'

'It's madness to stay here. I'd rather die fighting the jungle . . .'

'You'll never get off the island.'

Ben leant against the wall, considering this. After a few moments, he said, 'That would be a good caption to the Singapore series of drawings.'

'It's been used.'

'Already?' He turned his face to the wall, ashamed to let his friend see the extent of his despair. His face was much thinner now. Geoffrey thought he would draw him as a dark, wounded bird; but a bird of prey, still, fierce and formidable. How different they were! All he had to sustain him was the countryman's stolid, persevering patience. He guessed that, had they met in peacetime, Ben would not have spared him a second glance. He said gently, 'We'll get used to it.'

'I'd rather die.'

As Ben lay in the hospital, he had felt a sense of shame, outrage, anger, bewilderment, as if he had lost a vital race. Surely it was only a heat? There would be a re-run and this ludicrous result would be reversed; the Union Jacks would fly from the flagpoles again. He had never thought of himself as being particularly patriotic, but it had never for one moment occurred to him that British soldiers could be so comprehensively beaten. In particular, he had never imagined himself being beaten. He thought of his mother, her face drawn and old before her time because she had struggled so hard to give him a chance. That was a mistake! Life doesn't like planners; whatever happens you must not be seen to be too much in charge, otherwise the reins will be snatched from your hands. Then, interrupting all this self-pity, the Japanese had burst into the hospital, performing in a few minutes infinite variations on the theme of terror. Afterwards, he had crawled out on his belly, glad to be alive.

He could not stay here, shut up in this confined space, with such memories. He had to get out, beyond those hills. 'I'd sooner die.'

'That *is* going to be the alternative way of escape.'

Geoffrey spoke so soberly that Ben turned to look at him. 'I believe these are the conditions in which men may think themselves into death.' He did not meet Ben's eyes, and Ben could see that he was frightened for himself.

Ben said sharply, 'You are still doing your drawings?'

'I lost most of them. But I've started again.'

They were both going to need the drawings to keep them sane. They were at Changi for several months, during which time they became accustomed to hunger and brutality. The hunger was the more destructive because it never went away; and if you weren't careful it dominated every moment, walking and sleeping, so that a man could get into a state where there was nothing, however ignominious or vicious, he would not do to obtain extra rations. They thought they were living like animals and that their conditions were as bad as they could be. Tandy had talked his way into the cookhouse, proclaiming himself an expert at cooking rice. As rice was all there was to cook, he was made welcome. Ben and Geoffrey went out on working parties. Sometimes they worked on the roads, but occasionally they had to repair houses to make them habitable for Japanese officers. They became adept at looting, although their efforts were not always successful. Geoffrey once presented Tandy with what he took to be cooking oil, and was only discovered to be some kind of lubrication after the entire evening meal had been burnt to cinders.

When the news came that some of them were to move north into Malaya and beyond, they greeted it with relief. The Japanese painted a beguiling picture of the conditions they would enjoy — better climate, fresh flowing water, plenty of fruit and vegetables. While not entirely convinced, they were disposed to be mildly hopeful.

'It must be better,' Tandy said. 'It stands to reason. How could it be worse?'

That night, Geoffrey wrote to his family; and Ben, feeling the need to communicate his misery, wrote to Judith, telling her what a waste it had all been. It was of himself that he was thinking as he wrote, of the years going by, years in which his energy should have been expended on his career, years in which he would have reached his peak. As he bent over the paper, his face had a look of intense, impatient absorption, as though time itself was something to be consumed before it got away from him.

As Geoffrey wrote, he thought of his family. His mother would pour out her anxiety and grief to friends and neighbours, while endeavouring to keep the spirits of her dear ones high. His father's would be a quieter sorrow which he would keep to himself, unable to share it; probably he would find difficulty in mentioning his son. The two girls would be confused and irritated by their parents' behaviour, unable to conceive the possibility that their brother would never return. He realized as he wrote that he seemed to know and love his family much more now that he had moved outside the frame of their lives.

For part of their journey, they travelled in railway trucks. Then, when there was no railway, they marched. As they marched, they clung grimly to the belief that they would eventually find themselves in a better place. Once, it crossed Ben's mind that he was headed for Alice's mythical Kashmir. At the memory of Alice, he began to laugh. He did not laugh often. Tandy said, 'If there's anything funny, man, you ought to share it.'

'I was thinking of a girl I know. She came to the door one evening to let us in – I had been walking her older sister home. There was a howling wind and it blew her nightdress right up over her head.' Tandy sucked in his breath, visualizing something rather different from the young Alice's podgy form.

It was the beginning of the wet season. The rain hissed on the leaves of trees, and from time to time it surged as though a gigantic fan had been switched on which drove it now in this direction, now that. Occasionally, it came with a sharp little patter and Tandy muttered, 'God, it's raining bloody rice now!'

The ground was like black treacle. Geoffrey was already walking barefoot. Ben had bound his boots up with leaves, tending them as gently as mutilated flesh, but at each step he could feel them breaking apart; if he could not doctor them again he would soon be bootless, too. Tandy had managed to obtain new boots.

When they rested at night, the Medical Officer came to see how they were getting on. Geoffrey said he was a good sort. Ben thought him a fool.

'If ever there is a chap who won't get out of this alive, that's the one!' he said scornfully. 'The product of a good public school, more concerned with being gentlemanly in adversity than survival! What good does he think he is doing himself or any of us, rushing hither and thither, encouraging the weak and faltering!'

'Whereas you wear yourself out with anger.'

Geoffrey had his own personal scheme for survival: don't expend too much energy hating the Japs, or being ashamed of defeat; don't sweat about what happens tomorrow or try to be brave today. 'Energy is going to be as important as food and water,' he warned Ben. 'There isn't much we can do about food and water – but we can try not to squander energy.'

He looked affectionately at his angry friend: six foot one of spare flesh and bone, a mere exclamation mark in a world in which Nature had run riot. The jungle was the enemy and it was little use being angry with it. It was like a child's painting where everything has been overdone; trees with vines twisting in the branches and cascading down the trunks, huge fungi rising above a tangle of vegetation. Everything was clotted as though each inch of space must be used up. There was too much creation here, he thought uneasily; life and death were in danger of becoming one. He looked at Tandy, squatted beside him. His jaw was thrust out; every now and again, his tongue flicked out and licked the water which ran down his face. There was something saurian in the movement. Unconsciously, Geoffrey's drawings began to show man in the process of reverting to the primeval.

They marched for many days and had little rest. Soon, Ben found himself trying to concentrate his mind on the miseries of his boots in order to save himself rather than them. He was in a state of exhaustion, but other men were managing to keep going and so must he. It was only later he would come to realize that there was hardly a man who did not feel he had reached the extreme limit of endurance. During the next months the limits would be pushed further and further. It was good that at this stage they did not know what lay ahead of them.

In June, Tobruk fell. Alice remembered her father saying what magnificent fighters the Dutch were; and then, 'It will be Belgium again; we shall hold them in Belgium' – the Maginot Line had been side-passed before he had had time to consider its holding power. People were more used to defeat now. The ships of the French fleet, inactive in Alexandria harbour, were a constant reminder of the fall of France. More recently, the Japanese had taken Malaya and Singapore. Once Tobruk fell, there seemed nothing to stop Rommel getting to Alexandria. The Great Flap was on. Where were they, Alice wondered, those cool, tight-lipped, purposeful men who never panicked and had the air of knowing exactly what they were about? Perhaps they had been sent to some other arena of the war.

At the end of June, the Wrens were evacuated under conditions of the utmost confusion. Alice, sitting on her luggage, looked out of the train at the verdant green of the Delta, and wondered what was in store for her. A tent in the desert? She waited in vain for that rolling expanse of sand to appear. It seemed that nowhere was anything done as thoroughly as in Hollywood. The country through which the train eventually passed was little more than scrubland. The palm trees were thin, their branches like upturned feather dusters; in the town, their trunks had been like giant pineapples.

Once, as they passed through a gimcrack place reminiscent of a wild west shanty town, she saw a detachment of soldiers, resigned, blank-faced, leaning against a wall, no doubt waiting for transport. It seemed unlikely that at this moment they thought much of King and country; yet something in their stubborn, immobile faces, a certain kind of steadiness, sobered and touched her. What would become of them when the transport came to carry them into battle? A hot little gust of wind sent a swirl of sand into the air, and set a song going in her mind: 'Sherman's dashing Yankee boys will never reach the front/So the saucy rebel said, and 'twas a handsome boast/Had he not forgot, alas, to reckon with the host/While we were marching through Georgia . . .' She remembered that she and Ben and Guy had sung this, walking on the sand of a Cornish beach. She wondered what had happened to Ben; he seemed to have dropped out of sight.

Guy was on his way back from forty-eight-hour leave in Alexandria. He had tried to find Alice, but she was no longer at the address which Louise had given him. Everyone was on the move now, and Alice was probably at sea. He had heard that the Wrens had been evacuated. He was not sorry to have missed her. He found interruptions in the pattern of service life unsettling.

At the present moment, he was suffering a particularly irritating interruption. A journalist who was doing a series of Men at War photographs for the Ministry of Information, was sharing his jeep.

The man should have been in the charge of a liaison officer who had gone sick with amoebic dysentery. Guy had been pressed into taking him as far as Mersa Matruh; but the man had insisted on going further, and when Guy had asked whether he was authorized to move about as he chose, he had replied, 'Don't be so bloody pompous!' He was a leery-looking individual with mournful eyes sodden with strong drink. Guy felt ill-at-ease in his company. He wondered what his driver thought of the fellow.

In the distance, they could see a village. Nearby, sheep clustered like toadstools around a tree and men lay on the ground in what little shade they could find. The photographer pointed at them, 'Bedouin?'

'It's not the name of a particular tribe,' Guy said. 'It's a term for the nomadic people of the region.'

The man sucked in his breath. 'So they *are* Bedouin.'

'Probably.' Guy was doubtful himself. He did not know much about the indigenous people and this worried him inexplicably, in the way that some half-forgotten neglect can nag the mind.

Heat bands shimmered on the gritty road. Further on, a boy herded goats, a blue hood over his head; he had a dark, unsmiling face, none of the city urchin's gamin impudence. The photographer said, 'God, how they must hate us, kicking up all this racket!'

Guy said, 'Their life is so remote from ours that he probably does not know how to respond to us.'

'How would you expect him to respond?'

They travelled in silence for a while. Guy stole a look at the face of his driver, but it was enigmatic as the goat-herd's. He fretted about the goat-herd. I need too much reassurance, he told himself; I expect the whole world to open its arms in order to assure me that I am doing all right. He was startled by his self-awareness, and thought, this won't do at all!

The jeep drove on into the desert. Guy said to his companion, 'Did you enjoy your stay in Alex?'

'You could say that. I got myself a Greek girl. I suppose they're fairly safe?'

'Safe?'

The man turned his head to look at Guy in amusement. Guy flushed, understanding his meaning. 'I spent most of my leave trying to find my sister-in-law,' he said.

But he remembered now, that as he was walking along a street in Stanley Bay, a woman had emerged suddenly from one of the cafés. As she walked towards him, the sea breeze lifted chestnut hair and she tossed strands back from her face. He had felt a pain so intense it had seemed to dislocate his whole body. He had stood gasping in the street, tears blurring his eyes. When eventually he walked on, his vision still seemed to be blurred. The experience had been akin to drowning, except that it was not his past so much as what might have been which swam before his eyes: the years he had missed with Louise; the children growing up, the stages of their lives he would never share; all the joys of lover and parent denied him, which could never be recaptured. Usually, he succeeeded in holding Louise and the children framed in his mind, like the still of a film. He imagined them waiting for him, untouched by time, thinking only of him, planning what they would do 'when Daddy comes home'. The agony of longing and loss had shaken him. He could not stand too much of that.

He looked towards the desert. 'You won't find it comfortable out here, you know,' he said to the journalist. 'Thirst is the worst thing.'

'I believe you.'

'Did you know that in the desert, a soldier's water ration is just under a pint per day? And after using some of that to shave and wash, he is lucky if he has as much as a half-pint to drink.'

'Does that include officers?'

'Of course. There is no distinction in the desert.' The man irritated Guy. '*And* salt must be added to that to replace the body salt lost in the heat.'

The journalist stared moodily out at the sand without making any comment.

Guy said, 'When you're not in action, you can't think of anything else but your longing for water. You sleep whenever possible, just to forget.'

His insistence reminded the journalist that he had brought his own supply of liquor. He took out a flask and made a brief gesture in Guy's direction. Guy shook his head. The journalist refreshed himself, and continued to do so at frequent intervals.

They came to a place strewn with the wreckage of battle, now half-covered in sand. 'Tank.' The journalist pointed to something which now resembled a half-submerged submarine. 'You know their tie – brown, red, green – you know what it stands for? Through mud and blood to the cemetery beyond.' The driver gave Guy a sideways glance. The journalist tapped him on the shoulder and told him to stop. The driver looked at Guy, who nodded.

The journalist got out of the jeep to photograph a bayonet stuck up in the sand with a billycock hitched to it – a rough joke outlasting its laugh. 'It will all blow over,' he said when he returned. The smell of his breath preceded him into the jeep. 'It has blown over the glories of lost civilizations.' He waved a hand at the vast expanse of sand. 'So it will blow over this. *Won't it?*' He glared at Guy.

'I suppose so.'

They drove on. The journalist had become morose. 'All gone. The cocky laughter, the blasphemies, all buried in sand.'

Guy pleated his lips and looked ahead.

7

July–August 1942

'Alice!' Claire wrote. 'It seems so strange. Where is everyone? Daddy dead. You and Guy and Ben so far away I can't even imagine the places where you are. Even Mummy and Lou are in different places now that Lou has gone back to London. There isn't anywhere where I belong. I'm a floating person. There is a place in my tummy that aches all the time. It's no use praying about it. God isn't there. I expect you have found that out by now?'

She was writing from Dorset. It was July. She was eighteen and in a few weeks she would leave school for ever. In the autumn she would go to Oxford. She had known this was her destiny ever since, at the age of ten, she had heard her father telling the minister, 'Of course, Claire is the clever one. My dearest wish is that she may get an Oxford scholarship.' She had imagined it would bring her happiness as well as him. Now, she was less sure. In her childhood, supported by home and school, her abilities had presented her with more rewards than problems. In Dorset things had not gone so well. She had encountered challenges of a different order.

When Claire was billeted on the Armitages, Mrs Armitage wrote to her sister, 'We have such a funny little gnome with us. Her late father seems to have been one of those Bible-thumping Methodists – I recall them in our childhood but I hadn't realized the species survived into the Thirties. Our young Claire has a brain, but her capacity for rational thought is hampered by all this godly nonsense. It's quite pathetic, but of course one mustn't *say* anything. Even so, I think we come as quite a surprise to her. I see her looking at the book shelves and wondering where the Bible is! She is to read history, so I suppose one is permitted to do a little gentle *guiding*.'

Mrs Priscilla Armitage was a woman of advanced ideas. She had no missionary zeal, however, and had little wish to convert others, since general acceptance must have made her ideas the less advanced. Her only aim in discussion was to lay waste the ideas of others without setting anything in their place. 'My husband and I are humanists,' she told Claire soon after her arrival. She spoke as though there were only the two of them. Mrs Armitage impressed Claire. Claire suited Mrs Armitage very well. Professor Armitage was too exhilarated by his present much-publicized quarrel with a fellow biochemist to register Claire – or his wife, for that matter – very clearly. Mrs Armitage, lacking her husband's assured place in the world of academic contention, needed to exert herself rather more in small matters.

On her first Sunday with the Armitages, Claire had said, 'I usually go to chapel.'

'Do you, my dear?' Mrs Armitage had been as amused as if Claire had said she went to the circus. 'Then of course you must go, and we will point you in the right direction.'

From then on, although never overtly challenging Claire's beliefs, she brought religion out for an airing every day to inspect its condition and find it ailing. Her idea of what Christians believed was based on what she would have liked them to believe – namely, that God was a benevolent father-figure who rewarded the good and punished the bad; and was always on hand to offer comfort, and ensure that the members of His flock never had to come face to face with the more unpleasant aspects of His creation. Any more mature idea of religious belief, she would have dismissed with the words, 'Well, I would like to *think* that was so, but I'm afraid it is not what the majority believe.'

Claire hated Mrs Armitage, not so much for her non-belief (her beloved friend, Heather, was not a believer) but for her amused attitude. Above all things, Claire needed to be taken seriously. She prayed to God to help her to overthrow Mrs Armitage; but day by day, Mrs Armitage prevailed. There is very little one can do with a person who accepts any argument one puts forward with an amused smile. 'You have plenty of enthusiasm, my dear,' Mrs Armitage assured Claire. 'And if you are a little short in analytical thought, I daresay this will come in time.' Claire lacked the expertise to test Mrs Armitage's own capacity for analytical thought.

From time to time, she applied to Heather for sympathy, but Heather was not helpful. 'It will do you good!' she said. 'Other people had to listen to an awful lot of talk about religion when they came to your home. Now it's your turn to have an earful of atheism.'

'But she's not *fair*! She keeps telling me what I think, and then she picks holes in it. But it's *not* what I think – and she won't listen.'

'That's the way people argue, silly! You create a weak case for your opponent, and then knock it down. I expect we'll spend years at university doing that sort of thing.'

'I wish it was all really as simple as that,' Claire said miserably. Her problem with Christianity was not at all what Mrs Armitage imagined. It was not that Christianity offered certainties which Claire was finding it increasingly difficult to accept; but rather that the further she ventured, the more she discovered that whatever was being offered, it was not certainty. And it was certainty that Claire needed. Not for her the journey into the unknown, the quest for that other continent whose existence depends on a few unconfirmed travellers' tales. The risk of failure was too high. Mrs Armitage would have been mortified had she known that Claire envied her the certainty of her unbelief.

This was a climax in Claire's life. Her beloved father, who could have sheltered her in his arms, was gone. Throughout her childhood, when she came home from an outing, one of her parents would be waiting for her, and always they would embrace; the warmth of physical love was never lacking in her home and now she missed it sorely. She longed for the companionship of her sisters – even their quarrels seemed precious now. Theirs had been a noisy, talkative house. Why, over dinner and supper of one day, they would have tucked into Mrs Armitage and disposed of her!

Sometimes at night, before she went to sleep, Claire imagined her father still alive, visualized him striding up the path to fetch her away from this bleak place; and she went to sleep comforted. In the morning, she would wake heavy with the knowledge of his death.

When her mother came to visit her, she tried to tell her something of this; but her mother, grieving in her own way, was unable to help her. Instinctively, then, Claire knew that no one would ever love her again as her father had loved her, that no one else would shelter her as he had sheltered her. All that warmth and security was in the past. From now on, everything gained in the way of love and understanding would have to be earned.

Judith was at a loss as to how to help Claire. She had lately begun the painful procees of reassessing her life with Stanley. When he took Judith away from Falmouth, he had said to Ellen Tippet, 'We may only have met a few times, but I *know* your daughter.'

'We'll see what you make of her, then,' Ellen had retorted. Wise in her fashion, she understood that by 'knowing' a person we impose on them the duty of being the person we would like them to be.

During their marriage, Judith had often seemed to be the strong one. Stanley relied on her love and attention. She was resilient where he was easily discouraged; she was not quick to take offence while he was all too readily diminished; she breasted storms in which he floundered. Yet now, it seemed that it was only his incessant demands which had drawn her into being, and without them she was not sure who she was.

She was a small packet in a large parcel, gradually being unwrapped of the things she was not. After Stanley's death, a person he could not imagine would eventually emerge. Her development appeared to consist of a series of stages in which the things she was not were stripped from her. Would Stanley himself be one of these? It sometimes seemed to her that a widow must either live in the shadow of her husband or move beyond him.

Claire, who had looked at her mother to sort everything out with brisk efficiency, was dismayed to find her strained and inattentive as a person listening to a conversation in another room.

'You don't care about me,' she accused.

Judith said, 'I'm sorry, my love. This is something you will have to work out for yourself. It will be happening all the time when you are at university, so you may as well get used to it.'

Claire hung her head. After a pause, she said, 'Do you think we shall ever see Daddy again?'

Judith turned away. 'We don't know, do we?'

'We're *told* we will.'

'But not in what form,' Judith said indifferently. It was now that she needed Stanley, not in eternity; she needed the sheer thrusting bulk of him *now*!

Claire shivered, contemplating life with no one to blame for its awfulness.

Judith said, 'There's only a week of term left. I'm going to take you back to the farm with me. I don't like to leave you in this place.'

It was the answer to everything. 'To think,' Claire wrote to Alice, 'that we went down to the farm so many times when we were young and we never appreciated them! Alice, I have learnt so much while I have been here, just talking to Uncle Harry and Aunt Meg. Particularly Uncle Harry. I think he is the finest, best person I have ever known.

'He never tells you what to think, but you feel that whatever you are talking about, he *knows*. It is all inside him; his face glows with it. We had a long talk yesterday about the meaning of suffering. He *feels* so deeply about all the injustices in the world – the people in the slums; the black soldiers expected to fight for the Americans and turned out of all the cafés by the white Americans; all the poor people in India and China. It was – well, rather like God groaning over His creation! I think this is the only way I am going to be able to go on believing in God – seeing the great goodness in people like Uncle Harry.

'We talked about the miners, and the way people expect them to work so hard for the war effort, without asking for better conditions; while no one worries about munition workers profiteering! There is so much wickedness in the world, Alice; when you get to talking about it, it is quite overwhelming. Uncle Harry doesn't have any answers; but he doesn't have to provide answers because he is such a wonderful person that, in a way, he *is* the answer. I'm going to start trying to live more like him and see what I can do without.'

She took this very seriously, and one of the first things which she found she must do without she came upon unexpectedly. It involved a decision far harder than any she had anticipated.

While she was going through the little case she had packed of treasures salvaged from the wreck of her home, she found the exercise books in which she had written about the imaginary family, the Maitlands, which she and Alice had created when they were younger. She read the books, remembering how bleak Shepherd's Bush had seemed when they moved there from Sussex, and how she and Alice had comforted themselves by inventing this family. The Maitlands lived in an old farmhouse. It was the place of their dreams, full of unexplored nooks and crannies, with a wild, secret garden in which anything might be made to happen. As she read, the thrill of pleasure she had felt at the time returned: she could smell the Cornish pasties cooking in the oven, feel the coldness of her feet tucked beneath her as she scribbled in her bedroom. The London fog pressed against the window pane, but the light was clear and bright in the enchanted world she and Alice were making together. Sadly, however, she noted, as she read on, that the Maitlands were much better off than the Fairleys; the boys went to boarding school and the girls had fancy names, like Stephanie and Imogen. She knew then that the stories had too much of luxury about them. They must go. In the late afternoon, she went into the yard and made a small bonfire, well away from the stables where the straw might catch alight. On this she burnt the stories. When finally she turned away from the ashes of her imagination, she felt she had freed herself from a 'power'; the door to an unknown world had been closed. Yet she was sad; and as she walked in the twilight back to the farmhouse, a little shudder of fear went through her.

She told her uncle what she had done, and he said he was proud of her. Overflowing with joy, she wrote to Alice, 'I can't describe to you how he looked at me! No one has ever looked at me like that before – as though I was some kind of miracle. Now, I often see him watching me with such wonder in his face. Perhaps he feels I am the daughter he never had. I can hardly believe I have been singled out to mean so much to him.' She wrote of this wistfully, as though it was difficult to imagine herself singled out for special attention. Alice, when she read the letter, thought it was something which happened only too often to Claire. Claire concluded, 'I shall always remember this holiday as one of the most important times in my life. Although I must say I don't like Aunt Meg so much as I did – she is a bit on the brisk side.'

Her sacrifice was not as complete as she made out. For, as well as the stories, she had found two plaits of raven hair which she and Alice had made to adorn Rosalie, the eldest of the Maitland girls. Somehow, she had not been able to burn Rosalie's hair, and had pushed it away to the bottom of the suitcase.

'Daddy!' Catherine shouted as she saw a soldier passing by in the street below.

'You don't remember Daddy,' her brother said, clutching at one remnant of the superiority he saw daily slipping from him as his sister grew older.

'I do! I do!' She screamed at her mother, who was in the kitchen, 'I *do* remember Daddy, don't I, Mummy?' She had had a long walk in the park in the afternoon and the screaming turned to tears; by the time her mother came into the room she was sobbing drearily, 'Jameth thayth I don't remember Daddy.'

'You shouldn't tease her,' Louise said to James, not very severely. She picked up her daughter and carried her away to the bathroom. 'One of us is tired.'

'She called Mr Porritt Daddy this morning,' James muttered angrily to himself. He heard his mother running the bath water. When she came into the room for one of Catherine's toys, he said, 'When am I going to have a brother?'

'Not yet.'

'Great-granny told me I was going to have a brother and then *she* came.'

'That was silly of Great-granny. I want these soldiers tidied up, please, James.'

'They're holding a bridge.'

'Then you can take the bridge away as well.'

When she had put Catherine to bed she came back to find James still playing with the soldiers. Impatiently, she swept them up herself. His face went scarlet, more with hurt at her brusqueness than her action, which his sense of fairness told him was not unreasonable.

'Mummy, I had them formed up – I was *going* to dismiss them!'

She tried to keep her patience as she squatted beside him. 'Darling, I *told* you I wanted you to be quick tonight.'

'It's not *my* bedtime. I go to bed half an hour after *her*.'

'It's nearly that now. Aunt Irene is coming to look after you, and I want you both in bed by the time she arrives. Then perhaps she'll read to you while I'm out.'

'In here?'

'If Catherine is asleep by then, yes. But she won't be asleep if you don't go to bed soon.'

He accepted this without grumbling; he was a reasonable little boy. Louise's heart ached for him. He was the one who really missed his father; or perhaps that was no longer true – he missed a father to play with him. She looked at the photograph of Guy and felt a pang. Things were not going well in the desert, and here was she looking forward to an evening's outing.

'Don't forget to say your prayers,' she said to James. 'Pray for Daddy. He loves us all so much.'

By the time Irene arrived, both children were in bed, Catherine fast asleep and James hopefully awake.

'I am grateful,' Louise said. 'I've got a lodger, but he is out a lot, and anyway, I wouldn't want to leave the children with him. He's a policeman – Sergeant Fletcher. I always feel he's making an inventory of the room when he comes in here.'

'You don't mind if Angus joins me? He won't even notice the furnishings, let alone make an inventory!'

'Enjoy yourselves! Once you've done your duty by James, he'll go to sleep. They won't be any trouble, they both sleep like the dead. Proper little Fairleys.'

'You're lucky, Louise.'

'Yes.'

Lucky! Louise thought. There is Irene, waiting for Angus, and here am I *running* along the street because I am so eager to meet Daphne Drummond! Anything, in fact, to get out of the way of my children for a few hours. She adored the children and she was a good mother. Some women would have been satisfied with that: to them having children was the mainspring of life. But it wasn't! Now, as she hurried along the road her heart leapt at the sight of the plane trees in evening sunlight; and she looked eagerly towards the Uxbridge Road, anticipating the people and the traffic, as though she was heading for the first time for Fifth Avenue, or the Rue de Rivoli, instead of an ordinary thoroughfare along which she walked daily with her children. She had even put on her best navy linen dress in honour of the occasion. It was a little tight and she could feel it pulling beneath her arms; but this did not worry her because the dress had suited her very well when she bought it several years ago, and she had not given its appearance a thought since then. When she was younger she had been so lovely it had not been necessary to think about making the best of herself; and this had given her a confidence she would take through life with her. She would say, 'I don't need to wear a suspender belt . . .' long after this had ceased to be true. Now, hurrying along the street, she looked so warmly grateful to life for being so good to her that most people – certainly most men – would be prepared to accept her as a beauty.

The restaurant was in a side-street off Notting Hill Gate. It had two tables on the pavement outside a Moorish-style bar. Louise could see Daphne Drummond sitting at one of the tables. She had never thought much about Daphne or Irene until recently. Younger sisters' friends were not people one considered. Then, when they had met in one of the shops in Notting Hill, the children had been tugging at her, and Daphne had said, 'We can't talk now. But I would love to have news of Alice. Would it be possible for us to meet one evening?' And here she was. And there was Daphne, waving from the far side of the road. Daphne was sharply in focus and had the effect of making the people around her seem blurred. Louise could not imagine why she had not noticed Daphne before.

Daphne had gin and lime and Louise a shandy. They talked about Alice. Louise was the older of the two by some four years, but in Daphne's company she began to feel simple, as though there was some important but unspecified area of life in which she was not proficient. She could hardly blame Daphne for this, since she was doing most of the talking while Daphne listened more than politely. From time to time, however, Daphne would glance around her at the busy street, the people strolling by, and there was something in her cool gaze which suggested she was equal to anything. Why, Louise wondered, should this unmarried, and presumably inexperienced, young woman imagine she can upstage me in this way? Although she had had sexual intercourse before marriage, Louise regarded hers as an exceptional case and would not readily have countenanced such behaviour in another.

Daphne's eye rested briefly on two Army officers who were walking slowly in the direction of the restaurant. They did not hold her attention for long. Perhaps they were piqued by this, or perhaps they had intended to stop in any case. They stood talking, their shadows falling across the table where Louise and Daphne were sitting. After a pantomime of indecision, they decided, disdainfully, that they could do worse than this place. Louise and Daphne, who had now lost interest in each other, found it necessary to converse with a vivacity which had previously been lacking in their exchanges. The two men, while appearing to study the menu, made their assessment and decided that the straightforward pick-up would not do in this case. Over their beer, the men talked about the fighting at El Alamein; while Louise and Daphne talked about their friends – 'What has happened to Jacov, do you know? He seems to have disappeared.' Louise was aware, without turning her head, that one of the officers was lively, slight and dark, while the other was a big, craggy man. She said, 'I met him in the park in May. He made the usual improper suggestions, and I haven't seen him since.'

The craggy man said, 'It was an attitude of mind that lost us Tobruk. If we are not careful we shall condition ourselves to defeat.'

His companion said easily, 'Oh, the English always lose every battle but the last.'

'No, it only seems so because that is the way we write our history.'

Conversation died down. All four looked into the darkening blue of the evening; the cooler air gave impetus to flagging spirits. It would be a waste if things went no further. The dark soldier turned suddenly to Daphne. In the diminished light his face was shadowed, but the eyes, in contrast, seemed brighter. 'Would you think it impertinent if I spoke to you?'

'I suppose that would depend on what you said.' She was still as an ivory figurine: a receptive stillness, though – he would not feel repulsed.

'I'm sure we must have acquaintances in common.'

'Whatever makes you think that?' She smiled; she had a wide mouth and the smile transformed her face. The suspicion of coquetry was swept aside. Her glance was frank enough to startle Louise.

'I have this feeling that we have so much to talk about.' There was a slight lilt to his voice – Welsh, perhaps, but not obviously so. ' "Of shoes – and ships – and sealing wax – of cabbages – and kings . . . " '

Louise said to the big man, 'Does he go on like this all the time?'

It was a friendly enquiry, she was a friendly person. But she could see that she had lost favour in his eyes by jumping a move ahead; she should have waited for him to speak. A pity, because she thought he was the more interesting of the two men. His blue eyes had a far-away look, the look which had once attracted her to Guy. But the face was different; this was a man capable of realizing his dreams. The impression created – though goodness alone knew why this should be so, since the dreams might be mundane enough – a suggestion of impending danger. Louise saw danger (as she saw all excitement) in sexual terms.

'We are thinking of dining here,' the dark man was saying to Daphne. 'Would you take pity on us?'

His companion allowed him to undertake negotiations which he obviously found distasteful, although he appeared to have an interest in the outcome. His eyes watched Daphne with more than casual curiosity. Louise shrugged him aside. There's something to be said for the one who can ask for what he wants, she thought.

The dark soldier made the introductions. He was Ivor Ritchie and his companion was Peter Kelleher. Louise and Daphne responded. Louise saw Ivor look at her wedding ring and back to her face.

They went into the restaurant. A group of RAF personnel had pushed tables together in the middle of the room. There was an air of celebration about their party. Louise remembered afterwards the radiant face of a girl who normally was probably rather plain.

Ivor said, 'Oh dear, they'll start singing soon – "You can't get to Heaven in an old string bag" – or is that the Fleet Air Arm?' He steered his party to a table by the window. Peter Kelleher had not yet spoken. But he could not be accused of indifference. Shock waves rippled between him and Daphne Drummond. Until then, Louise had believed that love at first sight only happens in one's teens. Peter Kelleher was quite old, thirty at least. He looked at Daphne with the bewilderment of an explorer who finds, on a search for a group of islands, that his compass has pointed him to a whole new continent. Daphne was quiet – one might almost have said modest, had she not been so electrically female. If she had subsequently told Louise that words were never exchanged between them during their entire courtship, Louise would have believed her. Certainly, at this moment, the current was strong enough to make words irrelevant.

An RAF sergeant was proposing a toast: undoubtedly an engagement party. At their table, Louise and Ivor did most of the talking. Companionship developed between them because they recognized, and were amused by, the agitation of the other two. Ivor had a quick sense of humour and Louise, who believed in adapting herself to the reality of her circumstances, began to like him more than his silent companion. He was sensitive to what happened around him, no nuance of behaviour eluded him, no facial reflex escaped his notice; but whereas this sensitivity might in another person have produced a morbid anxiety, with him it seemed to provide food for a constant inner mirth.

The air raid siren sounded. The proprietor said, 'This never happens now,' as if it was an affront to his establishment.

Ivor's eyes darted from one person to another with the glee of a child at his first encounter with the clowns. He appeared to believe that others must share his merriment, for he looked them full in the face, inviting laughter. Louise did not think this was the laughter of the person who must forever disguise a state of nerves; he seemed very far from nervous. Perhaps he simply found life a farce? Only on one subject was he briefly serious. To her delight, she discovered that he, too, enjoyed music. His manner changed when he talked about Bach, a subject on which he evinced genuine passion. 'You listen with your heart,' he accused her.

'What else would I listen with?'

'Your ears, woman!'

The throb of approaching planes could be heard now. One of the RAF men said, affecting Welsh, 'On the way back from Cardiff, man.'

Louise was thinking of music. She had an unmusicianly theory that those who sing flat are the people who are afraid of getting things wrong, so instead of striking out boldly for the golden note, they reach up to it gingerly; whereas those who sing sharp are the intrepid spirits, who soar to meet the challenges of life, who launch themselves into the great void of the air careless of consequences. She was sure Ivor sang sharp, as did she.

He was talking about a series of lunchtime concerts which would be held in London soon. She was pleased that he was not above using music as a means to an end.

'You'll probably be posted by then,' she said.

He shook his head. His work, about which he had not spoken, seemed to offer a degree of permanence; he was confident that he could plan ahead.

Louise said, 'We'll see.'

The guns at Wormwood Scrubs opened up. It was never a reassuring sound. In the blitz, people had maintained that the guns made the planes jettison their bomb loads. The RAF were singing now,

> 'And on her leg
> She wore a purple garter
> She wore it in the springtime
> And in the month of May.'

Suddenly, Louise felt faint. 'I'm not liking this,' she thought. 'It's because of Daddy. If it goes on much longer, I shall have to get out of here.'

The planes passed. They were indeed on their way home. Ivor said, 'Do you want more of this?' He stirred the dregs in his cup. 'What do you suppose it's made of?'

Daphne said, 'Acorns?'

They heard the drone of a solitary plane. Ivor said, 'A straggler. Probably winged.' He grinned, triumphant at having got the remark in first. The men at the RAF table raised their glasses to him. The guns started up again. Someone said, 'Oh, let the bugger go!'

One of the RAF men had his arm round the girl and she was gazing up at him. Louise thought, 'I know just how she feels!' Then she saw the girl's eyes dilate with horror.

The ceiling came apart, making way for sky and a tilting chimney.

Louise was on her back with Ivor on top of her. He seemed to weigh several tons and one of his buttons was engraving itself on her chest. She could move her head, but nothing else. She moved her head and saw Daphne's face, quite near, dead white with a trickle of blood running down from the temple. She said, 'Daphne's dead.'

'No, I don't think so.' Ivor sounded calm, his face close to hers.

'I can't move! Oh God, I can't move!'

'Neither can I, but it's all right. There's nothing more to come down. They'll get us out soon.'

The greater part of the building was heaped near by, where the RAF group had been sitting. But above, through a haze of dust, Louise could see a jagged promontory of brick from which grit dribbled continuously. If one or two bricks were to be dislodged, a cascade of masonry would smash straight down on her face. She would be helpless, unable to move. The air was thick with dust and grit. She began to cough. Panic made the cough worse. 'I'm going to die,' she thought. 'Oh God, if they don't get me out of here quickly, I'm going to die! The children . . .'

Out of the darkness, she heard Peter Kelleher's voice, curtly commanding, 'Hold your breath!'

For the children's sake, she clenched her teeth and held her breath.

The coughing eased, but her throat was raw and she was terrified it would become bad again.

A young voice asked, 'Are there people in there?'

A woman's voice replied, 'I don't suppose so, dear. Come away.'

A whistle was being blown; and now men were shouting as they moved carefully amid the rubble. Peter Kelleher called out to them. Someone scrambled in their direction. 'Have you any idea how many people were in here?'

Kelleher spoke as though he was working it out at a desk. 'Eight at a table in the centre. The waiter, the proprietor. I don't know about kitchen staff.'

The man said, 'Strewth!' He looked down at Louise and Daphne. 'All right, my loves. We'll have *you* out soon.'

A flask of tea was produced. Louise longed for it, but Ivor said, 'Better not. Or you really will choke.' He did not have any either; whether for the same reason, or for her sake, she did not know.

The ambulance came. A doctor crawled over to Daphne and remained with her, although she appeared to have no need of him or anyone else. The men worked very slowly. If there was to be any hope for those who had been completely buried, they must be careful not to bring down further masonry.

Louise said, 'This happened to my father.' She *must* talk about her father. Ivor listened. Afterwards, she joked about this, saying he had had very little alternative, the way they were placed; at the time, she was comforted. Daphne lay peacefully through it all, composed and enigmatic as an Asian god. She would be recalled as having behaved in an exemplary manner. It isn't fair, Louise thought: Why couldn't I have gone out like a light?

Little bits of plaster spattered her face and she cried out. Ivor said, 'Keep your eyes and mouth closed.' She realized she had lost her dinner. Oh well, better that way than being sick and choking. God, but she was in a mess!

After a time, she began to feel much better and seemed to be floating free of the masonry. Light-headed, she whispered to Ivor, 'What an introduction!'

He answered, lips close to her ear, 'It does away with the preliminaries, I'll say that for it.'

He was quick-witted and effective. She thought how much she liked this in a man. And his laughter! Was he laughing now? Laughter bore her upwards . . . A long way away, someone was saying, 'Let her be. It's probably better for her that way.' She went round and round and up and up.

As the men set about the immediate task of setting them free, Louise realized that Ivor was hurt; his pain shot through her own body. She had an arm free now; she held his head against her shoulder. She soothed him, and seemed to carry them both away on a spiralling ascent. Afterwards, she could not remember what she had said to him, and was embarrassed. But it was too late by then.

In the ambulance, she came to herself and protested, 'The children! I must get back to my children!' They assured her that a message had been sent to her home, but she continued to feel desperately concerned about the children.

Irene, on this particular evening, was thinking of finishing with Angus. The idea of finishing inevitably heightened her feelings, so there was a sense in which she was close to loving. Had she finished with him, she would have admitted subsequently that he had not a lot to talk about, had few interests, was, in fact, rather dull. In future years, one of her sayings would have been, 'Never believe still waters run deep!' repeated with gaiety untinged by bitterness. Should things not go well with her, she might have been tempted to regret lost opportunity, to wonder whether she had made a mistake. Common sense would soon have asserted itself, however, reminding her that, in fact, there was little to regret – other than the anticipation of pleasure never realized in his company.

When he arrived, the children were asleep. The two adults were alone. In profile, Angus looked more handsome than ever in his static way, like a sketch for the Byronic hero, with his strong patrician nose and wry mouth. Full face, one noticed that the pointed chin weakened the lower half of the face and gave an impression of instability. It soon became apparent that their aloneness had inhibited him still further. As he talked, he looked round the room warily, swivelling his eyes without moving his head – just as if Louise might be hiding somewhere to catch him out in an indiscretion! Irene promised herself that at the end of the evening, she would tell him she saw no point in their meeting again. And yet . . . This inability of his, frustrating though it might be, was undoubtedly intriguing. The face promised a sensuality the eyes flinched from. Someone so deeply wounded must have been through experiences more harrowing than those which befall the ordinary person. He was a man who invited endless speculation.

The late evening sun, falling aslant the trees, cut soft swathes of mellow light across the living room. Angus talked about Stalingrad. 'Not much mention of the fighting there in the press.'

He was beginning, Irene noted, to be gratified by the shortcomings of country and individuals alike. Yet he did not strike her as a bitter person, but rather as someone who found refuge in constantly confirming the general unsatisfactoriness of life. The great battles to be fought — whether at El Alamein or Stalingrad — would not move him. He felt safer with defeat: it demanded less of him. What am I doing sitting here, if I can see these things in him? she wondered.

'I don't suppose there is much in *their* press about *our* Russian convoys,' she retorted.

He smiled at this indication of her incapacity to understand his feelings. He is mean and miserly, she thought angrily; he would rather be excluded from love than risk sharing himself. And so their friendship might have ended, but for the knock on the door. The knock was tentative — not Louise returned home early and having forgotten her key.

Irene looked at Angus. He seemed disconcerted, perhaps unsure of his position in Louise's house should the caller be a neighbour. It was Irene who went to the door.

The man on the doorstep was small. His was the smallness of someone who has not had the opportunity to develop; his impoverishment, intellectual and physical, was the one thing about himself he sought to project. The impression of deprivation was so strong one imagined for him reach-me-down clothes, although in fact he was not poorly dressed.

It was a warm evening and windows were open; the sound of dance-band music carried on the still air. A neighbour was mowing his lawn. Irene and the small man held their positions. Did Louise have lame ducks? she wondered. In case this were so, she tempered firmness with a brief smile as she said, 'I am afraid Mrs Immingham is not here.'

The sun was going down beyond the roofs of the houses opposite, and the heavy foliage of the trees already darkened the street. The man peered into the interior of the house, looking to where Angus stood in the doorway of the living room. 'If I might have a word with you, Captain Drummond?' His dismissal of the woman was the more offensive for being instinctive rather than deliberate.

Irene was so startled that she continued to stand with her hand on the door, preventing him from entering. In a garden near by children were playing, and a ball bounced into the street; a portly dog ambled after it. Angus said awkwardly, 'If you wouldn't mind, Irene? It won't take a minute.'

Absurd though it seemed afterwards, throughout the scene which followed the thought which was uppermost in Irene's mind was that this was Louise's home. Although nothing was said – or, as far as she could judge, done – to which Louise might properly have objected, Irene had a strong sense of betrayal when she saw the small man sitting in Louise's fireside chair. It distressed her beyond reason and accounted for her refusal to leave the two men alone in the room. There was something here she must guard. She made a mental inventory of the objects put in her trust: the photograph of Guy in army uniform, smiling shyly from the work table; one of James's soldiers lying in the hearth; Catherine's little red sandal half-hidden under a chair; the theatrical prints which Louise collected, neatly framed and badly hung . . .

Her presence upset Angus. He might, earlier on, have taken little notice of the pleasing effect of late sunlight falling into the room; but of the dimming of the light, there was no doubt of his awareness. He sat still. He seemed always afraid of movement, as though it gave away things about him; but his eyes turned constantly to the figure of Irene. She was wearing a dark green dress which merged all too readily in the fabric of the settee. Gradually, as the dusk deepened, the precise outline of her form was lost, so that only the oval of the face remained clear. In a few moments that, too, would recede and the whole person would be muffled in shadow. There was a light switch in the skirting board beside him. If only he could lean forward, at one touch the light would come on; she would be there, in all her precious clarity, beneath the standard lamp. But the tension in the room was considerable. It immobilized him, as so often he had been immobilized in the dining-room of his home, not daring to turn his head to look at the clock to see when his father would allow them to rise from the table. The past held him in its bony grip. The last thing he saw clearly of Irene was her eyes, which looked enormously alarmed – or was she angry? How little he knew what to expect of her.

The small man said, 'It is just that the proof has arrived from the printers and it will have to be back by tomorrow morning.' He continued with a certainty which emphasized his authority, 'You will have time to look at it tonight.' He delayed handing over the brown paper envelope to Angus, fingering it as though power must drain from him once it had left his hands.

Irene witnessed the scene with incredulity. However secret Angus's office work might be, she was sure it could not involve enterprises of this nature. She was herself now working at the War Ministry in London and knew that HM services do not conduct their business in a manner which could best be described as furtive. Furtive and amateur.

The small man did not want to leave. He seemed to have become interested in his surroundings; turning around, so that he was in danger of falling off his chair, he squinted at the badly aligned prints. He was like a bailiff, about to take possession. He gave a little snigger, devaluing what he saw.

It was possible, Irene supposed, that Angus might be engaged in work requiring him to assume a double identity. In which case, she herself, as she sat here listening to them talking about their silly proof, was now accidentally involved.

At last, gathering himself and the contents of the room together, the man rose to his feet. He handed over the 'proof' and left. The accidentally acquired knowledge remained.

Angus said, without looking at Irene, 'I'm sorry about that.'

'It was like something out of Dornford Yates!' He was so unsuited to cloak and dagger nonsense. She hoped there was no idea of dropping him over France.

He said, 'One of those rather sad little working men's groups. You know the kind of thing.'

'No, I don't.'

'Oh well . . . it's not my niche, either, really, I suppose . . .'

'How did he know where to find you?'

'I gave them lectures at one time.' He vouchsafed this remark as though it was an explanation. 'Now they like me to keep in touch.'

'Is that wise?'

'Probably not, in view of this evening. Do you think you will be able to forget about it?'

'I shan't talk about it, if that is what you mean.' The knowledge was irrevocably hers.

The air raid siren went and he said, 'I'll draw the blinds.'

'No.' She could not bear to see the room in all its untidy simplicity, the unaligned prints on the wall, the photograph of Guy on the work table. 'We don't need to put the light on.'

'Louise will wonder what is up.'

'She will think we have been sitting here on the settee holding hands in the dusk, like sensible people.'

He laughed uncertainly and remained by the window, fingering the black-out material. The long summer evening was drawing to a close. Louise would be back soon. Irene felt it was more than the evening which was slipping away. What was she to do? She had lived a rather solitary life with her parents. Now, on the threshold of maturity, it was particularly necessary that her adult relationships should be fruitful; if no man took her hand at this stage and coaxed her forward, there was the danger that she might tend to withdraw from intimacy. As she sat looking at Angus, troubled by what had happened, she had a sense of something in the balance. She had meant to finish with him, and it would have been better had she done so. But he looked so forlorn, it stirred her. Suddenly, she found herself on the far side of the perimeter which had bounded her feelings for him, in a place where there were no calculations – how much, how far, will it work?

'You're not a happy person,' she said.

'Happy?' He shrugged his shoulders. 'What is certain is that I'm no good to a woman. There was a girl once . . .' He was looking into the street, imagining Katia walking beneath the trees, grown older and more dynamic than ever. More Jewish. 'I treated her badly.'

'I don't believe you would know how!'

He came to her, stung by this. A pulse beat in her throat. She said, 'Oh, my darling . . .' Once again, there was someone at the front door. As they sprang apart, the front door opened and the hall light was switched on. Irene said, 'It must be Louise.'

The door of the sitting room opened and a man stood there. In the light from the hall, they saw a big man with a flat, rosy countryman's face, crowned by a hard brush of tow-coloured hair clipped close. Irene remembered that Louise had a lodger. 'It's Sergeant Fletcher, isn't it?'

He nodded, and said in a slow voice with a faint country burr, 'Did I disturb you, missie? Mind if I pull the blinds?'

He pulled the blinds and then switched on the standard lamp. He did these things very deliberately, continuing to look amiable, but making no apology for his intrusion. He was not unused to making his presence felt in other people's rooms. He said, 'I saw that joker leave here. I wondered if anything was wrong. Just say the word, m'dear, and I'll . . .'

Irene said, 'No, it's quite all right.'

He made no move to go. It was difficult to tell whether he was stolid or stupid. Physically, Irene found something threatening about him, so massive and inflexible, with that well-scrubbed face and the small, light eyes.

Angus said, 'He had to pass a timetable to me – nothing important. Something to do with evening classes. I told him where he could find me.' Irene thought it odd that he found it necessary to give this man the explanation he had refused her.

The policeman turned his head and looked at Angus. There was a pause while he committed the face to memory. 'Oh, I see, zurr. Well, that's that, then, isn't it?' He spoke in the mindless way of one not at all convinced. 'It just so happens I knows the rascal. You want to watch out for our Charlie, zurr.'

'Thank you, I will.'

'Proper little Bolshie, he is.'

'Really?'

How long he would have stayed had they not heard the sound of oncoming planes, Irene had no idea. He said, 'Probably on their way back. But you never know. I'd best go to the station. I never wants to be off-duty when there's a raid on. Got a gammy leg, you see. If it wasn't for that, I'd be fighting the bastards.'

When he had gone, Irene said, 'I bet he enjoys digging out the bodies!'

Angus looked at her in surprise.

'He's the sort of blind zealot storm troopers are made of. Didn't you feel it?'

He smiled and shook his head. 'All policemen are nosey.'

Irene turned out the light and drew back the blinds. 'Let's watch, shall we?' The fanlight window was open; the evening breeze wafted into the room the smell of newly-cut grass. One or two people were at their front gates, looking up at the searchlights weaving about the sky. Angus came and stood beside Irene. She said, 'Why did you tell that little man where to find you?'

'As I said. The evening class timetable. There go the Scrubs guns!'

James called out. Irene went to him. Catherine was still asleep.

'Where's Mummy?'

'She's out, darling. She'll be back soon.'

There was a noise like a great tearing of silk above the roof of the house, followed by a muffled explosion. Catherine turned on her side, and snuffled into her pillow. James was frightened. Angus had come into the room. 'I've found one of your soldiers,' he said. 'Shall we go and see if we can find the others?' He lifted the boy from the bed and carried him into the sitting room. Irene followed and drew the blinds. Angus, surprisingly tender and understanding, was making a good job of amusing James.

'I'll make tea,' she said.

They had had tea and she was washing up when Fletcher returned. He came and stood in the doorway to the kitchen. 'I've got bad news.' His little eyes fixed on her face as if it was a nice cream bun he was about to consume.

131

When he had told her, she said, 'Sergeant Fletcher, I would offer you tea, only James is in there, and I don't want him to know there is anything wrong.'

Fortunately, he reacted with genuine benevolence to this. 'I don't want to upset the little fellow. And anyway, I'd best go back and help. Now, don't worry, m'dear. *I'll* keep you informed.'

James was asleep in the crook of Angus's arm, one hand clutching a toy soldier. They discussed what they should do in whispers, then Irene tiptoed away to telephone her parents.

Her father answered the telephone. 'Do you want me to do anything?' he asked, when she explained. 'I could go along there and see how things really are.'

'No, no.' Enough had happened for one night, without his taking any risks. 'But perhaps if Louise isn't back by the morning, Mummy could come round.'

As she put the receiver down, she suddenly realized that she had not told Angus that Louise had gone out to meet Daphne. She sat on the stairs for a few moments, feeling overwhelmed by the demands of the coming hours.

They managed to put James back in his bed without waking him. Then Irene told Angus about Daphne. He looked at her so incredulously he might have forgotten he had a sister; had his face not gone so white, she would have thought he did not care.

'What do you want to do?' she asked, nervously irritable.

He seemed not to know.

'Do you *want* to go along there?'

'But what about you?'

She was very tired by now and dreaded the children waking and screaming for Louise. Angus, caught in a nightmare of demands, none of which he felt able to meet adequately, waited slackly for her decision.

'You'd better go,' she said. 'If you . . if you *can* manage to come back, I'd be glad. But you must see how things are.'

After he had gone it seemed very quiet. She sat by the window looking out into the night. She felt low-spirited. She wished Alice was not so far away. Alice was the only person she could have talked to about this.

Angus returned within a quarter of an hour, whiter than ever, to say that Louise and Daphne had been taken to hospital; from what the ARP men had said, it seemed that Daphne was suffering from concussion and Louise from shock.

'What about the other people?'

He shook his head, unable to reply. They looked at each other, deeply troubled. He said, 'You look tired. Shall I make tea?'

Later, while she dozed on the settee, he made a few notes. He judged that Police Sergeant Fletcher would report that Captain Drummond had received a visit from a suspicious character this evening. It was important that he should also report this. His superiors were aware that he was in touch with this group; but it was as well to record his own version of this incident.

8

September–November 1942

The fortunes of the Allies seemed at their lowest ebb. Day by day, the Germans were moving towards Stalingrad. From the desert the news of fighting was conflicting, rumour abounded: at one time, it was said that Rommel had reached the outskirts of Alexandria. It actually passed through Alice's mind that the Allies might be defeated, that the war could conceivably be lost. The weakness was only momentary – the testing of a nerve. But until now she had been unaware of the existence of this particular nerve. The doubt clouded a whole day.

She was too happy, however, to be troubled for long. Love coloured everything in rose and gold, abetted by the Egyptian sun. Added to love was Adventure: now, evacuated from Alexandria, she was sleeping under canvas not far from Suez. It was excruciatingly uncomfortable and the desert wind which whips up in the autumn made matters worse. But Alice accepted these minor hardships readily. She was emerging as one of the tougher of her group, able to cope with discomforts which drove other people to distraction.

'I believe you actually enjoy this!' Madeleine accused her. 'It must be that dreadful hair-shirt upbringing.'

Alice laughed. 'I don't think my headmistress thought she was preparing me for this!'

She was aware, even at her happiest, of her incapacity to come to terms with the reality of war, of the dubiousness of her determination to abstract from it personal satisfaction. But there was nothing she could do about it – plagued by flies, unable to sleep on the straw palliasse, enveloped in sand, she was persistently happy.

Irene wrote that she had seen a film about the defence of Stalingrad. Alice, looking out of the window of the Nissen hut where she worked, eyes red-rimmed from the stinging sand, tried to imagine that grim, snowbound struggle. 'Suppose it was Lewes, or Falmouth . . .' Whenever she thought of the snow and cold and hardship, of the distant booming of guns, she remembered Gordon with his arm around her waist as they strolled along the Corniche. She could only hope that somewhere in Stalingrad there was, in spite of the desperate nature of the struggle, some dark-eyed Natasha as happy as herself.

Irene's letter, she noted, lacked the usual sparkle. The references to Angus were muted. Oh poor, poor Irene! Alice's own experience of love was so great a contrast, all sunlight and warmth. Gordon's letters were increasingly tender and full of concern for her welfare. He confessed to feelings he had never been able to reveal when they were together. She recalled their first encounter. She had been with Gwenda and two other very attractive girls; Gwenda already knew Gordon slightly and Alice had assumed he had come to take her out. But after chatting to them all for a few minutes, he had asked Alice . . . She could not now recall the pretext on which he had borne her away. The memorable – the unbelievable – thing was that he had singled her out. Afterwards, in spite of his reserve, there had been times when she had seen her own happiness reflected in his eyes. She had never imagined such power to be within her compass. He spoke in his letters of a time when they would always be together. 'But you must be patient, my darling. I promise you that we shall be together; only we must not snatch at happiness. Promise me that you will be patient?' She supposed he did not approve of hasty wartime marriages; and, warm in the glow of his love, she assured him that she was content to wait.

She had reason to be grateful to him. He had eased her passage into the adult world; he had made the rough places smooth. She believed his love had transformed her, and so it had. She was very popular now.

'All the men like you, Alice,' Madeleine told her. 'You are so jolly.'

Alice was not best pleased by this. 'Jolly' in her understanding, related to people over forty, of proportions not less generous than those of Margaret Rutherford. In future, she must tone down her exuberance. She did not want Gordon to find her 'jolly' on her return to Alexandria.

They were never short of male company and spent much of their off-duty time swimming at the French Club near Suez. Alice was a good swimmer. These hours of swimming, and lying on the sand, gave her a hedonistic pleasure she had seldom experienced – she, for whom pleasure had tended to be something which had to be inspected and accounted for.

'You're much nicer than I used to think,' Gwenda said, wriggling her toes in the sand.

'How did you used to think of me?'

'Oh, a bit better than other people. Not that you seemed to be trying to impress – just that you actually *were* better.'

Their male escorts were still thrashing about in the water, and the two girls lay quietly. Alice was pleased to know that she now met with Gwenda's approval. The acceptance of one's fellow Wrens was important. It seemed appropriate that it should be Gwenda, herself one of the most acceptable by virtue of her prowess with men and her conviviality with women, who should bestow honour on Alice.

'However do you handle Arnold?' Alice asked, feeling homage was due from her. 'He is so sexy he always seems quite beside himself with it.'

Gwenda looked towards the water, where Arnold was displaying his manliness for her benefit. 'He is going tomorrow.'

'You'll miss him.'

'I rather think something might be starting with that curly-haired Frenchman – the very dark one. A touch of the tar-brush there, would you say?'

Alice was surprised. Gwenda was noted for lack of selectivity in her relationships – Madeleine had once referred to her as 'the last Wren in Alex to go out with a matelot'. But a touch of the tar brush?

'You prefer Arnold?' she asked cautiously.

'While he's around. One at a time is my only principle. I have to be true to someone – even if only for a little while. And thanks to all this toing and froing in the desert, it *is* only a little while.'

'Don't you ever think you'll fall?'

'Now, Alice, don't start being superior. I, too, have had my moments.'

Alice watched the water lapping gently at her feet, wondering whether to go in again. 'You wouldn't marry a half-caste?'

'I don't see why not. What's wrong with it, Alice? Your chap did.'

'My chap?'

'Gordon. Didn't you know? I thought everyone knew.'

Later, she said to Jeannie and Madeleine, 'I don't know what made me come out with it. Except that I had been quiet about it for so long. And when she sounded priggish, I suddenly felt it just wasn't worth the effort of keeping it from her any longer.'

When she saw how badly Alice was taking it, she said, 'She shouldn't have poached.'

'Alice didn't think she was poaching, Gwenda,' Jeannie said. 'She wasn't out here when you had your thing with Gordon.'

'Well, she knows about him now. She shouldn't take up with a fellow if she can't accept him the way he is. *I* wasn't bothered about his marriage.'

'That is the difference between you that made Gordon choose Alice,' Madeleine said sweetly. 'He is the kind of man who can only love a woman who doesn't approve of the way he behaves. You ought to know that. It's been going on for centuries.'

'Fuck that kind of man!'

'Oh, such language I never did expect to hear from the lips of a woman.'

'You weren't brought up in the Bristol docks.'

'I offer up thanks for that every day.'

Alice wrote to Gordon, 'I have heard a rumour which has upset me, so you must forgive me, dearest, for being doubting. . . .' She crossed the words out. There was too much of her hurt feelings there; she must seem to shrug it off. 'It is scarcely worth repeating, but as it *has* been said. . . .' She crossed these words out, too. It was totally insincere to say that it was 'scarcely worth repeating', when she was thinking of nothing else day and night.

As she struggled over the letter, so she came to accept Gwenda's story. It was not the way Gwenda had spoken, nor the manner in which some of the others had reacted, that convinced her: it was that the knowledge slid too easily into her own mind. The reasons for his reserve which she had recited to herself – that he did not wish theirs to seem like just another wartime romance, that something had hurt him badly in the past, making him unduly cautious – were spurious. She had always known that Gordon was not free.

Love was pain as well as joy; how could she ever have imagined it possible to cross this threshold without pain? This, she told herself, was the reality of loving. She must be proud of the pain. For a few hours she felt quite exalted.

It was particularly hurtful that Gordon should have discussed his affairs so freely with Gwenda. Could she be lying? When tackled, Gwenda readily admitted that she had found out about Gordon's marriage from a fellow officer. He had told her that Gordon had got a girl in Mauritius into trouble; and, being Gordon, had married her when no one, least of all the girl or her family, expected it of him. Alice could believe this. It had probably done the girl no good, but Gordon would have been untrue to himself had he behaved dishonourably. She began to hope.

Such an unsuitable attachment could not last, surely? He had felt that, in all honour, he could make promises for the future to Alice.

So, if she was wise, they could still be happy together. Yet something *had* changed; and the change was not in Gordon, but in her. He had not been able to tell her. She would have liked to think that he was prevented from fear of losing her; or because he was concerned for her. He had wanted to sort out a few things before he felt free to commit himself entirely to her. But she could not acquit him of pride. That inner pride which had made him so complex, so worthwhile because it gave him added depth, was now the rock on which she stumbled. Was he more proud than loving?

At last, she wrote briefly to him, 'My dearest, I have been told about your marriage. It must have given you a lot of pain. I long for us to be together again so that we can talk about this. Your loving, Alice.' It was in his hands now. She waited to hear from him. If he loved her, he would waste no time in replying. He would know how wounded she must be and he would not let a moment pass before he attempted to console her. She felt sorry for the agony she was causing him, but excited by the prospect that all the barriers between them would come down.

Days passed and turned into weeks.

'Alice, you must get out,' Madeleine said. 'You are quite gaunt. It does not become you. Neither does all this silent suffering.'

'I shall hear from him soon.'

'He's a sod. Why not accept it?'

Alice shook her head. The conditions in which she had grown up were for her the natural condition of life. Subsequently, she might learn that this was a fallacy and her intellect would accept it; but in her inner heart she would still regard it as the reality. Just as she regarded the one photograph which flattered her view of herself as being really 'like' and all others as yet another proof that she did not photograph well, so Alice persisted in thinking of life as a period of sunlit calm occasionally disturbed by freak storms. She was waiting for this storm to die down. Then she would hear from Gordon, who had in the meantime been making strenuous efforts to sort out his life (Mauritius being some distance away, notwithstanding).

Finally, a package came from Alexandria. It was a large package and when she opened it, she saw that it contained her letters to Gordon, two of them unopened. She sat staring at them for a long time before she picked up the letter which accompanied them. It was from a fellow officer in the intelligence section. He wrote to tell her that Gordon had been killed several weeks ago. A shell had fallen on a restaurant where he was eating. Gordon had been badly wounded, but in spite of that he had insisted on helping to pull other people from the wreckage. On the way to hospital, he had had a haemor-rhage and had died of loss of blood.

It seemed to Alice that the door to life had been shut in her face. Overwhelmed by this great negative, she could not talk about her feelings. She would have liked to lie on her palliasse day in, day out; but the Royal Navy would have none of this. Activity was thrust upon her. It was now late autumn. Rommel had been held at El Alamein and it was considered safe for the Wrens to return to Alexandria. Within a week of learning of Gordon's death, Alice was back at the convent.

The fortunes of the Allies were on the mend. The good news had not travelled to Northern Siam. Matters of less moment were of conse-quence here.

Ben said to Tandy, 'You do that again and I'll kill you.'

They were standing in the cookhouse, watched by Tandy's mates, who were unlikely to come to his rescue if violence was attempted, but who would make sure that their own interests were not put at stake.

Ben had come back late from emergency duty to find that no food had been saved for him. He knew that there had been an egg allocation. Eggs provided the best nourishment and were seldom available. He felt that Tandy had eaten a day of his life.

Tandy said, 'Careful now. You'll do yourself a mischief getting worked up over things can't be undone. This place would be just the same when I was gone. All you'd have done was to give yourself a lot of nasty thoughts.'

'I've plenty of nasty thoughts as it is, a few more wouldn't worry me.'

'Murder would worry you, boyo.'

'No more than killing that snake we ate last night.'

'Would you eat me, then? Now that is one thing I might not be able to bring myself to. I've thought of it, but I can't be sure of myself. I don't believe I've the taste for human flesh.' He was disappointed in himself, and, from his point of view, with reason. Gomer Tandy was now a small, sharp, rat-faced man. He had grown in self-knowledge daily, sharpening his wits and putting them to use for his own salvation. The small rodent was what he had whittled himself down to; and in doing so he had revealed the born scavenger within.

His wits having nothing else to occupy them now that night was coming on, he set about defending himself. 'I have to give a lot of thought to what I do. You could say, I work very hard at it.'

'Yes, you certainly could say that.'

'What about our officers, then? All *they* have to do is hold their plate out! I tell you, boyo, you see life in the cookhouse. You make all that fuss about one egg – where do you think all the others go?'

'And you just stand by and watch, I suppose?'

'Oh, I take my pickings. And why not?'

'If I saw them having so much more than us, I'd take it up with the CO.' Ben was only half-inclined to believe Tandy.

'And much good that would do you! The MO carries on about it, and they don't take any notice of him. Look at it from their point of view. They *need* more food than us. They've got all that brainwork to do, haven't they? Organizing work parties, making sure the men fall in and get off pronto; it must be very exhausting. And then, while you're all out hacking down the jungle, they've got their speeches to prepare – those rousing talks about keeping up morale and the importance of clean living to a healthy body. I tell you, boyo, all this brainwork taxes a man.'

'They're not all bastards. At the camp across the river, they say the officers go out on work parties with the men.'

'You try selling that to our lot.'

'How about my selling it to you?'

Tandy made no reply to this. He was dedicated to survival. All his intelligence was bent to this one end, which he pursued with the single-mindedness of a man possessed by a great enterprise. Indeed, Tandy would have said that living was *the* great enterprise. He bartered, fawned when it suited his purpose, always got more than his share, feigned sickness, and stole. He was adept at avoiding emergency duties, such as clearing away a fallen tree or moving boulders. He had ingratiated himself with the men in the cookhouse and seldom went out on working parties; and had never been known to do a latrine duty. Most men accepted their work conditions as a matter of chance, of being in the wrong place at the right time. Not so Tandy.

It was the stealing which gave Ben pause for thought. His mother had been ambitious for him; but she would never have stolen for him. Even the will to success must be subordinated to 'Thou shalt not steal'. It was a matter not only of moral precept, but of self-respect: whatever else might be said of one, it must be known that one paid one's way. Ben was having to rethink some of his ideas about survival. 'If I could only survive by stealing, which, in these circumstances, might well mean at the cost of another man's life – what then?' He had not come up with the answer to that yet.

'I hope you rot in hell,' he told Tandy. But there was little venom in the observation. Tandy's resilience and energy were astonishing. It was not possible to dismiss him with contempt; his industry was too formidable.

The two men walked through the camp together. An emergency operation was being performed in the open, by the light of a bonfire and a hurricane lamp. The patient was stretched out on a roughly constructed bamboo table. Three doctors were there and several Japanese guards were watching avidly.

'Dave Pearson is having his leg amputated,' Tandy said. 'The MO borrowed our meat saw. Sterilized it, of course.'

'I hope you sterilize it when you get it back.'

'It's no laughing matter, a saw. At the camp down the river they say the Japs lay about with them whenever they get angry. Decapitation is one of the punishments.'

Ben made no reply. Tandy exaggerated, but he, too, had heard these stories and believed them. Here, the usual punishments were beating, sometimes with barbed wire, or being made to stand in the sun holding a rock above one's head. Violence was a part of their lives. Yet, even here, they had a little precious time in the evening at their own disposal. Discussion groups had been started, many of a light-hearted nature. A few men preferred to be serious, however, and they passed a group debating the interpretation of the parable of the Good Samaritan.

'Yours would be an interesting contribution!' Ben said to Tandy.

'I might have a few thoughts to offer, at that.' Tandy strolled across to the group.

Ben went on to his tent, which provided cover for twenty men sleeping on bamboo beds. Here he found Geoffrey, who had returned from the hospital after a bout of dysentery. At first, Geoffrey had suspected that he had cholera, and this had frightened him. The hospital consisted of a few huts in which the sick lay on bamboo slats, many receiving no treatment because, apart from quinine, there was little medicine available. There were few to care for them and in their weakness they frequently fouled themselves. Ben had visited Geoffrey whenever it was possible and had helped to keep him clean. But he had not gone out of his way to reassure him about cholera. A fright would do Geoffrey no harm, in Ben's opinion. In contrast to Tandy, Geoffrey showed a quirky indifference to his own – and others' – welfare. It seemed it was not in his nature to take precautions. He was more likely than most to fail to dip eating utensils in boiling water before using them; and Ben had had occasion more than once to snatch meat from him on which a fly had settled. To the angry question, 'Do you want to get cholera?' Geoffrey would shrug, 'I forget.'

The longer Ben knew Geoffrey, the more he realized how infinitely variable a man is. Geoffrey had revealed an unexpected gift as a mime. The Phantom Dog, with whom the prisoners enjoyed mystifying the Japanese, was a game which Geoffrey played with a difference. He insisted on being the dog. Although this destroyed the illusion in so far as the Japanese were concerned (they simply thought him mad), the men forgave him because his performance was so convincing that it was possible to guess the breed of the animal, whether dancing greyhound, lugubrious bloodhound, or brisk terrier. Yet, although he seemed able to keep his spirits up as well as anyone, he had odd lapses when he failed to concentrate on the business of staying alive. Ben, who had respected his steadiness and sobriety, loved the man for his maddening inconsistency.

Geoffrey showed Ben the drawings he had done when he began to recover in the hospital. Most were in his usual style: the sick, lying on their bamboo beds, while two men tried to support one another on their way to the latrine – at least, that was what Ben supposed them to be doing, since there was little else that would rouse them to such effort. There were two drawings which were unlike anything Geoffrey had hitherto done. One was of a tree framed in the door of the hut. It was bare, now that winter was come, and the tracery of branches was fine and intricate as hieroglyphics in an unknown language. In the other drawing, the perspective had changed. The hut was a minute cube, a peripheral area of darkness, beyond which the tree and the mountains were held in the great curve of the sky. Ben thought the effect was of an enormous eye.

'How am I supposed to find a caption for that?' He flung the drawing down. 'They've amputated Dave Pearson's leg. You haven't got a drawing of an operation.'

'I haven't watched an operation.'

'But *I* have!' Ben was shaking with fury because his own experiences were not being recorded. Rage flared easily in these conditions.

The next day, great good fortune befell Ben and Geoffrey. They were detailed off to guard a truck which had broken down in the hills some five miles from their camp. They were to remain with the truck until such time as the Japanese had made arrangements for its removal. Geoffrey was by no means fully recovered – the Japs did not allow men to stay sick for long. This special duty was a godsend for him.

They set off in high spirits: stripped of clothing, save for a piece of cloth which covered the genitals, their jerky movements gave them the appearance of marionettes carved in bone. Ben wore a rattan coolie hat. Geoffrey, who never seemed able to prolong the life of his possessions, had lost his own hat but had been fortunate in inheriting an Australian felt hat. Beneath its shade, Geoffrey's eyes were sunken and his skin fell in withered, papery folds.

The rainy season had ended, but the tracks through the jungle were still a morass of glutinous mud which concealed the vicious bamboo spikes. Ben, whose feet were already lacerated, sometimes stumbled and cried out in pain. In a small clearing they came upon a group of Thais sitting around their bullock carts. Geoffrey wanted to communicate with them because he was always trying to find materials with which to do his drawings, and hoped they might have a dye which he could use. 'After all,' he said to Ben, 'they paint their own bodies.' But in spite of Geoffrey's miming, which was entrancing, they only succeeded in alarming the Thais, who thought they were after food.

When they reached the truck, two Japanese guards were there. They had got a fire going of logs and bamboo sticks. 'No let out!' they said as they prepared to depart. 'Many tiger.' But they left no matches to rekindle the fire if necessary. As soon as they had stumped off down the track, Ben went over the truck thoroughly to see whether there was anything worth purloining. There was nothing. The truck was weighed down with heavy equipment, and had developed a mechanical fault which it would take more than muscle power to correct. 'With any luck, we've got a couple of days' rest cure before they come back with engineers who can do anything about this!'

They set about preparing their evening meal, which consisted of a tiny piece of dried meat and the inevitable rice. They fetched water from the stream which ran some way below the track and boiled it thoroughly before cooking the rice and meat in it. Both ate sparingly, thinking of the morrow.

They sat cross-legged, looking down at the swift-flowing stream, so crystal clear that Geoffrey said he was tempted to run down and drink its waters. Ben told him not to be a fool. Nevertheless, the stream was good to look upon. The thought of several days with no one to shout at them or to belabour them was pleasant. They relaxed warily, anxious to get as much as possible out of every moment.

Geoffrey threw a stone into the stream. The water rippled, just as the Welsh Border streams of his childhood had rippled. 'A snare and a delusion,' he said sadly. 'I would give anything for a drink of pure mountain water.'

Ben looked at the jungle with its teeming life of plants and creatures. A vivid crimson flower was thrusting through the bamboo bush; and nearer, a snake, brilliant green mottled with red, slid from the base of a tree stump and disappeared in leaf mould. The monkeys set up a clamour in the swaying branches. There was something destructive in the very livingness of the jungle; and the constant smell of rotting vegetation made it seem impregnated with death.

That night they talked by the light of the fire, on which they had heaped more bamboo sticks. 'I've only met one fellow who said he saw a tiger,' Geoffrey said. 'And I'm not sure I believed him.' The night was velvet, pricked with stars. Geoffrey told Ben about the Border country. 'We'll do a walk along Offa's Dyke when we get out of here. We'll start at Prestatyn and do the whole length of it.' He described the country through which they would pass so vividly that Ben could imagine himself lost on Denbigh Moor, wet and cold in the Black Mountains, but rewarded by his first glimpse of the Wye winding through wooded hills.

'It's lush, the Wye valley,' Geoffrey sighed. He began to talk about women, which was unusual, as the sensual images which tended to come most readily to prisoners' minds were connected with food. He was engaged to a girl named Jean. Although he spoke warmly of her, it seemed that his capacity for fidelity was limited. As in the matter of hygiene, he lacked discipline; the stolen waters beckoned and Geoffrey yearned for their refreshment.

Ben, looking up at the spangled sky, saw the form of Daphne, glowing with a soft inner light. A strange place, this, in which to celebrate the beauty of the human form! And yet, was it so inappropriate, here, where he had seen the body's endurance tested as never before? He remembered that moment in Daphne's bedroom as clearly as if it was the Ben of now who had felt so humble, so overawed. She had said to him when they parted, 'You helped me.' Now it seemed that it was he who had received something of which she was unaware, in which she was, in a sense, a random participant. In that moment of incandescent loveliness Daphne's form had been the instrument through which the gift was passed to him. The gift of what he hardly knew. He looked at Geoffrey sitting beside him, ulcerated legs folded about his hollow belly. The sense of awe was not diminished. For a few brief moments, sitting here very nearly at peace, Ben was grateful.

Geoffrey said, 'It's cooler already. Maybe we'll be out of here before the next rainy season. I heard a rumour the Japs were going to move us south.'

Judith wrote to Alice telling her that she had heard that Ben was a prisoner of the Japanese. She gave an address. 'We must all write to him and hope that at least some of our letters will get through.'

Alice read the letter when she came off-duty, sitting on her bunk in the dormitory. She read it through several times without taking in its contents.

'Alice!' The Wren quarters assistant stood at the top of the stairs and called. When Alice did not reply she stamped angrily along the landing, thus breaking two hallowed rules in as many seconds – no raised voices, no heavy footsteps. She stood in the doorway, sweat streaming from her bright pink brow.

'You might answer when I call.' She was breathless with heat and annoyance.

'I'm sorry.' Alice lifted her head and contrived to look both contrite and attentive.

'There's an Army officer downstairs asking for you. I couldn't get my tongue round his name.' She turned and went back along the corridor, soft-footed, muttering under her breath that this sodding place would be the death of her.

Alice, who had spent some time wondering if the room would somersault were she to put weight on her feet and stand up, now performed this feat without ill-effect, other than the gentle swimming of her head which went on all the time. Guy! It must be Guy: Immingham was indeed not a name to trip lightly off the tongue.

She put her mother's letter to one side and crossed to the mirror. She raked a comb through her dank hair and hastily coiled it into a knot at the nape of her neck. The result was to make her look like a Brontë heroine who has lost herself on a bleak upland and emerged in the wrong century. But, Alice thought, as she tried to make the best of herself so that Guy would not be shocked, at least I know I have a bone structure now! When she had finished her brief toilet, dabbing her face with cologne, she stood for a moment breathing deeply. Tears came only too readily of late, and the thought of seeing Guy threatened a deluge if she was not in firm control of herself.

She went down the stairs, holding tight to the banister rail. Her heart thumped so strenuously it seemed she must burst apart. The quarters assistant had asked him to wait in the little sitting-room which the nuns had kindly set aside for the Wrens. As Alice went into the room, tears were already dimming her vision. She could see well enough, however, to realize that the man standing with his back to her at the window was not Guy. She halted, desolate. Then he turned and held his arms wide with the most unmilitary theatricality.

The quarters assistant, who had been watching from her desk, was surprised to see what she took to be a passionate embrace. 'All that refusing to go out with anyone because she couldn't trust men any more!' she said dourly to the quarters PO. 'She was just waiting for something exciting to come along.'

The something-exciting held Alice back from him and studied her with interest. 'You are very thin, Alice. Is it the heat? I think I liked you better plump. And you've grown your hair again.'

'Oh, Jacov!' The tears came. He accepted them without embarrassment, apparently seeing them as a fitting tribute to his arrival.

'How long have you been in the Army?' she asked when she was calmer. 'Since we're being honest, I liked *you* better out of uniform.'

'The uniform is a disguise. I am engaged on work of national importance.' He put a finger to his lips and whispered, 'I am here with a company that is entertaining the troops. Guess what we are doing.'

'*Hamlet.*'

'Don't be so gloomy, Alice. *The Barretts of Wimpole Street.* Now, don't you think that is splendidly inappropriate? But they all enjoy it; and they hiss Papa Barrett as if he was the villain in *Maria Martin*! Especially the sailors. Sailors are very emotional men. I remember that once in Portsmouth they stormed the platform to prevent Othello from killing Desdemona.'

'Are you Browning?'

'Of course! Who else? No, no, I am the organizer on behalf of HM Forces.' He ran a finger along Alice's cheekbone. 'We shall have to do something about you. Shall I make you drink porter?'

'You could take me out and make me eat.'

'This was my whole purpose in coming to Egypt.'

When she had changed into the most becoming frock she had, he looked at her approvingly. 'That is better. Now, we will eat, and you can tell me all about your exiciting life here which has made you so thin.' He took her arm and linked it through his own. As they passed the quarters assistant, she leant forward and said, 'I am so sorry, I didn't get your name.'

'Jacov Alexei Anton Vaseyelin.'

As they left the convent they could hear her muttering, 'I still didn't get it.'

Although Jacov had only recently arrived, he already seemed to belong in Egypt more than Alice. He might, with his dark, curly hair and bright eyes, have passed for an Egyptian, save that the skin, which had seemed dark in England, here was too pale and fine. He was thin as wire still, in spite of a manner increasingly suggestive of opulence. He took Alice to Pastroudi's, assuming she would never have been there before. He had a long discussion with the waiter, although his requirements would not seem to have presented any problem to the kitchen. Alice, uninterested in food, looked about the crowded restaurant, and saw several people whom she knew, including Madeleine, who was at a table with three naval officers.

When the waiter departed, Jacov produced cigarettes for Alice, who did not smoke, and lit a cigar for himself. She was not sure whether this behaviour was now normal to him, or whether he was hoping to impress her. He said, 'Tell me about him. He was married, of course.'

Alice stared at him. While she was formulating a reply which would shame him out of this mood of cheerful insensitivity, he went on, 'It happens all the time. And to men, too, let me tell you.' It was obvious he had every intention of telling her; he rattled on without drawing breath. 'I had a passionate affair with Greta Coburn – you know her, of course?'

'I have never heard of her,' Alice said coldly.

'She was in *Diamonds Became Her* – and a host of other whimsical light comedies. You would certainly know her – she advertises a hair shampoo. I produced her in *Regimental Duties*. She was very demanding. Every interval she needed reassuring – in a certain way, you understand – that she was good. I can talk to you like this now, can't I, Alice? And then one day, the dressing room door is flung open and there is this major. A dreadful fellow with butter-coloured hair and a face like an overripe plum. He was supposed to be the last man out of Crete; but, in fact, I have since heard on good authority that he was the first man out of Tobruk! The scene he made! If it had been a play no one would have accepted such a performance from a betrayed husband. And I didn't even know she was married! They had to call the police or she would have missed her entrance in the second act.'

'Did he knock your teeth in?'

He stabbed his cigar in her direction. 'Ah, there's still some spirit there, then?'

A waiter arrived with champagne, followed by another waiter with lobster in a rich cream sauce.

Alice said huffily, 'I'm afraid I can't compete with your performance.'

'It was just a curtain raiser.' He waved a hand above the lobster. 'Now we have come to the important matters.'

The champagne disposed Alice to lenience. She began to speak haltingly about Gordon. But soon the sad truth was borne in upon her that no one understands anyone else. If she had asked for one person to come here to comfort her, it might well have been Jacov that she chose. Dear, lovable, gentle Jacov! And it was only too apparent that he did not understand the first thing about her feelings for Gordon.

'You are making his motives too complicated, Alice,' he was saying, as if addressing an incompetent actress at rehearsal.

'He was a very complicated person.'

'He had got himself into a complicated situation, that doesn't make *him* complicated. It sounds to me as if things just moved too fast for him.'

'In what way – too fast?'

'He meets you, likes you, gets to know you. And before he knows where he is, he has let things go on too long without telling you. When it begins to matter, it is already too late. What you might have accepted had he told you at once, had become a deceit. To deceive Alice Fairley!' He clicked his tongue. 'He didn't know how to set about it; so he kept putting it off.'

'I don't think Gordon was like that.' She preferred to think of him racked with agony, rather than merely procrastinating. 'It's so final.' Her lips trembled. 'I shall never know if he loved me or not.'

'Perhaps he didn't know either? If he was still alive, you would accept that. Why must it be all or nothing?'

'Because I can never ask him now.' She was over twenty and no man had yet loved her. The hopelessness of her situation welled up in her eyes.

'But *asking* doesn't solve anything, Alice! He would have made some sort of reply – yes or no or maybe – and you wouldn't have been any wiser than you are now.'

She sipped more champagne and essayed an unsteady gaiety. 'You're not being very kind about my broken heart.'

He reached across the table and patted her cheek. 'Hearts don't break so easily, Alice. You know what is wrong with you? You never had the chance to tell him how mad you are with him. Now he's dead, you have to pull a long face and keep saying respectful things about him.'

It was on the tip of her tongue to ask him if he had ever lost anyone, but she remembered just in time that he had lost everyone – more or less. She looked at his dark, monkey face, and saw the bright eyes fixed on her as though he could read her thoughts. He said, 'I am not married. So I am perfectly free to do anything you like when we leave here.'

'I'd like to go for a walk.'

'Oh, well . . .'

They walked in the Nouhza Gardens. Either the champagne or the lobster had made Alice feel rather ill. She held tightly to Jacov's arm, trying to fight down bouts of sickness and despair. She said, 'Things will get better. All men aren't like that, are they? It will be better next time.'

'What makes you believe that?'

'I hope.'

'Why, if it only leads to disappointment?'

A groundswell rolled her stomach about uneasily. 'One *must* hope, Jacov.'

'For what?'

She said faintly, 'There must always be *something* to hope for.'

'Oh, Alice!' He gave a little laugh, as though she were an inept pupil in the game of life.

Yet he was very good company. During the next week she saw him several times, and gradually he restored both her spirits and her digestion. His was the gaiety of one who, hoping for nothing, is released from the need to be serious. Hers was the gaiety of spirit of one who, in spite of everything, will always hope. If they were to meet, each setting out from their position, surely they would effect reconciliation leading to a consummation on the far side of hope? Alice wondered if it would be too big a task to hope that she might redeem Jacov. By which she meant making him more like herself.

There was no doubting that he was genuinely fond of her. As they walked in the Nouhza Gardens – she avoided the Corniche because it reminded her of Gordon – he told her about his life in the theatre. It seemed important to him that she should know how successful he was, and he let drop several well-known names. In spite of his boasting, he was never dull, being quite a raconteur. In some ways, he was like a boy coming home to talk to his family, showing off his cleverness and independence, yet still very much in need of their unchanging presence. The members of the Fairley family were, perhaps, the only unchanging presence Jacov had known. Alice felt alternately naive and motherly with him.

149

In the Nouhza Gardens they sat under a tree, talking about Louise and Irene.

'Do you think she will marry Angus?' Alice asked. She hoped so much that Irene would be happy. Yet there was no doubting the relief she experienced when he replied, 'I don't think Angus will ever marry.'

'And Daphne?' she asked, feeling more relaxed now that she was assured of a comrade in misfortune. 'I seem to have lost touch with Daphne.'

'I haven't seen her recently either. Angus says she is not living at home any more.'

'I'm glad of that. Her father was . . .' She stopped, surprised at having come so incautiously to a subject she never mentioned now.

Jacov said, 'Yes?' He prompted because he was curious about other people's fathers. Had Alice referred to Daphne's mother, and then stopped, the conversation might never have taken place.

He was not the only one to give Alice his attention. A ring of urchins was studying them from a distance, giggling and making salacious comments. Automatically, Alice pulled her skirt down over her knees. Other of her escorts would have driven the children away – never an effective gesture, they always came back. Jacov prompted again, 'What about Commander Drummond?'

'There was a woman who came to our chapel. Her name was Dolly Bligh. Her husband interfered with the children and they took the children away from her. They lived in one room – all of them. I thought it only happened because of that – I mean, to people who lived in those conditions.'

Whenever she had tried to speak of this, she had started with Dolly Bligh. She remembered, in particular, that she had tried to tell Ben, and then Louise. In both cases, she had got no further than Dolly Bligh. But perhaps this time she had been more explicit, for Jacov was looking at her speculatively; and he did not interrupt to comment on the sad case of Dolly Bligh.

'Then, when I was at Crusaders, I heard a girl talking about the Drummonds. This girl's aunt had worked at the Drummond house, and she said she had had to leave because she didn't like the atmosphere there – she said he paid too much attention to his elder daughter.'

Jacov said, 'You mean incest?'

'No, no!' she protested, unprepared to apply such a word to a friend. 'But later on, Daphne said something about his twisting her arm . . . and I knew inside me that there was something else . . . I don't mean that anything actually happened . . .'

'They just played games?'

She looked down at the grass. How strange that this should have come out, here, under the Egyptian sun. She thought, shocked more by herself now than the Drummonds, that she would have preferred to have left it at incest. Playing games seemed much nastier.

'*You're* not shocked,' she accused Jacov, but smiling, because she wasn't feeling as bad as she had expected.

He thought it more unnatural that a father should take no interest in his wife and children, and infinitely more cruel. As for incest . . . 'I suppose it may be bad for our advanced society to adopt the practices of antiquity.'

'You're laughing at me!'

'Nothing shocks me, Alice.' He studied her face. 'And *that* doesn't shock you?'

She shook her head, uncomprehending.

'You don't know, do you, what that means – being unshockable? If the nerves of our body fail to register shock, our whole system is at risk. If there should ever be an entire race of unshockable people, the world would come to an end.'

'You never take anything seriously, Jacov.'

'That, too.'

She shifted so that she was sitting sideways, her skirt primly covering legs and ankles. Suddenly, she remembered a dream of long ago. A boy and a girl, sitting on the grass, making a garland of flowers: an idyllic picture, yet in the dream, there had been a sense of something dreadful awaiting these two beyond their formal border of flowers. She put her hand in his and they sat quietly for a few minutes, each with their own thoughts.

Jacov's company was performing in Cairo the following week. He asked Alice to join him there for a few days. She did not think she could get leave, but it was granted. Her ill-health had been noted; there had been talk of sending her back to England if she did not recover.

She had spent a few hours in Cairo during the Flap. Now she looked forward to a longer stay and was not disappointed.

Cairo seemed much more lively than Alexandria. It had not been bombed, although the front line at Alamein was less than a hundred miles away. The street lights, painted blue, shone all night giving the city an eerie gaiety. It was also much hotter than Alexandria, where there was always a sea breeze. Already tired from the journey in a crowded, stinking railway carriage, Alice had a headache, which never seemed to clear while she was in Cairo. Nevertheless, she set about making the most of her time there. She was sufficient of the seasoned traveller by now to consider headaches and stomach disorders a part of being abroad, along with sand and flies and palm trees.

She stayed at the YWCA. In the morning, she woke to cries from the minarets as the muezzins called the people to prayer. She dressed, breakfasted on figs, and then took a tram to the centre of the town. She was to meet Jacov later. There was a rehearsal this morning; one of the minor parts had had to be recast owing to the illness of the player concerned.

As she walked through the main streets, crowded with service people of all nationalities, she wished that Ben was with her. He would revel in this dusty, clamorous city with its wealth of medieval buildings! Nothing would escape him: mosques, tombs, caravanserais, stone fortifications would all be examined as well as the more famous monuments. He would drag her down side-streets, loiter in the bazaars, when all she wanted was coffee. By the end of the first morning, she would be tired out and exasperated with him beyond bearing! It was so real to her that she laughed aloud. No such energy could be expected of Jacov. She hoped, however, that she could persuade him to take her to the Pyramids.

This proved impracticable. His contribution to seeing the sights of Cairo was to take her to Groppi's. The needs of the touring company precluded his being away long enough to leave the city.

'If we went it would have to be in the afternoon. The heat is terrible then. You would find it quite unbearable after Alexandria.' He ignored the fact that she had spent some time in the desert. 'And there is always a haze. You need to see them at sunset.'

'But there may not be another time.'

'Alice, *you* are the hopeful one. Look to the future. Here we are! You will enjoy this much more than the Pyramids.'

'Have *you* been?'

'Everyone insisted on going as soon as we arrived. It nearly killed us. Elizabeth Barrett nodded off on her couch during the evening performance.'

Alice noted selfishness in him, which was a surprise as he had always seemed so ready to please others. The dedication with which he made his selection of pastries was also a revelation. Perhaps the lobster and champagne had not been a treat especially for her benefit? She wondered, as he consumed an excessively sticky confection, what was his taste in women. He had confided a lot to her about his theatrical ventures, but had made only a few references to love affairs. He knows more about me than I know of him, she thought. She was persuaded to have another pastry. Her headache was worse when they eventually left.

It persisted throughout the performance of *The Barretts of Wimpole Street*. Nevertheless, the excitement of being in a theatre again, and of knowing the producer, quite outweighed this.

They were to go to a party at the flat of a diplomat who was friendly with one of the members of the cast. Alice was shy at the thought of meeting theatrical people, but she need not have worried. She had the qualities they cherished, enthusiasm and a desire to please.

'It seems rather an odd choice, don't you think?' Browning asked. His tone was tentative; his brown, doleful eyes waited for reassurance. In case it should not be forthcoming, he laughed wearily, 'Goodness knows what they made of it.'

'They *loved* it. It's so romantic.'

The audience had consisted mainly of sailors. 'I suppose almost anything is welcome after so much time at sea,' he pouted. 'They would probably have been moved by *Jack and the Beanstalk*.'

'Not at all.' Alice undertook to defend the emotional integrity of the Navy. 'I remember seeing the film of *New Moon* with Jeannette McDonald and Nelson Eddy. They thought the love scenes in that were hilarious. Then there is that song which goes

"Give me ten stalwart men
    Who are steady and strong
    Who will fight for the right
    To be free . . ."

When all the men began to line up behind Nelson Eddy, one of the matelots shouted, "Liberty men, fall in!" It was uproar after that.'

'I see. "Liberty men, fall in!" Yes, very amusing. At least no one shouted at us.'

'And it *is* romantic. In real life, I mean. The way they fell in love, and those wonderful letters, and the elopement. They went through with it; they didn't hold back, or cheat . . .' Tears filled her eyes.

Browning, accepting her emotion as a tribute to his performance, said, 'Much better than Nelson Eddy, eh!' He put his arms around her and called to Jacov, 'Alice thinks I am better than Nelson Eddy.'

The diplomat said ambiguously, 'No comparison, my dear fellow.'

They all loved one another throughout the evening.

'You were a great success,' Jacov told her as he walked back to the YWCA with her.

'I thought it was a lovely party.'

She would not have wanted too much of it, though; they were all a little unreal. To Jacov, this was the reality: the food, the drink, the noise and laughter, the generosity of the emotions of people constantly constructing a special world in which they could belong, however momentarily. He longed for, treasured and respected the dull ordinariness of life as lived by the Fairleys; but he had no idea what it was that really mattered to them. He mistook the symbols for the things symbolized; and he was grieved and perplexed that Alice should have preferred a visit to the Pyramids to tea at Groppi's. Family life, to him, depended on afternoon tea and a well-trimmed hedge.

'I will call for you tomorrow,' he said when they parted.

'I thought I would take myself to the Pyramids. It will be my last opportunity.'

'No, no. I am taking you to Shepheard's. You can't come to Cairo and not eat at Shepheard's.'

He kissed her goodnight. A surprisingly chaste kiss. She thought that he was being careful of her because she had not yet recovered from the loss of Gordon. In fact, she represented something of a problem to him. She was the embodiment of all the Fairleys: kissing a whole family is difficult.

Over lunch at Shepheard's, he said to her, 'You are beginning to look better, Alice. But this life out here doesn't suit you. Will you marry me? Then you could get out of the Wrens and go home.' He seemed to be adopting the style of the actor—manager, taking a paternalistic interest in the lives of his troupe.

Alice said, 'But I like being in the Wrens.'

'Do you?' This gave him pause for thought; his plate was empty, in any case, and he was waiting for her. 'Why?'

'I meet new people and see different places.'

'You don't want the old people and the old places?' He was distressed. He valued unchangingness in the Fairleys.

'Eventually, I want them, of course. But not until after the war.'

'Then will you marry me and stay in the Wrens?'

This time Alice paused to finish her soup. She put down the spoon and said, 'Are you in love with me, Jacov?'

'I don't know what you mean, exactly. Is it that you want our relationship to be more than a matter of going to bed with each other?'

'Well, I'd like to know about that as well.' It was not to be assumed that the matter did not arise.

'Are you a virgin still?'

Alice went red.

He said, 'I see. Is *this* what is troubling you?'

They were both becoming confused, neither sure what was being offered or what was the more important to the other.

'I don't know if I could,' he said, wrinkling his brow over a dish of sea food. 'I promised your father once that his daughters would be safe with me. It was a matter of honour. I let him down over Louise.'

'Really, Jacov!' Alice said with asperity. 'It is me you are involved with now, not my father.'

'I will marry you.' He spoke with resolution. 'I will marry you tomorrow.'

'You didn't know my father very well if you think he would have been happy about *that* kind of arrangement.'

'What kind of arrangement?'

'A marriage without love.'

'But I do love you, Alice.'

'And Louise, and Claire. And Mother as well, probably.' She was eating fast; she would regret this all the way back to Alexandria.

'But I always had a special feeling about you.'

'*What* special feeling?'

He spread out his hands in a gesture of helplessness. 'It is not possible to be specific in these matters. You, who are so romantic, should realize that.'

'I don't see anything romantic in offering to marry me so that I can get out of the Wrens and go home!'

'I do not understand you.'

They drank their coffee in silence. On their way to the station, Alice said, 'I think we both need time to think.' He seemed as glad of a pause for reflection as she.

On her return to Alexandria, Alice reflected. For several days she went about her work in a state of confusion. There was something to be said for getting this business of being a virgin over and done with; and she could think of no one better suited to perform this office for her than Jacov. But although she had accommodated herself to many new ideas, she found that in some respects she had changed little. She did not want to treat sex as an initiation, a kind of tribal rite to be

155

performed at a certain age. She knew several girls who had behaved in this way and had had little pleasure from it. The enjoyment of physical love, she had noted, could be destroyed as readily by indulgence as restraint. These, however, were the arguments of the head. The heart still cried out foolishly for the love of one man, for the consummation of their love in marriage.

These, and kindred matters, were often the subject of discussion in the dormitory. Alice usually remained silent, not wishing, as Madeleine put it, 'to cast her few small pearls before swine'. One evening, in a moment of weakness, she confessed her predicament.

Madeleine said, 'Alice, you must make the most of life *now*. By the time the war is over, we shall all be quite old. There will be some other little innocent to play the girl in the gingham gown.'

Girls from the next dormitory drifted in. Alice received little vocal support. Several of the girls who agreed with her held back only for fear of having a baby.

'I used to be like you, Alice,' a fair-haired girl with the face of a Botticelli angel said. 'It's the way we've been brought up.'

'I think that's true,' Alice conceded. 'But we *were* brought up like that. It moulded us.'

'For Heaven's sake! Break the mould!' Madeleine said crisply.

'I think that might damage me more than not breaking it.'

'I don't feel all that damaged.' The angel cast a sideways glance at the mirror. 'My fellow is a psychiatrist. And he says it is impossible to really enjoy anything without sex — music, art, even food. You're only part alive without it.'

A heavy-eyed brunette said, 'This idea that a man likes a girl to be a virgin is nonsense. You should hear the jokes they make.'

Jeannie said, 'I think you are all being squalid. Alice is a nice girl. And men *do* care about that.' Jeannie made much of being the wholesome, girl-next-door type, while signalling sexual availability. It was a fiction which she maintained rigorously, never for one moment relaxing, even among her fellow Wrens, who were all well aware of her activities. Sometimes, it seemed as though she herself believed in her virginity.

Alice said, 'I'm not bothered about being a nice girl.'

'That's just as well,' Madeleine said. 'You're still young enough to carry it off. But if you go on much longer, you'll find yourself nursing a virtue no one is trying especially hard to take from you.'

The brunette said, 'And the longer you wait, the more difficult you will find it.'

Alice could see that a time might well come when she would be too afraid of being unsatisfactory to take the risk. 'I'll think about it,' she promised.

'This actor fellow would be better for you than Gordon,' Madeleine told her. 'With Gordon so knotted up, and you so inexperienced, the whole thing would probably have been a disaster.'

'I loved Gordon, though.'

'Alice! If you are going to wait for what you regard as true love, you'll be too old to enjoy it when it happens – if it happens.'

When the others had gone, Jeannie remained behind. 'I don't like to say this, Alice; but you want to beware of Madeleine. In my opinion, she is a very bad influence. She has led a lot of girls astray.' She sat on the bunk and put an arm round Alice's shoulders. Alice was uncomfortably aware of the vibrance of her tawny body. 'I've always felt we had a lot in common. Madeleine is just a high-class tart and Gwenda isn't any class at all. *We* come from the same sort of background.'

Alice said, 'Thanks very much, Jeannie,' in a tone which she hoped was more valedictory than obliged.

Jeannie squeezed Alice's arm. 'Don't let them change you, Alice. I think you are sweet the way you are. You might do something with your hair, though, if you don't mind my saying so. If you had it cut, and properly shaped, you might not look so old-fashioned. And if you *should* . . . well, don't tell them. It's a great mistake to tell.'

'All right, Jeannie. Thanks.'

Jeannie kissed her. 'If you want to know anything at any time, Alice, you can always come and talk to me. I'm not crude, like the others.'

When she had gone, Alice sat in front of the mirror staring at her image. I *am* a puritan, she thought sadly; but I can't toss it aside because other people tell me I should.

She felt very homesick. Although, in fact, the same discussion with her mother, Claire and Louise would not have yielded a unanimous verdict, it would have been conducted within a framework of shared values. There was something else, too. She strained to reach it, and felt it was almost within her grasp when the quarters PO flung open the door.

'There's two Aussie soldiers downstairs wanting to take a couple of Wrens to a dance. Can you come, Alice?'

'Sorry. I'm on late duty.'

'I don't know how I'm going to get rid of them, short of getting Reverend Mother to exorcize them.' She padded quietly down the corridor.

Alice sat on her bunk, reconstructing her home within her mind, which was something she did when she had a quiet moment. It had been difficult at first, but gradually, as the shock waves of her father's death died down, it was becoming easier. Soon, the house would be the reality, the heap of rubble the fantasy. It helped if she went far back into her childhood. Claire swore she could remember being in her push-chair; she said it had almost tipped over once outside Warren and Beck's in Acton, and she had been terrified. Alice could not go back as far as this. One of her earliest memories was of the coming of Claire.

The convent bell rang. The nuns would be making their way to the chapel. PO was probably still trying to convince the Aussies that she didn't have any Wrens hidden away anywhere. Alice could remember Clai 's christening. They had gone back to the house afterwards for a tea party and had discovered that the dog, Badger, had licked the top off all the fairy cakes.

The christening robe: the same christening robe for all three of them, and for Catherine and James. She herself, being godmother, had held Catherine in her arms wearing the robe. It had been the loving work of many hands; her great-grandmother had made it, some of the crochet work had been added by her Fairley grand-mother, and carefully repaired by her own mother. There was a smell of lavender about it: the smell of being cherished that had been about her in infancy. The joy at Claire's coming (she could remember that because she had been jealous) must have reflected her own coming.

She had lost the house now. All she could bring to mind was the attic where they had gathered on the last occasion that they were all together, turning out their treasures. They had thrown away so much that she would like to have kept, and they hadn't saved the house. But she realized now that, although the house had gone, its potentiality was within her.

She wanted the christening robe for her child. She wanted the child to be born of loving parents who had waited, hoped, and prepared for it. She wanted joy and reverence for the making of the child. And so, she wanted that long walk up the aisle; the feeling of fear and awe at the commitment she was about to make, risking herself, not just for one mad moment, but for the whole of her future life. This giving of herself at the altar was, for her, the gesture she must make, in order to receive the gift of the baby.

The convent was quiet. The nuns were at prayer and the Aussies had presumably been persuaded to leave. She experienced a few minutes of peace. Well, perhaps not as long as that – one and a half minutes?

Oh, were that all, how well it would sound! But there were other things to be taken into account. She was so inexperienced. Was it this which held her back, the fear that she might not be good in bed? Or was the dread of having an unwanted baby paramount? She had seen how much that had upset her parents. Was it the thought of her mother's pain, should it happen to her as well as Louise, which prevented her? The more she probed her motives, the more she wondered: is 'goodness' ever entirely good?

She had admired Louise so much for going against the climate of her time. Yet now, only a few years later, the climate favoured Louise. Moral values, it seemed, were more constantly in a state of flux than she had suspected as a child. It was all a question of standing where it seemed right for oneself, and abiding by the consequences. But who was oneself?

She had had another gift which had been handed down in another family. She remembered the brilliant shawl which Jacov had put round her shoulders one Christmas. It had seemed so alien, then, so unfitting. She seemed to have been reconciling herself to its silky rainbow splendour ever since. Now, the thought of it stirred her strangely.

It was so confusing – the christening robe, the shawl, nights at home when the frost cracked in one's ears and the world had a diamond-hard clarity; the brilliance of this coming night, when everything would dissolve in warmth and scented turbulence. How could all this be bound together into one life?

The evening breeze at last began to move the curtains, the first easing of the heat of the day. The sun was going down; she went to the window to watch the darkening of the brilliant crimson sky to violet. The whole world seemed to heave over into night and within her there was such yearning she cried aloud, 'Oh, what am I to do?'

If Jacov were here now . . .

But it was a week before he returned. Apparently, he saw his role in her life as husband rather than seducer.

'You asked me if I was a virgin,' she said when he proposed again. 'How many girls have you had?'

He seemed to regard this as an unfair question.

She said, 'I've been in love with one man who kept part of his life secret from me. I'm not going to let it happen again. How much would you share with me, Jacov?'

'Share?'

'You don't know what I am talking about, do you? I want a husband who is prepared to share himself without reservations.'

He looked puzzled. After a few moments, he said, 'You don't like it that I am an actor?'

She wondered if he was being deliberately evasive; and then she realized that, intentionally or otherwise, he had come near to voicing her uncertainty about him.

'That's as good an answer as any. I should always want to know what went on inside you, once you walked through the stage door.'

'You make me sad.'

'We should both be sad if we got married.'

She had expected him to accept this with relief and was surprised to see real sadness in his eyes. Had he wanted her so much? And why? She herself longed to be understood; but she had not thought it mattered about understanding Jacov, who, she had assumed, was deliberately misleading. Could she have been wrong?

'I do love you,' she assured him.

He laughed and took her hand and raised it to his lips. They did not talk any more of marriage.

It was only after he had left Egypt that Alice remembered to write to Ben. She decided to make her visit to Cairo the main topic. It was difficult writing to someone in captivity. Probably he would not want to hear about her enjoyment of the freedom of life in Alexandria; she would tell him how she had missed his company in Cairo. She made much of the antiquities of Cairo and of her disappointment at not seeing the Pyramids.

Hers was one of the few letters which reached Ben. He read it crouched in the latrine. He was weak from dysentery and he wept as he read.

9

Winter 1942–Spring 1943

It was pitch dark. Judith sat in the train with an uneasy feeling of being abandoned. There was no sound from the engine, not even an expiring sigh. Five minutes ago – or perhaps longer? – there had been some bumping and a sound which she had taken to be the coupling on of further coaches. Now, the unpleasant thought occurred to her that it might have been the uncoupling of the engine.

She found the idea of the removal of the engine profoundly unnerving. True, she had not been entirely satisfied she was travelling in the right direction; but, since most of her life motion of some sort had seemed preferable to inactivity, she had accepted this as a necessary hazard of wartime journeying. Unconsciously, she had adopted the maxim: don't worry where you are going as long as you are moving. She was not well-equipped to cope with stillness.

A lot of people had got out at the last station; but there was at least one other person in the compartment. She could hear the tapping of fingers on the far window. She said, 'Are there only the two of us?'

A few moments' silence, then a man's voice answered, 'It would seem so.' He did not sound disposed to be companionable.

Judith wound down the window and leant out. Little was achieved by this, other than making the compartment colder than ever. There was no gleam of light in earth or sky. It was as if the world had run its course. 'What are we going to do about this?' she said.

'I suppose I could get out and see what is happening?' He sounded irritable. Perhaps he thought she should have offered?

To cement his resolve, she said, 'Be careful. I don't think we are at a station – there may be a long drop.' Her own voice was as brusque as his, but she was unaware of that.

He opened the door at his end of the compartment; some effortful breathing, accompanied by exasperated exclamations, ensued. She thought this not entirely necessary. The voice was not that of a young man, but it had a resonance which did not suggest old age and decrepitude. Eventually, he called from somewhere below, 'We seem to be in a siding.' She heard him moving laboriously over stones; he obviously intended to make heavy weather of this. As the sounds became more distant, it occurred to her that he might not come back. He did not give the impression of being a particularly chivalrous man.

The blackness and the silence were dense. There was sweat on her forehead. A siding! Shunted off into a siding! It is all over, she thought in panic; my life is all over! She had refused to see what was happening to her; but now the bleakness of her situation, so heartlessly symbolized by the Southern Railway, was inescapable. Louise did not need her; she was a nuisance to Harry and Meg; Claire was at university; and Alice was enjoying herself abroad. She was alone. She looked out of the window again. Blackness pressed against her eyeballs.

The man was returning. 'There's just two coaches,' he said, accusingly, as though it was her fault. 'I didn't hear anyone make an announcement, did you?'

'I *heard* an announcement, but it was incomprehensible – as usual.'

He hauled himself back into the carriage and slammed the door. More heavy breathing.

Where are we? Judith thought, trying to distract herself with a little local geography. Trains branched off at certain stages in the journey to Lewes – she was always afraid she might end up in Storrington or some other God-forsaken place. She had thought she recognized the words Haywards Heath in that announcement, but could not be sure. If that last station *had* been Haywards Heath, and supposing she was – or had been – on the right train, then the siding was probably somewhere near Plumpton. Were there any sidings near Plumpton?

She said, 'I think we may be near Plumpton. If only the moon was up, we could see the Downs.'

Her companion was not prepared to speculate about Plumpton. A few minutes later, however, he said, 'I have some spam sandwiches, if you would care . . .?'

'Oh, I couldn't deprive you . . .'

'I really think you had better.' He was more irritated than ever. 'We don't know how long we may be here. If you don't eat, you may become faint.' This would be too inconsiderate, his voice implied.

She groped and received two spam sandwiches. 'I've got a flask of tea,' she said. 'I didn't bother about bringing food because I thought it was going to be a short journey.'

'It is rather cold,' he acknowledged. Taking this for acceptance, she poured tea into the cup of the flask. 'I've got a mug for myself,' she said, as they negotiated the exchange.

They munched and drank in silence. The utter darkness robbed her of any sense of companionship. I am alone, she thought. Alone! She was one of seven children; she had married and had three children, and a demanding husband. What she had hitherto thought of as being alone was the luxury of having an afternoon to herself. The blackness was becoming suffocating.

'Why is there no one about?' she asked sharply.

'I expect the entire railway staff has been put into a munitions factory.'

'Wherever you go, everyone seems to be away doing useful things.'

'The whole bloody world is actively employed!' he responded vehemently. But she could tell that his feeling was of a different quality from her own: he was exasperated by the dislocation of his journey, in no way was he afraid.

She ate the second spam sandwich, which was warm and dry. The lack of activity was the worst thing of all. She was a practical person, life had formed her that way. There had always been so much to do. If you took the sewing machine, vacuum cleaner and cooker away from her, there wouldn't be a person there at all. She felt full of rage against life.

She said, 'I have been staying with my daughter.'

'Yes, so have I.' The cause of his irritation was now apparent. He added, in a tone of almost sepulchral gloom, '*and* my grandchildren.'

'It can be difficult, can't it?'

'My daughter is one of those implacable females.' He became quite expansive. 'It's impossible to be of any help to her because she doesn't *listen*, she knows everything. Absolutely no experience of the world, mind you, she just *knows*.'

Judith, thinking of herself and Stanley, said wryly, 'She must have got it from somebody.'

'My wife, probably. She tended to live by Divine revelation.'

Either his wife was long dead, or he was a very cold fish.

What was she to say now? 'I have been staying with my daughter . . .' Was this to be her conversation over the coming years, the relating of details of her visits to Louise and Alice and Claire; and when she was not visiting, would she be anticipating their invitations, or hoping they would spare the time to come to her? And where would she be living? She could not stay forever on the farm with Meg and Harry Braddon. Oh, this awful blackness!

'Children *do* tend to make use of one, don't they?' she said. 'I suppose it's our own fault, for wanting to be needed.'

'But I *don't* want to be needed!'

You're needed now, though, she thought savagely. I have to talk to someone.

'You have only the one child?'

'I had a son. He was killed at Dunkirk.' The statement was made with a brevity which invited no comment. Nevertheless, she said, 'My husband was killed in the blitz.'

Such a stupid thing, she wanted to tell him; trying to open a door for a crazy woman who lived next door. It wasn't as though he was ever any good at household jobs. She almost choked with rage.

The man said, 'Your visit to your daughter wasn't entirely successful?' His voice sounded different, not exactly sympathetic, but as though they had arrived on common ground.

'Her husband is in North Africa. I'm afraid something is not right there . . .'

'At home, I take it – not in North Africa, where everything seems to be proceeding so splendidly?'

'Yes, at home.'

'A man?'

'I suspect so. She didn't say anything, of course – but she didn't need to.'

'Ah! "The fig tree putteth forth her green figs and the vines with the tender grape give a good smell . . ."?'

'Yes.' She gave a long sigh. Yes, she thought: I am jealous of Louise! It takes a stranger to tell one these things. After a few moments' silence, she said, 'Her husband has been away since 1939 – she hasn't seen him since Dunkirk, and then only briefly. It's a long time, when you're young.'

'It's a long time at any age, damn it!'

Judith leant back in her corner and closed her eyes to examine her own inner darkness. I am jealous and angry, she repeated to herself. I am in my late forties, and I still have desires; but everyone assumes *that* is over for me. For the rest of my life, I shall be expected to sit in a corner, knitting for my grandchildren and being careful not to make a nuisance of myself – but always being on hand when they need me. She repeated to herself, I am jealous, jealous . . . She still felt angry, but not so afraid.

There was the sound of movement dislodging stones. Judith looked out of the window. A dim blue light was swinging towards the coaches. The man had become authoritative. 'Let me!' He leant out of the window and shouted, 'Ahoy!'

An aggrieved voice answered, 'What you doing in there?'

'We could well ask you that!'

'Didn't you hear what they said about the last two coaches?'

'Not one single word, I assure you.'

'You'd better come along of me, then.'

The man said to Judith, 'We are indeed fortunate. This must be the last porter in England. Cherish him!'

As they followed their guide down the track, they learnt that a passenger had reported that two people had remained in the compartment. '"I suppose that is all right?"' he said. Bloody twit! Whyn't he tell *you*, instead of the ticket collector, and save all this.'

'The Englishman's unwillingness to interfere!'

Judith sensed that her companion was relishing this. Her own feelings fell somewhat short of enjoyment. 'Just where are we?' she demanded.

'Haywards Heath. Where do you think you are?'

'But we left Haywards Heath. I remember that.'

'You left it so we could shunt you in 'ere.'

They had been walking past a high hoarding which separated the shunting area from the main station. When they rounded it, dim lights immediately became visible. Judith had a glimpse of her companion – a tall, broad man, probably in his early fifties. She noted, with compunction, that he walked with a limp.

A train came creeping in almost as soon as they arrived on the platform. A desperate struggle ensued as soon as the doors opened. The porter led them to the guard's van.

'No room!' The guard said.

'You've got to take them, mate. They got shunted orf.'

Wedged into the guard's van were two calves, several soldiers with kit bags and rifles, three naval officers, and a handful of civilians, one of whom was a young woman whose children had been disposed at random among the service personnel. A corporal was potting an infant with phlegmatic professionalism, while a less experienced naval officer was attempting to change a nappy. The young woman, who had a pronounced Irish accent, was explaining to a disapproving elderly woman, 'I bear them and me mother breeds them.' As if by magic, she produced a spare infant and deposited it on the chest of Judith's companion. Judith liked the fact that, although he did not make a fuss, he made no attempt to pretend he was pleased by the arrangement. Neither did the infant. The two seemed to have something in common – they had not learnt to dissemble.

At Lewes, when they had extricated themselves from the train, Judith's companion asked, civilly, but without being pressing, 'How will you manage from here?'

Judith could see Harry advancing towards her. 'My brother-in-law is meeting me, thank you.'

She said to Harry, 'It was good of you to wait.' But it transpired he had not waited, he had mistaken the time of her train.

'You travelled with one of our local celebrities,' he said, as Judith's companion limped past them to another waiting car. 'Austin Marriott.'

'You know him?'

'Only by sight. He is not our sort of person – he's a publisher.'

'Why do you say that?' Judith was tired and disposed to be fractious. 'What sort of books does he publish?'

'I have no idea. But they are a rather rackety lot, publishers.'

'Shouldn't you assume the best until you know the worst, Harry?'

He made no reply, either because he was having so much trouble starting the car, or because he was annoyed. Judith wondered how much longer they were going to be able to tolerate each other.

In the spring vacation, Claire came down to stay on the farm. The train in which she travelled did not shunt coaches into a siding, but it did have an unscheduled stop at a nameless country station. It seemed to Claire, as she looked out of the window, to epitomize all the country stations of her childhood. Beyond the deserted platform was a low bridge where one or two children stared unmoving at the train. In a field near by cows were contemplating a move which might – or might not – be made in the remote future. Far in the distance came the sound of sheep bells; a sound which seemed, to Claire, to be the echo of all the tranquil moments of her life. If only Alice were here! There were a lot of school children in the train. Claire, so lately escaped from school, had felt acutely their giggling silliness; but now, this ceased to irritate, and became a part of the timeless peace of a country railway station on a warm spring afternoon. Why did I have to grow up? she thought, envying the schoolgirls the joys she imagined to be theirs.

A guard had now got out of the train and was gesticulating wildly, presumably to the engine driver. Beyond the bridge, Claire saw a bird, coming in low and arrow straight. She remained at the window, transfixed, as something spurted from the bird. There was a deafening rattle of noise and dust fizzed up from the platform. Someone dragged her down on to the floor. Children were screaming. Hands grasped the seats and pulled them over their bodies. Afterwards, Claire was never sure which had been worse — being machine gunned, or the appalling discovery of what lay beneath the seats of Southern Railway trains.

The plane did not return. After a time, the train went on. Some of the children laughed and others cried. Claire, who was extremely fastidious, was nearly hysterical with distress at the filthy condition in which she now found herself.

She was late arriving at Lewes station, and no one was waiting for her. There was, however, an army utilicon which picked up a few soldiers; and the driver agreed to go a mile out of his way to leave Claire at the gate of the farm. The soldiers were concerned, but had nothing practical to offer in the way of comfort. One of them carried her case as far as the yard. 'I'll be all right here,' she said, feeling that his presence would inhibit the exhibition which she intended to put on to shame her relatives for their desertion.

In fact, she had no need of histrionics. When she burst into the kitchen and found Harry there, in the act of taking off his boots, all her tumultuous emotion gushed forth spontaneously.

He looked at her aghast. In the dim light, thickly coated with grime and clotted with the putrefying remains of discarded food, she had all the appearance of one risen from the grave. 'Oh, my darling, my darling!' he cried. 'My little Claire, what have they done to you?' He took her in his arms, grappling to rid her of the 'they' who had done this wicked thing. As they clung tighter and tighter to each other, it was difficult to tell which of them was the more transported.

Meg, coming into the kitchen to investigate all this sound and fury, was immediately aware of feeling which went far beyond the requirements of comforting a distressed young woman.

'What a disgusting noise you are making, Claire!'

'My dear . . . Surely you can see . . . something dreadful . . .' As he had no idea what in fact had happened, and was, moreover, ravaged by lust, Harry was hampered in going further.

'I can see very well.' Meg spoke in the tone of one to whom explanation would henceforth be superfluous.

Claire became hysterical, and Meg slapped her face with an application which suggested she had been waiting just such an opportunity. 'Now, go upstairs and get yourself clean!'

There was much that each had been waiting to say to the other, but it would have taken a poet to render their emotions into suitably

167

elevated language; and, being rather ordinary people, they had to make do with commonplace phrases.

Claire screamed, 'You vile woman!'

Meg replied, '*And* you can leave this house tomorrow.'

Harry tried to intervene, and Meg told him he was a whited sepulchre.

By the time Judith returned, having waited on the wrong platform for Claire, the situation was beyond retrieving.

'We are at the mercy of terrible forces!' Harry said. This, it transpired, was not a simple acknowledgement of desire, but a reference to some more exalted state. His eyes strained from his white, hatchet face. Judith could see that pushed a little further, he might well take to mysticism in order to justify himself to himself. She did not think he was much concerned with anyone else.

It was impossible to reason with Meg. Judith, whose sympathies were with her sister-in-law, was sorry about this. After years with Harry, she supposed that resorting to reason would be a negation of the whole of their life together.

Claire, while proclaiming her intention of killing herself, had discovered that her overriding need was to get clean. She was standing naked in her bedroom, sponging herself while she wept. She still had the slenderness of a child. Judith noted with a pang how appealing she was and how vulnerable. Her body did not as yet seem ready to cope with the responses it aroused.

Claire said, 'I want to die, Mummy.'

Judith unpacked her suitcase and put out fresh clothes. 'We'll go into Lewes when you have dressed and find somewhere to eat. Do you want me to wash your hair?'

'I want to die.'

But while Judith was washing her hair, she said weakly, 'Anyway, how can we get into Lewes?'

'I shall take Harry's car, with or without his permission.'

'The train was machine-gunned, Mummy.'

'Yes, I know, darling. They told me at the station.'

They had a meal in a hotel near Lewes. Afterwards, they sat in the car in a country lane overshadowed by the Downs, watching the last of the light fading.

Claire said, 'How was I to know? I shall never be able to be natural with a man again.'

'Don't be silly, Claire.'

'This has probably ruined my life.'

'You are just like your father. You dramatize everything.'

'What about Aunt Meg, then?'

'You were partly to blame for the way she behaved. You have been making rather too much of Uncle Harry lately.'

'But he's my uncle.'

'He is also a man. Men aren't sensible about this kind of thing.'

'I hate men!'

Judith, a little worried about her daughter, said, trying to choose her words more carefully than was usual with her, 'Claire, you are older now. You must try to be responsible for the way you behave with other people.'

'Why aren't I responsible?'

'You tend to work on people's feelings without knowing what your own feelings are. You used to do this with friends at school. You asked a lot of them, more than you were prepared to give yourself.'

'I *loved* my friends.'

'You wanted them to love you. Once they did, you sometimes stopped being interested.'

Claire began to cry. 'You love Alice and Louise more than me. You always did.'

'That's not true. *You* saw to that!' Judith gave her a little hug. 'I'm sorry, pet. You've had a dreadful day. I shouldn't have said so much.'

The next day they left the farm. Judith went to see the minister of the chapel which she attended near Lewes. His wife offered accommodation for the week of Claire's stay. Judith hoped that during this time she would be able to find more permanent accommodation for herself. She was determined not to return to London, and it was certain she could not remain at the farm.

Claire, enjoying the luxury of having her mother to herself, behaved entrancingly throughout the week. The minister's wife said it was like having an angel round the house. Claire was now at Oxford, and the minister had been at Balliol. They had long talks about Anglo-Saxon history. Claire read them *The Dream of the Rood*. She read it in Anglo-Saxon, which only she and the minister understood. To have read it in English would have been easier for all concerned, but then anyone could have read it in English. The minister told Judith that Claire would go far.

When they parted, Claire said to Judith, 'I shall remember what you said to me.' By this time, her mother's words had been translated into acceptable form. Claire was adept at extracting from advice that small particle which she could assimilate without difficulty and with profit to herself. She now interpreted her mother's words as a warning that other people might try to manipulate her, not that she was herself the manipulator. Claire had long ago cast herself in the role of the victim of others' treachery; and it would have taken a radical revision of her nature to alter this view of herself.

She was to spend a few days at the YWCA near Marlow with Heather. She was the first to arrive and, having deposited her suitcase at the hostel, she went for a walk along the towpath. It was a beautiful spring day. As she walked, she looked forward to telling Heather of all that had befallen her. In a field on the far side of the river there was a group of Free French soldiers. They called to her and she waved in reply. One of them began to sing a catchy French tune in the manner of Maurice Chevalier. She tossed her head, so that her curly red hair floated around her face; her lips parted slightly; she walked as in a dream, noting how utterly, utterly lost she was in the wonder of this glorious day. The Frenchmen also noted this. Further on, there were GIs picnicking with some very silly girls. She did not want to be disturbed by people. So she turned and walked back again. The Frenchmen cheered and waved. What a beautiful race they were! She must improve her French.

In the distance, she saw Heather coming towards her. Her heart lifted at the sight of her beloved friend; she skipped and waved, so that the whole of her small form was animated by excitement. Heather was an ambulance driver. Uniform suited her long, raw-boned frame; but she was now wearing a summer frock, which had all the femininity of a sack draped round a lamp-post. Claire allowed the golden goodness of her love to pour like a benediction over poor, ugly Heather. Heather, delighted, ran to her, scooped her up and swung her round and round. The Frenchmen wailed outrage.

Claire, unprepared for Heather's joy to leap beyond her own, wavered. She was aware of the French soldiers indulging in mimes unworthy of such a beautiful race. She felt embarrassed and stood back from her friend, breathless, pushing her hair from her face. A slight flush made Heather's sunburn even redder. She said, with a cheerfulness that was not without effort, 'My, but it's good to see you again!'

Claire said brightly, 'Aren't we lucky it's such a lovely day?'

Heather took her arm. 'Let's get out of range of the Frogs, shall we?'

They walked the way Claire had already been, passing the GIs and their girls, now a distasteful tangle of arms and legs. Further on, they came to an unfrequented meadow where they could lie and talk, still having a view of the river. The sun was hot for the time of year. It had brought out the freckles on Claire's face and arms. Heather teased her, and said it wouldn't be possible to get a pin between them. Then she stretched out, and sighed, 'Oh, I have been looking forward to this!'

Claire stretched out beside her, calmer now. 'Yes,' she thought, 'I have been looking forward to it, too.' As she listened to the droning of insects in the long grass, a feeling of sheer goodness quieted her spirit, and made her very nearly forgetful of herself. 'I am happy,' she thought, which was strange because she was always telling herself she was happy (or desolate), so why should she feel so surprised by this happiness? Somewhere, deep inside her, there was a cool delight, quite unlike her usual nervy rapturousness. This delight made her think of the first concealed sparkle of water in a cleft of rock; water that would run down into a hidden stream; and then become the river, running broad and free between green banks.

'I'd like to swim,' she said.

Heather said, 'Why don't we?'

'I haven't got a costume. Besides, no one else is.'

'My old Claire!' Heather mocked. 'Do you suppose there is a notice up somewhere telling us it is forbidden?' She took hold of the hem of her dress, pretending to be about to raise it. 'I will if you will!'

'Heather, don't!'

Heather lay back, laughing her gusty laugh. 'All right. I didn't think you would.'

'Would *you* have done?'

'Probably not. It would be icy cold.'

They lay in silence, half-dreaming in the warmth of the sun. Then Heather said, 'Well, come on! Tell me about yourself. Are there any young men at Oxford?'

'Just a few.'

'The halt and maimed?'

'There's one who is quite passable. He's got bad eyesight.'

'I see. So that's all, is it? One passable bloke with bad eyesight?'

The need to dramatize was awakened now. Claire told Heather about Harry and Meg.

Heather said, 'The sod! So that is why you were so buttoned up when we met. And I thought you were in one of your mean moods!'

A mean mood, Claire might have accepted: 'one of your mean moods' she did not at all like. She said, 'Harry's not a sod. He loved me. I hadn't realized what it is to be loved like that.' She felt that Heather had not grasped the unique quality of this experience.

Heather said, 'The dirty old man! You must have had an awful time and I haven't been a bit sympathetic.' Repentant, she flung her arms around Claire. Her elbows dug into Claire's ribs. She smelt of sweat.

Claire, looking up at the tilting sky, was not sure how she felt about this. There were people coming along the towpath; she could hear them exclaiming about the pussy willows.

'I can't breathe,' she said touchily. 'And anyway, you mustn't speak in that way about Harry. He *is* my uncle.' Heather's family was common; it did not behove her to speak in this way of a Fairley connection, even though not one of the blood.

It was more than that, though. There was something so unselfconscious, so without guile or affectation, so unqualified – in fact, so unambiguous – about Heather's friendship . . .

Heather was saying in a different voice, 'But then, you're all sods, randy old Uncle Harry and all.' She was sitting looking away over the river, hands clasped round her knees.

Claire said, trying to be chirpy, 'Who's in a mean mood now?'

Heather put her head down on her knees and did not answer.

Claire said, 'Well, if you're going to sulk, I'm going for a walk.'

She began to walk along the towpath, looking back from time to time to see if Heather was following her. Heather was not. Claire was more put out than she had anticipated. She realized that her friendship with Heather was getting quite a hold on her. 'I don't think I have ever felt so unhappy,' she thought. 'And only a little while ago I had never felt so happy.'

Further along the towpath, she sat beneath the pussy willows, looking down at the river. A current chafed the smooth blue surface so that it looked like shirred silk. She had real trouble now. She had grown up in a world where the boundaries of loving were not blurred, and the lines of demarcation were armed frontiers. The air was very still, but the reflection of trees trembled slightly. Once look beyond those frontiers and all was over with you; the mirror cracked from side to side, and there was no way back.

Mummy was right, she told herself. I *do* need to be careful; Heather will just sweep me up otherwise. Tears came; tears that, for once, she did not particularly want but could not hold back. She remembered how she had burnt her stories of the Maitland family. There were other people – *real* people – one must also do without. She owed it to dear Harry to remember that.

By the time she met Heather at the YWCA she had herself well in hand.

Judith stayed another week with the minister and his wife, during which time she found rooms in a large house on the outskirts of Lewes. The owner of the house was away in North Africa. His wife was in the WVS, an activity which seemed to occupy her day and night. Although active in good works, she was not communicative on the purely social level, and was glad to find a lodger who kept herself to herself.

The memory of the railway siding stayed in Judith's mind; but gradually, because she was not a poor-spirited woman, she ceased to blame life for her troubles and began to question her own attitudes. Perhaps she had chosen a road which led to a dead end? If so, it was now up to her to fight her way out.

10

===

Spring–Autumn 1943

By the spring of 1943, the tide of battle had turned; yet to the ordinary soldier there never seemed to have been a particular moment when he discovered it was flowing in his favour. Stalingrad was a world away from North Africa; the Coral Sea and Midway Island he had never even heard of. His horizons were limited by what he could see.

In July, Guy Immingham, who was now in Sicily, could see Italy across the Straits of Messina. He viewed it with mixed feelings. The desert had provided an ideal background for fighting. Sicily had brought him a stage nearer to places which were part of a known civilization which he associated with his own way of life. He liked the Italians, and did not look forward to wreaking havoc in a country which had formed the background to much of his classical studies in school. The crimes committed in Abyssinia had made little impression on him; he associated Italians with laughter and gaiety, Titian and Dante.

His companion had other thoughts in mind. 'All those señoritas!' he said, gazing avidly as though he saw voluptuousness in the contours of the coastline itself.

'Signorinas, I believe,' Guy corrected gently.

The other man rubbed his hands together. 'Naples, that'll be the place! Oh, boy – Naples!'

Guy wrote to Louise, 'All that seems to concern some of these men is brothels – their availability or otherwise! You must not think I share these feelings. I am not tempted in this way. I have only to think of you . . .'

Louise ran into the hall and cried to the children, 'We're going for a walk.'

'*Again*, Mummy.'

'Yes, yes, James! We mustn't miss a moment of this sunshine.'

'You won't walk so fast this time, will you?'

There were a few items of interest which Guy omitted from his letters to Louise. For one thing, he had hopes of further meetings with a WAAF officer whom he had met in Cairo. As he had done nothing of which he need be ashamed, he did not consider there was any need for him to tell Louise about this. Had she known his feelings, however, she would have felt a little less guilty. Guy *did* experience a certain pleasure in being with an attractive woman other than his wife: an undoubted sense of having put something over on 'people' whose identities he did not specify. He would have something to smile to himself about in future years, a secret. Until now, his emotions had been mortgaged to pay debts to others — his parents for his good home and schooling; Louise for loving him and bearing him children. *This* was something for himself, his very own.

Her name was Monica Ames. She was dark and slim and had a skin like a peach. But for all her undoubted beauty, most men found her company unsatisfactory. They said they were never sure if she was enjoying herself. Her eyes were rather lifeless. To Guy, wanting nothing more than a personable companion, her beauty was a bonus. She, for her part, was unconcerned by his lack of enterprise. For Monica Ames, the scented evening air, the coolness of a drink, were not preliminaries, but a part of sensual pleasure as authentic as the presence of a man. This was an unacceptable attitude to most men, who felt they must be at the centre of the mystery. Even Guy, had he understood her better, would have found a threat to his masculinity in the idea that Monica might experience a moment's sensual pleasure unrelated to himself. When they were together, he assumed that every adornment was worn for his benefit; the dress chosen because *he* might find it attractive, not because the feel of it sent a delightful shiver through *her* finger tips. Happily unaware of the true state of things, he congratulated himself on finding a woman who seemed content with an arrested love affair. They made a handsome couple and were well-pleased with each other. Guy very much hoped she might find her way to Naples.

Louise walked up Hampstead High Street with the children. Shop windows reflected her flushed face and the too-bright eyes. On the Heath, the merciless impatience which had taken possession of her body drove her on. The children called after her, 'Mummy, Mummy! You're going too fast!'

At home, later, she was unable to sit still and must rush out to post a letter, buy an evening paper, weed the garden . . . She had prayed for Ivor to be posted. Now, he had had to go away for a week and she prayed for his return.

Alice wrote to Ben, 'I am going home soon. Believe it or not, I have been recommended for a commission as a Signal Officer! As I'm a coder, I know quite a bit about signals. But I shall have to do a few months at one of the big communications establishments in England before I go to OTC. I can't say I have any great desire to wear a three-cornered hat; but it is nice to be going home. It has been a wonderful experience, of course; and I am terribly disappointed at not seeing the Pyramids. But I do long to see Mummy and my sisters. I expect I shall notice quite a difference in Catherine and James. Whatever will it be like for Guy? He has missed their childhood.'

How small my world is, she thought, looking at what she had written. She paused to wipe the sweat from her hands. I wonder what it will be like to feel cold again; and to have lots of grey days and rain. She dreaded the grey days, but could have waxed lyrical at the prospect of the smell of wet earth, the freshness of English fields.

The convent bell sounded. She would miss this, too, this strange sensation of a sustaining rhythm going on beneath the little activities of daily life; the feeling of being, however uncomprehendingly, a part of the cycle of the seasons of God.

She picked up her pen and wrote, 'How tiresome all this must be to you, Ben. My war so different from yours. It sometimes seems to me as though the whole war will go by without my having made a moment's sense of it.'

Now that she had it in writing, she realized what a daunting indictment it was. She had shed a few illusions. She had learnt a lot about people and something of herself. But what had she been *doing* all this time? She had seen men going to battle, had visited some of them in hospital; she had lost a man whom she had loved; she had heard the guns getting nearer, had slept in the desert. Yet, the one abiding image of war which she carried in her mind was of the woman with the cat in the smoking ruins of Coventry. She remembered her dream. Was *that* reality? That terrible rushing stream into which she had felt urged to jump? If so, she was still on the bank; and Ben it was who had jumped.

Irene had been writing to Alice but had put the letter aside for want of subject matter. She was at home with her parents, listening to the rain – soft, summer rain pattering on the leaves of the plane trees. There was already some blue in the sky. The sun would blink through soon.

It was a Sunday afternoon; a precious time they spent quietly together, seldom disturbing one another. It seemed questionable, at these times, whether she loved Angus for himself, or because he shielded her from more demanding men who would have taken her out of this peaceful household. She opened the sash window gently, because her mother was dozing over *Barchester Towers*. The smell of rain-wet earth was pleasant – particularly pleasant to a Londoner whose small garden was of special importance. A country garden would be impossible, she thought; all those fields and woods waiting to take over. Here, one had only bricks and mortar over which to triumph. Further away, she could see a bombed site, bright with marigolds, lovingly planted. How tenacious is the will to make things grow! How tenacious, indeed, is the will to grow! Were the marigolds not there, the willow herb would have taken over.

Her father put down his paper. 'So, it's all over with Mussolini.'

'Do you think the Italians will fight without him?'

'Of course not. They'll be out of the war in a matter of weeks. But it won't save their country from being a battlefield. Ah well, I hope *we* shan't behave like barbarians, whatever the Germans may do.'

'You're thinking of all those lovely old towns? But people are more important than buildings, surely?'

'I suppose you may be right.'

She looked at him, cherishing him because he would never adopt the expected attitude. There was a certain excess of human feeling against which he must always stand.

'We don't own the treasures which have survived for thousands of years. After all, we are only here in the blink of an eyelid. Yet, we strut about as though the world was made for no other purpose than to answer our immediate needs.'

'It is hard to equate the need to save human life with the requirement to be good stewards of the world's treasures, isn't it?'

'Our masters don't even do the equation. They are much too arrogant for that.'

Mrs Kimberley, who was *not* dozing, said, 'My dear, and us? Our way of life . . . to be preserved or . . . ? It's what we are fighting for, I take it. But I have the feeling . . .' She paused, not sure that she could commit herself to a feeling, then went on, 'In terms of what you have been saying, is it important, the survival of our way of life?'

'I don't suppose so. Only to us.'

'I find that very dispiriting.'

'We've had a good run. I'm glad I'm not young, though.' He took up his paper and Mrs Kimberley returned to *Barchester Towers*.

Irene wondered idly whether her mother noticed that even in Barchester, the way of life seemed always to be under threat.

Angus Drummond was attending a briefing at a country house in Berkshire. It was all rather rushed because a number of British agents in France had disappeared recently. It must be assumed that they were permanently out of action. In one particular case, a replacement must be sent without delay – or so the French maintained, and at this moment it was important to play along with the French. So, for one reason or another, no delay. Angus was aware that, given different circumstances and more time, he would not have been the first choice for such an enterprise. Emergencies tend to make nonsense of selection procedures more often than is generally supposed: his main qualifications were availability and expendability. In addition, he had a quick mind, a cool, unruffled appearance, and a manner which hinted at inner reserves of something which his companions must hope was strength. He was a man on whose reliability it was permissible to gamble. Only one person present had serious doubts. It wasn't that the almond eyes gave a certain obliqueness to the face, it was more the pointedness of the chin. There was something about these faces which taper away – fragile, handle with care . . . But it was too late for speculations of this kind. One could not expect the others to back down because the fellow had the wrong-shaped face. And, in any case, he was not convinced of the importance of the operation.

Angus was studying photographs of Jews being rounded up in a village. This was only a small part in a picture which Intelligence was building up of the activities of the German secret police and the organization of concentration camps. While his companions were talking statistics, he found it impossible to move his mind beyond this single image.

On his way to this briefing, he had called at the corner shop in the village near by. As soon as he entered he was aware of an unaccustomed restraint. The shop was usually full of people queueing and complaining. Mr Snaith was not the jovial, much-loved store-owner, doing his best in trying circumstances. He was known to be doing rather well, having discovered a mysterious source of supply which enabled him, at a price, to dispense certain commodities, such as bacon, off the ration. He had his favourites. This had undoubtedly been his downfall. One of his least favoured customers had been to the police. The local police tended to be beneficiaries. The complaint had been made at a higher level. The two policemen who were talking to Mr Snaith were not local officers, and had all the virtue of men who have never seen an illicit side of bacon. Their manner, as sometimes happens with the disadvantaged, was not pleasant. Had Mr Snaith been found to be harbouring a German spy complete with secret radio in his attic, a greater sense of impending doom could scarcely have been conveyed. One could only imagine the firing squad to lie ahead of Mr Snaith. Mr Snaith stood, a policeman on either side of him, hitching his upper lip above his dentures in the same mirthless smile with which he was wont to announce his regret at being unable to oblige. The policemen were having none of this.

There were several people in the shop, behaving with all the discretion of extras in a film who have been told to hang around without letting their presence impinge upon the main characters. Although Mrs Snaith, quivering and tearful, was waiting to serve them, none appeared to be in a hurry to come to a decision as to their purchases. The newspaper stack was particularly favoured. In happier times, Mr Snaith would have reminded them that this was not the reading room in the public library.

Mrs Snaith must have come hastily from her bed to take over while her husband acquainted the police with the intricacies of his stock books. Her hair had not been disturbed since the rollers were recently removed from it. She wore an overcoat from beneath which trailed a long, puce garment which was presumably a nightdress. Usually, she was meticulously groomed in the style of a Renoir barmaid. Her humiliation was such that no one in the shop felt it quite nice to say anything to her.

Angus, acutely embarrassed, grabbed a newspaper and held out a shilling to Mrs Snaith. Face to face, he found himself more afraid of her than the police. He did not dare do other than look her in the eye.

'Oh, am I glad to see you Major, dear!' Mrs Snaith's tone was automatically arch, but the urgency of her situation now invested it with a compelling appeal. Angus was dismayed, fearing the police might imagine himself to have been the recipient of her favours. Mrs Snaith's favours, though of a different order, were as well-known as her husband's. He smiled nervously, waiting for his change. He had put himself in her power by not giving the correct money. If he walked away, she would shout after him that he had forgotten his change, thus drawing attention to his retreat.

'You find out who your friends are at times like this,' Mrs Snaith said, embracing Angus in a watery gaze.

'Oh, really . . . I hadn't realized . . .'

'Well, I don't usually stand here like this, dear, straight out of my bed. Where's your eyes?'

One of the policemen looked up. Angus said, 'And I'll have ten penny stamps, please.'

'The post office isn't open, dear. I couldn't cope with that now, could I?' She seemed set to make further scathing comments on his deductive powers.

Fortunately, the question as to whether legally the post office should be open now exercised the more aggressive of the two policemen. In the ensuing argument, Angus made his exit, leaving Mrs Snaith in possession of his shilling. A venerable old man, standing outside the shop, said to him, 'Caught up with old Snaith, then, have they?' He spat prodigiously.

It was all very unpleasant. But then, the Snaiths had themselves exercised power, giving food to friends, withholding it from those in greater need. The Snaiths deserved their fate. Angus looked down at the photograph, where people stood in the village street, heads turned away, while the Jews were rounded up. How far, if really stretched, would one extend licence to the police? There would be no problem about guilt. Some small crime can be made to stick on most of us, if people set their minds to it. If all Snaiths were sentenced to wear some symbol – an equivalent appropriate to the Snaiths of the Star of David – on their jackets, would people say they were 'getting away with it lightly'? Would the villagers of Little Heaton have turned their heads away if the Snaiths within their midst were marched down the road with a few possessions in a sack over their backs? 'Caught up with the Snaiths, then, have they?'

Before the SS came to this village in Eastern Europe, would the Jews already have been in hiding? Or had they thought themselves, within the confines of their restricted lives, safe here? What must it have felt like? Whole villages had been razed to the ground in Russia and elsewhere. But that, terrible though it must be, was different from this scene, where the life of the village would go on peaceably enough once the Jews had been weeded out. It was the complicity of ordinary, decent people which made this crime so peculiarly dreadful. How had it ever come about that it could be regarded as irrelevant whether a person was innocent or guilty provided he was a Jew?

He looked at them, standing there like so many sheep. Cry out, damn you! he thought angrily. When the pastors of the German Confessional Church had been taken away, the congregation had not stood idly by; they had gone into the street, singing hymns, loudly drawing attention to what was happening. The Jews were so passive. It was as if they colluded in their own destruction. The whole thing – the victims, the persecutors, the passers-by – was a monstrous act of collusion. He had thought this often enough in the past, had almost argued himself into a frame of mind where he could believe that the Jews had only themselves to blame.

But now, looking at this photograph, it seemed that the faces *did* cry out! The terrible acceptance of all concerned in this unemphatic scene, cried out 'Shame!'

The photograph showed the moment of the dividing of the ways. The villagers would continue with the small change of daily life, talking in bread queues, walking a dog, bathing a baby. While those others, who would never see a quiet street again, or sit with families in a house, would move beyond the daily task, the common round.

Had they understood what was ahead of them? The doleful little girl, dragging at her mother's hand, had she been complaining about some toy left behind? And the mother, what had been her expectations? And Katia . . . When she, at some time past, stepped into that other street, had she already been as cowed as these people seemed? Or had she, restless, ebullient creature that she was, gone resentful at another diminishment of her freedom; though still imagining the nightmare to have an ending which would leave her with a stake in the future? It could not have been. Katia's appearance would have marked her down. Had he himself not been aware of her ripening? In his mind, he saw her depraved, humiliated, the object of obscene sexual play.

'I am assured your French will stand up to it.'

Some poor devil had bought a trip abroad! It took him a few seconds to recall that it was himself.

When he came out of the briefing, the sun was shining through rain, jewelling trees and roses in the gardens which surrounded the building. The gardens provided a setting of formal peace for this network of nerves and arteries which reached out across Europe. He would never walk happily in such gardens again; henceforth, visits to places such as Hampton Court would be accompanied by severe attacks of migraine.

He wondered whether he should go up to London to see Irene; but decided he could not, after looking at that photograph. It would contaminate her. He decided instead to visit his Aunt Millie, whom he did not see as being in any danger of contamination.

Melancholy thoughts absorbed him as he drove into Hertford. Melancholy had a fairly firm grip on him now. Perhaps it attracted certain events to him, or perhaps it was chance that when he parked his car the police should be questioning a motorist near by. A matter of petrol coupons was being debated. The motorist's friends were showing a tendency to fade away. Angus sat in the car for a few minutes pondering the fact that respect for authority can create an atmosphere in which people cease to monitor the manner in which authority is exercised. Having satisfied himself that England was well on the way to fascism, he called upon his aunt. He was not, therefore, a witness to the knocking off of authority's helmet and the disrespectful mêlée which ensued.

Once inside his aunt's house, Angus discovered that authority had suffered a graver blow than any being inflicted on the county constabulary at this moment. 'Your poor mother has been distracted trying to get in touch with you,' he was informed. His mother was invariably distracted. His Aunt Millie, on the other hand, maintained an air of unruffled, if often inappropriate, calm. She told him with commendable composure that his father had been badly wounded. His boat had been sunk (she spoke as if it was something he played with in his bath) and he was in hospital in Plymouth – the natural consequence of such infantile capers.

For the first time that he could remember, Angus was more concerned for his father than his mother. Without his realizing it, his hatred of his father had become one of the mainstays of his life.

'What does Mother mean by "badly wounded"?' he asked, his tone conveying an uncharacteristic criticism of his parent.

'One of your father's sailor chums has been in touch with her. He does sound to have made rather much of your father's injuries without being specific.'

'There is nothing I can do.' Angus realized with relief that fate had performed yet another office for him; whoever must sit by his father's bedside, or console his mother, it could not be he.

'I have been posted,' he said.

'Yes, but that was before your father got himself into this mess.'

'That will make not the slightest difference to HQ.'

'Surely, on compassionate grounds . . .'

'Not when I have two sisters. Who is with Mother now?'

'Cecily. A broken reed if ever there was one.'

'Daphne is in London somewhere. She will have to cope with this. She is the one who is devoted to Father.'

'I have never thought of Daphne as being "devoted". And, in any case, it is *you* that your mother wants.'

'You must reassure her, Aunt Millie. You are always so good with

182

her. And she has probably exaggerated. It will be better if I don't try to get in touch with her immediately. She will accept my absence much more easily as a *fait accompli*.'

'Are you off abroad on this jaunt?'

'No, no. But I have to go north tomorrow. With any luck, I shall be back again in a month. Try to console her with that, be a dear.'

'Yes, all right. Your uncle always used to say you didn't manage these things well. You'll be too early for grouse. I don't know about trout. Your uncle used to trout fish all the year – but I sometimes thought this was an excuse for getting away.'

Angus was not entirely cowardly in his motives. This mission was one in which he dared not fail. He was not so positive in his thoughts as to imagine any act of his could redeem the past; but to turn aside would have been yet another rejection of Katia. The business of his father's injuries, and the effect on his mother, could be dealt with on his return – if he returned.

The rain had stopped, but clouds were brimful of further grief. The smell of rotting vegetation was as strong as if all the stale cabbages in the world had been dumped here and boiled. Bodies must not suffer a similar fate. The funeral pyre was lit and soon, in the camp below, men could see the smoke rising.

The body, lying stiff on the bamboo stretcher, a rice sack over head and shoulders, was lifted and placed on the pyre. The bugler sounded the Last Post. Here, by the pyre, as in the camp below, men stood silent for a few moments.

When it was over, another wooden cross was driven into the yielding mud. Ben laid his wreath. Between the tall grasses and fallen leaves which bound it together, he had twisted a few yellow lilies and blue-trumpeted convolvulus.

In a few weeks, the monsoon rains would be over. The best time of the year lay ahead. 'Why couldn't he have held out?' he said to the MO as they walked back to the camp in the rear of the funeral party.

The MO said, 'He made a good end.'

'I can't believe it, you know.' Ben looked at the MO as though the fact of Geoffrey's death was something that had been thrust upon him against his better judgement. 'It doesn't seem at all credible to me.' He stopped, overcome with weakness and emotion, and the MO waited quietly beside him while he recovered himself.

In the days following his mother's death, Ben had walked about the house, looking in rooms as a person might who is engaged in a treasure hunt. But there were no clues. Apart from its cleanliness and order, her personality had not expressed itself in her home; it had remained her secret and she had taken it with her. They had loved each other, but had found no way of expressing that love; and they had lived too close to know each other very well. It would hardly be true to say that he had missed her. She had left a blank in his life, disturbing as a half-completed sentence which poses a question that will never be resolved.

His mother died a comparatively young woman; he might have expected years of her company. But he had seemed to accept her death stoically. Geoffrey had died of cholera in a camp where seventy-three men had perished in the epidemic. Yet Ben, who had helped to nurse him at some risk to himself, was totally unprepared for his death. 'We were going on a walking holiday when we got out of here,' he told the MO, as though their conjunction with Offa's Dyke was fixed and immutable as stars in the firmament. And, since his friendship with Geoffrey had become his universe, so it had seemed.

The MO put his hand on Ben's shoulder and guided him forward. 'He was a good man.'

'He was a damn fool! If he had looked after himself he would be alive now.' He felt Geoffrey's death as a desertion.

When he got back to the camp, Ben saw that Tandy had been through Geoffrey's few possessions. There was nothing there of value to Tandy, but he had come across the drawings. 'You'd best get rid of these,' he advised Ben. 'Or you'll be in trouble, with some of the choice things you've written about the Nips.'

'Then I'll be in trouble.'

Tandy shrugged. 'All right. I shan't give you away.' This was probably true, since there would be nothing to gain by betrayal and Tandy was not vindictive. 'Just so long as, if they're found, you take the blame, see?'

'I'll take the blame.'

The bedding was soaked by the rain which had fallen during the day, but the drawings, wrapped in part of an old gas cape, were still dry. Ben resolved that they were going out of the jungle with him, or they were going to be buried with him. He wrapped them up more securely, knowing it would be some time before he could bear to look at them again.

That night he read the Old Testament. Reading material was limited, but there were other possibilities open to him – such as Agatha Christie or the New Testament. He sat in the ring formed round the fire. While the fire flamed brightly he was able to read –

familiarity with the text seemed to enlarge the print. The men on either side of him had formed a debating group and took their discussions seriously. The future of parliamentary democracy was in question tonight. Somewhere beyond the circle of fire a Scots soldier with a good, strong voice was singing 'Bonnie Mary of Argyle'.

The Old Testament had a special appeal for Ben. It abounded in people who did dreadful deeds and yet were not necessarily rejected by their fellows, or, it seemed, utterly damned by God. The great David sent a man to his death so that he might have his wife. Much such a man would have thought of stealing his neighbour's rations! David had been caught out, of course. The prophet had drawn a picture of a man he had not recognized, and then had come the denunciation, 'You are that man.' But David was also the man who had loved Jonathan.

The flames were sinking by the time Ben closed the Bible. Men were drifting away, though a few zealots remained to argue the case for a socialist state. Across the river, an Australian emergency party had been called out. No doubt in protest, they were singing as they went, 'They'll be dropping thousand pounders, when they come . . .' A few voices on this side of the river sympathetically took up the refrain. Ben wondered if the Japs thought it was some kind of Anglo-Saxon hymn to the night.

As he lay on his sodden bedding, he thought about what was to become of him. In his present state of shock and bewilderment, the choice seemed to lie starkly between life and death. He thought of Tandy as representing life and the MO death.

Sometimes the MO came out with one of the work parties and returned to complain about conditions. He seemed to have decided against life, so the mechanics of survival played little part in his behaviour. He made gestures others feared to make and he got away with it. Even the Japanese respected him. When Ben first met him, he had dismissed this man's unfailing courtesy as 'easy enough if you are a product of the public school system'. He had waited for the façade to crumble; but it seemed the façade was the man.

On one of the first comparatively cool days in December they were passing lumps of rock down a long human chain. Owing to some human frailty further up the chain, the supply broke down for a few blessed minutes. The clouds were high now, like sky palaces, forming and reforming.

'You know,' the MO said, and stopped. It was a habit of his which Ben found excessively irritating. The MO looked around him at the riot of wild flowers which, even at the onset of winter, carpeted the jungle, before he went on, 'This is the place where the whole of my life's work was meant to culminate.' He could never let such a pretentious statement stand without qualifying it; and immediately, talking fast and apologetically, he continued, 'Such as it is, of course . . . my work, I mean. I would never have made a good GP. I'm hopeless at diagnosis. Here, it's easier – if it's not cholera, it's malaria, or one of the dysenteries, or pneumonia . . .'

Ben interrupted what threatened to be a lengthy catalogue of tropical diseases, 'And if you make a mistake, your patient won't report you to the BMA.'

The Japanese guard lashed Ben across the shoulders with his stick and screamed, 'Speedo! Speedo!' It was the fact of there being nothing to speedo about which was fraying his nerves. Later, they discovered that an overhanging boulder had been dislodged, cutting a swathe through prisoners, one of whom was killed, and injuring a Japanese guard. As a result of this delay, they had to stay out longer than usual and it was late in the evening when the party made its weary way back to camp.

This long day's work had taken its toll of Ben, who had not been well since Geoffrey's death. On the way back he felt dizzy. He had pains in his back and legs and could hardly stand up straight. The MO made him stop and rest. Ben wondered whether the cooks would keep food for him; he did not care much.

'So, you've decided to die in this place,' he said, feeling within himself the sickness which might dissipate his own will to live. 'Is that what you are telling me?'

The MO had been a plump, florid man; he had lost a third of his weight, but still looked well set-up in comparison with most of the men. Ben's remark shocked him.

'No! I haven't decided anything. It is simply that when I came here, I recognized the place at once. Not externally – I have never imagined anything like this. I'm not an imaginative man. It was inside myself – an interior condition that was waiting for me. Do you understand?'

'No.' Ben got up. His head didn't like the movement involved; it hammered an angry protest to his legs, which promptly buckled.

'I don't understand myself when I speak about it,' the MO said, as he supported Ben down the track. 'I'm not particularly articulate.' Ben did not think anyone should be allowed to be as humble as this. 'Action,' the MO said, 'is all that I have ever really understood.'

'You have nothing to offer but blood, toil, tears and sweat?' Ben asked sardonically.

'I don't know that I would put it like that.' He sounded offended. Ben was sure that if he had had the energy to raise his head, he would have seen the frown, and the perplexed look in the pale blue eyes. The man hadn't Tandy's sense of humour; but he suspected he was being mocked.

Ben was glad enough of his support on the way down. The MO took him to the hospital and gave him quinine tablets. 'If you're no better in the morning, you must report here.' He also offered some of his own food. His orderly hovered in the background, prepared to make a meal of Ben if he accepted. He need not have worried. Ben could not face food. Even so, the man followed him outside to tell him that the MO and his fellow doctors would be up most of the night because there had been a bad accident when a temporary bridge collapsed.

'The silly sod shouldn't have come out with us,' Ben snapped.

'He has to, then.' The man primped up his little rosebud mouth. In civilian life he had been a dresser, and his attitude to the MO was much the same as to the great actors with whom he claimed to have worked. 'How can he know the conditions you work under if he doesn't see for himself?'

'Why doesn't he get Colonel bleeding Brown to move his fat arse off his office stool? He's the camp CO.'

'Do be realistic, dear!'

Back in the tent, Ben's sick mind went over and over the conversation they had had on their way back. Amid all the verbiage the MO had talked, there had been something which made sense of a sort.

'I am my acts.' It was a concept Ben had no difficulty in understanding. The problem came with the acts themselves – in the case of the MO, the tireless giving of time and strength, the sharing of food, the patient care of the sick, even those who abused him and tried to trick him. Still, he was in a special position, wasn't he? Ben sat up in bed and said to the man next to him, 'It *is* his profession, after all.'

'What profession, chum?'

'Any profession. It's all the same thing.'

'If you say so.'

Men in the act of their profession – that was it! The great violinist, with nothing on his mind but the music; the surgeon operating; counsel pleading; the farmer delivering a calf; all the energy and intellectual drive poured into the one performance. Was *that* what was happening with the MO? Only, with him, it went further because he was sustaining the performance. It was not a case of a man trying to be good, but of a man living totally in his acts, draining everything out of himself so that there was no 'afterwards', no time for sloth, envy, greed, covetousness ... All forgone, not out of prudish choice, but because the man had become the act and *there is nothing of him left over*.

The man next to Ben said, 'Take it easy, soldier.'

'But he's not even an interesting man, not amusing or particularly intelligent.'

How is it done? Let go of yourself, is that it? Ben's mind zoomed obligingly so that he had the sensation he was floating somewhere up above the tent. Decide against self-preservation. But that was offensive. The MO is offensive. With Tandy, one may feel a superiority in oneself; his lack of dignity increases one's own. But goodness is abrasive, implacable; it leaves other people very little room in which to manoeuvre. It was surprising, when you came to think of it, that Christ found as many as twelve men who were willing to follow him and that only one betrayed him. He must have been more than just good. He must have had some of Tandy's artistry, even his effrontery? Or are we back with the man being his acts again?

He was climbing higher and higher, up stairs in a narrow old house, so rickety you wouldn't have thought it could have borne so many stairs. And now here he was in a room with a dizzying view over roof tops with pointed spires thrusting between them, and all far, far below. He was up in a brilliant blue sky. It was too high for him. The whole edifice was shaking; better get down before the gimcrack house collapsed. It should never have been built so high.

'Here!' The man next to Ben had produced a dish containing a concoction of rice and limes which had been devised by the cook in a rare moment of inspiration. 'I saved this for you.' It was not true, of course; he had taken it for himself, only to be moved by Ben's plight. Ben could not get the food down, but afterwards he remembered with surprise the generosity of this man; a man to whom he had hitherto paid little attention, not an intelligent man.

The next day he went into hospital. As his temperature came down, he began to sort out his thoughts. These two men, Tandy and the MO, were the poles between which some delicate balance must be maintained.

Other men, such as Geoffrey, seemed instinctively to keep that balance: men who sometimes got out of doing a duty, who grumbled and cried with pain; but who did not cheat their comrades, or seek special favours; who could give comfort to those worse off than themselves; who kept some compassion, a little cheer, and who, when their time came, made a good end.

He could not add to the drawings, but he decided that from now on he would keep a diary.

II

Autumn 1943–May 1944

Guy had thought of the landings in Italy as being a joyful event. The Italians had recently surrendered and he saw himself as a liberator, which roused everything in him that was chivalrous. He envisaged (even as he advised his men against such expectations) a warm welcome. The Italians would take the Allies to their hearts. It was the high point of his Army life, its meaning made clear. Evil was vanquished and he had played his modest part.

A warm welcome had indeed awaited those who landed at Salerno. The Germans had mown men down on the beaches, and the attitude of the Italians to the Allies was no different from that of any other people who find that their land has become a battlefield. Reinforcements were urgently needed, and as the Eighth Army advanced up the toe of Italy with desperate speed, it became apparent even to Guy that all was not well.

He had never been conscious during his long war service – at Dunkirk and in the desert – of any strain involved in keeping his illusions intact. He had also remained remarkably fit. Yet now, engaged in this grim race, he felt he had been struggling for too long.

He was back in Europe and closer in spirit to England than he had been for several years. Yet he was uneasy. It was as though he carried within him a precious potion which must be delivered safe at home without one drop being spilt; and only now, in the manner of all good fables, did the tension begin to tell, his feet to stumble.

It was partly the fact of the countryside being so at odds with the war that undermined him. Whenever they rested, it was as if the clockwork machinery of army life had run down. When they set off again, it became more and more difficult to get back into the military rhythm. He did not want to go on. He was seized with the most dreadful lethargy and found it difficult to think clearly. He wondered whether he had sleeping sickness (about which he knew very little) and almost hoped it might be so.

He was so tired, that was the trouble. He was so terribly tired. He had seen dreadful things happen to men in the desert; perhaps this had sapped some vital energy from him without his being aware of it. Yet, at the time, the desert had seemed to have healing properties. Beneath that wide, stupendous sky, he had been freed from some unacknowledged constraint which had always held him prisoner.

Things were different here. The countryside exercised a fascination for him. It was a landscape of passionate contrasts: strong light and deep shade; richness of colour, harshness of contour; poverty of soil, yet people deeply rooted in the land, the precariousness of their existence seeming to have called forth a tradition of great strength. It was a place which knew nothing of the compromises which had turned Guy into the quiet, moderate man he was. Sometimes, in his bewilderment, he wondered what it was he had moderated. Here, he felt irrelevant − not in the manner of a stranger, but as a human being.

The people watched the troops going through their countryside without a great deal of interest, then turned back to their work in the fields as though the war was an aberration already forgotten. At times, Guy wished he had spent the war there, where they worked in the fields. He wished he had deserted, all that time ago in France, and worked his way to some such place as this. It was a very poor life, he could see that; but it had a continuity. He was a townsman, had not put down roots anywhere, had no sense of family stretching beyond mother and father. He had no strong feeling of attachment to Holland Park or Shepherd's Bush, or even London. His childhood had been centred in the small suburban house of his parents; his adult life was centred in Louise and the children. Suddenly, it did not seem enough. There was nothing strong enough to protect him from this terrible weariness. It was not just the war which was called in question: the framework of his life had been too small. Daily, terrifyingly, the feeling of his own irrelevance grew upon him.

Daphne Drummond married Peter Kelleher at the end of October. It was just over a year since their first meeting, and they had been lovers for most of that time. Louise was surprised they should decide to marry. Daphne had seemed unconcerned about marriage. It was Kelleher, apparently, who had strong feelings on the subject. Ivor said that he liked to have his possessions registered in his own name. Ivor could be sharp, even malicious. Not a reliable friend, perhaps. But whatever Kelleher's feelings, he had not reckoned with the fact that Daphne would be inconsistent enough to insist that, if she was to be married, then she would not line up in a registry office alongside the pregnant girls in a hurry to make sure of their GIs. Kelleher had loved her courage and been attracted by her boldness, but in his heart he preferred a woman to be submissive. Daphne, who was sure that in him she had found the only man she would ever love, took care to meet his demands on every aspect of the ceremony, other than its venue. There were three witnesses in the church: Mrs Drummond, Ivor as best man, and Louise as matron of honour, in Alice's stead. Daphne was loyal to her friends. As he looked at Louise, standing beside Daphne, Peter Kelleher wondered about the absent Alice. He hoped she would not intrude in any way into his life with Daphne. Perhaps the debt to friendship might be honoured if they took her out to dinner once when she returned to England?

Daphne wore a close-fitting sheath in buttercup yellow and a wide-brimmed navy hat and navy gloves. The outfit seemed tailor-made for the occasion, although in fact a counterpane had provided the dress, while hat and gloves had been retrieved from an old clothes trunk and dyed.

Louise, her resources already exhausted in providing for the children, wore the navy linen which had proved so serviceable over the years. It now fitted her well as she had lost weight. In the restaurant in Shepherd's Market where they had lunch, Mrs Drummond said to her, 'You're thinner, surely, Louise?'

Ivor's eyes flashed from the speaker to Louise. She felt herself blushing as she replied, 'I walk a lot.'

'As long as you eat enough.'

Mrs Drummond, Louise noticed, was eating well. Louise was surprised by the change in the woman, whom she had recalled as a genteel, faded lady, always ill. She still looked genteel in a flimsy dress with a rose buttoned at the breast, her face shaded by a gauzy concoction which must have spent long years in a hat box. Ill, she most certainly was not. Her skin, though still pale, had a glow as though blood was beginning to flow again; the brightness in her eyes as she talked about her husband betokened alertness, not hysteria. 'We did try to persuade Jumbo to come. He is paralysed from the waist down – you knew that, of course? I am sure we could have managed to get the wheel chair here – or we could have had the reception at home. But he wouldn't even discuss it.'

'It must be terrible for him,' Louise said, shocked.

'And for you.' Ivor's interjection was not entirely tactful; he was watching Mrs Drummond with interest.

'Yes, indeed.' She acknowledged his sympathy complacently, as she slid the fish knife expertly beneath the bone, levering it up gently so that little of the flesh would be wasted. 'He was always so active. I am afraid he does find it difficult to be completely dependent on other people.'

'You must have found it hard to leave him behind today.'

Louise looked uneasily at Ivor. He was not always a comfortable person to be with on social occasions. His mind was too quick for his own good and his tongue too ready. He saw other people with clarity unsoftened by charity.

Fortunately, Mrs Drummond appeared in no need of charity. She said, 'Cecily is with him. She can manage for an hour or so. But most of the time, I have to be there, of course. There are some things he would not want anyone else to do for him.' She sipped wine delicately and looked about her with interest. It might have been she who was recovering from a disabling illness. She gave the impression that all experience – food, drink, the fashionable restaurant and its clientèle – breathed new life into her.

Daphne was angry. The tensions of the Drummond household were inescapable, even at the wedding feast. Louise heard Peter say to her, 'Well, *you* wanted this, my dear.'

But, if he could not resist making his point, he did then proceed to redeem the situation effectively. Although he was not by nature a talker, when the need arose he could be entertaining. 'I believe your husband is in Italy?' he said to Louise. 'If so, I envy him.' He had once walked from the toe of Italy to Tuscany. The circumstances had been different from those in which Guy now found himself. Kelleher had been alone and had lived rough. He seemed to have a natural affinity with more primitive peoples and spoke of them with respect untinged by sentimentality or condescension. There was a coldness about him which repelled Louise; but nevertheless, listening to him, she could understand that Daphne might find him attractive. Kelleher had little to say about Rome and Florence. Culture meant nothing to him; the more a particular civilization overlaid the landscape, the less he cared for it. Something harsh and rocky, fierce but not barren, emerged from his talk, and Louise involuntarily wondered how Guy was faring.

While coffee was being negotiated, Mrs Drummond whispered to Louise, 'Do tell me, what do you make of this man of Daphne's?'

'I hardly know him.'

'He isn't a man who wants to be known.' Mrs Drummond took the point at once. 'Oh well, I don't suppose we shall see much of them in future.'

After what passed for coffee, she said, 'I must be getting home to

Jumbo. He can't be left for too long.' She explained this as though she was speaking of a child. Daphne looked at her with stony hatred.

'Your mother seems to be taking things very well,' Louise said to Daphne when they were in the cloakroom together.

'She is relishing every minute of it.'

Louise had always thought that Alice exaggerated the situation in the Drummond household. She now saw that this was not so.

'You'll be glad to get away from home,' she said.

Daphne looked at herself in the mirror. 'I am the happiest woman in the world,' she said, in a tone of surprise.

Louise felt weak with jealousy.

It was late afternoon when they left the restaurant. Louise and Ivor walked together through Green Park into St James's Park. Ivor said, 'Peter has done better than me!'

Louise answered sharply, 'The bomb knocked you on top of the wrong girl!'

He took her hand. 'Never think that! Whatever happens, you mustn't think that.' The intensity of his feeling brought tears to her eyes.

Guy's slow, charming incomprehension had touched her; she had been moved by his way of looking at her as if she was a revelation to him. Ivor pounced. He was in among her thoughts before she herself had formulated them. And not only her thoughts. Now, hand in hand, a longing was transmitted between them which could never have found adequate expression in words.

'It's not that I don't love you,' she said. 'It's because . . .'

'You are the last person I would have expected . . .' He broke off, exasperated.

'Did you expect an easy lay?'

'I didn't have it in mind to wait over a year!'

They walked, holding on to each other, unaware of the people around them, imagining their passion to be something generated by themselves. It was much more than that. They were in the grip of a force as strong as that which Louise's grandfather, Joseph Tippet, had seen blow suddenly out of a calm sea. And nothing to be done about it, save heave to, until it had abated its fury.

'It's been agony for me, Ivor.'

'Then why – in Heaven's name, *why*!'

It was agony because she knew that once she gave herself to him there would be no going back to Guy. Had it been Jacov, she could have maintained her belief that Guy could not be harmed by sexual infidelity. She would never love Jacov as she had loved Guy. But it would be different with Ivor. Even now, her whole being seemed to be involved with him. No part of her mind wandered idly, wondering were the children all right, had she remembered to hide the precious tin of syrup; no single part of her body drew attention to itself with some small irritation. She was consumed by him. Yet, were she to cry out, he would respond by drawing still more from her. Guy had left a residue of passion in her, unexplored, growing in mischief. Ivor would ask more than she had ever expected to be demanded of her.

It was a crisp, cold day; there would be frost tonight. Already a bluish film was forming on the dead leaves. When he spoke, she could see his breath. 'Now,' he said.

'Give me time.'

'I don't think I've been niggardly of time.'

'You've been away a lot.' Her resentment burned, thinking how long Guy, too, had been away. 'It's all right for you men – you go away and enjoy playing at being soldiers . . .'

'I don't enjoy one single moment when I'm not with you.'

'Not *one* moment! Ivor Ritchie, you're not the man I think you are if that's true!'

He laughed, as if she had won her point; although in fact it was nearer the truth than he cared to admit.

He stood warming her hand in his as they halted on the bridge looking towards the Admiralty. The water had been drained from the lake and the islands harboured no birds now. The late afternoon light was pale and cold. The sun was furred in the mist. He felt unsure of her because he sensed that reason would play little part in her judgement of a situation; she would make up her mind in an instant, and then nothing would change her purpose. It seemed to him a matter of chance which way the decision would go. She was wilful and highly unpredictable, passionate, yet on occasions capable of a surprisingly puritanical severity. He felt helpless.

Later, as they turned back towards the dimly lighted streets, he said, 'I've brought presents for the children.'

'I don't want you to give them presents.'

'Why ever not?'

'Because Guy isn't here to give them presents.'

He flinched and his face went white as salt. If she had hurt Guy like this, she would not have known; he would have crept away, holding it to himself. But now she felt Ivor's pain as she had felt it lying in the wreckage. Only this time, she was responsible. They were on danger-ous ground here.

'I *have* to be fair to Guy,' she whispered.

He said stiffly, 'I'm sorry. I should have thought of that.'

If he had pressed his advantage, he might well have won her; but because he was so unsure of her, he played safe. They walked slowly to the underground station, more in love than ever, and less able to make sense of their feelings.

At home, when she had put the children to bed and was doing the ironing, Louise tried to think of Guy and not of Ivor. But his voice did not reach out to her across the distance which separated them.

Years in the suffocating house in Shepherd's Bush had given Guy an air of quiet placidity. His strongest feelings lay in the deep well of his being, scarcely ever stirred by visitations from the daylight region in which most of his life was passed. On the rare occasions when he remembered a disturbing dream, he recounted it with distaste as though it emanated from someone other than himself. Even Louise was deceived into thinking him more phlegmatic than most people.

Ivor was prepared to live far more dangerously. She was in no doubt of that. He would not go out of the room whenever tempers became frayed, returning when he hoped the emotional temperature had dropped. Had she married Ivor, her children would have had a turbulent atmosphere in which to grow up. She did not take this further, wondering how much it would have hurt them, asking how sheltered children should be. The children were Guy's. She must not involve them in her love for Ivor.

Later, she prayed, first for Guy and the children; and then for herself and Ivor. She believed implicitly that God was on her side. It would be blasphemy to imagine that what she so clearly perceived, He could not. She did not, however, try to manipulate Him. Where she had doubts (about her own affairs, her doubts were never theological) she allowed that it might be He who had sown the seed.

She had loved Guy, and she had made her vows before God. Her God tended to be the God of the Old Testament, who looked upon men who sometimes did wicked things with a forbearing eye. This God, however, was also the Covenant God, who, having made His covenant with His people expected them to keep to its terms. Louise had promised to care for Guy in sickness and in health, for better or for worse. And this, at the time, she had intended to do. She had foreseen his sickness, perhaps even that he might turn out badly, and had known she must abide by him. What she had not foreseen was that she might cease to love him, might one day love another. This, surely, was a different matter altogether? Another love allowed a fresh start. Love, after all, could not be forced, cultivated, learnt. Once it ceased – it ceased.

Unfortunately, she heard at this moment, not the voice of God, but of Granny Tippet, saying to her as they stood in the kitchen at Falmouth, 'You won't always think he's wonderful. That will be the time to talk about loving him.'

Granny Tippet. Married all those years to a sailor in the Merchant Navy, who seldom set foot on land save to beget children, and then was off again – leaving her with seven children to rear on her own. No time for discontented whining about 'what might have been', only time for making the best of what was. How well she compared with Grandmother Fairley, who had had a much easier life and now spent her time bemoaning the past and looking forward to being taken into glory. Louise had always been proud to come of Granny Tippet's stock.

Grandmother Fairley had another severe stroke and died early in December. The funeral service was held at the Methodist Chapel in Holland Park which she had attended during the long years of waiting to be taken into Glory. There was a good congregation, more in honour of Aunt May and Louise than of the old lady, who had made few friends.

Neither Judith nor Louise had ever liked Grandmother Fairley. They were both honest women who found it hard to dissimulate. The occasion was made more difficult for them by the fact that Guy's parents, who also attended the chapel, must be included among the mourners. It seemed to Judith that all the good things of family life were gone, while its defects remained.

Fortunately, at the last minute, the party was augmented by Judith's youngest brother, Silas, who was on embarkation leave in London; and by Claire and a boy friend who had hitch-hiked from Oxford. Claire cried sufficiently to make up for any lack of tears on the part of other members of the family. She had not been close to her grandmother, but was reminded of her father's funeral. Alice, who alone had had an affection for the old woman, was on her way home; and, unaware of her death, was even now writing a letter to her grandmother.

The minister had called on Grandmother Fairley as a matter of duty; but she had never accepted him because he was a pacifist. It had grieved her that he should set foot in the house – 'all smiles and pleased with himself' – while Alice and Louise's husband were away fighting for their country. Aware of her dislike, and its cause, he made a rather faltering business of his address.

While he spoke, Aunt May wondered desperately what was to

become of her now that her mother and Stanley were both dead. Judith and Louise stared at their clasped hands and Silas at his cap badge. Mr and Mrs Immingham gazed at the minister with the appropriate expression of muted grief which those least concerned are readily able to assume.

The most notable of the mourners was definitely Claire's young man, who patently had no idea how to behave in chapel, let alone at a funeral. He was in turns embarrassed, alarmed by Death, affronted by the idea of God, and deeply anxious to please Claire. This complex of conflicting emotions produced in him an uneasiness so profound as to divert the attention of his nearest neighbours from what was due to Grandmother Fairley. He wore huge horn-rimmed glasses which constantly signalled a peak of distress by misting up. He would then take them off and polish them with all the desperate application of a Lady Macbeth before replacing them. His face, the while, was so white and moist that Louise thought he would be sick.

It was only on leaving the chapel that they became aware of the ultimate misfortune. Meg had felt she must attend her mother's funeral, while dissociating herself from Judith and her children. She had, therefore, arrived late and had sat in the front row of the gallery, where her presence was conspicuous. On leaving the chapel, she refused to speak to Judith, but remained on the pavement talking to a distracted Aunt May and delaying the departure to the cemetery – thus giving cause for much speculation to members of the congregation.

'At least she has asked me to go and stay with them,' Aunt May said tearfully when she joined Judith and Louise in the first car.

'I shouldn't if I were you,' Judith said. 'It's a very uncomfortable house. Why don't you go down to my mother in Falmouth? She would make a great fuss of you and you would enjoy seeing all the grandchildren.' As she said this, she realized that she, too, would gain much from this. Her joy in Silas's unexpected arrival was a reminder that she had cut herself off for too long from her own roots. It was arranged between them that she and May would go to Falmouth together.

In the other car, Claire was saying to her young man, 'That's the aunt I was telling you about – the one who was so beastly to me.' He put a protective arm around her shoulders. Mrs Immingham savoured the incident with Meg as yet another indication that the Fairleys were a bad family. Indeed, more than that, that family ramifications were themselves bad.

After the burial service, they returned to Louise's house. This had been the home of Grandmother Fairley for most of her life since the death of her husband. Mrs Immingham said to Louise, 'You must often think of her sitting here.'

'She didn't sit here,' Louise said. 'She had the rooms upstairs as her sitting-room and dining-room.'

The neighbour who had been looking after the children delivered her charges, whose advent Mrs Immingham greeted with, 'Here come the little darlings!' This phrase had delighted them as toddlers and she expected it to serve until puberty changed them irremediably. Mr Immingham's face glowed with a quieter pleasure. But the children were concerned only with Silas, whom they greeted rapturously. The Cornish side of the family was particularly important to them, since it provided so many holiday playmates of their own age — to say nothing of notably tolerant elders.

'He must be nearly twenty years younger than Judith,' Mrs Immingham whispered to her husband.

'She *was* one of seven.'

Mrs Immingham flushed, disturbed by these living proofs of the grossness of Granny Tippet's life. Both she and her husband were only children, although he had had a sister who was still-born.

Claire was introducing her young man, whom she regarded as a rival — and superior — attraction to Silas. His name was Terence Straker. The purpose of her visit had been to draw him into the family. Now, he had attended the funeral, and as a result of this gesture of solidarity must henceforth be accepted as one of them. She spoke of him as a person long known to them; and she told the children he was Uncle Terence, as though reminding them of a much-loved figure in their past. Louise thought he was an awful weed, which was sad, as Claire wanted very much to impress her elder sister. Alice was the beloved companion, but Louise was the high-priestess of physical love.

In spite of inevitable talk of the war and news of relatives who were fighting, this was essentially a family gathering. The presence of her brother, little though she had known him as a child, gave Judith a feeling of continuity, a wider sense of her own place in the pattern. The relationship between brother and sister was far less painful than other familial bonds. She had dreaded this reunion in the house of which Louise was mistress, but, buttressed by Silas, now found herself able to appreciate a place where she was honoured and had little responsibility.

'Are all your people Methodists?' Terence asked Claire, while the rest of the family was talking about Charlie's boys, and Mrs Immingham was trying to attract her husband's attention so that they could leave.

'The whole clan.'

'What do they imagine has happened to your grandmother?' He had been deeply shocked by the burial service.

'*Grandma* thinks she has gone to Glory.' Claire was deliberately flippant.

He pleated his lips.

'I know it's all nonsense,' she said. 'But we can't go into that today.' Her manner was at once propitiating and domineering; he was to understand that she respected his superior intellect, but did not expect him to give it an airing today.

He blinked, wriggling his heavy glasses on the bridge of his nose. He was extremely uneasy when unable to control her thoughts; but he comforted himself with the promise of the long trip back to Oxford, during which time he would expound the religious fallacy. Meanwhile, he sat silent, having little gift for light conversation. He would like to have played with the children, but Silas monopolized their attention. The children apart, he did not much care for Claire's relatives. Had they shared his views, it would have made little difference. These people had known Claire long before he discovered her; he felt threatened by them.

In order to escape from this uncongenial atmosphere he offered to help when Louise collected the tea things together. She accepted because she thought this would give her mother an opportunity to talk to Claire without this glowering young man intervening.

'What are you studying, or reading, or whatever you call it?' she asked cheerfully, when he was installed at the sink.

'Economics.'

'Goodness, isn't that frightfully dull?'

'I would hardly be doing it if I thought it was dull.' His glasses misted up with the steam from the water and he took them off; he looked young and rather helpless without them.

Louise said kindly, 'No, of course not. That was silly of me. I expect it's the sort of thing that appeals to a man's mind.' In spite of her good intentions, she made it sound a masculine silliness, akin to playing with trains.

'It explains a great deal which is wrong with society today,' he said.

Louise picked up a plate and wiped it. 'Are you from London?'

'Isleworth,' he said bleakly, as though admitting a failure.

'I had a drink at the *London Apprentice* last week . . . with a friend.'

He peered into a milk jug. 'Does this mark come off?'

Later, when they were alone, Judith said to Louise, 'Do you think Claire is serious about this young man?'

'I don't see who could take him seriously, other than himself.'

Alice arrived in England in January.

When she was packing in Alexandria, she had looked forward with longing to coming home; but with every stage of the journey, the prospect grew less attractive. Colourful remembrances changed imperceptibly into monochrome reality as the ship pursued its slow course. Almost unlimited opportunities had seemed to lie ahead of her when she went abroad; nothing, she had felt, would ever be the same again. Yet here she was returning, the same Alice Fairley, a couple of years older, having shed a few illusions and two stone, and with little else to show for her experiences. She felt a sense of failure. A friend had given her a copy of the banned *Lady Chatterley's Lover*. When her fellow Wrens talked of sex, they made it seem trivial. Lawrence was a great awakening, lifting the subject to the realm of the sublime. As she read, Alice's sense of personal failure increased.

On her arrival, she learnt that her mother was staying in Falmouth. She had looked forward to a family reunion in London, and had already made plans to see Irene and Jacov. Jacov was acting in a play at the Q Theatre, and had promised to take her backstage. It was important to do interesting things, and see as many people as possible during her leave. Otherwise depression would be total. Although she was welcome to join her mother in Falmouth, she decided to stay with Louise in London.

January was the worst possible month in which to return. England was grey and chilly. Louise's house was not warm and Alice soon developed a streaming cold. For the first time, she realized how much the civilian population had to put up with. When she offered to do the shopping on the first day of her stay, she had anticipated getting it over with quickly, and then finding a congenial café in which to have coffee and take stock of London life. She spent most of the morning queueing and had little to show for it by the time she returned. There was a letter from Daphne waiting for her. Daphne was in Scotland. When she returned she would look Alice up 'wherever you are, and we will talk and talk!'

Meantime, Alice talked and talked about Egypt. Wherever Louise took her, she made invidious comparisons. For two days, Louise was forbearing. On the third, she announced at breakfast, 'And I don't want to hear *that place* mentioned once during the next twenty-four hours!'

Irene was more patient. She had a first-class degree and was now working at the War Ministry. Alice nevertheless assumed her own experiences to be of greater interest. How could events at London University possibly compare with the wonders of Alexandria, Cairo, Suez, and an unhappy love affair? Irene listened; but she did not enter into Alice's adventures as once she would have done. Alice felt that something had happened to Irene's mind. She seemed more objective and analytical, examining thoughtfully statements which were not intended to bear the weight of scrutiny. She had accumulated a company of unseen academic witnesses on whom she could call to endorse her statements. Alice was not interested in what the great brains of London University – or indeed what Heidegger or Kant – had said, but only in what Irene herself thought. Alice let her own thoughts fly out indiscriminately. It seemed to her that no sooner had she embarked on an interesting subject than Irene put out a foot to trip her. True, she could sometimes hear herself speaking nonsense; but, in friendly conversation, this did not seem to her to matter. It was a way of venturing. Later, alone, she might examine more seriously what had been said and get it into some kind of order. Irene seemed intent on preserving order from the outset. The result was that Alice felt herself ill-considered and uncontrolled; while Irene was aware that, without meaning to do so, she was constantly dampening Alice's enthusiasm. They were both disappointed in the reunion, having expected too much from it. In their times of loneliness and unhappiness, each had longed for the one friend who could really understand their feelings. Now, it proved impossible to broach the matters nearest to their hearts. But their friendship had deep roots and neither one of them allowed herself to consider the possibility that it would dwindle. Irene thought that Alice would be less excitable and irrational once she settled down; and Alice thought that Irene would be able to let herself go more when they saw each other frequently.

They went together to see Jacov at the little theatre by Kew Bridge. This was their most successful outing, as they both thought the play pretentious and Jacov unsuited to his part. When they met him afterwards, it was Irene who was most prepared to compromise her opinions.

'Well, I do congratulate you!' she said. 'It would have been tedious without that great extrovert performance! You kept the whole thing alive.'

His performance had certainly been wilfully extrovert. They had a drink at the *Star and Garter*. Irene and Jacov talked about the theatre. She was well-informed and able to express her views concisely and wittily. He was scurrilously amusing. Alice looked out of the window. The river was at its lowest ebb, dun-coloured water petering into mud.

On the last day of her leave, she hitch-hiked to Oxford to see Claire. In a chill wind, they walked in seemingly endless quadrangles while Claire pointed out architectural features. It seemed to have escaped her notice that Alice had been abroad.

At lunch in a British Restaurant, Aiice was introduced to an owlish young man who was as unimpressed by her as she by him. While she was with them, Alice began to realize that there was more than absent-mindedness involved in their dismissal of her service abroad. Her presence in uniform was an affront to their susceptibilities.

'How long have you been a pacifist?' she asked Claire.

'As long as I can remember. Certainly, as long as I was mature enough to think clearly.'

In spite of this, when they were alone in the cloakroom of the restaurant, Claire said to Alice, 'Daddy would be proud of you being recommended for a commission.'

'He'd be proud of you, too, at Oxford.'

They hugged each other before returning rather shamefacedly to the boy friend, who gave every indication of resenting even this brief separation from Claire.

It was a relief to report to Plymouth, where she was to do her preliminary signals training. Alice was pleased to find herself quartered in a large Victorian house on the outskirts of the city. Here she discovered that Felicity Naismith, with whom she had shared that harrowing experience in Coventry, was on the same course. Felicity was away for the week-end, but had left a message to the effect that she was very much looking forward to seeing Alice again. This made Alice suspect that Felicity was finding life in Plymouth dull.

In the services, one was seldom alone for long. No sooner had Alice installed herself in her cabin, than one of her new companions suggested they should have supper together.

'We'll go to The Magnet,' the girl said. 'They do lemon sole, believe it or not!'

More astonishing than the lemon sole was the devastation of the centre of the town, which her companion now took for granted. The roads ran between heaps of rubble and the café was one of the few buildings left standing. Alice had never seen anything like it.

She and Felicity met on duty in the Moat, that network of communications built into the rock face. Alice was standing over a machine which was supposed to decode messages and was at present sending out Jabberwocky. Felicity came up behind her and said, as if they had last met yesterday, 'You've got the code for the day wrong. What day did you think it was, Alice?'

'Tuesday.'

'It's Wednesday. Whatever happened to Tuesday? I hope it was worth such a grave error as this.' She readjusted the coding and the machine began briskly to disgorge information of the whereabouts of ships.

This was not a busy time and the other Wrens were playing a guessing game under the indulgent eye of a PO.

Felicity said, 'They are madly dull. I'm so glad you have come.'

They picked up their friendship easily, as though no time had intervened. Alice said, 'I don't think I shall ever get my commission.'

'My dear, it's simple as can be. Otherwise they would never have put me forward for it.'

'Do you care much about it?'

'Passionately! I've been doing admin. recently. If I don't change to cypher, I'm never going to get abroad and find myself a man.'

Alice, who considered that she had matured, was amused to find Felicity still talking in this way. 'It doesn't always work – abroad and getting a man.'

'Not in your case, perhaps. You never did seem to *mind* enough. *I'm* desperate.'

'What is it about marriage that appeals to you?' Alice asked, thinking that, after all, this was not a very sexy woman.

'I've been bred for it,' Felicity said glumly. 'What would become of me if I didn't marry? I should end up teaching games at a girls' public school. You may laugh, but that actually happened to a cousin of mine.'

During the next few days they were together often, both on and off duty. Although when they first met, Alice had thought that Felicity must be attractive to men, this assumption had been based largely on Felicity's conversation. She could now see that the games mistress might well be Felicity's fate. Her scattiness was of that order. In the two years since they last met, her long face had grown more horsy. The other girls were amused by her, but half the time they were laughing at her. The men, so much talked of, seldom materialized. Alice, contrarily, found herself liking Felicity more now that she appeared less successful.

'You don't need to worry,' she consoled. 'People who are single-minded usually get what they want.'

'Not if it's in short supply, they don't. The number of men who can keep up a country house with decent stabling is diminishing. I should know. My father had to go into the professions. English country life has been declining ever since the Industrial Revolution. All I've ever been able to do is look over the hedge at the gentry. My chances of finding a man to keep me in the style to which I am unaccustomed are not good.'

'What about love?'

'That is neither here nor there. It is marriage we are talking about. I don't care about love. In fact, I don't really care all that much for men.'

Alice thought Felicity's ideas on marriage pre-dated the decline of English country life.

There were several girls whose company she preferred to Felicity's, but she was too good-natured to make this apparent. She and Felicity spent much of their off-duty time together, bored and bickering. She had looked forward to working in the Moat, about which she had heard all sorts of rumours: the work was intensive, the atmosphere so unhealthy one was not allowed to spend more than six months there, it was 'worse than the Tunnel at Rosyth'. This had created an impression of a place some way between a coal mine and Aladdin's cave. In fact, once past the rather impressive entrance in the rock face, the place had about as much mystery as a fish tank. As in most large establishments, the atmosphere was impersonal and there was more formality than she had been used to. Worst of all, there was a preponderance of women.

When she moved to the signals section, however, she found herself working as hard as she had ever done and enjoying it. At the end of a watch, she had written so many messages that her arms were dyed purple to the elbows by carbon paper. Quantities of methylated spirits – no doubt intended for some more important purpose – were used to remove the stains.

Once outside the Moat, it was all very depressing. Alice could not get over the devastation of Plymouth and Devonport. Reports of the air attacks by the Allies on the Ruhr did nothing to lift her spirits. She was home in England, but did not feel at home, and was not sure she was going to manage very well.

Judith saw Alice briefly when she and Aunt May passed through Plymouth on their return from their holiday in Falmouth. She thought Alice looked the better for being thinner and noted that she had matured during her two years abroad. Aunt May thought Alice was not well because she was 'touchy'. She was too charitable to ascribe this to anything other than ill-health.

Judith said, 'Alice is the most obstinate of my children. It will take her a long time to accept my move to Sussex.'

'But you haven't *moved*, dear. You'll be coming back when things settle down, surely? You must want to see more of your grandchildren.'

Judith bit her lip, feeling the pressure on her and determined to resist it. May's train arrived, and in the struggle to get her a seat the matter of Judith's return to London was forgotten.

Judith had an uncomfortable journey. The train was packed with service personnel, with kit bags, rifles, gas masks and other paraphernalia. She was glad she had decided to break the journey to stay with friends in Hampshire. As a result of this break, she arrived in Brighton in good fettle.

The first person she encountered was Austin Marriott. He addressed her as though they had just emerged from their ordeal in the siding. 'There is a bomb on the line. The Southern Railway is delighted to inform us that there are unlikely to be any trains to Lewes tonight.' He looked at her thoughtfully, perhaps wondering whether it was her presence which exercised such a malign influence on the Southern Railway.

'I suppose we can get a bus,' she said.

He looked at his watch. 'A meal might be a better idea, I think, don't you?'

Judith could not remember the last time a man, other than her husband, had taken her out for a meal; and Stanley had done it seldom enough. She scarcely knew what to say. He took her silence for acceptance, picked up her suitcase and limped towards the street. She hurried after him, embarrassed by the case but suspecting he would be annoyed were she to suggest he should not carry it.

'There's a little place in a side street near here that provides reasonable food,' he said as she joined him on the pavement. 'Unless you would prefer a hotel? It will be further to walk, but we might get a taxi . . .'

Judith said the little place nearby would do very nicely.

There were only a few people in the café. They had a corner table. When they were seated, he gave her a rather wry look which seemed to say, 'I suppose we have to go through this process?' Or perhaps he wasn't saying that at all? Yet, in spite of her uncertainty, she was aware of having immediately answered the look.

They drank sherry while they studied the menu. He tasted and made a face. 'This sherry is like cat's pee.'

'I'm not a judge of either, I'm afraid,' she said. 'I was brought up strictly teetotal.'

'Did you actually sign a pledge?'

'I think I pledged myself when I was young. But it's rather gone by the board since the children grew up.'

'You must forgive my interest. It's so different from my upbringing. Everything in moderation was our motto.'

'Very bland.'

He smiled at her. There was a relish in that smile which was quite unmistakable. She was glad to be sitting down, otherwise her knees might have betrayed her weakness. This was inconceivable. She was in her late forties. He turned his attention to the menu, and she drank half a glass of sherry rather quickly.

'I think the fish seems the least of all the evils, don't you? Good gracious!' He considered what he had just said. '*Am* I bland?'

'I hardly know you well enough to answer that.' She was distinctly more at ease, and beginning to savour the pleasures of being with a man again. He seemed a more sophisticated person than the usual run of her acquaintances, but she felt she could hold her own, at least during this meal. She had undoubtedly put a check on any complacency he might have about his childhood. When it came to a contest, there was nothing like a puritan upbringing to toughen the muscles. Over the fish, he began to talk about his childhood – obviously determined to make it clear that there had been a great deal more to it than moderation. She gave him a civil hearing before speaking of the rigours of life in Falmouth – 'a father always at sea, and me the eldest of seven!' It was remarkable that in so short a space of time they should seem to be in contention: now he was telling her of the harshness of his life at boarding school, waking in winter with snow on the sheets because there must always be an open window. She was finding it quite hard not to appear aggressive.

As he spoke of his university life at Durham, and explained why he had decided against an academic career (while making it clear that one would have been open to him), she studied his face. Now that she could see him in a good light, he was impressive. A big man, with a head to match, broad and strong. The face was not as forceful as one might have expected; impatient eyes counteracted a slight suggestion of self-satisfaction about the mouth. Perhaps by fifty one might be allowed some cause for satisfaction? Yet something about him made her feel that this was a man who had, perhaps temporarily, lost his impetus.

He began to speak of more personal affairs. His wife had died twelve years ago. 'I thought I shouldn't marry again until the children were old enough to leave home. I had unhappy examples of my friends who had introduced stepmothers into the home. It was bad for the children and hell for the unfortunate woman. So I had a series of housekeepers, each more determined than the last to achieve marital status. It became quite a challenge.' He allowed a pause before he said, 'But that's all over now. The children have departed. No more housekeepers.'

Judith made her contribution. 'My children have departed, too.'

If he is sensible, she thought, he will leave it at that for the moment. He was sensible. When they parted he made no suggestions for future meetings. She was pleased to have time for reflection. There was no doubt of their mutual attraction. He might be difficult, but she had had experience of a difficult man. In his favour, he was not entirely selfish. Whether his decision had been right or not, he had done what he thought best for his children at some cost to himself. When he told her about this, he had been leading up to the fact of his being free now and had not been trying to impress her. She was the more impressed. In her eyes, his lonely battles with amorous housekeepers counted for more than his distinguished performance at Durham University; or the fact that he had launched several well-known writers whose talents others had failed to appreciate.

Time passed. He will wait until what seems the right moment for him, Judith told herself, without giving thought as to whether it is also right for me – but that is the way of mankind.

She settled down to her own affairs. For the first time in her life, she had a room of her own. The room pleased her. It had the simplicity of rooms in her childhood with its low bed, white-painted wicker chair, and ottoman covered in faded blue with patchwork cushions. The threadbare rug was blue and rose, and the floor boards had been painted white. The room was cool, uncluttered and peaceful. It looked out across fields to Lewes. Judith knew that she would not wish to spend the rest of her life alone; but she was reassured at finding herself able to take advantage of this quiet interlude in the middle age of life.

During the day, she was busy working with the WVS. Her landlady, Mrs Chace, had a car but did not like driving. It had become the practice for Judith to drive her to the local WVS headquarters where she spent the day. Judith was then available to drive the car to whatever emergency might present itself. This was an arrangement congenial to the WVS organizer, who had become alarmed by the number of accidents recorded by Mrs Chace. On two occasions, when taking sick children to hospital, Judith had to visit the downland village where Austin Marriott lived. To her disappointment, she failed to find his house.

In the spring, Alice and Louise came to visit her. Louise stayed in the house and Alice in a neighbouring YWCA. Now that they had their mother to themselves, each showed a tendency to revert to childhood. In Louise, this was unusual.

Why does she want to be a child again? Judith wondered. James and Catherine were staying with Aunt May. Was Louise enjoying an innocent freedom from responsibility? Motherhood had come naturally to her; she had never made a burden of it, as some women do. Judith did not think that Louise was feeling released from the small daily acts of cherishing. No, she thought, it is more than that. She is enjoying being on her own because she can imagine herself free – just as I am free now. But I am well into middle age and must limit my expectations; while she may look to a second flowering.

Alice was torn by the desire to be her mother's child, and the equally compelling need to be accepted as a mature woman. In the interests of the latter, she spoke much of *Lady Chatterley's Lover*. From her manner, one would have supposed the freedom to speak explicitly to represent greater sexual maturity than the actual performance. Certainly, she imagined herself much superior to her mother, if not to Louise.

Judith thought that Alice would outgrow all this nonsense without coming to any harm. Alice felt more deeply than her sisters, and she made heavy going of things which came easily to Louise. But Judith felt in her bones – or in her mother's heart – that Alice would be all right. But Louise? She could not be sure of Louise.

'It is the greatest driving force in Nature,' Alice assured her more experienced listeners when they were on a picnic together, surrounded by Nature at its most temperate. Moreover, she assured them, it was as natural as food and drink, and should be part of the daily diet. She looked expectantly to her mother, wanting her respect, yet needing her dissent. It was important that her mother should remain old-fashioned in these matters. A sexually adventurous mother was the last thing she wanted.

Alice was sitting on the bank of a stream, dangling her feet in the water. In her white blouse and black tie and skirt, she looked more like a penguin than a priestess of sex. Louise, humming a tune, gazed across the stream towards the water meadows on the other side, carpeted with celandine. It was doubtful whether she had heard much of what had been said.

Judith said, 'The greatest driving force in Nature? Well, if it's as powerful as *that*, I'm surprised you should think it can be played with at will.'

Alice, taken aback by her mother's vehemence, said, 'Man converts power to his own use daily.'

'*Harnesses* it.'

Alice took her feet out of the water, which was ice cold. She contemplated them as they dried in the sun. She had tended to think of her own generation as uniquely circumscribed by sexual taboos. It had not previously occurred to her that limits had always been imposed, by the tribe, the race, the church, the state . . . 'If we don't free ourselves of all that, we shall never be really adult,' she pronounced gravely.

'What *are* you looking at out there?' Judith asked Louise.

'I was thinking that that is mimulus down by the water's edge. Do you think it would grow in the damp crack in Mrs Chace's yard?'

'What a splendid idea! She is always complaining that it looks so dreary. But is this the time to transplant it?'

'It has to be. It's the only time I'm here.'

Alice said, 'I *am* hungry. What have you got in that hamper?'

'Bacon sandwiches.'

'Bacon!' Louise exclaimed. 'Has Farmer Giles killed a pig or something?'

Alice stretched out her arms. 'Oh, I am so happy! I shall always remember this day.'

Louise took a sandwich. 'You'll soon be able to make a book of your memorable days.'

'You shouldn't laugh at her,' Judith admonished.

'I'm not laughing at her. I think it's wonderful to be only her age and have had so many days she will always remember. When she is old, she will be forever telling her grandchildren about her happy life.' She rounded her shoulders and spoke in a croaking voice, 'My dears, there was that day down by the river, when we had *bacon* sandwiches . . .'

The next day was happy, too. Judith had to collect a child from Austin Marriott's village. Alice and Louise accompanied her. On the return journey from the hospital, she took a different lane into the village and here she came across Marriott's house. It was not large, but, standing in half an acre of land, it seemed impressive to Judith – an old, red-tiled building which had the look of a place which pre-dated the garden and most of its neighbours. An old man was clipping the hedge, and from one window a plumpish woman in an overall shook a duster – a 'daily', definitely not a housekeeper.

Louise said, 'Do you know any of the people here?' It was an idle question, yet Judith sensed that something had communicated itself to her daughter.

Alice said, 'What a lovely old house! Do stop.'

Judith stopped the car in the shade of an ash tree. 'We mustn't seem to stare.'

Alice was enchanted by the house. Here, she felt, the work of man – in this case, the house – grew from the earth like the trees which surrounded it, not aggressively imposed on the landscape, but a partner with fields and hills. She thought of the smoke rising from the house in winter as the leaves turned and the trees became bare. The life of the house would send its light into the winter darkness.

The remainder of their time together was not so enjoyable. It was apparent to Alice that her mother was becoming increasingly involved in local affairs. She knew a lot of people at the chapel, and was active there as well as with the WVS. For the first time, Alice saw herself and her sisters as part of her mother's life, but not everything. Although she herself sought to break free of the ties of family, Alice expected to remain everything to her mother.

On the Saturday evening she announced that she would prefer to go to the Church of England service the next morning. She made this announcement in good time, anticipating argument.

Her mother said, 'Yes, I think you should have experience of other services.'

In the face of such ready acceptance, Alice herself must assume the burden of disapproval.

'You used not to think like that,' she accused.

'Well, your father had very definite ideas, and it was better for us not to argue too much. You were all much better off living up to his beliefs. I should have made a mess of your religious upbringing if it had been left to me.'

Alice was upset that they should talk in this dispassionate way of her father. It seemed that her mother, perhaps unconsciously, was conveying the impression that in reality she had been the wiser of the two. Alice felt her father was being robbed of his dignity and was shocked that her mother could so forget her loyalty to him.

'Don't you miss Daddy at all?' she asked.

'Miss him?' The question had taken Judith by surprise and her eyes filled with tears. '*Miss* him?'

'I'm sorry, I didn't mean . . . I didn't know . . .'

The momentary loss of control was soon over, but Judith did not turn from her emotion. Perhaps she realized what had prompted her daughter to behave in this way. She said, 'I would give everything to have those years again.' She paused and seemed to consider this statement; and then, its veracity tested, nodded her head. 'Yes, everything.' The brisk, sometimes formidable woman was momentarily gone, and in her place Alice saw a rather careworn, lonely person.

'That was awful of me.' She fumbled for words. 'Why don't you live with Louise . . .'

'Because I don't want to.' Judith was brisk again, but affectionate. 'I can manage this way much better. Probably because it *isn't* just managing, marking time, getting through the days somehow, which is what some widows do. I am finding out things about myself. Sometimes, I can be quite surprised by what I do and say. This is right for me. I'm not meant to spend the rest of my life being Stanley's widow and your mother, my love. Though, goodness knows, the things we *are* meant to be, aren't always what we want to be.' She paused, seeing Louise in the garden. Louise had been planting the mimulus in the crack, and was now lingeringly surveying her work – Judith thought: she is preparing herself for something.

Alice said, 'You aren't happy, are you?'

'Happiness, in the sense in which you mean it, is irrelevant.'

'I don't think I understand.'

'No, I don't suppose you do. But you will one day.'

The next morning, they went their separate ways. Alice attended church in Lewes, while Judith went to her chapel. Louise said she would like to go to a country church. She walked across fields; and, as usual, allowed herself to be distracted by lambs and wild flowers, and any other pleasant sight which claimed her attention. Her dalliance, however, was a charade; even as she lingered, enchanted by wild daffodils and cowslips, she felt her impulse drawing her strongly across the fields. Although she was habitually late, she always meant to arrive.

As she walked up the path to the church, the few people who had attended the service were leaving. On the threshold, she hesitated, coming from sunlight into shadow, and began to shiver. By the time she took her seat in one of the pews, the church was empty save for the vicar and the churchwarden, who were counting the collection in the vestry.

She sat quietly, composing herself to her task. She did not pray regularly, but only when she had something to say. She imagined God probably found this quite refreshing. Lately, there had been rather a lot to say. Perhaps she had overdone it. The words would not come now. Worse than that. Her thoughts, of which she was usually complete mistress, refused to address themselves to this business of acquainting God formally with the fact that, as she could only reach true fulfilment with Ivor, she must renounce her marriage vows. But it was Guy, and not Ivor, who occupied her mind. Guy, so diffident, so self-deprecating, had somehow succeeded in holding his own against his more forceful rival. How had this come about?

She looked around her, as though the building itself might explain this waywardness. She did not know the name of the church, or the village which it served. But she realized she had been in it before. It was small, bare and rather dark. A Saxon church which in past centuries must have served a poor farming community. There were no plaques commemorating the lords of the manor; not so much as a humble esquire was immortalized here. She recalled the hymn sung at school on Commemoration Day: 'And some there be which have no memorial, Who are perished as though they had never been . . .' In like manner would she have cast off Guy.

Her eyes travelled. There were three small stained-glass windows beyond the altar; the side windows were clear glass. Her eyes were drawn to one of the side windows. She remembered that when she was last here, there had been a flower festival. This had been the Magdalen window. She could see the flowers now: all the reds arrayed, from the pale crown to the dark hem, in a flowing robe of gaiety, love and joy, deepening into passion. She had had some kind of vision as she looked at the flowers. They had told a story, older than words. But she had misinterpreted it, and had gone out celebrating her love for Guy.

And now? Now, here she was, about to explain to God that this choice of Guy had been a mistake, he hadn't lasted well once she had got him home. She had thought to shrug him aside like a bad buy because she had found something which suited her better. And she had expected God to condone this bargain basement approach to marriage.

She had been happy when she last came to this church. Now, she was full of pain. Yet, the image of the flowers was still the same, only the colours that made up the swirling hem of the garment had deepened.

There was a stabbing in her breast. It was so bad she thought she would be unable to move. The churchwarden came out of the vestry. He would make a fuss, probably he would want to fetch a doctor. She forced herself to her knees, bowing her head, holding to the pew in front. His footsteps stopped for a moment, while he wondered whether there was anything he should do. Then he passed on to Sunday lunch. After all, there was still the vicar in the vestry.

The vicar, when he came, asked if she was all right. There had been that girl who had crept in unobserved, pregnant by a GI, and had delivered herself of the baby on the chancel steps, of all places. He cleared his throat and said, 'Is there anything . . . ?'

'Might I stay here a little while?'

He looked at her dubiously. Even had he seen her when she came years ago, decked in all her hope, he would not have recognized her in this heavy-faced young woman. Of course, the light was bad and shadows smudged her face, but even so . . . He straightened his shoulders. One must not imagine every unhappy young woman to be in need of a midwife.

'Of course you may stay.' He wondered if help was required of him, and was unsure of his ability to give it, should he make the offer. He said again, 'Is there anything . . . ?'

'I should like to be alone.'

He touched her shoulder, and was gone.

Sunlight danced on the wall at the side of the altar, shone on the lectern turning the brass to gold, shafted through the stained-glass window, green as sap rising up the stone pillar. Outside, birds twittered quarrelsomely.

Louise knelt. She seemed no longer to be thinking. The decision, when at last it came, was presented to her in terms of flowers and music. Her marriage was a sacrament; she had pledged herself and, in return, she would find fulfilment. There was no other way for her. She had always known what she wanted and dismissed alternatives; so it did not seem unjust to her that she should find herself on a road with no side turnings. There was a rightness about it, impeccable as a Mozart sonata, not a note out of place.

She managed to raise herself to her feet. She went slowly out into the sunshine. She did not question why she should have been drawn to this church, or go over in her mind the story of the flowers. It had happened; she accepted it. She could see her path ahead across the fields. It seemed a very long way; but there wasn't anything for it, save to set out.

She was so pale on her return that her mother wondered if she was pregnant, but decided this was unlikely. She did not look as if she was carrying new life within her.

Alice wrote to Ben when she returned to Plymouth. She told him briefly about her stay with her mother and Louise, and mentioned the house which she had thought so attractive. Then she turned to matters of more particular concern to him.

'I can see Cornwall from here. Sometimes we take the ferry and go to a village called Cawsands. There is an old Cornish woman there who does teas with crab sandwiches. Her man was in the Navy, and, however busy she is, she will never turn a sailor away. Later on, I am going to stay in Falmouth with Granny Tippet.

'And there is one thing I must tell you. There are a lot of GIs in Plymouth – indeed, they swarm all over the south of England. Only swarm is rather an active word for such remarkably inert men! One gets awfully tired of them, mooching around, contemplating too much money and not enough to spend it on. People don't respect the Americans because they think they can buy anything (and there is quite a lot they *can* buy!). The other day when I was walking on the Hoe, I realized something else about them. There was the usual crowd milling around, being knowledgeably inaccurate about the ships in the Sound. Near me was a child, crying bitterly; his mother was bored and took no notice. A GI came and squatted down, trying to comfort the child. From his expression, one would have thought nothing in the whole world so bad as an unhappy child. A few moments before he had given the impression of a seasoned old warrior who could look on carnage without batting an eyelid. Yet here he was, shocked almost to tears himself! As I was watching him, lost to everything but the needs of the child, I suddenly thought of your father. Your poor father, Ben! He only saw you as a tiny baby. You probably hardly ever think of him. But he must have been so thrilled to see his own baby. I expect he was thinking of you and planning for you when he went down on the *Lusitania*. I don't know why I'm telling you this, except that at the time, it seemed important. If life goes on, in some way, then the loving must go on, too, mustn't it?'

The railway had been finished in October; the last sections had joined on October 17th. But there was maintenance work to do, roads to re-make, even new camps to be built for those who would service the railway. Ben's camp was to be dismantled. By February, many men had already left it. Now, in May, preparations for the final departure were underway. Soon, the jungle would reclaim this clearing where so many men had lived and died.

A bad attack of fever had swept through the camp, and Ben was down with it. A doctor was operating on a man, cutting out ulcers; the man's cries were terrible to hear. A dysentery case was staggering back into the tent, supported by a cholera case who had gone to help him.

Tandy came in. He was getting over the fever and was doing light duties in the hospital. His idea of cheering those of the sick who were able to take in what he was saying, was to tell them a man had been beheaded for being in possession of a radio.

'I don't know what they do with men who conceal diaries,' Tandy said. 'It probably depends whether they understand what a diary is. That mound of paper – they might think it was all military stuff, mightn't they? They'd behead you then, I expect.'

Ben tossed and turned on his bamboo bed, his mind going to and fro over what Tandy had said. He saw his life slipping away like sand running through an egg-timer, all running away and he hadn't even begun to get a hold on it. Tandy was right about the diaries. It was too much of a risk. But the drawings were different. They represented a shared life: it was only the decision as to their retention which belonged to him alone. He would be bound to be searched when they moved camp; at the first kit inspection, the drawings would be found. The MO was the man to do it! He would have privileges denied to the ranks. Also, he would have equipment to be packed and the right to superintend its subsequent unpacking.

The fever soared away with him. He was in a landscape of fire. He saw Tandy's face, the teeth bared, snarling from the flames; in the flames, he also saw the MO. He was climbing a red-tongued mountain by a route that went round and round and up and up – the route always spiralled when he had fever. As he climbed, Tandy held the drawings in front of him, just out of reach. It came to him as he climbed that the north face of love is evil.

He reached a plateau where, briefly, he was conscious. Even in his consciousness, he was on fire; but the figures around him were not yet touched by the flames. He realized that he must speak to the MO about the drawings. But when the opportunity presented itself, he got confused and asked the wrong question. 'Did you ever ask yourself whether you wanted to be a doctor?'

'I was supposed to be going into the Colonial Service. I stayed with my uncle, who was a District Commissioner. The people used to come to him with their problems, like children, and he sorted them out. He was a good man and he loved the people. But when they were sick, he didn't have anything to give them. I thought I would be better at giving people something they needed than at telling them what to do. I was always stronger on the practical side.'

Ben noticed that a change had come over the MO. His once florid face was hollow, the skin yellow; he seemed smaller, yet harder, more compact. There was a little stone there in the centre of him, like the stone of a fruit, and all his resources were gathered about it. Ben said, in a panic, 'You should get that seen to! After all, you're a doctor.'

'What should I "get seen to"?'

'That thing, that stone . . .'

It was no use. He couldn't make them understand. The plateau was only a brief resting place; he was spiralling again.

Someone was laughing. His mother! His mother was young and laughing! His father stood beside his mother, cradling the baby. But the minister wasn't christening the baby, he was shouting, 'Baby too ill to work, then baby need no food. Speedo, speedo, speedo . . .'

Daphne was ahead, naked, arms stretched wide. As he looked at her, he saw that her feet were growing from the ground; gradually, the outstretched arms branched and blossomed. The blossom opened to reveal faces, Tandy and the MO, his mother and father and the Japanese guard . . . so many faces, yet all held in the one form.

When he was conscious of his immediate surroundings again, he saw the MO standing beside him. He raised himself on one elbow and croaked urgently, 'You should look after yourself.'

The shrunken head swivelled, the mild eyes looked at him. 'I have been more fortunate than most—because I have been able to carry on my profession here. You might say, even, that I have had unique opportunities. Sometimes, I have felt guilty about it; as though all these men had been sick to keep me occupied and healthy.'

And so it wouldn't be right to come out of here alive, was that it? Ben was moaning with weakness and anger. Now, when he most needed his help, the man was going to die! He watched the MO continuously during the next two days. It was the eyes that told the story. The eyes were patient as those of a sick animal, uncomplaining, looking at the men with a kind of adoration as he tended them. He reminded Ben of the dog he had sat beside one night when he was young. It had licked his hand, grateful, loving to the last, as though it owed *him* something; when the reality had been that it had given him most of the childhood joys he had experienced. Now, the MO looked at him with that same incredible gratitude.

Damn the man! Rage gave way to despair. They would leave the MO behind, another cross, hastily driven into the ground, before they went away. The bloody fool! If he had taken more care of himself he would have stood a better chance than most. He had the right physique; he was an officer – moreover one whom the Japanese listened to with respect. But the wrong attitude of mind. You didn't mean to leave here, Ben fumed. You meant to die, make a martyr of yourself. When what I, Ben Sherman, had in mind for you was a different kind of martyrdom. If you had been caught carrying the drawings, they might have beheaded you. Wouldn't that have assuaged your thirst for martyrdom?

That night, the MO sat down on the ground beside Ben. Slowly, with infinite pain, he crossed his legs. His hands came to rest on his knees. The effort involved took his breath away and some minutes passed before he said softly, 'Do you know what my vision of heaven is?' His head bowed, meditating bliss. 'A couch. A couch with a thousand cushions on it!'

Ben said, 'I would settle for just one cushion.'

The MO did not answer. A few more minutes passed before Ben realized he was dead.

The next day Ben was out of the hospital. The work of clearing the camp was under way. Only a few men were left in the hospital. Some of these were men who had feigned sickness so long they would now never recover their health – they were physically wrecked or mentally unbalanced.

'A terrible thing they've done to themselves!' Tandy said virtuously.

Ben volunteered to help with packing the hospital equipment, hoping he might hide the drawings in one of the crates. But the MO's orderly would not have him.

'I don't want you in here, dear. You were always so beastly to him.'

'I respected him.'

'Then you had a funny way of showing it, dear, that's all I can say. He was a good, forgiving man. I wish I could be more like him; but since I can't, you just get out of here.'

Tandy it was who helped in the hospital. Ben was singled out to pack the Japanese CO's equipment. It was an opportunity of a kind. He could not imagine what would be the consequence of discovery. He tried to convince himself that he had become obsessed with the drawings, that they had served their purpose and were now worth-less, that Geoffrey would never have expected him to take such risks to preserve them. But, at the last, he found he was more afraid of leaving without them than of being caught with them. Either they had come to represent something more important than survival; or they contained the means of survival.

He hid them away, and, since the risk had now been taken, put the diaries with them. He wondered what he would do if they were found and another man was blamed. He was not sure he could trust himself to step forward at such a time. It seemed wiser to make the position clear now, when the gesture would cost less. He said ingratiatingly to the Colonel, 'I see to everything personally,' and spread out his hands, drawing attention to his handiwork. He had indeed managed very neatly. The Colonel was impressed and said that Ben was to travel with the equipment. He had, at one instant, given himself the chance to retrieve the drawings, and cut his escape route should anything go wrong. During the long journey south he would have plenty of time to realize that he was not by nature a gambler; if he got away with this, he would never, never do anything so foolhardy again.

The train carried them away. The jungle receded. Ben, looking from the window, saw the mountains, like hooded figures, turned away from them. He had come here, and he was leaving, one of the lucky ones. He very much wanted to live, but did not yet dare to give way to hope.

12

≡

Claire and Terence Straker were married in June. They had long
discussions about the wedding. 'It will upset too many people if we
marry in a registry office,' Claire insisted. She also admitted that she
would not *feel* married in such circumstances. 'It would have upset
Daddy so much,' she said. 'I've pushed myself a long way. I can't go
any further just now.'

Terence thought he understood. He was afraid that he might
undermine their marriage if he insisted on having his own way over
this. He did not doubt for one moment that he *could* have had his
way, but told himself that true strength often lies in forbearance. He
loved Claire very much and wanted to see her happy on her wedding
day. As far as principles were concerned, time was on his side.

It was agreed that they should be married in chapel. The possibility
that they should not marry at all was not discussed. This would have
been as unacceptable to Terence's parents as to the Fairleys, if for
different reasons. Although his conversation might lead one to
suppose that he came from a working-class background, the fact was
that he had grown up in a mock Tudor estate in Isleworth, where his
parents were pillars of the local country club. Mr Straker was a
commercial traveller, something of which Terence was deeply
ashamed. At first, Claire had put his revulsion down to inverted
snobbery, but she had come to realize it had its origins in an unhappy
childhood.

He had described to her how his parents would go out several
evenings a week to the country club. He and his sister had wondered
what went on there, imagining exotic, not to say erotic, rites into
which they would be initiated when they grew up. Then, one evening,
there had been an urgent business call for his father, and eleven-year-
old Terence had gone to fetch him. He had pushed open the door of
the club and had seen the room, wreathed in smoke, full of people all
of whom seemed to be wearing grinning masks. His mother and
father were standing in a group near the door. His mother had a

painful, ingratiating smile fixed to her lips; her face was rouged and diamanté ear-rings and necklace flashed as she tilted her head archly, but her eyes were as anxious as ever. In spite of the glitter, his mother would never be a social success. His father was reduced to his effects – drink in the one hand, cigarette in the other, ruby ring on the little finger, smart grey suit encasing the rotund body. The fond smile which Claire might have seen break over her father's face, had she interrupted him at some adult gathering, had not greeted Terence. His father had looked at him with glazed indifference. His mother, when someone had said, 'This is your boy, is it?' had given a squirming smile while her frightened eyes implored Terence to be civil.

'Why do you and Mummy go to that place?' he had asked wretchedly on their way home. He had seen, with the merciless clarity of the child's eye, that his parents were trying to be acceptable and were not succeeding. It was how he had felt when he went into the transition class: he had imagined this kind of ordeal to be peculiar to childhood.

'You've got to be seen around.' His father had made no pretence that pleasure was involved.

It was not entirely for business, however, that he went so often to the country club. Subsequently, Terence realized that to his father, bored by his mother, the club was an escape. When Terence was older, his father said to him, 'I married a silly woman. Be sure you don't do the same. If a girl giggles a lot, ask yourself if you want to listen to it for the rest of your life.'

His mother giggled because she was nervous; it was her response to any situation which she could not handle. His father, by his contempt, had turned her into a compulsive giggler. Terence saw this clearly, and knew that there was no remedy for it.

His parents were lower-middle-class people hoping to raise them-selves. Gradually, Terence had constructed an alternative family which he much preferred, based largely on the activities of paternal grandparents who had died when he was young. His grandfather, he told Claire, was one of Nature's scholars, and a sturdy agnostic. If he could imagine him worshipping anywhere, however, it was in a Methodist chapel, where so many working-class men had had their first experience of debate on social issues. It was of this he thought on his way to his wedding, and not of his mother's: 'Chapels never look right, somehow, with no central aisle for the bride to walk up.'

The Allies had landed in France, Rome had fallen, and there was jubilation in the air as Terence and Claire planned their wedding.

Although both were confirmed pacifists, it was impossible not to be affected by the renewal of hope. Claire's only sadness was that her dear father would not be there to support her. She had written to Harry, asking him to give her away, but had received a letter regretting that he was unable to leave the farm. 'Unable to leave Aunt Meg, more like!' she had said angrily. So, it was on the arm of one of her Cornish cousins, fortuitously stationed at Uxbridge at this time, that she entered the chapel.

June was to be remembered not only for the invasion of France, but for the advent of Hitler's 'secret weapon'. The wedding ceremony concided with the first flying bomb incident in Acton. The ominous drone could be heard while the couple made their vows. The engine cut off as the congregation rose to sing 'Love Divine, all loves excelling'. Most of those present prostrated themselves in a style not normally acceptable to Methodism. Several seconds passed and then the floor seemed to shift slightly. A pile of hymn books stacked on the back pew fell down and someone screamed. Outside, whistles were blown and there was the sound of running feet. Terence's father said crossly to his wife, 'Why get hysterical now? It's all over.' Jacov began to pick up the hymnbooks. The congregation resumed the vertical and sang with fervour:

> 'Come almighty to deliver;
> Let us all Thy life receive;
> Suddenly return, and never,
> Never more Thy temples leave.'

When the newly-married couple came out of the chapel, the emergency services were at work digging bodies out of the rubble. Had Claire and Terence been married in the registry office, they would have been decently removed from the incident.

Claire vowed she would never set foot in chapel again. The flying bomb had completed the alienating process set in motion by the bomb which had killed her father. Terence was relieved to have played no part in this. Although it was important that she should share his views on all intellectual issues, he had no wish to appear a destructive element in her life.

The wedding guests returned to Louise's house, where Terence applied himself earnestly to the business of being convivial. At some stage in the festivities, he was alone with Alice, and took the opportunity of assuring her that, rather than losing a sister, she had gained a brother. 'I want you to know that you will always have a home with us.' He and Claire were still at university and had no home, but in his view it was the goodwill which mattered, the bricks and mortar could wait.

The goodwill, conjuring up as it did the picture of the unmarried sister who must be allocated her place in the corner, disturbed Alice. Only a few moments ago, Aunt May had said, 'It will be your turn next, I suppose, Alice.' She had sounded comforting rather than confident.

Alice said to Terence, 'I expect to have a home of my own; thank you, all the same.'

'We shall all hope for that. But you mustn't be too proud to come to us whenever you feel lonely.' He could see in Alice the one member of Claire's family with whom he might establish, if not a friendly, then at least a practical relationship. He was anxious to secure her as an ally.

Claire joined them. 'I am so glad to see you two getting together. I have told Terence how close we have always been.'

'I have been telling Alice I want that to continue,' Terence said.

Claire looked at Alice, her eyes shining. Alice could see that she was expected to be grateful to Terence, not only at this moment, but from now on. They would not expect Louise and Guy to be grateful for each gesture of affection. Pairs had an immunity not extended to the single, from whom the due of gratitude must be exacted.

Alice replied with as good a grace as possible, 'I'm sure we shall all be good friends.'

She could see that Claire had expected rather more.

The weather was sunny, and some of the guests were sitting in the garden. In the kitchen, Judith said to Louise, 'Why don't you go out? I can take over in here.' She thought Louise looked strained and supposed she had period pains.

Louise said, 'I'm better if I keep going.'

Judith opened the dresser drawer to look for a tea cosy. Tidiness was not one of Louise's merits, and she had to rummage. After a minute, she exclaimed, 'Why, there's a letter in here from Guy!' She turned the envelope over as if she expected it to tell more than the names of the sender and addressee. 'Not even opened.' She looked at Louise.

Louise said, 'Put it away. I can't read it now.'

There was a photograph of Daphne's wedding in the drawer: the bride and groom, Mrs Drummond, Louise, and a dark man who looked into the camera, one eyebrow raised above alert, amused eyes. Judith put Guy's letter down on top of the photograph. 'I guessed there was someone else.'

'There's no need for you to look like that. It's all over. Nothing came of it.' Louise twisted the dish cloth, grimly intent on wringing every drop of moisture from it. Judith put an arm around her shoulders. It was a gesture which these two could seldom exchange, and Louise was taken by surprise. The tears came in spite of herself.

'Did you want him so much, my love?'

'After it was over, I didn't know it could be so hard, just to go on living.' Judith accepted the words as the kind of thing all unhappy lovers say. She could not have visualized the well in which Louise had found herself trapped, nor have known how much stronger was the pull of the dark water than the distant daylight. 'That letter . . .' Louise was more in control now, her voice husky with the strain on throat muscles. 'I'm terrified it's to say Guy is on his way home. That's the truth of it.'

Judith said quietly, 'It won't be easy, even without this affair. He's been away a long time. But once you've both got over the strangeness of being together again, you'll manage.'

'That's all very well for you. You wanted Daddy back. I don't want Guy. I don't! I don't want him!'

'Your father and I didn't know each other very well when we got married. We only had five days together, and then he went back to the Front. I wondered what I had done, marrying a "foreigner" as my mother put it. You and Guy have a lot to build on, even if you can't see it that way now.'

'I can only see Ivor now.'

She had not seen him very clearly the last time they met.

They had sat in the restaurant, the untouched food on their plates.

'But *why*?' Ivor shouted as if to make his voice carry above a high wind. The waitress, lolling against the wall, agitatedly chipped varnish from her nails. Louise had looked as if she had gone into a trough in a wave which obscured her vision; she was having difficulty with her breathing, too.

He had foreseen that she would be inflexible. He had imagined himself amazed that something so adamantine should be concealed beneath the softly rounded flesh; he had heard himself shouting at her, 'Refusing to give an inch is a sign of weakness, you do realize that, don't you? It's the last resort of the feeble-minded!' She would shout back, 'You're well rid of me, then,' and they would have a wild scene ending in love-making. That was how he had visualized it.

The reality was somewhat different. There was wildness, certainly, but she was in the centre of it, without any apparent need of his presence. Her face was scoured by a harsher abrasive than the rasp of his tongue. Every few seconds she snatched for breath, but the frantic straining of her breasts indicated that she gained no relief. There was something she could not quite swallow; she tried again and again, and after each attempt she tossed her head back and blinked her eyes rapidly. How could he expect that she, engaged in this grim struggle, should be aware of him, let alone heed his words? He put his head in his hands and groaned. The waitress thought this was better than the cinema. What could he do? There was something so awesome about this distress that, although he was not lacking in conceit, he could scarcely credit himself to be responsible. The creation of such havoc belonged to realms beyond mortal man. His own grief was bitter, but so small in comparison that there was no hope of bringing it to her notice. He said, 'Let's get out of here' and paid the bill, although they had eaten nothing.

When they parted, he said, to satisfy himself, 'I am Ivor, and I love you, Louise. I am not on a mountain top, or in the depths of the sea. I am here at Victoria Station. Won't I do?'

She dashed the back of her hand across her eyes. He saw that the fingers clutched a crumpled handkerchief.

So it had ended between them.

Judith said, 'You will get over it in time.'

Louise, who had by now wrung the dish cloth dry, draped it over the taps. The kitchen door opened and James edged in. Judith guessed from the aimless way he behaved that he was worried about his mother, and uneasy when she was out of his sight. 'You can help me with the tea, James,' she said. 'Mummy is going to sit in the garden and have a well-earned rest.'

Louise made a few dabs at her face in the scullery and then went into the garden. Most of the people there were friends of Claire and Terence whom she did not know. She sat on the stone steps leading down from the French windows. After a few moments, she sensed that someone was standing behind her, and looking up, she saw Jacov. He knew her too well for her to be able to hide her unhappiness from him, and she did not try. He sat down beside her. Neither spoke.

Louise had loved Ivor in every way it was possible for her to love. All her senses were involved with him; he was as much in the joy of the first cup of tea at breakfast as in the lilac coming into bloom in the garden. He was in the rain splashing the backs of her legs and the music of Mozart. He was in the smell of bacon cooking and the dusty sweetness of mown grass. Perhaps she exaggerated, but this was how it had seemed to her.

Yet now . . . The sun was going behind the trees and a breeze sent a shiver down her spine. As the air began to cool, she experienced a sharp pleasure which had no other source than the smell of night-scented stocks. She was aware of the randomness of the erotic impulse. 'I need a bridge,' she conceded. 'If ever I am to come to Guy again, I need a bridge.' There are some messages the body can convey more unequivocally than words. Louise, leaning against Jacov, was conscious of a great relief.

At the end of September, Guy was in the foothills of the Apennines. To those who followed the progress of the fighting in Europe from GHQ, a grand scheme must now seem to be unfolding. But for Guy, the war had been reduced to one solitary farmhouse. He had been put in charge of a raiding party and instructed to take the farmhouse and hold it pending further instructions. This had been achieved after a sharp exchange with German soldiers. What was expected of them, they had no idea. Nor had they any idea how the war was proceeding beyond the bounds of the farm. A week had passed and no instructions had reached them.

Guy had written to Louise describing the kind of country through which they had passed on their journey from the south of Italy. It was a rather prosaic description, in part due to the requirements of censorship, and in part to his inability to articulate his feelings.

It had been beautiful, of course, the country through which he had fought his way. But there was too much of it and he had come to resent it as he might have resented a woman who over-dressed on an informal occasion. On the road from Salerno, there had been lemons and oranges hanging from trees like onions. The lemon trees were a crude, nightmare green. It was a claustrophobic landscape. He remembered a road twisting endlessly with sheer drops on one side; it had gone on and on, like a thriller in which the climax is too long delayed. Sometimes he had felt tempted to walk over the edge. They had passed through small towns, stupefying in the heat, not a leaf stirring; petrified places, waiting with decreasing hope to be brought to life by rain. It had not rained for four months, they had said. Further north, there were villages clinging to hillsides, the houses close-packed, like a pattern of dominoes.

Guy was glad to have reached the farmhouse. He was weary of travelling. As he looked from one of the shattered windows, he knew that in the scrubby fields outside Englishmen and Germans were buried. They had buried them hastily, their graves indistinguishable. It had surprised Guy to realize that as he thought of these dead men, he himself made no distinctions. The union of soldiers in death had long been a theme of poetry, but it was an idea at which he had only just arrived. With this recognition came the knowledge that the war had ceased to have any meaning for him. He was still convinced that it mattered – but to other people, in another place. Looking back, he could see that this stripping-down process had been going on for quite a time.

His view of service life had been endorsed by films in which gallant Naval officers roused the spirits of frightened stokers, or young lieutenants in dug-outs quieted panic-stricken corporals. The advent of the Americans had offered an alternative mythology. At their camps, he had seen many films in which gallant stokers took over from frightened young officers. Majors, calm and capable on the parade ground, had proved unfitted to lead a group of men lost in the desert; in such circumstances, the immortal sergeant must take over.

There were two Americans with him now. Somewhere in the confusion of the long fight in Italy, they had become lost and eventually attached themselves to his company. He looked at them from time to time, ready to meet any challenge they might make to his authority. At this moment, they were playing cards.

A strange people, the Americans. Although they looked so mass-produced, they seemed to have little sense of esprit de corps. They preferred their heroes to be lone men, at odds with their fellows, proving themselves against a landscape hostile to man. Perhaps it came of living in a country where there was so much space? Whatever the reason, at this stage these two seemed no more inclined to play the immortal sergeant than Guy the gallant young officer. Here, at the farmhouse, only the fact of their being so far from home reminded them that they were soldiers.

Guy started to attention suddenly, and at the same time one of the look-outs called, 'Men coming across the field, sir – there, to the left.'

Two men, not in uniform, carrying rifles much as men out for a day's hunting might. They halted some distance from the farm and called out in Italian. Guy sent two of his men to bring them in.

They were like most peasants, suspicious of the stranger. But they had not that look of belonging to the soil on which they stood. Their eyes made calculations which had a certain inwardness, which suggested to Guy that it was not primarily food and shelter with which these men were concerned. At first, they affected to speak only Italian. Then, after a brief exchange, one of them spoke in English. He said he was a school teacher and English was his subject. He and his companion were partisans. His hearers received this statement with some reserve: it was their experience that all Italians now claimed to be partisans. The man said they were on their way to join a band of partisans in the hills to the north. It would be a hard journey and they needed food.

'We can give you food now, and we'll talk later.' Guy dispatched them with two of his men.

Once they were out of the way, he looked at his sergeant. 'How do they strike you?'

'Never trust an Eytie, sir.'

Guy looked at the two Americans. One of them said, 'If ever a guy was a loner, it was Mussolini. He sure didn't have any followers!'

'But there *are* partisans to the north. We know that.'

The sergeant said, 'Commies, most of them.'

The other American said wearily, 'What the hell! So, we *don't* give them food and send them on their way—what then? We shoot them?'

Guy bit his lip. 'I think we need more information from them.'

When the men returned, something had been decided between them. The older man said to Guy, 'You do not trust us? I will show you something that makes you believe we are no friends of the Germans.'

'Show me something?'

'You come with me. You and . . .' He pointed to one of the Americans. 'This is something you both should see — to tell your people.'

The sergeant said under his breath, 'Not on your life!'

Guy said, 'I'm not so sure. How far away?'

The man shrugged his shoulders. 'One hour.'

Guy looked at his lieutenant, who was standing very straight, looking startled — a posture he seemed to have been holding for several days. Guy thought irritably, 'I hope *I* never look like that.' He pointed to the older man. 'You come. Your companion stays here.'

It was an obvious precaution. The man spread out his hands. 'Of course.'

Three of them went with the Italian — Guy, a sturdy young Scot who was plainly eager to come for the walk, and one of the Americans. They climbed steadily through scrub and bush into woods, and beyond, where there was only rock. At each step the land fell away behind them, and a great panorama was unrolled like a huge canvas by one of the old masters. This aerial view was at once liberating and cautionary. In the farmhouse, they had led an isolated existence. Up here, they could see the connections: a camp down in the plain; smoke spurting from a small town; a train crawling towards a bridge over the river, light sparking from gunmetal. Guy reflected on a time when men had lived in small units unaware of the existence of other units not so far away. Awareness was a burdensome thing. The Scot said it wasn't a patch on the Trossachs.

Ahead, there were gashes in the rock with dust spewing out, like gaping mouths, crying for rain. They climbed up, into land that resembled a giant stonemason's yard. At yet another gaping mouth, the Italian stopped. 'A cave.' A smell one might encounter at the mouth of hell emanated from the cave. Instinctively, Guy stepped back. The Scot and the American were watching him. Conformity made its last stand, and he did what was expected of him. He said to the Italian, 'You first.' The Italian entered the cave, and Guy followed him. It was a big, deep cave and the slanting light of the sun penetrated only a little way, but far enough to shed some light on the pile of rotting carcasses.

The Italian said, 'These are people of my village, not partisans. Look, Inglese – children. See the children.'

Guy, on the threshold of the unimaginable, wondered why this should happen to him, this random encounter resulting in an experience which he, of all people, was particularly unsuited to bear. He stood there, looking down; a man brought up in a home where a misplaced ornament was a threat to order, the breaking of his school's memorial window a symbol of disintegration. He had thrilled to the deeds of the heroes of his tribe – Nelson and Scott, Lawrence and Wingate; something of their glory had touched him and made him walk with pride. Now, he seemed to breathe a primeval corruption into his own body. As he gazed at the corpses of children, who in life were probably little different from his own, he understood that this was not the result of war, that it was something in man himself, and that he was not immune. Whatever it is that begets war, was in that cave; and he was looking down on it. And he knew that, simply by having looked on it, he was in some way part of it, not only of the dying, but of the doing.

He was not sick. That was really surprising. The others were sick, but he did not manage to retch anything out of his system: he ingested it.

Outside, they walked silently down to the tree line. Here, they rested. The light was still strong. Guy saw how relentlessly it exposed the stone beneath the sparse grass. He said to the Italian, 'How did you know about this?'

'I was on my way home. I saw the Germans going towards my village. Something here' – he touched the back of his neck – 'told me bad things. The partisans had been with us a few weeks ago. I ran into these woods. If I had run to the village, it might have saved someone.'

'How could it have done?'

'One person, perhaps two. A child? Yes, for certain. But I ran away. And I watched, up in the hills. I saw the smoke and I heard the screams. They brought them up here, men, women, children. There was shooting. Afterwards, I made myself go in. But they shoot good. All dead.'

Guy wondered how long afterwards he had gone in. But he was in no position to condemn. 'And your companion?'

'He is of the village, too. But he was away, hunting. We met in these woods.'

The American asked, 'How would the Germans know about the cave?'

'They had – how do you say – a man of . . .' His hands embraced the landscape, making a miniature of it.

'A local man?'

He nodded. 'Bad man.'

The American said, 'You?'

He did not feign anger. Perhaps he felt he had no right to it. He simply said, 'How would I get away? The Germans leave no one behind to tell.'

The American looked away. Guy was inclined to believe the man. He had put himself in unnecessary danger by bringing them here; there was no one to corroborate his story, and he was intelligent enough to realize that blame might fall on him.

They entered the wood and walked slowly through the undergrowth. Whenever they stopped, it was silent, there seemed to be no bird life. The last of the light filtered through the trees. By the time they came to the farmhouse, the air was cool; and looking up, Guy saw that the sun and the moon shared the sky – the alpha and the omega.

That night he took a statement from the two Italians. Afterwards, he and his men argued among themselves.

The sergeant said, 'There must be a reason.' Once you can find a reason, you are well on your way to excusing, even to condoning. If you can't find a reason, life is going to be that much more uncomfortable for you. 'You can't trust an Eytie. They were happy enough to go along with Jerry when things were going well.'

'There were bairns there, sarge,' the Scot said.

The sergeant was not listening. He was looking to where they had buried the Germans who had defended the farmhouse. Good fighting men, they had been, and he had respected them. A soldier stands his ground – the Italians ran away.

The Scot said, 'How do we know it wasn't him led the way to the cave?'

The American said, 'He'd have a hell of a lot of trouble proving he didn't.'

Guy said, 'I believed him, though. Did you?'

'I didn't disbelieve him so much I'd want to hand him over.'

The sergeant thought the men should be detained. Guy could see that the lieutenant agreed with him. While they were debating, the Italians escaped. The soldier who was guarding them had had no very clear instructions, and was tired and confused; he had made the mistake of allowing them both to go to the bog at the same time. For form's sake, a search was mounted for them. As he set out, the American who had been in the cave said, 'I guess this is one movie I don't have to see through to the end.' No one paid any attention to him. He failed to return with the search party and they never saw him again.

Guy was later severely reprimanded for having failed to obtain sufficiently detailed statistical information; and for allowing the Italians to escape and the American to desert. He had displayed serious lack of judgement. Two facts alone saved him from court martial: his own record; and the failure of his senior officer to explain satisfactorily why the raiding party had been left so long at the farmhouse without relief or further instructions. Guy was surprisingly unconcerned about his fate. For once, he was uninterested in what those in authority thought of him. All his life he had had a certain innocence, which he had now lost. Shortly after this affair, he sustained his first incapacitating wound – a chest injury, so that it was as a physical casualty that he was treated in hospital. While all the time a change was going on inside him. Questions which he seemed powerless to resist presented themselves constantly to him.

Those who don't let the questioning get out of hand survive, become the stable, well-adjusted people who fit into the structure of their particular society; they die in their millions defending it. These people will suffer incredible hardships and will only break down if their society is radically changed. Guy had been groomed all his life to be one of them. But breakdown can also result from an awareness of evil, which most people manage to ignore. As he lay in hospital, he tried very hard to fight his way back to that company of stable, well-adjusted people from whom he had become separated at some stage during his campaigning.

In October, Alice received her first letter from Ben. For several years he had lived in that limbo peculiar to prisoners and had only the past to write about. His letter was full of reminiscences. 'There are times here when I would dearly love to talk to your father, argue with him. We used to laugh sometimes because he felt things so intensely – it seemed a bit embarrassing to us youngsters. But, Alice, I have learnt to value him so much. I hope I grow old like him and never learn that kind of wisdom which seems to have arrived on some lofty peak where it looks serenely down on the struggles of less composed mortals. God save me from serenity! I want to be "a foolish, passionate man" – like Yeats and your father . . .'

Towards the end of his letter, he wrote, 'I should like to see you, Alice. It would be good to have something to aim for. What about getting yourself drafted to Ceylon? We'll have a drink at that hotel everyone talks about in Colombo.'

Alice wept. Since she had been back in England, she had missed her father more than ever, and Ben's letter made her realize the extent of her loss. She resolved that she would indeed meet Ben in Colombo. He was important to her; he was part of her family. But a meeting in Ceylon, with Ben free, looked to the end of the war. What then? Where would she go? What would she become? All her life there had been something bigger than herself to which she belonged – family, chapel, school, the WRNS. Community was important to her. She was going out with a Petty Officer who very much wanted to marry her. Apart from a strong physical attraction, they had little in common. D. H. Lawrence notwithstanding, her ideas about love and marriage had become more, rather than less, old-fashioned. She had dreamt of the love that blots out everything else; but had found that in reality the idea of two people turning in on one another repelled her. When she married, she wanted it to be part of a shared way of life, including relatives, friends, neighbours, stretching out into the larger community. It seemed hard that she should arrive at this understanding of her needs at the time of the break-up of family life.

She pinned her hopes on Falmouth, which she visited in December with Felicity. This, she told herself, was where her roots were. 'I mean to come and live here after the war,' she said to Felicity. 'I'm going to write a history of my forebears.'

When she arrived, she found Granny Tippet very frail, but with the strong jaw more resolute than ever now that the flesh had fallen away; and the long-seeing blue eyes quite as unnerving. Grandchildren constantly erupted into the house. But the feel of a rooted life was not there. Perhaps this was the fault of her grandfather. Joseph Tippet, crippled by arthritis, sat in his chair by the window, looking out to the Carrick Roads, and dreaming of his days in the Merchant Navy. Alice realized that if she pinned her hopes of family on Cornwall, she must accept that her roots were made of seaweed. The thought that she came of a breed of rovers was not without its appeal. Her grandmother, who had been watching her intently since her arrival, said, 'You've got yourself into a fine old muddle, haven't you? You don't know what you want.'

'I think I want to settle down,' Alice said. 'But I mean to get to Ceylon before the war is over.'

'That's the trouble with you young people. There are too many choices open to you. I had to settle for what was offered and get on with it.'

'But you don't regret it?'

Alice hoped for a resounding affirmation, but all her grandmother said was, 'What's the point of regretting?' She had not thought of life in terms of expectation, but rather of what was available to her: you accepted the gifts of life along with its demands. Regret was irrelevant.

Joseph sighed, 'Ah, the China seas!' There was such a world of longing in his voice that Alice felt she must regret it all her life if she did not get to the East.

When she left, she said impulsively to her grandmother, 'After the war, I shall have had enough of travelling. Then I shall come here and live in Falmouth.'

'Not you!' Her grandmother put her arms around her. 'I'll tell you something, Alice. You'll never be satisfied. Never, all your life.'

Alice, suddenly aware of how much she loved her grandmother, was alarmed at the thinness of the arms which held her. As the bus carried them into Truro, all her hopes of a life here seemed to be receding as the bus tunnelled between the high hedges. It was not so much that she wanted it less, as an understanding that Granny Tippet's world was no longer available for her to live in.

'I thought your grandmother was *fascinating*,' Felicity said. 'But Falmouth is the dreaded end.'

'I *must* get to Ceylon, Felicity. When do you think we shall go to OTC?'

Felicity had her mind on other matters. At Truro, she insisted that there was no need for them to catch the afternoon train. 'We shall be sure to get a hitch back. Let's go for a drink and assess the possibilities. There must be a decent hotel somewhere.'

'We haven't got time, Felicity.'

'We've got twenty hours!'

'But there aren't twenty trains.'

'We're not going by train.'

A stroll along the main street enabled Felicity to identify the hotel which would attract the officer trade – never a difficult task in any small town. They went first to the cloakroom, where Felicity made the most of her short, dark hair by flicking it into wispy curls across her forehead, giving a festive look to her long face so that it resembled a milkman's horse on carnival day. She looked at Alice, who was piling up her long hair, and said sharply, 'Come on; we haven't got all day. Let's go and survey the field.'

Within a few seconds she was saying to an Army captain, 'Well, that's very hospitable of you, I must say. Gin and It will be just the thing.' She always contrived to sound as if she was being entertained in a private house. She looked round the dingily respectable room and said, 'Not bad, eh?' as if she was congratulating the captain on his choice of furnishings.

'Not a place to stay, though,' he warned. 'Beds haven't been aired since Queen Victoria slept here.' He cocked an interested eye at Alice, who asked for beer.

His name was Rodney Stowe. He had a long face with good features, but so thin it looked as though it had been clamped in a press. The rest of his body had the same elongated, tortured appearance. Alice could imagine him in effigy, lying with fingers piously steepled in some dim cathedral recess. Felicity seemed to find him eminently acceptable. They took their drinks to a table where his companion was waiting for him. Stowe made introductions. Barney Crocker, a captain of marines, had none of Stowe's attenuated breeding. He was a compact man with an impatient, leathery face, and a body which looked strong enough to burst out of its uniform at any moment. He and Stowe were taking refreshment prior to driving to Gloucestershire, where they both lived. Felicity, allowing some elasticity to county boundaries, said that she rode to hounds in Gloucestershire. Stowe said his family farmed there. Felicity said then he must know the Maplehursts. He said he did know the Maplehursts; whereupon Felicity changed tack smartly and began to talk about Ralph Heneker-Howell, whom he did not know. Crocker lit a cigarette, and made a pessimistic assessment of how long it would take to bed Alice.

'Are you stationed at Falmouth?' he asked.

'Plymouth.'

They drank in silence for a few minutes, then he said, 'You'd better come with us.' He sounded resigned, but when she hesitated, he jerked his head in Felicity's direction. 'Your friend has it all wrapped up, anyway.'

'Can you imagine!' Felicity said to Alice some moments later. 'These chaps are insisting on going out of their way to take us back to Plymouth. I call that a jolly good show.'

Crocker looked at her as though he would not be surprised were she to balance a ball on her nose. They went out to the car. Stowe held the back seat door for Alice, but Felicity said, 'Alice has to travel in front or she gets car sick.' In the back, she and Stowe talked about Bonnie Bravely, whom Alice assumed to be a horse until Felicity said she had married Edward Phillimore. Alice soon ceased to listen to their conversation. Barney Crocker was a typical marine driver: no doubt the marines' assault course included a section on reckless driving.

'I'm sorry we're taking you out of your way,' she said, as he slewed round a corner on two wheels.

'Makes no odds.' He saw little in this for himself and was in a hurry to get the journey over. The miles sped by in record time. Then, as they came towards Bodmin Moor, they got behind an army convoy, moving slowly through the narrow lanes. Crocker lit a cigarette and drove with one hand on the wheel; his swearing relied heavily on the anatomical, as befitted such a physical man. Felicity said, 'Why don't we stop? Stretch the cramped limbs, eh?'

They had tea at a farmhouse. The convoy was still on the road when they emerged. Perhaps it, too, had stopped for a brew-up? 'Who the hell is in charge of this circus?' Regardless of any traffic which might come up behind him, Crocker left the car and strode off in search of someone to browbeat. Alice walked a few paces from the road. Ahead, the land stretched away, unbroken by house or hedge, as far as the eye could see. She never stood on the edge of wilderness without a sense of having escaped from somewhere, or something. Service life had been the great liberation so why, now, should she be breathing this harsh moorland air as though her lungs had long been constricted? She realized she was becoming bored with service life; its repetitions now outweighed its capacity for surprise. The view stretched vision, and she found herself wishing it went on forever – but then *that* would become very boring indeed. If she wasn't careful, life was going to resolve itself into a matter of balancing boredom and surprise. Was her grandmother right in saying she would never be satisfied?

Felicity came up behind her. 'How are you getting on with yours? Mine's a distinct possibility. We're going to stop for a drink at Jamaica Inn.'

'If we do that, we shan't get back tonight.'

'All the better.'

'I thought you wanted your commission?'

'As the most likely means to a husband. If I could get one without all that fag, I'd be only too pleased.'

'Well, I want to go to Ceylon; and I'm more likely to do that in signals than anything else.'

'Alice, this is very important to me. Rodney is related to the Smalls of Nether Wishford.'

They returned to the car. Neither of the two men was there. 'A nice pickle we shall be in if they just disappear,' Alice said.

'Do all your family have this gift of foreseeing calamity?'

'It doesn't need special powers to see that this is going to end badly.'

Crocker returned, got into the car, and started the engine. It occurred to Alice that he was on her side; he could not wait to get to Plymouth and find something more promising.

'Rodney isn't here,' Felicity protested.

'Gone for a pee, I expect.' He was turning the car off the road. 'This convoy goes on for miles, but apparently there's a minor road we can pick up about a mile and a half due west.'

By the time he had manoeuvred the car into position, Stowe had joined them. They bumped about for what seemed much further than a mile and a half.

'I've always wondered what happened *after* the characters rode off into the setting sun,' Alice said, as she was thrown against the windscreen.

They came at last to the minor road, which was little more than a track. As they turned on to it, Alice saw the sun going down somewhere behind her shoulder and was glad that at least they were heading in the right direction. It was nearly dark when the track ran downhill into a good-sized village.

'And a hostelry!' Felicity exclaimed.

It was a long, low stone building. The trucks and jeeps parked outside indicated it was much favoured by service personnel. Alice said, 'Our turn. What are you drinking?' The men gave their orders without demur and made for the gents. Felicity, who was close with money, departed in search of the ladies. Alice went to the bar and took her place beside a Negro soldier. The man behind the bar, a burly, bald-headed fellow, gave Alice a smile which was the more genial for seeing someone he actually wanted to serve. In most circumstances, she would have been pleased enough to catch his eye – it was usually difficult for a woman to get service at a bar. It was apparent, however, that she was now in the presence of someone even less privileged. She said, 'This soldier was before me.'

The barman, finding her less to his liking, said curtly, 'What are you having?'

Alice gave her order, then turned to the Negro. 'What will you drink?'

A GI sitting near by said, 'He's not drinking anything, sister. Not while we're here.'

The Negro was for departing with dignity, but he had an ATS girl with him, a little strutting hen, with frizzy peroxided hair and bulbous eyes either side of a formidable beak. She went up to the table where the GI was sitting and shouted, 'They come over here and fight for you buggers, don't they? They're good enough for that!'

The GI reacted with the wild uncontrol of a wounded animal. As he struggled to free himself from the restraining hands of his comrades, Alice was reminded of how her beloved dog, Badger, had reacted when a kitten had been introduced into the family – a betrayal which had roused him to a frenzy of fear and fury. Reason was as irrelevant to the GI as to Badger. The man's desperation would have been comic had it not been so frighteningly intense.

The landlord said to the Negro, 'Get out. Go on. Both of you. I'm not having any more trouble in here.' The Negro, a tall, quiet man, wore his humiliation with a fortitude which added to his stature. His girl was more strident. She made her exit screaming at the GIs, 'I wouldn't dirty myself with any of you . . .'

Crocker had come out of the gents and had taken in something of the situation, though not Alice's part in it. 'There's a table back there,' he said. 'You get out of the line of fire. I'll manage this.'

Alice sat down beside Felicity and Stowe. Felicity said, 'A bit overdone, don't you think? Even for an At. A cook-steward, I expect.' Alice was full of admiration for the courage of a girl who could take on so many hostile men. She herself felt weak at the knees.

Stowe said, 'The Americans should keep all this feuding for their own country.'

When Crocker returned to the table, the GI came with him. 'You seem to have made a conquest,' Crocker said indifferently. 'He wants a word with you.'

The GI stood looking down at Alice, shaking his head reproachfully. 'You shouldn't interfere in things you don't understand.' His rage had subsided, and his expression was that of a well-meaning man who is continually confronted with people who do not understand him. The fact that he was one of life's failures was already etched on the earnest, wrinkled brow. 'If you had any idea what this is all about, you'd know you British are really responsible.'

'Us!'

Crocker frowned at Alice. 'Easy does it.'

The GI raised an admonishing finger. 'Who shipped them over in the first place, tell me that?'

Stowe said to Alice, 'Humour him. He's just a crank.'

'I reckon the time's come when you should take them back.' He had the gentle, persuasive manner of a door-to-door salesman peddling an unmarketable commodity. Crocker found him amusing. 'In fact, I'm not sure they don't already have some scheme for you to take them back.'

'And the Red Indians, too, I expect,' Felicity said.

'No, no.' This made him more mournful than ever. 'The Red Indians belong, whether we like it or not.'

Crocker said, 'So, Geronimo stays.'

'I favour the Red Indians having certain rights,' he said seriously. 'But the blacks were shipped over by you British.'

'You've got a problem there,' Stowe said peaceably. 'We all sympathize with you, old chap.'

Alice said, 'I don't.'

His eyes implored her understanding; they were dark and unfathomably sad as a chimpanzee's. 'Look, sister, you have a class system here in England that's like nothing I ever came across before. You put up barriers and create reservations to keep *your own people* separate.'

'What nonsense!' Felicity exclaimed. 'People just know their place, and what is expected of them. It isn't something that has to be imposed, it happens naturally.' She looked at the GI with disfavour, and added, 'Bred in the bone.'

He paid no attention to her, but continued to press for Alice's conversion with all the evangelical zeal of his Pilgrim forefathers. 'Our problem is quite different. The blacks aren't the same as us. I'm not saying they're not human, but they are way down the evolutionary scale. You can't turn back. Even Darwin knew you can't turn back.'

Barney Crocker said to Alice, 'What did you do to start this?'

'I just offered to buy him a drink.' Alice wished she didn't sound so placatory when talking to Crocker.

'Who? Not the Sambo, for Pete's sake!' As she said nothing, he raised his eyebrows. 'Really? You are one very silly little girl.' He turned to the GI. 'Come on, my friend. You've made your point and we all agree with you.' He looked imperiously at Alice, who remained stubbornly silent. He said to the GI, with an edge to his voice, 'The English are an easy-going people, but *most of us* know tolerance can be stretched too far. I'll buy you a drink, and that's an end to it.'

He hauled the GI towards the bar, but the man twisted out of his grasp and came back to Alice. 'Do you go out with them? Look, I have to know. That girl — she was trash — but *you*, do you go out with them?' He gazed at her as though civilization was in the balance — which perhaps, for him, it was. The others waited impatiently for Alice to make her peace.

Alice's mouth was dry. 'No. But then . . . I don't go out with just any white man, either.' The truth was, she had felt embarrassed when she danced with a Negro; she would have made any excuse rather than go out with one. As Crocker hauled him away again, she said in a rush, 'And she wasn't trash. It was true, what she said — they're good enough to fight for you.'

This was too much for the GI's comrades. They decided to rescue him from Crocker. The marine was a hard-trained man, and he reacted quickly. Several of the GIs landed on the floor, and one of them came up with a piece of broken glass. A party of sailors, who had been drinking quietly in a corner, ignoring what was going on, now noticed that two Wrens were present. Never must it be said that the Navy failed to defend its own. They weighed in purposefully.

There followed a scene which was the staple ingredient of every Western and common to much farce. In the cinema, it would be greeted with applause or laughter. But here, witnessed in the raw, without benefit of cutting or shift of angle, the sight of so many able-bodied men mindlessly slugging away at one another, was sickening. Stowe alone stood back from the fray. An expression of mild disdain on his patrician face, he said, 'Allow me to escort you ladies . . .' He was hit on the temple by a flying chair, and sank gently between Alice and Felicity, lying at their feet rather as Alice had imagined him when she first saw him. A sailor grabbed hold of

Felicity, and pushed her towards the side of the room where there was a small window. He was joined by several of his mates, and between them they managed to get the two Wrens out of the window.

Alice landed neatly, but Felicity twisted her ankle, fell and gashed a knee. 'How you could get yourself involved with that dreary little lunatic, I simply don't know!' she fumed at Alice. 'I only hope someone sorts him out, maundering on in that hectoring way.' She accepted Alice's handkerchief and bound it round her knee. 'I expect he comes from some little mid-West town which sprouted up a hundred or so years ago, where they think civilization started with the Declaration of Independence.'

'I didn't mean to get involved with him.'

'My dear, you were shovelling away like a stoker, feeding his fire. And just look at *that* . . .' She pointed to where a van was speeding up the road. 'The Military Police! I hope you're satisfied.'

'I didn't mean . . .'

'Why do you take things so seriously? At the best of times it makes you a bit of a bore. On occasions like this, it's positively dangerous.' She limped off towards the van, which had stopped outside the inn. 'Some awful little American had a brainstorm,' she informed the first of the MPs to emerge. 'And there is an *Army officer* badly injured in there. We came here together. You must help me to get him out.'

Alice sat on a bench. Near by several ATS girls were leaning against an army truck. She had wrecked their evening, and they regarded her with dislike. She wished she could sort her feelings out as easily. She was angry for the Negro; yet sorry for the GI who, within his own racial group, would probably be just as downtrodden. She felt guilty about Felicity and a little afraid of Barney Crocker. Why couldn't she have given vent to her feelings as the ATS girl had done? Oh, for the days of childhood, when heroes and villains were readily identifiable, and one's response to them uncompromised by ambiguity!

An ambulance had arrived. Several sailors and GIs were being herded into the van by the military police. Barney Crocker accompanied them, looking masterful. No doubt he had imposed his version of events on the MPs and was now on his way to see that injustice was meted out. Two men appeared carrying a stretcher. Felicity limped beside them. She waited until the stretcher had been lifted into the ambulance and then climbed in. Alice hurried over to the ambulance.

'There's no room for you, Alice,' Felicity said firmly. 'And, anyway, you must get back to Plymouth and explain all this. I rely on you to think something up. You're so good at thinking.' She shut the door in Alice's face.

The driver of the ambulance said to Alice, 'Sorry, Jenny. I've stretched a point as it's her fiancé, but I daren't take you as well.'

Alice walked into the street. There was a signpost but the place names had been blotted out. She called to the ATS girls, 'Which is the way to Bodmin?' They pointed, and then relented. 'You can have a lift with us when our blokes come out.'

When Alice arrived at Bodmin station, the last train had gone. She spent the night in the waiting room with several sailors and a very drunk Scots soldier. She arrived at Plymouth at ten in the morning, and at half-past ten she was explaining her difficulties to First Officer. Although she incurred no punishment, she was left in little doubt that in First Officer's view she lacked those qualities so essential to leadership – judgement and initiative.

On the whole, Alice thought this a fair assessment. Hers was not the authority which, steadfast in the face of oppression, can reduce those around to shamefaced silence. Nor did she possess that lucidity of expression, that powerful emotional integrity, which leaves no unbiased onlooker in any doubt as to the rightness of a cause. It seemed rather to be her fate that, given a cause to espouse, her voice should rise a nervous couple of notches; and her mind fail to extract from the turmoil of her emotions that one statement which would incisively demolish all argument. She wished Ben had been there. Dear Ben! He was always so *trenchant*.

Felicity returned in good spirits, which First Officer's coldness failed to dispel. She told Alice that she was unofficially engaged to Rodney Stowe. When the next batch of trainees went to do their officer training, Alice and Felicity were not among them.

Alice wrote to Ben, 'You are so right about Daddy being passionate. Why is it we are made to feel we should admire people who are *restrained*, who guard their speech as if nothing must come out that hasn't passed a fitness test; and lock their emotions away in some little private chamber, like jewels so precious they must be kept in a vault!

'As for Ceylon, sadly . . .'

13

Autumn 1944–Spring 1945

France was all but free. Paris had been liberated in August. Daphne and Irene had celebrated in a Kensington restaurant to the strains of 'The Last Time I saw Paris' soulfully rendered by Judy Garland. Daphne suspected that Peter was in Paris. About Angus's whereabouts she had no information.

'I thought you might have heard?'

'Good Heavens, no!' Irene spoke as if she could imagine nothing more unlikely.

Daphne did not probe, perhaps saw no reason to. She enjoyed the company of her friends, but had no wish to learn the intimate details of their love lives.

'Yesterday I visited a friend of Peter's who is in hospital,' she said. 'Ivor Ritchie. He went over on D-Day, and said it was the most fantastic experience of his life. Then, a few weeks later, he was on a special mission that ran into trouble. His companions bought it; he was the lucky one, and only lost a leg.'

'Let's hope he will always think himself lucky.'

'Oh, he will! There is nothing mean-spirited about *him*. One meets some marvellous people, don't you think? It makes me quite ashamed. I meant to do so much; and I've had a dull war.'

'You've married a man who sounds anything but dull.'

'I just wish he wasn't my proxy on this occasion. Don't misunderstand me; I'm not complaining. But can you imagine how it must have felt, these last months? Like Agincourt.'

Irene nodded. 'I'm glad I've lived through these last days. That feeling won't come again in a hundred years. It's what's going to happen afterwards that worries me.'

'So long as we don't start talking about a land fit for heroes, and all that sanctimonious cant that went on after the last war. Men coming back knee-deep in self-pity.'

Irene stilled the retort which came to her lips, remembering Daphne's father. He was never mentioned now, but she sometimes wondered whether some of Daphne's remarks might not be addressed to him.

She raised her glass. 'Here's to a safe homecoming for all husbands and lovers!' At least Daphne could not quarrel with that.

But she underestimated her friend. 'Peter wouldn't want that. If things go badly, he'd sooner come home *on* his shield. Here's to a victorious homecoming!'

As Irene had no quarrel with that, they drank to it.

By November, the Germans were still in the Ardennes. The sound of gunfire could be heard continuously in the small town where Angus Drummond waited in vain to meet a German informer, about whose reliability there were doubts. The German was either dead, detained, or had been warned away.

Angus was usually good at waiting. Perhaps because he had not enjoyed his own life, he was able to absorb himself in the small affairs of his adopted lives. His unhappy home life served him well in other ways. He reacted coolly in danger – its effect on him was that of delayed shock, so that he went on functioning with an appearance of complete normality in circumstances in which others might have panicked. It sometimes seemed he had concealed his feelings for so long that he himself was no longer sure what they were.

He had been very successful in his original mission to investigate the activities of rival Resistance groups in a sensitive region. He was convinced he had been right in recommending that the Communist-organized group was the more likely to be effective. After that, he had successfully carried out other missions. Thanks to the many times in his life when he had wished himself invisible, he had developed a gift for not drawing attention to himself. Now, with a minimum of disguise, he had come to this small town, where he was accepted as the brother-in-law of the chemist, a morose widower with few close friends. Angus had seen pictures of the man whose identity he had assumed; and of his wife, child, house, dog. He was well-rehearsed in all aspects of the man's life. The chemist assured him there was no danger that enquiries at the man's home would find his brother-in-law there. He had indeed started out on a visit to the chemist. Angus did not know what his fate had been. Nor was he curious.

One matter did arouse his curiosity.

The chemist's house was down a rough track which led to a farm. It was an isolated place with only a few outhouses and a dilapidated old stone house in sight. From his bedroom window, Angus looked across the track to the old house. Since he arrived, there had been a lot of rain. Then one morning when he woke, the skies had cleared. Raindrops still hung in the grass and the black branches of trees glistened; the ruts in the track were full of yellowish water. But the sun was out. The door of the old stone house swung on rusty hinges. There was no one there – he had been told that the house was unoccupied. But the movement of the door, the shift of light and shadow, gave a momentary illusion of life within. He had imagined the house to have been empty for years; but now he saw that only a few slates were missing from the roof, and none of the shutters hung loose from the cobwebbed windows.

'Who lived in that house?' he asked the housekeeper when the chemist had left to open his shop. The woman, though as taciturn as her employer, was less grudging of information; and for some reason, he wanted this particular information. He was sure she knew everything that went on here, in this house, and in the town.

She was a dark, dour, middle-aged woman, with the eyes which can sometimes go with such looks, suggesting that resentment fuels an inner fire. Angus was never sure where her loyalties lay. It seemed unlikely that it was patriotism which motivated her, and he did not think she had any great affection for her employer.

As she answered him, her eyes went to the place at table where the chemist usually sat. She spoke as though he was there to be defied, or taunted.

'They were Jews. They had connections with important people in Paris who thought they would be safer here. The farmer let them have the house. I expect their wealthy friends made it worth his while.'

Angus accepted the statement without surprise. It had long seemed possible to him that our obsessions can alter life, take control of events. 'Something happened to them?'

'The Germans were becoming suspicious. Someone thought it necessary to create a diversion.'

'They were betrayed?'

She shrugged her shoulders and turned towards the stove, where she was making soap from pig's fat. 'They would have been caught anyway. It bought time, when time was needed.'

He took the crockery to the sink, and began to wash it. 'But it shocked you?'

'No.' The suggestion angered her. 'They put all our lives in danger, just by being there. Someone used them to advantage, that is all.'

He said nothing, guessing she would interpret his silence as dissent

244

and that, with her temperament, she was more likely to respond to this than any probing. He was right. Perhaps the chemist, too, answered her by silence.

'They belonged here no more than the Germans.' He had been mistaken if he thought she would need to defend her attitude. The single statement seemed to her to be justification in itself. 'He has become a Communist. It is all he thinks about now. Before the war, no one thought of such things. Communists, Germans, Jews – what are they to us?'

Hers was the peasant's hatred of the stranger; the deep, instinctive awareness that in any exchange he will be the loser. Probably there were other people like her in this small town; people whose passions were rooted in something older than the idea of country.

I am a stranger, he thought. How safe am I? He wanted to survive. He feared capture. His nerve was good when playing the game of suspense; under physical pressure, he would crack. There were German soldiers in the town, but the Allied armies were getting nearer. Soon he would be safe. Why, then, must he do something so foolhardy on this day?

When he had fed the chicken, he did not return to the house. Instead, he walked across the track, and pushed open the door of the Jews' house. It smelt of damp and dust. Had he expected something more, a smell of putrefaction, the charnel house? He went slowly up the stairs. There *was* a smell on the landing, oily, perfumed, which triggered memory. He stood sniffing, moving his head from side to side, but could not catch it again. The memory was vivid though: Katia, standing outside a cinema, on an April day. It was his own reactions he remembered, his envy of her vitality. About Katia herself, he had forgotten more than he had ever known. The slovenly schoolgirl with the crude make-up and the tight-fitting, shabby clothes was no part of his vision. In his mind he saw her as a mature woman, magnificently endowed with sexual energy. Which she might have become – or might not.

Yes, he thought. I am approaching understanding. He walked from room to room, hoping for what? For stone walls to cry out, to make the inexplicable surrender to his reason? He found bird droppings, dead mice; a table, a few broken chairs; no personal possessions.

And yet, surely he was nearer to Katia than he had ever been, standing in this place from which Jews had been taken? They must have heard the soldiers coming. He could get that far in understanding. He knew about the steps that fall regularly through all our nightmares, which cause us to wake in terror, or rouse us to take charge of our dreaming so that the unthinkable never happens. He recalled a waking moment, in a shop doorway. It was a rule that no pupils should leave the school during break period. He and his friend had gone out to get cigarettes, and on their way back had seen a master walking down the street. They had dodged into the doorway of a gents' outfitters. As he heard the footsteps coming nearer, he had experienced a moment of sheer terror which had nothing to do with any punishment likely to be meted out at school. The master, at that moment, was the archetype of the irrational terror which forever stalks abroad; if one gets in his path, the civilized façade will give way to the dark reality that lies beyond. On that occasion, the archetype had passed by.

Yes, he was near to knowing. It was the Jewishness which prevented him from completely entering into her fate; a thousand years and more of being a stranger in every land on the face of the earth.

In the downstairs room, there was a cat with a litter of kittens. There were no books, no pictures, nothing to give a clue to identity. Only on the wall, near the ground, some words had been scrawled. He studied them with that vicarious thrill of horror, never entirely free from self-indulgence, which the gruesome can arouse. Not French, perhaps not words at all? What did they signify, these hieroglyphics? Praise of God, fear of Death? A game? Why on the wall? So that it might outlast them? Or had someone come in afterwards – a child, perhaps, leaving this proof of daring?

The kittens were rubbing round his legs, screeching and clawing. Starving, probably. He shrank from them, but they persisted. Their tiny heads seemed hung at an odd angle from their sticklike bodies, giving the appearance of deformity. Their mother watched, crouched in the corner, a skeleton creature too exhausted to meet the needs of her young. She opened her mouth in faint entreaty. It was most unpleasant. He felt tempted to take them all out and drown them, to put an end to their discomfort and his own. But when he bent down, he found he was afraid to touch these wriggling bundles of bone.

Suddenly, he was aware that someone was coming along the track. He went to the window and saw an SS officer. It was too late to get out. The worst possible mistake is to be seen retreating; however dangerous the situation, it is wiser to stand one's ground. But it would be bad to be found here. No one came to this house, and the Germans knew it and knew why. What could he say to explain himself? Would it serve to take a risk, to say, 'I was curious. I have never been in the house of a Jew. I wondered if it would be different . . .'

The steps came nearer. This time it was going to happen; he would not wake, and the footsteps would not pass on. For one moment, it was as though all life ceased, and he was suspended out of time. Then the shadow fell across the doorway. It was a big, blond man with a full mouth and bright, dancing eyes. Angus knew of him. He had a reputation for cruelty. Prisoners had died under this man's hand, women among them. He said, 'What are you doing here?'

Angus replied conversationally, but with the requisite hint of subservience in the pitch of his voice, 'It was the cat. She was having kittens; today I noticed she had had them. So, I followed her . . .' He pointed, wondering as he did so if he would have used another human being as a diversion as readily as he used the cat.

The man looked down. The kittens were already fawning about him, opening their hideous pink mouths. Angus stood in the shadows, watching while the boot which could crush to a pulp toed one of the kittens. Shall I, Angus taunted himself, at the first downward thrust of that heel, spring forward and rid the earth of this creature while he is engrossed by the prospect of brutality? The man bent down and prodded the kitten in the stomach; it curled around his finger in a furry ball. The mother came towards him, mewing desperately. Angus remained still; as always, the onlooker. The man put out his other hand and stroked the head of the mother. 'There, there!' he said reassuringly. 'Such a good little mother! But so thin!'

Angus said, 'I was going to drown them. They'll die anyway.'

'Ach, no, no! Think of all the effort she has made to keep them alive. I will get milk for them. I am on my way to the farm, anyway.'

Angus and the SS officer walked out of the house together. Angus accompanied him down the track to the farm until he reached the chicken coop, where he made an excuse that he must feed the chicken. He watched the German walk away. The sun still shone on the wet grass and a few birds were singing. The cat and her kittens would survive: the indecipherable writing remain on the wall.

And he must go. He sensed that this place was no longer safe for him.

A sharp November evening; the grass already coated with hoar-frost and cold air rasping in the throat. Judith and Austin had had several walks together in recent months. In spite of his lame leg – or perhaps because of it – he was a resolute walker. 'The next best exercise to rugger,' he had told her. Although it had crippled him, his devotion to rugger was absolute. On this particular day, they had walked further than usual and it was dark by the time they came to the field footpath which led to his village. Judith glowed with that sense of virtue which comes from winter exercise, of having challenged cold and disinclination and come through triumphant. For Louise, lonely and frustrated without Guy, wartime Sussex had been a place under siege, hemmed in by dark hills and barbed wire. Judith would remember the vast expanse of the night sky shimmering with stars; there would never be such skies again once the war was over. 'Look at that!' she exclaimed, seeing the brilliant flash in the sky. A split second later, there was an earthbound roar, and she and Austin were lying face down in the field, while echoes rumbled all around them.

'It must be the thing Louise wrote about,' she said, raising her head cautiously and peering through the wet grass. 'They say it's gas mains – but gas mains can't be blowing up all over the country, can they?'

'Something has gone up in the village.' He pointed to a cottage, flames streaming from its thatch, eerily resembling a cartoon figure with hair on fire.

It was, in fact, an adjacent barn which had been fired, but by the time Austin and Judith reached the scene, the fire had a hold on the cottage thatch. In the field beyond, a torn tree marked the crater where the weapon had come to earth. It stood up-ended, its chalky roots spraying out, as grotesquely indecent as an old woman dragged precipitately from her bed. The elderly couple who lived in the cottage were huddled, dazed, in their small garden, while neighbours handed out what furniture and prized possessions could be extricated. Judith and Austin hurried into the cottage.

Here, they were greeted by a man who had appointed himself director of removals. 'Two more pairs of hands and we'll have that settee out. Not you, Momma, sit down!' He was greatly excited and kept up a barrage of encouragement, interspersed with catchphrases from BBC shows which were not always appropriate. 'Make way, make way for the lady with the china dog. After you, Claude!' . . . 'The glass decanter? I don't mind if I do, sir!'

The room pulsed with rosy light which gave a Wagnerian intensity to the activities of the removers. At any moment, the music of *Götterdämmerung* might rise above the roar of flames and the director's inanities.

Judith and Austin took hold of one end of the settee. As soon as they did this, however, the man who had been tugging at the other end desisted. 'Why, Austin Marriott! I have been trying to get hold of you for days. I've been going through those letters of my father's . . .' He was dressed in a velvet smoking jacket – the explosion had probably interrupted his perusal of the letters. The flickering light reflected in his pince-nez and gave to his thin, scholarly face a look of mild insanity.

Austin said, 'Suppose we get this settee out?'.

'Ah, yes.' He strained ineffectively. 'I was once told that it is possible to lift a heavy piece of furniture with two fingers, if leverage is applied in the right place. Now, where, I wonder . . .' Judith went to his assistance.

The director shouted, 'Make way, make way for the lady and gents with the settee. After you, Cecil!'

The stairwell was now a smoking chimney. As they struggled, half-blinded, to get the settee through the narrow doorway, Judith's helpmate said, 'He is quite affectionate about Lloyd George; whereas you will recall that in the essays he has nothing good to say of him.' One leg came off the settee and this enabled them to manoeuvre it out into the open.

Austin said to Judith, 'This is Harry Makepiece.'

Harry Makepiece shook hands with Judith, then, excusing himself, he darted back to the cottage and returned with the leg of the settee. 'You might like to have a glance at them. There are some amusing anecdotes . . .'

An Air Raid Warden came running up the garden, arms thrashing like a veritable Don Quixote. 'Get that stuff out of the way! The firemen can't get through.'

'But, my dear chap, *where* are we to put it?'

'I am not your dear chap, Mr Makepiece, I am an *Air Raid Warden*.' He inflated as he made this announcement, standing on tip-toe as if about to levitate.

'Yes, yes, I know perfectly well who you are, my dear . . .'

'You take your instructions from me, see.' He danced from one foot to the other. 'Put it out in the lane.'

'Then we shall block the lane. But if that is the way you want it . . .'

'Yes, that is the way I want it. I know more about this than you, even if I didn't go to Eton. Put it out in the lane. How do you think the firemen are going to get through, you silly old sod.' He whirled into the cottage, where he engaged in furious debate with the director of removals.

'How extraordinary these people are!' Mr Makepiece wiped smuts from his pince-nez. 'I have lived here for twenty-five years and all that time he has been harbouring the suspicion that I went to Eton.' He spat on the glass and rubbed vigorously. 'Eton, indeed!'

Firemen came stumbling through the cluttered garden, their hose falling foul of chairs and china cupboards, which seemed to arouse the old couple from their stupefaction – a broken cup being so much more within one's capacity for grief than the loss of a home. There was a disorganized attempt to clear the area around the burning cottage. Austin and Judith, salvaging china, lost contact with Harry Makepiece.

'What an interesting life you must have!' Judith said, piling willow-pattern plates on one of the cushions from the settee.

'Well now, I am glad you have said that.' He added a Toby jug to her collection. 'Because I had been intending to ask you to share it.'

'I'm not used to your sort of person.' She stood by the sundial, embracing her bundle, and feeling like a peasant victim of aristocratic assumption. 'Where am I to put this down?'

'No one is used to Harry Makepiece. I should think over there, under the hedge, wouldn't you? Much better than blocking the lane.' He guided her through trampled shrubs and rows of squashed cabbages. 'You mustn't take writers seriously. Their books are life to them. Literature is all they know about – when they talk shop, you should see it as their equivalent of women exchanging recipes.' Burning straw drifted on the night breeze and Judith smelt her hair singeing. Austin put out the spark with his hand.

She laid her load down gently, just as a ceiling caved in, rendering up its burden with an agonizing crack of timber. The fire fanned out to claim new territory. Austin took off his jacket and put it over Judith's head to protect her hair. She said fiercely, 'Women do *not* spend their time exchanging recipes!'

'Make way there!' The director, worsted in his battle with the Air Raid Warden, was now taking charge of the clearance of the garden. A couple edged past Judith and Austin carrying the settee piled precariously with rugs, cutlery and silverware. 'You're doing splendidly, my dears, you're . . . wooah! Obstacle to be circumnavigated. Steer her to the port side, madam . . . the *port* side! Ah well, and they call us a seafaring nation!'

The warden erupted onto the front path, shouting, 'Get out, all of you! Get out into the lane.'

'That is what we are doing.' The director turned to Austin, momentarily shedding the mask of comedy to speak from the heart. 'Officious little bugger. Can't control himself, that's his trouble. I was at school with him. Always getting into a tantrum and wetting himself, even then. His mother was a decent sort, though. Married beneath her.' He resumed his responsibilities. 'We'll have to store this stuff for the old folk. Could you take some of it at your place?'

'Yes, of course. But, which seems more to the point, where are *they* going?'

'The vicarage. Then they will go to their daughter in Crowborough tomorrow.' He walked away, singing 'This is a lovely way to spend an evening'.

'The vicar has them for the night, and I have their effects for the duration,' Austin said glumly, as a small, burdened procession began to make its way towards his house.

The helpers, rewarded with tea and stale biscuits, showed a natural inclination to relax and relive the events of the night.

'I said to him, "Now, Vicar, I know you want to help like everyone else; but it's those two poor souls who really need you now." I wasn't having him in there with his two left hands.' '

'Well, how much do you reckon we salvaged, then?'

'I was surprised at what they'd got in there, I'll tell you that! And her always acting as though they hadn't two-ha'p'orth to rub together!'

'Glass decanter! And both of them teetotal!'

'Her old father never signed no pledge!'

Judith, an outsider, was hardly noticed. But at one moment, as she dispensed further cups of tea, she was aware that, during a lull in the conversation − no one having further revelations to contribute − more than one person was watching her. When the eyes had made their inventory, they turned to Austin. No judgements were made. These people were not involved, they merely noted with indifference something which was happening outside the framework of their own lives. Judith thought, alarmed, 'This has gone too far.' She must have time to think.

It was now very late and she knew that Austin would insist that she could not bicycle back to her lodgings. 'How are you going to get back?' she asked a man whom she recognized as a farmer.

'I've got my old van. Want a lift?'

'If you can take my bike?'

'No trouble.'

He was a good-natured man and had promised a lift to a couple who lived at the far end of the village. 'I'll drop 'em off and come back for you,' he said.

So, when everyone had departed, Judith was left alone with Austin. 'We must get all this cleared up for you,' she said, as though addressing an unseen assembly. She began to stack cups and saucers.

'We must indeed,' he said. 'So stop fiddling with the crockery.'

She looked round the room, which seemed full of books now that the people had gone. Stanley had had a lot of books, but nothing to compare with this. 'You bring your work into the house,' she said. 'I should get bored with it.' If he had been a farmer treading muck, it wouldn't have worried her.

'I get bored, too,' Austin said. 'Do you realize that for every book we publish, I read dozens we don't accept?'

'I don't mind about the books, or your reading them.' She spoke as if his intellectual pursuits were toys left lying about. 'It's the people. When I don't find them boring, I shall be overawed by them.' She screwed up her eyes, thinking of Tolstoy and Gide and others who might be relied upon to create awe.

'Nothing overawes you for long,' he said drily. 'But I concede it may cause difficulties.'

She could visualize the people who would come to this house, sitting here, exchanging literary small talk long into the night, when she wanted to go to bed, dropping names along with cigarette ash. Then there would be the others, people of greater stature, magnificent in their intellectual pride. And she would range among them, like a cat, picking its way amid treasures, tilting china in order to attract attention. Indeed, there would be difficulties!

He took her hand and drew her down beside him on the couch. 'The work doesn't have to come home. This is far enough from London for me to arrange my life in separate compartments which don't overlap, like a civil servant.' Stanley had always been earnest; Austin sounded as if he had some difficulty in taking himself seriously. Judith did not know which she found the more irritating. 'In London, I would be a publisher . . . But what would happen here? It would be a place I escaped to at week-ends. Would you build a life in the village? I expect so. And you would find little jobs for me to do so that I felt included, a part of village life.'

'Voluntary fireman?'

They both laughed, but without much zest. She said, 'I don't want just the part that's left over from your working life.'

'So what is the trouble?'

'We haven't heard what *you* want, have we?'

He seemed not to have imagined that he might be required to give account of himself. After several moments' silence, during which, judging by his expression, he might have been contemplating a disabling operation, she said, 'You must admit that we don't seem to have a great deal in common – unless you feel the need of an injection of good yeoman blood!'

He looked at her, surprised and appreciative, with that hint of relish which had shaken her once before. She felt as if, all unknowing, he had touched a secret spring and revealed things hidden away whose existence she, their possessor, had long forgotten; like the Christmas gifts of trinkets which were too 'fancy', their shiny brightness raising doubts as to what possible use they might be put to. And no respectable answer presenting itself, they must be put out of sight; the fact of their being gifts saving them from the waste bin, since gifts must not be thrown away, only buried.

What audacity is it you have uncovered in me? she wondered, while Austin addressed himself to more prosaic questions, under the impression that this was what was required of him.

'I suppose I have overworked – like a lot of older people, left to hold a business together while the young rattle around saving the world. Added to that, my emotional life has been dead for a long time.' Oh dear, oh dear! she thought, having brought him to this, and not now seeing it as important. They were already joined in a measure which had no need of words. But the mind cannot be left out of this exercise entirely, and must be allowed to come to its own decision, even though the conclusion be known. So she set her mind to attend to him. 'Things were getting quite bad at the beginning of last year. When I was with people, socially or otherwise, I didn't contribute anything. I heard myself thanking my hostess for a delightful evening; telling my daughter it had been good to see her again; I sat at my desk trying to say something positive to an author who deserved encouragement, and sounding grudging. Nothing seemed good, delightful, or worthy of praise. Then, you got into that railway compartment, and something happened. I have no idea what. I didn't think of you afterwards. But when I saw you again at Brighton station, I said to myself, "Here she comes!" as if I had been expecting you to arrive.' There was a long pause, then he said rather unhappily, as though his lack of eloquence had convinced him it was a matter of no great significance, 'I suppose you might say that I needed you.'

She felt depressed. She, too, had been through a distressing time. *Her* emotional life had been drained. Why should he assume that she was strong enough to meet his needs – comprising, as she understood it, restoration of the good life, delight, and the ability to think positively?

She looked round the room again, imagining that life here would definitely be too cerebral. How she would miss the shared jokes which she and Stanley had accumulated over the years; how long it would take for her and Austin to learn to accept each other's weaknesses!

And her children! They came to her on a thread of laughter and tears, unbidden as voices carried briefly on the night air to the dreamer by the hearth – a haunting, whether of time past or future the awakened dreamer scarcely knows. Nor whose the pain.

'Perhaps we should talk about this another time.' Austin, too, seemed filled with sudden apprehension.

Such a melancholy sight he presented that one might imagine his last breath to have sighed out leaving a face all puckers and pleats, like a doll drained of its sawdust life. Oh, you men! Judith thought. What a good thing we women don't leave our store cupboards in your keeping! And restored by the certainty of her own resourcefulness, she rose briskly to her feet. 'Do you realize we haven't eaten since lunchtime? No wonder we feel so dreary.'

They went into the kitchen. When the farmer came, she said, 'Do you mind? I expect you are hungry, too. It was all rather terrifying, wasn't it?'

'You would have been even more terrified if you had heard what I heard,' he answered. 'They hadn't cleared their attic, the wicked old dears.'

Austin said, 'You mean it was full of the accumulated treasures of their thirty years together, the weight of which might have brought the ceiling down on us at any moment?'

Judith recalled, 'We cleared our attic; but the ceiling came down just the same.' She felt sad, but held back the tears, thinking, I mustn't give way. It's too late. Too late for that now.

The dance must take its course, and doubt was a part of the pattern. She would be troubled, and lie awake at night thinking of the children and asking herself whether she was doing the right thing; yet knowing that somewhere, not too far away, joy awaited her. The pain and doubt were only stepping stones by which she would find her way to it.

In the spring of 1945, Jacov Vaseyelin had the use of a flat in London, which belonged to a journalist friend who was covering the fighting in Germany. In a surprisingly short time, Jacov had moved from near-poverty to affluence. The flat was in a block of Victorian mansions in Westminster.

Louise could hear the voices in the street and the rumble of buses. These busy sounds added to the luxury of being abed in the afternoon. The curtains stirring in a light breeze, and the glint of sunlight on the beads she had tossed down on the dressing table, added to her pleasure. She raised her arms, stretching her body from the tips of her fingers to her toes. She felt well-disposed to all human kind, and could have embraced the whole world but for the delightful languor which had eased out the tensions of the past week. She lay contentedly looking up at the pattern of light on the ceiling, until appetite began to oust languor. She called to Jacov, 'All I need is the smell of real coffee.'

He came to the doorway, shoulder hunched, one hand casually miming that in this respect alone, he was impotent to supply her need. 'Brandy, perhaps?'

'Ugh! Tea, then.'

It was cuttingly cold, as spring can be. There was no heating. When she got up she went into the bathroom to wash and then dressed quickly.

'When the war is over, it's going to take years to bring any warmth back into buildings like this,' she complained. Immediately, Guy intruded into her mind. She had a picture of him, standing on the doorstep, arms outstretched. It would not be the whole world he would want to embrace, but his wife and family exclusively. She might have felt differently had she known that at this moment, he was drinking coffee in a café in Florence with Monica Ames.

Jacov was bending over the stove. She stood beside him, nuzzling her chin into his shoulder. 'What have you got there? I'm ravenous.'

'An omelette.'

She watched him prodding delicately with a fork. 'You are more interested in food than in me.'

'To make a good omelette, you must give it all your attention.'

She ran a finger down his spine. He said, 'In a minute . . .'

He had always wanted her, but was not in love with her. She had no complaints about this, since she was not in love with him. They were old friends who had need of each other. Even 'friend' seemed to be claiming too much from Jacov. There was always a distance between him and other people. When he held her in his arms, Louise knew that there was a part of him which was totally disengaged. She sensed, however, that this was not of his choice, rather some kind of incapacity.

He plated the omelette with a flourish which would have been appreciated in the back row of the pit. 'If you're not careful,' Louise told him, 'you are going to become a performance.'

He kissed and fondled her, to demonstrate how well he performed, and then said, 'Omelettes must be eaten hot.'

She ate slowly. Nothing must be hurried; so much of pleasure lay in the savouring. 'You're a remarkably good cook. I can't think of anyone else who could do this with dried egg.'

'I used to cook for my mother and the twins after Anita died.'

'How are the twins? Still in Canada?'

'Yes. Praying they won't be fully trained by the time the war ends.'

'Do you miss them?'

This seemed to puzzle him. 'I haven't thought about it.'

'Jacov! All that has happened to you, and you can say that! Your only remaining family, and they may not come back to England!'

'They are very exclusive, the twins.'

'Don't you sometimes want to throw back your head and howl like an animal? I should.'

'No.' He looked apologetic, furtively helping himself to a further portion of omelette, leaving only a small piece for her. 'I'm afraid I don't.'

'How do you feel when you are on stage, then? Is it tragedy which gets the most out of you?'

'Goodness no! It's comedy I enjoy.'

'If it's comedy you're going to settle for, you had better stop over-acting. You can get away with belting out Shakespeare – there are lots of people who think that is rather good. But even they will begin to notice if you continue to play comedy like comic opera.'

This offended him. An attack on his character, he would have accepted meekly enough, but he expected praise for his acting. He said, 'I get good notices.'

'How much competition is there at this time?'

He leant forward and ran a hand down the inside of her thigh. 'I will worry when the competition comes along.' The gesture was made to deflect further criticism, but it put her on edge and spoilt the rest of their brief time together.

Even so, on her way home, her spirits were effervescent, and little tremors of laughter ran up and down her spine. His love-making was not ardent, but he never failed to stimulate her; teasing, but not malicious, he was an artful little monkey.

On the rare occasions when they could have a night together, there was an experience which she could share with him alone, a sharing of something outside themselves. This was when, after they had made love, they lay listening to music. Sometimes it would be Mozart; at others, Delius, Debussy, Schumann. Mostly, it was Mozart. They would lie quietly while the light in the room grew dim; and first the outlines of furniture dissolved, and then, as the city itself darkened, there was no window, and the material world was swallowed up in the music. As he lay beside her, Louise did not know whether Jacov enjoyed the music intellectually or dropped into it as a well. They never spoke of it afterwards. For her, this long descent into a darkness where there was only the deep throb of a cello or the sweet breath of a flute, was a return to that garden where God walked in the cool of the day.

After one such night in April, she went to collect the children, who had stayed with Aunt May. On arrival, she found her mother waiting for her. She went white with shock, imagining that there must be bad news of Guy. Aunt May said kindly, 'It's all right, dear. Nothing dreadful has happened.'

Surprisingly, Judith seemed too concerned with explaining her presence in London to notice her daughter's discomfort. She had travelled by train with a man who lived in some village near by – Louise had seen his house once and she seemed to think she should remember it. 'Red tiles . . .' she was saying. 'And a blue front door.'

'Louise was afraid we had had bad news of Guy,' Aunt May said. 'She has been so worried about him since he was wounded, haven't you, dear?'

'How could she think that?' Judith was irritated at being interrupted. 'You would have sent for her, not me.'

Louise had told Aunt May that she was going to the theatre and staying the night with a friend; she had not given a name or telephone number. Fortunately, Aunt May was too flustered by having said the wrong thing to pursue the matter any further. The children were playing in the garden. They could hear James shouting instructions to Catherine.

'Have they been good?' Louise asked, feeling wretchedly guilty.

'Yes, dear. James is very anxious to have a doggie.' Aunt May did not usually speak like this, but uneasiness made her adopt the vocabulary of the child.

'He knows he can't have a dog until the war is over. It would be terrified of the gunfire.'

Aunt May offered to make tea. They sat in the kitchen, where they could keep an eye on the children. Judith said she was surprised that Louise could not remember the country house with the red tiles.

'Why would I? Remember me? I'm Louise. Alice is the one of your daughters who imagines herself living in every period house she takes a fancy to.'

Judith coloured. The change of life affected her in this way, signalling heightened emotion unmistakably. She could feel her cheeks burning; colour spread from cheeks to neck. A light film of sweat broke out all over her face.

Aunt May said tactfully, 'Have a little more milk, dear. It's not good to drink anything so hot. I'm sure that is why people get ulcers.'

Louise was looking at her mother in astonishment. '*Why* are you in London?'

'I'm going to do some shopping.'

'There's a war on. Even if there was anything in the shops, you wouldn't have the coupons to buy it.'

'I want to look round. And then, I'm having lunch with the man who lives in the house I've been talking about – there's an orchard close by and . . .'

'What is his name?'

Judith offered up her secret joy with some reluctance. 'Austin Marriott.'

'I see.'

Aunt May, bewildered and uncomfortable, gave a little laugh. 'That's a funny name, isn't it? I mean, it sounds rather important . . .'

Judith said, 'He's a publisher,' as if this explained the name.

'Better than Joe Bloggs for a publisher, certainly.'

Aunt May looked anxiously from one to the other.

Judith said, 'I had hoped you would be more reasonable about this.'

'My goodness! You are really . . .'

'Not at all,' Judith interrupted sharply. 'It's just . . . a possibility.'

'Do you *like* him?'

'Really, Louise! How can you possibly imagine . . .'

'*Like* him?' Aunt May turned wounded eyes on Judith. 'You can't mean . . . it's not possible! Why, Stanley . . .'

'Stanley died over four years ago, May.'

'It seems only yesterday to me.'

'But not to me. I have had to live through every one of those days.'

'Yes, yes, Judith. Don't think I don't realize how hard it must have been.' It was apparent she had expected the hardness to last a lifetime.

'All this drama is out of all proportion,' Judith told them. 'I merely mention to you a man I have become acquainted with, and before we know where we are . . .'

'You didn't merely mention him!' Louise retorted. 'You told us all about his *house*.'

'I had thought you might like to come out to lunch with us.'

'Well, I wouldn't. Is he single? He must be very odd indeed if he is.'

The extent of her daughter's antagonism began to steady Judith. She reminded herself how long Guy had been away. It must be galling for a young woman, so deprived, to discover that her mother has been singularly — indeed, as Louise would no doubt see it — inappropriately blessed. She addressed herself to the business of introducing Austin.

'He is a widower. He was very fond of his wife, but she died a long time ago.' She smiled, remembering what Austin had said. 'I adored her. But she was always right. It is very difficult to live with someone who is always right. I didn't make a good fist of it.'

Louise, noting that smile, realized that her mother had already achieved intimacy of a kind with this man.

'He lost a son at Dunkirk. And he has one married daughter, who will probably like this no more than you.'

Louise, calmer now that Austin Marriott began to have more substance, said, 'You should have told me straight out, not kept on about red tiles and a blue door.'

'You won't come out to lunch with us?'

'I need time to get used to this first.' She could not bear to be a witness to anyone's happiness at this moment, let alone her mother's. 'Perhaps I could lunch with him some other time, if he works in London.'

Aunt May was crying, 'Oh Stanley, Stanley!' and Louise, thinking how they all betrayed him, found herself close to tears.

Aunt May went up to her bedroom to compose herself. Judith said to Louise, 'Didn't it ever occur to you that I might want to marry again?'

'No, it didn't. I thought you would probably come to live with us eventually.'

'That wouldn't have worked very well.'

'Is that why you are doing this?'

'No. I want to marry again.'

'Do you love him, this Austin Marriott?'

'When I married your father, I thought I loved him. I didn't even know him. The loving comes later.' She thought about Austin Marriott. In only one way did he resemble Stanley. They were both men who knew what they wanted. This was the kind of man she respected. 'The most I can say now is that there is . . . a rightness . . . about the way I feel.'

'I felt this rightness about Guy. You didn't think it was a sufficient answer then.'

So, Judith thought, all this time she has resented our attitude to her marriage; and now she sees me in her place, sueing for a blessing. She picked up her coat and prepared to leave. In the doorway, she said, 'If you are all against this, I can't do it. So you must think about it carefully.'

Louise brushed this aside with the impatience it deserved. 'You will do what you think fit. You always have. And I daresay I'm the same. But you must let us be against it, if that is how we feel – for the time being, at least.'

Judith left, not dissatisfied. That 'for the time being' was Louise's recognition that she would eventually come to terms with her mother's remarriage. So, too, would Claire, who would not long hold out against the prospect of finding another father figure – little though Austin might relish playing this role. Alice would be the one who would have most difficulty in acceptance.

As Judith walked along the street, her doubts fell away behind her. With every step she took, her body gave the affirmation she had sought from Louise. Happiness surged up from the very ground on which she walked, too strong to be refused.

14

Spring—Autumn 1945

The war with Germany ended in May. Alice was on duty in the Moat on VE Day and spent her time in a state of deep depression. Peace seemed a great anti-climax, an event for which people were even less prepared than they had been for war. A certain incoherence in the messages from ships spoke for the resentment of signals staff who must carry on as usual on this day. The signals office in the Moat was full of Naval personnel with very bad tempers.

The next evening was more memorable. Alice and Felicity set out in search of celebration. Several American sailors, waiting outside the Wrens' quarters, called out to them and held up bottles of gin as bait. For a dry navy, they were surprisingly well-supplied with liquor.

'I really shan't be sorry when they have gone back "over there",' Felicity said disdainfully.

'I wonder if they won't always be with us? People have adopted so many American ways since they came. I have an awful feeling we shall go on imitating them, and that in the end they will colonize the old country.'

'Watch it, Alice! This is becoming a little obsession with you. Whenever you see an American, you have a rush of prophecy to the head.'

'They corrupted me, that's why.' Alice declaimed dramatically, 'I spent my youth searching for Gary Cooper through the mean streets of Shepherd's Bush.'

Felicity said, 'I do wish Rodney could have got here,' conjuring up a mental picture of Captain Stowe straining nerve and sinew to reach Plymouth. In fact, he had not put in an appearance since he left hospital. Felicity wrote to him regularly. How often he replied, Alice did not know.

They made their way to the Hoe, where Lady Astor was encouraging a large crowd to sing. The sailors insisted on 'Land of Hope and Glory'; after which, they considered they had paid their debt to patriotism. Not so the man who had taken over from Lady Astor. It was his opinion that the proceedings would be improved by reminding his audience of the heroic efforts which men had made to win the war. The sailors, with the serviceman's unerring instinct that heroism must relate to someone other than himself, made rude noises. He persisted. The sailors turned their attention elsewhere. They began to stack wooden seats; and before anyone was aware of what they were doing, they had a sizeable bonfire going. It was almost dark now, and the ships in the harbour were dim shapes from which occasional sounds of jollity could be heard as a liberty boat set out for the shore. Every few minutes a searchlight swung across the water from Drake's Island. People had climbed the mounds around the fire and stood in tiers, the flames making their faces ruddy as a choir of Red Indian braves. 'Tipperary' replaced 'Land of Hope and Glory'. Several children, who had never seen a fire that was not caused by incendiary bombs, were terrified.

After a time, the NFS arrived to put out the fire. Plymouth, after all, was still under black-out regulations. 'Who do you think is going to bomb us tonight?' a sailor called out. 'The Japs?' The NFS men moved towards the fire. The sailors closed ranks; more than that, several of them grasped hold of the hose pipe. A tug of war ensued. A Petty Officer, who must surely have belonged to a male voice choir, sang, 'What shall we do with a drunken sailor?' and to cries of 'Hooray, and up she rises!' the Navy towed the NFS away. Lady Astor shouted ineffectively. The police and the NFS were very good-humoured about it all, and Alice and Felicity left before they ceased to be amused.

Lectures on aspects of civilian life now began to replace the diet of war films and documentaries. Alice attended one by an energetic Cambridge doctor who spoke uncompromisingly about democracy. There was, he said, no difficulty in people making their voices heard – the trouble with his own generation was that most of them had not bothered. 'When you leave the services, don't you make the same mistake. If anyone excuses inaction by talk of "post-war lethargy", remember that the lethargy that followed the Great War lasted for over twenty years.' After this, he gave a brisk run-down of the state of English life. Culturally, we lagged behind France and Austria; in education, we were inferior to Sweden, Norway, Canada and Holland; and our technical education was a disgrace compared to that of Germany and Italy. His audience listened enraptured, as only the English can, to this catalogue of failure. He was a County Councillor and could speak with authority on local government.

Take education: why couldn't young people learn in comfort without having to sit at desks? why couldn't they learn their lessons on a verandah in the heat of summer? why couldn't education be something to laugh about? couldn't youth be vigorous and eager? He was so vigorous himself that his hearers were convinced that he was providing profound answers to social questions. He went on to tell them about the committee structure, pausing briefly to ask why there were no women responsible for housing, and all maternity and child welfare committees. He emphasized the importance of each committee by pointing out what would happen without the service in question, painting a horrifying picture of a city where people had no houses in which to live, the education system had broken down because there was no money available for it, transport had come to a halt, and the sewage flowed in the streets. When the lecture was over, his audience filtered out onto the quarterdeck with a feeling of release as though they had attended some mass confessional. They stood, sniffing the warm spring air, and looking for further sins.

'He made local government sound quite interesting,' Alice said to Felicity as they walked across the moors to Yelverton later in the day. 'I wonder if I might do that? He seemed to think more women were wanted.'

'If all I had to look forward to was answering the call of local government, I should shoot myself.' Felicity looked as if she was ready to shoot herself anyway; she had been in a black mood for some time.

'The world seems to be getting smaller,' Alice said, thinking without enthusiasm that it might be necessary to transfer service from one's country to one's town.

They had tea in a hotel at Yelverton, where Felicity sat staring at an Army officer with a kind of despair, as though he was the last of his breed.

Alice did her own stock-taking. She had no doubt about the major aim of the war – Hitler had to be stopped. But about her part in it, she was confused. She had seen a bit of the world, met a wider cross-section of people than she might otherwise have done; her work had been varied, and for a few months her conditions had been uncomfortable, if not intolerable. But she was no nearer that reality she had glimpsed when she saw the woman standing in the ruins of Coventry.

What was she to do now? For three years, she had been something of a wanderer, travelling light, moving on before she had time to become bored. She had liked it. Some of her friends, certain they could never settle down to a routine life again, were trying to find jobs which involved travel – the Foreign Office and commercial airlines being particularly favoured. But recently, Alice had begun to notice that the scenery is not endlessly variable, and the stopping places have certain similarities. If some choice must be made, she could only say that she felt now was a time when she must stand still.

Guy was in one of the first groups to be demobilized. Louise met him at Victoria Station. He looked taller and thinner than ever. As he came close, she saw that his hairline had receded; and, as though a mask attached to the lower hair had been displaced, another face had appeared. The eager boyishness which Guy had retained into his thirties had been translated into an immature anxiety. The eyes smiled readily, but were too uncertain of their joy to hold the sparkling light long; the mouth showed signs of fatigue. For a moment, as she looked at him, it seemed to Louise that it was the father, not the son, who had returned from the war.

They embraced. He held her close, repeating, 'Oh my darling, my darling! How I have longed for this moment.' Beyond her encircling arms lay the accountant's office and a life which he dreaded. It would take more than a world war to effect any change in the ordered ways of Busby and Overton. The only difference would be that he was more out of place than he had been before. Whatever his war experiences might have done for him, they had not increased his financial acumen.

'I've got a taxi,' Louise said, gently disengaging herself. 'You are coming home in style.'

The taxi driver drove slowly because Louise, regardless of expense, had asked him to. She thought Guy would enjoy this leisurely homecoming; and she was right. He looked out of the window eagerly at sights he had not seen for so long. He scarcely noticed the bomb damage, he had come from scenes worse than this. It was the appearance of the children which amazed him. 'They look so bonny!' he kept repeating.

'They have all sorts of extra rations.'

'You must have found that very helpful.'

'Catherine and James are too old to qualify for a green ration book, I'm afraid.'

He winced. Neither had been too old when he last saw them.

Catherine and James were peeping through the curtains of the sitting-room when they arrived. They came down to the front door slowly, rather shy. Guy was visibly shaken at how much they had grown. He was unsure of what was due to children of their ages. Fortunately, the situation was unusual enough to excuse any inappropriateness in his treatment of these little strangers. He had brought presents, silk shawls and scarves, which delighted Louise and Catherine; nothing of much interest to James. He was himself sufficiently sensitive to understand his son's disappointment.

'Nothing much for you, old chap, I'm afraid. But Mummy mentioned in her letters that you wanted a dog. We'll see what we can do about that.'

James was more than mollified.

They had high tea together and soon afterwards the children went to bed early.

Guy settled back in his chair, more relieved than he would admit to be rid for the time being of their demanding presence. He wanted Louise to himself. He looked round the room; it was just as he had remembered it, only tidier – Louise had made a big effort on his behalf. 'I can't tell you how often I have thought of this,' he said. 'When I was in hospital, I used to assemble this room in my mind, starting with the mantelpiece. I could remember every ornament.'

'We shall need new curtains, now there is no black-out.'

He was not listening. He was checking the ornaments on the mantelpiece. It was apparent the unchangingness was of great importance to him in reassembling his own life.

'And you!' He stretched out his arms to her. 'You are just the same. Oh, my darling, I have thought of no one but you all these years! I can't tell you how often I have longed to be with you.' His voice was shaky. All emotion, of whatever origin, was focused on her now. And Louise, who had so dreaded his return, came to him.

She seldom anticipated events, but for the last months, this had been forced upon her. Now, she shook herself free of foreboding and came out joyfully to meet her crisis. Challenges physically embodied stimulated her to give of the best that was in her. So it was that when she saw her husband's need nakedly displayed, her heart opened to him. The relief of finding herself able to respond swept aside all reserve. She was convinced, as she had been years ago when she married him, that all would be well. She would *will* it so.

The children had been well-rehearsed for their father's homecoming and had accepted going to bed early with apparent good grace. It had been carefully explained to them that he would feel very tired after so much travelling. Even so, they were not entirely without resentment. As Guy and Louise embraced, Catherine sat on the edge of James' bed.

'It's only for tonight,' James told her. 'We shall go on just the same as usual tomorrow.'

'Did Mummy say so?'

'No, but she *meant* it.'

Certainly, they meant it.

Claire and Terence left Oxford proclaiming their relief at escaping from the suffocating environment of tradition and privilege; and their earnest desire to get down to the real business of living. They felt strongly about real people, real places, a real way of life; but found it easier to define the unreal – Oxford, Hampstead, commercial travellers and all academics, women who shopped at Fortnum and Mason's, and men who worked in merchant banks.

Both had gained good seconds. For Terence, this result represented the triumph of hard work over moderate ability. Claire, however, had been told by her tutor that she might have got a first had she been more adventurous in her thinking. A natural scholar himself, he had little idea how much she had hazarded in going to university. Once that decision had been taken, her resources of courage and initiative had had to be husbanded carefully to sustain her from one day to the next. 'Only a small gap separates you from the most interesting students of your year,' she had been assured; but the gap between intellect and emotion was steadily widening. Her university life was a perilous voyage during which she felt herself moving further and further from all known landmarks, until it seemed she was travelling in a glass globe, amazed at the nearness of stars, and the cosmic wonder of the universe unfolding; while somewhere in that steel blue void a voice of utter desolation was howling. The process of fragmentation had already begun before she went to Oxford; and there was a sense in which her good second was a mark of her striving for integration.

In spite of their professed delight at leaving university, Claire and Terence were daunted by the prospect of existence beyond the sheltering walls of home or an institution of one kind or another. They were very unsure of themselves. This necessitated their asserting independence in the most abrasive manner and rejecting all offers of help from their families. 'We're not going to live in an area like Holland Park, that is just rotting away in the past,' Claire said scornfully when Louise offered to make enquiries of a neighbour who might have a room to rent. Terence's parents were informed, 'We couldn't possibly live in suburbia – nowhere in the middle of nothing.'

As the extent of the housing problem became clear to them, so Holland Park and suburbia began to seem more possible; and it was with some dismay they discovered that accommodation suitable to their purpose and purse was not available. They were lodging with friends in Earl's Court, having refused an offer from Aunt May because 'Once she's drawn us into her web, she'll strangle us with love and we shall never get away.' It was apparent that the friends had no wish for them to prolong their stay. 'We've got to find somewhere, even if it's a converted garden shed!' Terence said miserably. At the beginning of August, they found unfurnished rooms in Hammersmith.

To be precise, they found one large room at the top of a four-storey house. An alcove on the landing, equipped with a sink and gas-ring, was euphemistically described by the landlady as 'the kitchen'. The bathroom and lavatory, shared by all the tenants, were two floors below. 'It's not quite what we were looking for,' Claire had said, rather in the manner of an unreal person turning over hats at a milliner's. The landlady had shrugged. 'Take it or leave it.' They had taken it.

Number 9 Rosemount Street was a Victorian house distressingly within sight and ear-shot of Hammersmith Broadway. The houses on either side had suffered bomb damage and were abandoned; while fissures in the walls of Number 9 gave rise to the suspicion that it, too, might not be safe for occupation. 'It *is* in the middle,' Claire said. 'Were there two separate incidents, or just the one, do you think?' She did not like the idea that they might be housed above a bomb cavity.

'It's not our worry,' Terence said. 'Even if the foundations are damaged, we shall be out of here before there is any serious subsidence.' He was beginning to despair of their ever finding an acceptable place to live.

Claire persisted, 'I'm not happy about being three flights up.'

'You'd rather be on the ground floor and have the upper storeys fall on top of you?'

On one matter, they were entirely in agreement; the room must be purged before they could move in. Beneath the dust caused by the bomb damage was the ingrained dirt of over a century. 'No one bothered about it when the servants lived up here, and no one has since!' Terence, roused by his sense of social injustice, was ready to rub his knuckles raw on that Victorian filth.

'We'll have to strip the wallpaper off first, in case of bugs,' Claire said.

The landlady, whom they always encountered when she was 'just on the way to the shops' – a phrase which she repeated with the look of one brazening out an accusation – said she had no objection to them doing 'a bit of tidying up, so long as you don't interfere with the cracks'.

They were both fastidious, Terence the more so. On the morning when they set to work, his first priority was to clean the lavatory, a task which he accomplished so thoroughly that he used up most of the disinfectant intended for their own room. It was only with difficulty that Claire dissuaded him from tackling the bathroom. 'As long as we wash under running water, we shan't come to any harm.'

'Suppose someone hears?' He would go to the barricades for his beliefs, but flinched from the thought of infringing the requirements of the Ministry of Fuel and Power.

Claire looked into the wash basin. 'It's all right. There's no plug, anyway.'

They set to work stripping the walls of their room. This had promised to be an easy task, since the paper was peeling away from skirting boards and ceiling. Elsewhere, however, it had formed into a greasy film which could only be removed together with rather a lot of plaster. The possibility that they were rendering the room uninhabitable occurred to each of them but was not voiced. Terence spurred himself on by hating the Victorians for incarcerating servants up here. Then he thought that perhaps the room had been a nursery at some time; and he was distressed by the picture of children, half-starved and beaten. Claire thought of the attic bedroom she had shared with Alice, of the smell of bacon cooking, of Louise playing her music softly and her father calling them to prayer. She thought of the bombed houses on either side, of the loss of her father, and her mother's coming marriage. As she stripped down the walls, she felt she was peeling off a skin. They worked in silence, each too appalled to speak.

Just before lunchtime, Terence went out in search of more disinfectant. Claire was left alone. She had worked hard and she was hungry. She had a pain in the pit of her stomach. The room now bore less resemblance to a place where one might live than it had before they started. Little rivulets of dust and grit were trickling onto the floor. Apart from that, it was quiet. All activity seemed momentarily to have ceased, here, and in the road outside. She could not remember the last time she had known such stillness. So much had happened over the last months and years that there seemed to have been a constant roaring in her ears, as people, places, events flashed by, moving too fast to make much sense. Now she had the sensation of having come to herself in a strange place, after being absent for quite a long time, and with a nagging suspicion that she had done something irrevocable while she was not in possession of her faculties.

She went to the window, standing sideways to peer down, as might a person suffering from vertigo. Opposite, there was a terrace of tall Victorian houses whose disrepair owed less to bomb damage than the changing patterns of life. The large families for whom they had been designed had dwindled, and the houses were let out, room by room, to migratory workers who had neither the means nor the inclination to look after them. In the Acton slum house, window boxes had proudly proclaimed that, whatever the dilapidation of masonry and the blistering of paintwork, this was a home. Here, the only flower to be seen was willow-herb on a bombed site. This apart, the contribution of war had been black-out curtains and chicken wire stretched across broken windows. Ragged children played amid rubble, taking no notice of a woman who shouted threats of punishment unlikely to induce them to come indoors. An old man sat on basement steps rolling a cigarette.

There was a public house on the corner of the street, and Claire could see their landlady, a shopping bag over one arm, making her way towards it with something of the absorbed dedication of the chapel-goer who has already left the outside world behind.

She had never before felt so lonely. To what had she committed herself in this period of her absence, during which her home had been destroyed and her beloved father killed? The answer, of course, was Terence. The past few weeks had given her no cause to regret this. In the teaching of school and chapel, sex had not been mentioned as a factor in the making of a marriage. Other sources, which she had come to later, were insistent that sexual satisfaction was the essential ingredient. On her wedding night, she had been surprised by her response to Terence's clumsy fervour. Self-control, discipline, frugality were qualities with which she was familiar, as exemplars, even if she had failed in their performance. Here, in an area of life where abandonment was laudable, untutored and unprepared though she was, she had been immediately successful. Undoubtedly, sex was what she had been waiting for, and its lack explained that tension and anxiety which had characterized her adolescence. She had looked at herself in the mirror the next morning and wondered how, confronted daily by that vivid hair and pale, agitated face, she had failed to realize that she was simply avid for sex.

269

Now, standing at the window of Number 9 Rosemount Street, it occurred to her that a vast amount of time had to be filled in while one was not actually making love. She could not, at this moment, imagine how this was to be done. She blew her nose and then, disgusted by the black mess on her handkerchief, began to cry.

In the first chemist's shop to which he came, Terence was unable to obtain the particular brand of disinfectant which he required. Although on principle he rejected parental example, in the matter of disinfectant he was his mother's son. It had to be Milton. So desperate was the expression on his strained, owlish face that oncoming pedestrians automatically stepped to one side, imagining him on an errand of greater gravity than the purchase of a bottle of Milton. The taxi driver who was cruising down the Broadway when Terence emerged from the shop where he had secured his prize, did not even notice him. Weak eyesight and an inability to judge distances made Terence a hazard on the road at the best of times; in a hurry, he was a potential calamity. The taxi must get out of his way; he was not himself a driver and saw no difficulty in this. Terence leapt forward. Momentarily, his dim eyes recorded a picture of the taxi driver, gripping the wheel of his vehicle as though attempting to get it airborne. Terence gave an even more spectacular leap and fell, rolling to one side so that he contrived to land on his back in the gutter, his precious package cradled against his stomach. The special constable who helped him to his feet insisted on seeing what it was that he had in the bottle. He looked at Terence sternly; but, having satisfied himself that the chap was not mad enough to drink the stuff, let him go on his way. The taxi had already disappeared in a cloud of blasphemy.

Terence limped on, moaning, not with pain but panic. Ever since he left the house, he had been haunted by the fear that Claire would not be there when he returned. She had looked so fragile, the beautiful red hair hidden beneath the scarf she had wound tightly round her head, as though preparing herself for the operating theatre. The eyes which watched him go had seemed wide with nameless foreboding. As he turned into Rosemount Street and saw the house, tears of humiliation stung his eyes. His first effort to provide for her, and he had led her to that dreadful room! How contemptuous she must be of his miserable failure! He must get her out of the place as soon as possible. Teaching was the answer; the country would be desperate for teachers when the war ended. He had dreamt of being a journalist on one of the more vituperative left-wing weeklies, where he would undoubtedly become a major influence on post-war thought. But dreams would have to wait; he loved Claire dearly and his first duty must be to provide for her. He did not see this as self-sacrifice, but as her due.

Claire heard his feet on the stairs, stepping carefully because he was no happier than she about the stability of the house. How were they going to live here if they couldn't even come up the stairs without fearing they would bring the whole structure crashing down?

'I've got it!' He held the bottle aloft. 'It took a bit of tracking down, but . . .' He saw that she had been crying and put his arms round her.

When she was calmer, they decided to eat their sandwiches in the open air. After she had washed her hands and face and put a comb through her hair, the elfin charm was restored; and he thought perhaps he would not have to teach. The sun had come out and it was a pleasant day. They walked hand in hand in search of a little park they had once seen on their way to the house. Terence looked about him, eager to find evidence of decent working-class people with whom he could identify – not himself being working-class, he had a clear picture of what he expected to find. Soon, however, they were in an area which had ceased to be residential. They passed a small factory where cheerful music competed with the whirr of machinery. A placard outside warned that careless talk costs lives. Further on, there was a row of lock-up garages where three men dressed in black suits were unloading a hearse. There was no one else about and one of the men came towards them saying, 'Lost your way?' He spoke pleasantly, while conveying the message that he owned the neighbourhood and they were trespassing.

'We were looking for a park,' Terence said. 'To eat our sandwiches . . .'

Claire felt impelled to hold out the sandwiches for inspection. The man was very sallow with dark, liverish eyes. The sight of the sandwiches affected him with such intense melancholy that Claire thought he might be sick; no doubt anxious to rid himself of nausea, he pointed, 'You see that alley down the side of the furniture store? You go down there, past Mr Jakes's Emporium; and beyond that, you'll see the park.'

Terence thanked him rather more warmly than was necessary, and they hurried towards the alley.

'What was it they . . . ?' Claire whispered. She had been afraid to look too closely.

'Meat.'

'Don't be so *beastly*, Terence!'

'Not human. Pork, by the look of it.'

'How could you possibly tell, with your eyesight?'

'It wasn't a cut of meat, it was a whole pig.'

Mr Jakes was standing outside his Emporium, as affable as the undertaker had been melancholy. 'I've got just the thing for you, my dear, with that lovely hair.'

'I'm afraid I haven't any coupons,' Claire said primly.

'I expect we could come to an arrangement.'

Claire laughed as though this was a splendid joke, and she and Terence hurried on. The few flower beds in the park had been dug up to accommodate an air raid shelter; squeals of laughter indicated that it was at present inhabited. They walked on to where there was a small patch of grass beneath a resolute oak. Here, they sat, using the tree for a backrest.

'We'll go back another way,' Terence said.

They thought of what they were going back to, then he said, 'Everything will be all right once we've got the furniture in.'

'It will never make a home.'

'Yes, it will. One or two bits and pieces will make all the difference, you'll see.'

But they had not been together long enough to accumulate bits and pieces which had any mutual significance. In spite of his nearness, Claire felt more alone than ever. I *must* have a baby, she thought; I must have a baby as soon as possible. *That* will make a home.

The sun was warm and they rested for a time and then walked slowly towards Rosemount Street, two frightened children strayed from some Arcadian world into a fairground, clinging to each other as they made their way between the bizarre attractions which jostled for claims on their attention, searching for a way out.

On August 9th, the inexplicable talk of heavy water installations resolved itself into something more explicit. An atom bomb was dropped on Hiroshima. The next day, while the shock waves were still felt, another bomb was dropped on Nagasaki. On August 14th, the Japanese officially surrendered and the war was over.

It was scarcely credible. As the realization of what had happened began to dawn on people, reactions were sharply divided. Services of thanksgiving were held. At least one West London vicar refused to conduct a civil service because of the enormity of the Allies' crime. Instead, he opened his church for a day of prayer. Claire and Terence, lacking any other means of demonstrating their feelings, were among the few people who attended.

'If I had been on leave, I would have gone, too,' Alice said to Louise.

'You don't give a second's thought to people like Ben,' Louise told her angrily.

It was true that Alice had not made this connection in her mind. Had the dilemma been hers to resolve, she would scarcely have known how to answer. She had, after all, thought the war against Hitler justified, and never more so than when the information of the conditions in Belsen was released. She realized her inconsistency; but she was not, and never would be, able to reconcile herself to the fact that the Allies should have been the first to use this worst of all weapons.

The dropping of the bomb cast its shadow over other events. It seemed to many of the men who had worked on the Burma railway that, from first to last, they were members of a forgotten army.

'Some of these men find it difficult to talk about their experiences, indeed cannot bear to do so,' wrote one of the doctors who interviewed the prisoners of the Japanese. 'They don't seem to have any idea how many of their comrades died – it is almost impossible to get reliable information out of them. I only pressed them because I knew that if I didn't produce records of a kind, they might suffer more determined interrogation by the Army's officers investigating war crimes. I am afraid it is going to be a long time before these men are ready to face ordinary life again. Indeed, some may never do so.

'One group I was particularly sorry for. They were the tubercular prisoners who were sent to South Africa to recuperate before returning to England. It was thought to be in their own best interests, but they were heartbroken when they discovered they would not be going home immediately. It was one of the saddest sights I saw there – watching them sail away. I can't help feeling it was a mistake.'

Ben went straight back to England. He was one of the lucky ones who had not returned to the jungle after the railway was finished. But it was not luck which kept him in Singapore. There had been a moment when the Japanese CO's equipment was being unpacked, when it seemed the drawings must be found. Ben had created a diversion by breaking the CO's radio. He had made a thorough job of it, first dropping it, then stumbling and trampling on it in his fall; he did not weigh much, but enough. He was severely beaten. It was Tandy who recovered the drawings. A terrified spectator, he had realized that if they were discovered, he himself, by his mere presence, would be implicated. While Ben was being reduced to something like the condition of the smashed radio, Tandy took the opportunity to hide the drawings in a discarded packing case. Subsequently, having had no opportunity to burn them — which would have been his preference — he brought them to the hospital, where a surprised doctor congratulated him on his loyalty and initiative.

Ben recovered slowly. Conditions in Singapore were much better than in the jungle, and by the time the war ended he was fit enough to return to England. Like many others, he embarked drunk with the prospect of liberty; but his jubilation had long worn off by the time he landed in England. He had left behind in the jungle, not only friends, but a part of himself.

His friendship with Geoffrey had given him a glimpse of a kind of life quite different from the one ambition had planned for him, a life in which companionship played an important part. Instead of the great courtroom victories, more homely scenes began to occupy his mind. A particular image had been the return from the winter walk, frost forming on the fallen leaves, making them crisp beneath one's feet; cottage windows with lights burning, giving an assurance of the comfort that lay ahead. Inevitably, food had formed an important part of the picture — the table heaped with ham and pickle, a crusted loaf, thickly buttered toast and jam, and a pot of tea in the hearth. But it was the sharing at the fireside which mattered most. He had lost his taste for solitude.

It seemed, however, that it was solitude which awaited him now. He had been a prisoner for the best part of four years; and he was returning to a place where his absence would scarcely have been noticed. He had always had to fight hard for attention. Now it was attention of a gentler kind that he needed, and he had no idea how to set about attracting it. In his worst moments, it seemed to him that he would never again be able to summon either the will or the energy to make himself noticeable.

When they came into harbour, all the ships saluted them. There were crowds of people on shore; relatives, friends, and members of associations who would look after those prisoners who had no family to go to. Everyone was anxious to make it seem that they had not been forgotten and never would be. But shame was to be their portion: to their fellows, a defeated army; to future generations, men implicated, however innocently, in the horror of Hiroshima. Back in Chungkai, the inscription on a memorial read, 'Their name liveth for evermore'. The jungle, already reclaiming the ground it had lost, was wiser.

Not long after he had returned to England, Ben and Alice met by chance in Piccadilly Circus. He would have walked quickly by, his head averted, had she not recognized him.

They had tea together in a café. Both were now demobilized and in search of employment. Alice, after a number of unsuccessful interviews, was aware of how little she had to offer a would-be employer. Before she was demobilized, she had made a lot of stipulations about what she would and would not do; the question of what she *could* do had not exercised her mind. The Navy, after all, had accepted her readily: it had taken one look and decided she was the right kind of person for the senior service. Civilian employers, with different standards, seemed less impressed by an education at the Winifred Clough Day School for Girls which had failed to include shorthand and typewriting in the syllabus.

'How long have you been home?' she asked Ben. 'We have been trying to get news of you.'

'Just over a month.'

'And you haven't been in touch!'

'I had to find somewhere to live.' He spoke bitterly, as though this was her fault.

'I'm living with Louise. She had a policeman for lodger, but he left, and I've got the room at the top of the house where I can see all the roof tops! Aunt May would give you a room, I'm sure.'

'I've found somewhere now.' He dismissed offers of help made too late with contempt.

'Are you back at your chambers?' Alice asked, after a pause during which he had nothing to say.

'No, I'm not going back.' He shut his mouth tight. He was better qualified than Alice to find employment, but had problems of emotional instability. He knew it would not be possible for him to return to the Bar. This was not something he wanted to talk about. The café was noisy, and the bustle of people and crash of crockery irritated and disturbed him. He had looked forward to seeing Alice and the other members of the Fairley family; but was not able to cope with encounters for which he had not prepared himself in advance.

'Claire is married,' Alice told him, filling one of the gaps in their conversation. 'And she's expecting a baby. Daphne is married to someone who did quite a bit in the Resistance. I haven't met him yet. They are looking for somewhere to live in Norfolk.'

'What is he going to find to resist in Norfolk, I wonder?' Ben said acidly.

'And Mummy . . .' She paused, crumbling a scone.

'Don't tell me *she* is getting married!' He did not for a moment imagine this could be so.

'Yes. I can't talk about it.'

He looked as dumbfounded as she herself had been; but all he said was, '*You're* not married, I take it?'

She did not like his 'taking it'. 'There was someone. But he was killed.' This did not seem to be the moment to tell Ben that Gordon had been married, so she said defensively, 'We had so much in common. He was a marvellous person.'

'Oh, they all were!' Ben was savage. 'Every mother's son of them. Not a bad penny among the gallant dead.' ·

'You shouldn't speak ill of them.' Alice tried to sound good-humoured. It was now apparent to her that he was far from himself.

'I very nearly joined them. And if there is one thing I know, it's that I wouldn't have wanted people drooling over my memory.' He was speaking loudly, his eyes protruding. The people at the next table were regarding him uneasily. 'After all, Alice,' he stabbed a pastry knife at her, 'if a man gets run over crossing a road, his folk remember him as he was. But get killed in a war and the state takes you over – provided you weren't in Burma.'

'I think people genuinely . . .' Alice lowered her voice and tried to sound calming.

'Alice,' his voice became the louder, 'the fallen of two world wars are going to be a pain in the arse to your children.' He collected the bill; he could not escape from this noisy, enclosed space soon enough. Alice followed him. 'You want proof?' he continued the argument on the pavement. 'Meet me here in fifteen years' time.'

It was obviously a mistake to get into any kind of discussion with him. Alice said, 'I fully intend to meet you before then, Ben.'

Tears came into his eyes and he turned away abruptly. She pretended not to notice and suggested they should walk in Green Park.

They walked in silence. Ben exaggerated the difficulty of negotiating a passage between the people on the crowded pavements. Once pointed in a particular direction, he seemed incapable of calculating the small adjustments of pace and thrust necessary to avoid collision. When they reached the park, he relaxed a little, and said, with an awkward attempt at sympathy, 'I'm sorry about your mother. Perhaps it won't be as bad as you think.'

'It couldn't not be.'

'You don't like him?'

'Oh, *he's* all right. In fact, he's quite interesting. He's a publisher.'

'What is the trouble, then?'

'We shall never be able to talk about Daddy together as a family, because it would exclude . . . this stranger. It makes me feel I've lost my father twice.'

It was this that hurt as much as anything: the need to be watchful, the curb to the tongue, the loss of that spontaneity which, though it could be abrasive, had been so precious a part of family exchanges. She had thought it would be a relief to tell Ben about this. But as he listened, with little to offer in the way of consolation, she realized that there could be no relief, only acceptance. My mother will take another name, she thought; and by doing this she will seal up a part of the past, not only her past, but mine as well.

And yet – the park was beautiful, its trees already bare, furred by autumn mist. Hope was hard to resist.

Before Ben left her, she managed to get his address. Although he gave it with bad grace, he insisted on writing it down because 'you'll only forget otherwise.'

'I'll be away for a little while,' he said.

'Are you going to Cornwall?'

'No. There is a family I have to see in Herefordshire. Then, I'm going for a walk. Along Offa's Dyke.'

'Wouldn't it be better to wait for summer?'

He turned away without replying.

She watched him go into Green Park station, moving with the awkward gait of a person unsure of his footing. She did not think he was fit enough to tackle Offa's Dyke.

She decided to walk back to Louise's house through the parks. People were sitting on the grass; it was warm for the time of year and one could almost imagine the summer flowers. The scene had the mannered elegance of a painting, static, tranquil; yet, by its very formality, invested with a sense of impending danger. The rush of traffic, though muted, never ceased, running like a river on all sides of the park.

She wondered what lay ahead of them all. She had joined up with an urgent sense that this was an experience she must not miss. Yet somehow, the reality had eluded her. And now that it was over, she still had the feeling of waiting for something to begin.

Elizabeth Berridge's crisp and distinctly English style of writing
established her as one of the most significant novelists of the post-
war years. Now that her best work is at last available in Abacus
Paperback, a new generation of readers will be able to discover the
quiet brilliance of her writing . . .

Elizabeth Berridge
ROSE UNDER GLASS

'*An eye for the beauty of humble and familiar things, and a gift for expressing it in
a language sharp yet delicate. She has a quiet, wicked sense of humour.*'
New Statesman.

ABACUS FICTION   0 349 10303 8   **£2.95**

Elizabeth Berridge
ACROSS THE COMMON

'*Entirely good and most beautifully written. I love her subtlety and observation and
impeccable characterisation.*' *Noel Coward.*

ABACUS FICTION   0 349 10304 6   **£2.75**

Elizabeth Berridge
SING ME WHO YOU ARE

'*One of the best English novelists presents something of a tour-de-force.*'
Martin Seymour Smith.

ABACUS FICTION   0 349 10305 4   **£2.95**

BILGEWATER
Jane Gardam

Shortlisted for the Booker Prize
Winner of the Whitbread Award and David Higham and
Winifred Holtby Prizes

'Superbly told . . . adolescent anguish has no better friend than this
poignant ode to its hopes and fears.' *Times Educational Supplement*.

'The best of all her novels. It is funny, beautifully constructed,
deeply moving, and I cannot get it out of my mind.'
Daily Telegraph.

'Jane Gardam has a deep, intuitive sympathy for victims of this age
group . . . not without an equally sharp comic appreciation of their
plight. Lively . . . excellent.' *The Times*.

'A very good book indeed, witty, enriching, and a pleasure to read.'
The Listener.

'One of the funniest, most entertaining, most unusual stories about
young love.' *Standard*.

GENERAL FICTION   0 349 11402 1   £2.50

Also by JANE GARDAM in ABACUS paperback:
THE PANGS OF LOVE AND OTHER STORIES
A LONG WAY FROM VERONA
GOD ON THE ROCKS
BLACK FACES, WHITE FACES
THE SIDMOUTH LETTERS

THE GLAMOUR
CHRISTOPHER PRIEST

All Richard Grey wanted to do was recover, to return to normal. For four long, painful months he had been convalescing after the horrifying injuries that he sustained when a car bomb exploded near him.

He could remember the years he spent as a cameraman, covering stories all over the world, and he could remember taking a break from his career – but there was a profound blankness where his memory of the weeks before the explosion should have been. It was as if his life had been re-edited and part of it erased.

But then Susan Kewley came to visit him and she spoke of those weeks. And what Richard wanted most was a glimpse of what that time had held for the two of them. But the glimpses he was afforded took him into a strange and terrible twilight world – a world of apparent madness, the world of 'the glamour' . . .

Christopher Priest's rich and subtle narrative is mesmerising and deeply moving, as compelling and deceptive as a Hitchcock film.

'One of our most gifted writers.' *John Fowles*

'A bizarre and intriguing book.' *Guardian*

ABACUS FICTION   0 349 128103   £2.95

The debut of an enormously gifted writer

Ease

■ P A T R I C K   G A L E ■

Domina Tey is one of life's success stories: an award-winning playwright, living with an equally celebrated writer in a magazine-featured home. A lucky woman, who knows and appreciates it. But at the moment, she's just not happy.

Convinced that a spell of seedy living – so far denied her by fate and circumstance – would give both work and soul a much-needed spring-clean, she elopes with her typewriter in search of la sleazy vita – discovering it in Bayswater's tarnished bedsit jungle. Within a week she has settled into the warm friendly world of Lady Tilly (landlady and ex-mortician), all-night sauna 'clubs' and midnight snack-land; and her search for a fresh start becomes an overwhelming desire to make passionate love to a much younger man. Quintus disturbs her. He's too innocent for such suffering. Domina watches his guilt changing shape, volume, direction, transforming him. Observing her, he carefully eases her out of her distress.

ABACUS FICTION   0 349 11400 5   £3.50

Patrick Gale's THE AERODYNAMICS OF PORK is also available in Abacus.